Hey, it was his first time. I wanted to scare him.

And I did, too. The dark-haired boy stood in a pentacle
of his own, smaller, filled with different runes, a metre
away from the main one. He was pale as a corpse,
shaking like a dead leaf in a high wind. His teeth rattled
in his shivering jaw. Beads of sweat dripped from his
brow, turning to ice as they fell through the air. They
tinkled with the sound of hailstones on the floor.

All well and good, but so what? I mean, he looked about
twelve years old. Wide-eyed, hollow-cheeked. There's
not that much satisfaction to be had from scaring the
pants off a scrawny kid.

Praise for *THE AMULET OF SAMARKAND*

'A rip-roaring read, hugely inventive, full of mood swings and featuring a fascinating central relationship between apprentice and djinni' *Wendy Cooling*

The djinni's wonderfully witty asides in the form of footnotes really make this novel something special and will leave readers salivating for the next instalment' *Grainne Cooney, THE BOOKSELLER*

'A complex, fast-paced and witty fantasy that Hollywood lapped up with relish . . . *The Amulet of Samarkand* has great cross-over potential' *Carl Wilkinson, OBSERVER*

'The action is thrillingly cinematic . . . Not since *Gulliver's Travels* has a children's writer managed to combine a thrilling tale of magic and adventure with such deliciously pointed comedy . . . The ending is perfect in ambiguity. Stroud's sinister world is imagined in baroque and energetic detail . . .' *Amanda Craig, THE TIMES*

'Drama, humour and hypnotically engaging storytelling' *Nicholas Tucker, INDEPENDENT*

'. . . the truly original touch is the way Stroud alternates Nathaniel's story with the djinni's own knowing and irascible first-person narrative' *Diana Wynne Jones, GUARDIAN REVIEW*

'Stroud's voice is distinct and confident enough to shake off waiting doubters. His cast becomes embroiled in a complex plot to unseat the government, resulting in a glorious set piece which will translate beautifully onto the big screen. But this is essentially an excellent children's thriller – full of fun, action, tension and magic . . . it could easily be the talk of the playground'
Lindsey Fraser, GLASGOW SUNDAY HERALD

'Both the djinn and the boy exist in a world described with great imaginative detail . . . The action-packed adventures of Nathaniel and Bartimaeus . . . are sustained over nearly 500 pages by the immensely enjoyable characterisation. The narrative slips skilfully from first person to third and back and Bartimaeus's voice is laugh-out-loud sassy, while Nathaniel's story has an engaging poignancy as he tries to prove himself in a world in which he has always been despised'
Nicolette Jones, SUNDAY TIMES

'Terrific stuff' *MAIL ON SUNDAY*

'This book gripped me like a magnet to metal . . . I don't have a favourite part of it because it was all brilliant. I can't wait for the next book. I would recommend the story to anyone aged 9 years and over'
Sam Baker (aged 10) IPSWICH

BARTIMAEUS

—THE—
AMULET OF SAMARKAND

BARTIMAEUS

—THE—
AMULET OF SAMARKAND

JONATHAN STROUD

CORGI BOOKS

THE AMULET OF SAMARKAND
A CORGI BOOK 978 0 552 56279 9

First published in Great Britain by Doubleday,
an imprint of Random House Children's Books
A Random House Group Company

Doubleday edition published 2003
Corgi edition published 2004
This Corgi edition published 2010

1 3 5 7 9 10 8 6 4 2

Copyright © Jonathan Stroud, 2003

The Random House Group Limited supports the Forest Stewardship Council (FSC),
the leading international forest certification organization. All our titles that are
printed on Greenpeace-approved FSC-certified paper carry the FSC logo.
Our paper procurement policy can be found at www.rbooks.co.uk/environment.

Mixed Sources
Product group from well-managed
forests and other controlled sources
www.fsc.org Cert no. TT-COC-2139
© 1996 Forest Stewardship Council

Set in Bembo

Corgi Books are published by Random House Children's Books,
61–63 Uxbridge Road, London W5 5SA

www.**kids**at**randomhouse**.co.uk
www.**rbooks**.co.uk

Addresses for companies within The Random House Group Limited can be found at:
www.randomhouse.co.uk/offices.htm

THE RANDOM HOUSE GROUP Limited Reg. No. 954009

A CIP catalogue record for this book is available from the British Library.

Printed in the UK by CPI Bookmarque, Croydon, CR0 4TD

For Gina

A note on pronunciation:

'Djinni' is pronounced 'jinnee', and
'djinn' is pronounced 'jinn'.
'Bartimaeus' is pronounced 'Bart-im-ay-us'.

Part
One

Bartimaeus

I

The temperature of the room dropped fast. Ice formed on the curtains and crusted thickly around the lights in the ceiling. The glowing filaments in each bulb shrank and dimmed, while the candles that sprang from every available surface like a colony of toadstools had their wicks snuffed out. The darkened room filled with a yellow, choking cloud of brimstone, in which indistinct black shadows writhed and roiled. From far away came the sound of many voices screaming. A pressure was suddenly applied to the door that led to the landing. It bulged inwards, the timbers groaning. Footsteps from invisible feet came pattering across the floorboards and invisible mouths whispered wicked things from behind the bed and under the desk.

The sulphur cloud contracted into a thick column of smoke that vomited forth thin tendrils; they licked the air like

3

tongues before withdrawing. The column hung above the middle of the pentacle, bubbling ever upwards against the ceiling like the cloud of an erupting volcano. There was a barely perceptible pause. Then two yellow staring eyes materialized in the heart of the smoke.

Hey, it was his first time. I wanted to scare him.

And I did, too. The dark-haired boy stood in a pentacle of his own, smaller, filled with different runes, a metre away from the main one. He was pale as a corpse, shaking like a dead leaf in a high wind. His teeth rattled in his shivering jaw. Beads of sweat dripped from his brow, turning to ice as they fell through the air. They tinkled with the sound of hailstones on the floor.

All well and good, but so what? I mean, he looked about twelve years old. Wide-eyed, hollow-cheeked. There's not that much satisfaction to be had from scaring the pants off a scrawny kid.[1]

So I floated and waited, hoping he wasn't going to take too long to get round to the dismissing spell. To keep myself occupied I made blue flames lick up around the inner edges of the pentacle, as if they were seeking a way to get out and nab him. All hokum, of course. I'd already checked and the seal was drawn well enough. No spelling mistakes anywhere, unfortunately.

At last it looked as if the urchin was plucking up the

---

[1] Not everyone agrees with me on this. Some find it delightful sport. They refine countless ways of tormenting their summoners by means of subtly hideous apparitions. Usually the best you can hope for is to give them nightmares later, but occasionally these stratagems are so successful that the apprentices actually panic and step out of the protective circle. Then all is well – for us. But it is a risky business. Often they are very well trained. Then they grow up and get their revenge.

courage to speak. I guessed this by a stammering about his lips that didn't seem to be induced by pure fear alone. I let the blue fire die away to be replaced by a foul smell.

The kid spoke. Very squeakily.

'I charge you . . . to . . . to . . .' *Get on with it!* '. . . t–t–tell me your n–name.'

That's usually how they start, the young ones. Meaningless waffle. He knew and I knew that he knew my name already; otherwise how could he have summoned me in the first place? You need the right words, the right actions and most of all the right name. I mean, it's not like hailing a cab – you don't get just *anybody* when you call.

I chose a rich, deep, dark chocolatey sort of voice, the kind that resounds from everywhere and nowhere and makes the hairs stand up on the back of inexperienced necks.

'BARTIMAEUS.'

I saw the kid give a strangled kind of gulp when he heard the word. Good – he wasn't entirely stupid then: he knew who and what I was. He knew my reputation.

After taking a moment to swallow some accumulated phlegm he spoke again. 'I–I charge you again to answer. Are you that B–Bartimaeus who in olden times was summoned by the magicians to repair the walls of Prague?'

What a time-waster this kid was. Who else would it be? I upped the volume a bit on this one. The ice on the light bulbs cracked like caramelized sugar. Behind the dirty curtains the window glass shimmered and hummed. The kid rocked back on his heels.

'I am Bartimaeus! I am Sakhr al-Jinni, N'gorso the Mighty and the Serpent of Silver Plumes! I have rebuilt the walls of Uruk, Karnak and Prague. I have spoken with Solomon. I have run with the buffalo fathers of the plains. I have watched over Old Zimbabwe till the stones fell and the jackals fed on its people. I am Bartimaeus! I recognize no master. So I charge you in your turn, *boy*. Who are you to summon me?'

Impressive stuff, eh? All true as well, which gives it more power. And I wasn't just doing it to sound big. I rather hoped the kid would be blustered by it into telling me his name in return, which would give me something to go on when his back was turned.[2] But no luck there.

'By the constraints of the circle, the points on the pentacle and the chain of runes, I am your master! You will obey my will!'

There was something particularly obnoxious about hearing this old shtick coming from a weedy stripling, and in such a rubbish high voice too. I bit back the temptation to give him a piece of my mind and intoned the usual response. Anything to get it over with quickly.

'What is your will?'

I admit I was already surprised. Most tyro magicians look first and ask questions later. They go window-shopping, eyeing up their potential power, but being far too nervous to try it out. You don't often get small ones like this squirt calling up entities like me in the first place, either.

The kid cleared his throat. This was the moment. This is what he'd been building up to. He'd been dreaming of this for years, when he should have been lying on his bed thinking about racing cars or girls. I waited grimly for the pathetic

---

[2] I couldn't do anything while I was in the circle, of course. But later I'd be able to find out who he was, look for weaknesses of character, things in his past I could exploit. They've all got them. *You've* all got them, I should say.

request. What would it be? Levitating some object was a usual one, or moving it from one side of the room to the other. Perhaps he'd want me to conjure an illusion. That might be fun: there was bound to be a way of misinterpreting his request and upsetting him.[3]

'I charge you to retrieve the Amulet of Samarkand from the house of Simon Lovelace and bring it to me when I summon you at dawn tomorrow.'

'You what?'

'I charge you to retrieve—'

'Yes, I heard what you said.' I didn't mean to sound petulant. It just slipped out, and my sepulchral tones slipped a bit too.

'Then go!'

'Wait a minute!' I felt that queasy sensation in my stomach that you always get when they dismiss you. Like someone sucking out your insides through your back. They have to say it three times to get rid of you, if you're keen on sticking around. Usually you're not. But this time I remained where I was, two glowing eyes in an angry fug of boiling smoke.

'Do you know what you are asking for, boy?'

'I am neither to converse, discuss nor parley with you; nor to engage in any riddles, bets or games of chance; nor to—'

'I have no wish to converse with a scrawny adolescent, believe you me, so save your rote-learned rubbish. Someone is taking advantage of you. Who is it – your master, I suppose? A wizened coward hiding behind a boy.' I let the smoke recede a little, exposed my outlines for the first time, hovering dimly

---

[3] One magician demanded I show him an image of the love of his life. I rustled up a mirror.

in the shadows. 'You are playing with fire twice over, if you seek to rob a true magician by summoning me. Where are we? London?'

He nodded. Yes, it was London all right. Some grotty town house. I surveyed the room through the chemical fumes. Low ceiling, peeling wallpaper; a single faded print on the wall. It was a sombre Dutch landscape – a curious choice for a boy. I'd have expected pop chicks, football players . . . Most magicians are conformists, even when young.

'Ah me . . .' My voice was emollient and wistful. 'It is a wicked world and they have taught you very little.'

'I am not afraid of you! I have given you your charge and I demand you go!'

The second dismissal. My bowels felt as if they were being passed over by a steamroller. I sensed my form waver, flicker. There was power in this child, though he was very young.

'It is not me you have to fear; not now, anyway. Simon Lovelace will come to you himself when he finds his amulet stolen. He will not spare you for your youth.'

'You are bound to do my will.'

'I am.' I had to hand it to him, he was determined. And very stupid.

His hand moved. I heard the first syllable of the Systematic Vice. He was about to inflict pain.

I went. I didn't bother with any more special effects.

2

When I landed on the top of a lamppost in the London dusk it was peeing with rain. This was just my luck. I had taken the form of a blackbird, a sprightly fellow with a bright yellow beak and jet-black plumage. Within seconds I was as bedraggled a fowl as ever hunched its wings in Hampstead. Flicking my head from side to side I spied a large beech tree across the street. Leaves mouldered at its foot – it had already been stripped clean by the November winds – but the thick sprouting of its branches offered some protection from the wet. I flew over to it, passing above a lone car that purred its way along the wide suburban road. Behind high walls and the evergreen foliage of their gardens, the ugly white façades of several sizeable villas shone through the dark like the faces of the dead.

Well, perhaps it was my mood that made it seem like that. Five things were bothering me. For a start the dull ache that comes with every physical manifestation was already beginning. I could feel it in my feathers. Changing form would keep the pain at bay for a time, but might also draw attention to me at a critical stage of the operation. Until I was sure of my surroundings, a bird I had to remain.

The second thing was the weather. Enough said.

Thirdly, I'd forgotten the limitations of material bodies. I had an itch just above my beak, and kept futilely trying to scratch it with a wing. Fourthly, that kid. I had a lot of questions about him. Who was he? Why did he have a death wish? How would I get even with him before he died for subjecting me to this assignment? News travels fast and I was bound to get some stick for scurrying around on behalf of a scrap like him.

Fifthly ... the Amulet. By all accounts it was a potent charm. What the kid thought he was going to do with it when he got it beat me. He wouldn't have a clue. Maybe he'd just wear it as some tragic fashion accessory. Maybe nicking amulets was the latest craze, the magician's version of pinching hubcaps. Even so, I had to get it first and this would not necessarily be easy, even for me.

I closed my blackbird's eyes and opened my inner ones, one after the other, each on a different plane.[1] I looked back and forth around me, hopping up and down the branch to get the optimum view. No less than three villas along the road had magical protection, which showed how nobby an area we were in. I didn't inspect the two further off up the street; it was the one across the road, beyond the streetlight, that interested me. The residence of Simon Lovelace, magician.

The first plane was clear, but he'd rigged up a defence nexus on the second – it shone like blue gossamer all along the high wall. It didn't finish there either; it extended up into the air, over the top of the low white house and down again on the other side, forming a great shimmering dome.

Not bad, but I could handle it.

There was nothing on the third or fourth planes, but on the fifth I spotted three sentries prowling around in mid-air, just

---

[1] I have access to seven planes, all co-existent. They overlap each other like layers on a crushed Viennetta. Seven planes is sufficient for anybody. Those who operate on more are just showing off.

beyond the lip of the garden wall. They were a dull yellow all over, each one formed of three muscular legs that rotated on a hub of gristle. Above the hub was a blobby mass, which sported two mouths and several watchful eyes. The creatures passed at random back and forth around the perimeter of the garden. I shrank back against the trunk of the beech tree instinctively, but I knew they were unlikely to spot me from there. At this distance I should look like a blackbird on all seven planes. It was when I got closer that they might break through my illusion.

The sixth plane was clear. But the seventh . . . that was curious. I couldn't see anything obvious – the house, the road, the night all looked unchanged – but, call it intuition if you like, I was sure something was present there, lurking.

I rubbed my beak doubtfully against a knot of wood. As expected, there was a good deal of powerful magic at work here. I'd heard of Lovelace. He was considered a formidable magician and a hard taskmaster. I was lucky I had never been called up in his service and I did not much want his enmity or that of his servants.

But I had to obey that kid.

The soggy blackbird took off from the branch and swooped across the road, conveniently avoiding the arc of light from the nearest lamp. It landed on a patch of scrubby grass at the corner of the wall. Four black bin bags had been left out there for collection the next morning. The blackbird hopped behind the bags. A cat that had observed the bird[2] from some

---

[2] On two planes. Cats have that power.

way off waited a few moments for it to emerge, lost patience and scuttled curiously after it. Behind the bags it discovered no bird, black or otherwise. There was nothing there but a freshly turned molehill.

3

I hate the taste of mud. It is no fit thing for a being of air and fire. The cloying weight of earth oppresses me greatly whenever I come into contact with it. That is why I am choosy about my incarnations. Birds, good. Insects, good. Bats, OK. Things that run fast are fine. Tree-dwellers are even better. Subterranean things, not good. Moles, bad.

But there's no point being fastidious when you have a protective shield to bypass. I had reasoned correctly that it did not extend underground. The mole dug its way deep, deep down, under the foundations of the wall. No magical alarm sounded, though I did hit my head five times on a pebble.[1] I burrowed upwards again, reaching the surface after twenty minutes of snuffling, scruffling and turning my beady nose up at the juicy worms I uncovered every couple of scrapes.

The mole poked its head cautiously out of the little pile of earth it had driven through the immaculate surface of Simon Lovelace's lawn. It looked around, checking out the scene. There were lights on in the house, on the ground floor. The curtains were drawn. The upper floors, from what the mole could see, were dark. The translucent blue span of the magical defence system arched overhead. One yellow sentry trudged its stupid way three metres above the shrubbery. The other two were presumably behind the house.

---

[1]   Once each on five different pebbles. Not the same pebble five times. Just checking. Sometimes human beings are so *dense*.

13

I tried the seventh plane again. Still nothing, still that uneasy sense of danger. Oh well.

The mole retreated underground and tunnelled below the grass roots towards the house. It reappeared in the flowerbed just below the nearest windows. It was thinking hard. There was no point going further in this guise, tempting though it was to try to break into the cellars. A different method would have to be found.

To the mole's furry ears came the sound of laughter and clinking glasses. It was surprisingly loud, echoing from very close by. An air vent, cracked with age, was set in the wall not half a metre away. It led indoors.

With some relief, I became a fly.

4

From the security of the air vent I peered with my multi-faceted eyes into a rather traditional drawing room. There was a thick pile carpet, nasty striped wallpaper, a hideous crystal thing pretending to be a chandelier, two oil paintings that were dark with age, a sofa and two easy chairs (also striped), a low coffee table laden with a silver tray and, on the tray, a bottle of red wine and no glasses. The glasses were in the hands of two people.

One of them was a woman. She was youngish (for a human, which means infinitesimally young) and probably quite good-looking in a fleshy sort of way. Big eyes, dark hair, bobbed. I memorized her automatically. I would appear in her guise tomorrow when I went back to visit that kid. Only naked. Let's see how his very steely but ever-so-adolescent mind responded to that![1]

However, for the moment I was more concerned with the man this woman was smiling and nodding at. He was tall, thin, handsome in a rather bookish sort of way, with his hair slicked back by some pungent oil. He had small round glasses and a large mouth with good teeth. He had a prominent jaw. Something told me that this was the magician, Simon Lovelace. Was it his indefinable aura of power and authority?

---

[1] For those who are wondering, I have no difficulty in becoming a woman. Nor for that matter a man. In some ways, I suppose women are trickier, but I won't go into that now. Woman, man, mole, maggot – they're all the same, when all's said and done, except for slight variations in cognitive ability.

Was it the proprietorial way in which he gestured around the room? Or was it the small imp which floated at his shoulder (on the second plane), warily watching out for danger on every side?

I rubbed my front two legs together with irritation. I would have to be very careful. The imp complicated matters.[2]

It was a pity I wasn't a spider. They can sit still for hours and think nothing of it. Flies are far more jittery. But if I changed here, the magician's slave would be certain to sense it. I had to force my unwilling body to lurk, and ignore the ache that was building up again, this time inside my chitin.

The magician was talking. He did little else. The woman gazed at him with spaniel eyes so wide and silly with adoration that I wanted to bite her.

'. . . it will be the most magnificent occasion, Amanda. You will be the toast of London society! Did you know that the Prime Minister himself is looking forward to viewing your estate? Yes, I have that on good authority. My enemies have been hounding him for weeks with their vile insinuations, but he has always remained committed to holding the conference at the Hall. So you see, my love, I can still influence him when it counts. The thing is to know how to play him, how to flatter his vanity . . . Keep it to yourself, but he is actually rather weak. His speciality is Charm, and even that he seldom bothers with now. Why should he? He's got men in suits to do it for him . . .'

The magician rattled on like this for several minutes, name-

---

[2] Don't get me wrong. I wasn't afraid of the imp. I could squish it without a second thought. But it was there for two reasons: for its undying loyalty to its master and for its perceptive eye. It would not be taken in by my cunning fly guise for one fraction of a second.

dropping with tireless energy. The woman drank her wine, nodded, gasped and exclaimed at the right moments and leaned closer to him along the sofa. I nearly buzzed with boredom.[3]

Suddenly the imp became alert. Its head swivelled 180 degrees and peered at a door at the other end of the room. It tweaked the magician's ear gently in warning. Seconds later, the door opened and a black-jacketed flunky with a bald head stepped respectfully in.

'Pardon me, sir, but your car is ready.'

'Thank you, Carter. We shan't be a moment.'

The flunky withdrew. The magician replaced his (still full) wineglass back on the coffee table and took hold of the woman's hand. He kissed it gallantly. Behind his back the imp made faces of extreme disgust.

'It pains me to have to go, Amanda, but duty calls. I will not be home this evening. May I call you? The theatre, tomorrow night, perhaps?'

'That would be charming, Simon.'

'Then that is settled. My good friend Makepeace has a new play out. I shall get tickets presently. For now, Carter will drive you home.'

Man, woman and imp exited, leaving the door ajar. Behind them, a wary fly crept from its hiding place and sped

---

[3] A human who listened to the conversation would probably have been slack-jawed with astonishment, for the magician's account of corruption in the British Government was remarkably detailed. But I for one was not agog. Having seen countless civilizations of far greater panache than this one crumble into dust I could rouse little interest in the matter. I spent the time fruitlessly trying to recall which unearthly powers might have been bound into Simon Lovelace's service. It was best to be prepared.

soundlessly across the room to a vantage point that gave a view of the hall. For a few minutes there was activity, coats being brought, orders given, doors slammed. Then the magician departed his house.

I flew out into the hall. It was wide, cold and laid with a flooring of black and white tiles. Bright green ferns grew from gigantic ceramic pots. I circled the chandelier, listening. It was very quiet. The only sounds came from a distant kitchen and they were innocent enough – just the banging of pots and plates and several loud belches, presumably emanating from the cook.

I debated sending out a discreet magical pulse to see if I could detect the whereabouts of the magician's artefacts, but decided that it was far too risky. The sentry creatures outside might pick it up, for one thing, even if there was no further guard. I, the fly, would have to go hunting myself.

All the planes were clear. I went along the hall, then – following an intuition – up the stairs.

On the landing a thickly carpeted corridor led in two directions, each lined with oil paintings. I was immediately interested in the right-hand passage, for halfway along it was a spy. To human eyes it was a smoke alarm, but on the other planes its true form was revealed – an upside-down toad with unpleasantly bulbous eyes sitting on the ceiling. Every minute or so it hopped on the spot, rotating a little. When the magician returned, it would relate to him anything that had happened.

I sent a small magic the toad's way. A thick oily vapour issued from the ceiling and wrapped itself around the spy, obscuring its vision. As it hopped and croaked in confusion, I flew rapidly past it down the passage to the door at the end. Alone of the doors in the corridor, this did not have a keyhole;

under its white paint, the wood was reinforced with strips of metal. Two good reasons for trying this one first.

There was a minute crack under the door. It was too small for an insect, but I was aching for a change anyway. The fly dissolved into a dribble of smoke, which passed out of sight under the door just as the vapour screen around the toad melted away.

In the room I became a child.

If I had known that apprentice's name, I would have been malicious and taken his form, just to give Simon Lovelace a head start when he began to piece the theft together. But without his name I had no handle on him. So I became a boy I had known once before, someone I had loved. His dust had long ago floated away along the Nile, so my crime would not hurt him, and anyhow it pleased me to remember him like this. He was brown-skinned, bright-eyed, dressed in a white loincloth. He looked around in that way he had, his head slightly cocked to one side.

The room had no windows. There were several cabinets against the walls, filled with magical paraphernalia. Most of it was quite useless, fit only for stage shows,[4] but there were a few intriguing items there.

---

[4] Oh, it was all impressive enough if you were a non-magician. Let me see – there were crystal orbs, scrying glasses, skulls from tombs, saints' knucklebones, spirit-sticks that had been looted from Siberian shamans, bottles filled with blood of doubtful provenance, witch-doctor masks, stuffed crocodiles, novelty wands, racks of capes for different ceremonies and many, many weighty books on magic that looked as if they had been bound in human skin at the beginning of time but had probably been mass-produced last week by a factory in Catford. Magicians love this kind of thing; they love the hocus-pocus mystery of it all (and half believe it, some of them) and they *adore* the awe-inspiring effect it has on outsiders. Quite apart from anything else all these knick-knacks distract attention from the real source of their power. Us.

There was a summoning horn that I knew was genuine, because it made me feel ill to look at it. One blast of that and anything in that magician's power would be at his feet begging for mercy and pleading to do his bidding. It was a cruel instrument and very old and I couldn't go near it. In another cabinet was an eye made out of clay. I had seen one of them before, in the head of a golem. I wondered if the fool knew the potential of that eye. Almost certainly not – he'd have picked it up as a quaint keepsake on some package holiday in central Europe. Magical tourism . . . I ask you.[5] Well, with luck it might kill him some day.

And there was the Amulet of Samarkand. It sat in a small case all of its own, protected by glass and its own reputation. I walked over to it, flicking through the planes, seeking danger and finding – well, nothing explicit, but on the seventh plane I had the distinct impression that something was stirring. Not here, but close by. I had better be quick.

The Amulet was small, dull and made of beaten gold. It hung from a short gold chain. In its centre was an oval piece of jade. The gold had been pressed with simple notched designs depicting running steeds. Horses were the prize possessions of the people from central Asia who had made the Amulet three thousand years before and had later buried it in the tomb of one of their princesses. A Russian archaeologist had found it in the 1950s and before long it had been stolen

---

[5] They were all at it – beetling off in coach parties (or, since many of them were well-heeled, hiring jets) to tour the great magical cities of the past. All cooing and ahhing at the famous sights – the temples, the birthplaces of notable magicians, the places where they came to horrible ends. And all ready to whip bits of statuary or ransack the black-market bazaars in the hope of getting knock-me-down sorcerous *bargains*. It's not the cultural vandalism I object to. It's just so hopelessly vulgar.

by magicians who recognized its value. How Simon Lovelace had come by it – who exactly he had murdered or swindled to get it – I had no idea.

I cocked my head again, listening. All was quiet in the house.

I raised my hand over the cabinet, smiling at my reflection as it clenched its fist.

Then I brought my hand down and drove it through the glass.

A throb of magical energy resounded through all seven planes. I seized the Amulet and hung it round my neck. I turned swiftly. The room was as before, but I could sense something on the seventh plane, moving swiftly and coming closer.

The time for stealth was over.

As I ran for the door I noticed out of the corner of my eye a portal suddenly open in mid-air. Inside the portal was a blackness that was immediately obscured as something stepped out through it.

I charged at the door and hit it with my small boy's fist. The door smashed open like a bent playing card. I ran past it without stopping.

In the corridor, the toad turned towards me and opened its mouth. A green gobbet of slime issued forth, which suddenly accelerated down at me, aiming for my head. I dodged and the slime splattered on the wall behind me, destroying a painting and everything down to the bare bricks beneath it.

I threw a bolt of Compression at the toad. With a small croak of regret it imploded into a dense blob of matter the size of a marble and dropped to the floor. I didn't break stride. As I ran on down the corridor I placed a protective

Shield around my physical body in case of further missiles.

Which was a wise move as it happened, because the next instant a Detonation struck the floor directly behind me. The impact was so great that I was sent flying headlong at an angle down the corridor and half into the wall. Green flames licked around me, leaving streaks on the décor like the fingers of a giant hand.

I struggled to my feet amidst the confusion of shattered bricks and turned round.

Standing over the broken door at the end of the corridor was something that had taken the form of a very tall man with bright-red skin and the head of a jackal.

'BARTIMAEUS!'

Another Detonation shot down the corridor. I somersaulted under it, aiming for the stairs, and as the green explosion vaporized the corner of the wall, rolled head over heels down the steps, through the banisters and two metres down onto the black and white tiled floor, cracking it quite badly.

I got to my feet and took a look at the front door. Through the frosted glass beside it I could see the hulking yellow outline of one of the three sentinels. It was lying in wait, little realizing that it could be seen from inside. I decided to make my exit elsewhere. Thus does superior intelligence win over brute strength any day of the week!

Speaking of which, I had to get out fast. Noises from above indicated pursuit.

I ran through a couple of rooms – a library, a dining room – each time making a break for the window and each time retreating when one or more of the yellow creatures hove into view outside. Their foolishness in making themselves so obvious was only equalled by my caution in avoiding whatever magical weapons they carried.

Behind me, my name was being called in a voice of fury. With growing frustration I opened the next door and found myself in the kitchen. There were no more internal doors, but one led out to what looked like a lean-to greenhouse, filled with herbs and greens. Beyond was the garden – and also the three sentinels, who came motoring round the side of the house at surprising speed on their rotating legs. To gain time, I put a Seal on the door behind me. Then I looked around and saw the cook.

He was sitting far back in his chair with his shoes on the kitchen table, a fat, jovial-looking man with a red face and a meat cleaver in his hand. He was studiously paring his nails with the cleaver, flicking each fragment of nail expertly through the air to land in the fireplace beside him. As he did so he watched me continuously with his dark little eyes.

I felt unease. He didn't seem at all perturbed to see a small Egyptian boy come running into his kitchen. I checked him out on the different planes. On one to six he was exactly the same, a portly cook in a white apron. But on the seventh . . .

Uh-oh.

'Bartimaeus.'

'Faquarl.'

'How's it going?'

'Not bad.'

'Haven't seen you around.'

'No, I guess not.'

'Shame, eh?'

'Yes. Well . . . here I am.'

'Here you are, indeed.'

While this fascinating conversation was going on, the sounds of a sustained series of Detonations came from the other side of the door. My Seal held firm though. I smiled as urbanely as I could.

'Jabor seems as excitable as ever.'

'Yes, he's just the same. Only I think perhaps slightly more *hungry*, Bartimaeus. That's the only change I've noticed in him. He never seems satisfied, even when he's been fed. And that happens all too rarely these days, as you can imagine.'

'Treat 'em mean, keep 'em keen, that's your master's watch-word, is it? Still, he must be fairly potent to be able to have you *and* Jabor as his slaves.'

The cook gave a thin smile and with a flick of the knife sent a nail paring spinning to the ceiling. It pierced the plaster and lodged there.

'Now, now, Bartimaeus, we don't use the s-word in civilized company, do we? Jabor and I are playing the long game.'

'Of course you are.'

'Speaking of disparities in power, I notice that you choose to avoid addressing me on the seventh plane. This seems a little impolite. Can it be that you are uneasy with my true form?'

'Queasy, Faquarl, not uneasy.'[6]

'Well, this is all very pleasant. I admire *your* choice of form, by the way, Bartimaeus. Very comely. But I see that you are somewhat weighed down by a certain amulet. Perhaps you could be so good as to take it off and put it on the table. Then if you care to tell me which magician you are working for, I might consider ways of ending this meeting in a non-fatal manner.'

---

[6] I'm no great looker myself, but Faquarl had too many tentacles for my liking.

'That's kind of you, but you know I can't do that.'[7]

The cook prodded the edge of the table with the tip of his cleaver. 'Let me be frank. You can and will. It is nothing personal, of course; one day we may work together again. But for now I am bound just as you are. And I too have my charge to fulfil. So it comes, as it always does, to a question of power. Correct me if I am wrong, but I note that you do not have too much confidence in yourself today – otherwise you would have left by the front door, quelling the triloids as you went, rather than allowing them to shepherd you round the house to me.'

'I was merely following a whim.'

'Mm. Perhaps you would stop edging towards the window, Bartimaeus. Such a ploy would be pitifully obvious even to a human[8] and besides, the triloids wait for you there. Hand over the Amulet or you will discover that your ramshackle Defence Shield will count for nothing.'

He stood up and held out his hand. There was a pause. Behind my Seal, Jabor's patient (if unimaginative) Detonations still sounded. The door itself must have long since been turned to powder. In the garden the three sentinels hovered, all their eyes trained on me. I looked around the room for inspiration.

'The *Amulet*, Bartimaeus.'

I raised my hand and, with a heavy, rather theatrical sigh, took hold of the Amulet. Then I leaped to my left. At the same time, I released the Seal on the door. Faquarl gave a tut of annoyance and began a gesture. As he did so he was hit square

---

[7] Not strictly correct. I *could* have given over the Amulet and thus failed in my charge. But then, even if I had managed to escape from Faquarl, I would have had to return empty-handed to the pale-faced boy. My failure would have left me at his tender mercy, doubly in his power, and somehow I knew this was not a good idea.
[8] *Ouch.*

on by a particularly powerful Detonation that came shooting through the empty gap where the Seal had been. It sent him backwards into the fireplace and the brickwork collapsed upon him.

I smashed my way into the greenhouse just as Jabor stepped through the gap into the kitchen. As Faquarl emerged from the rubble I was breaking out into the garden. The three sentinels converged on me, eyes wide and legs rotating. Scything claws appeared at the ends of their blobby feet. I cast an Illumination of the brightest kind. The whole garden was lit up as if by an exploding sun. The sentinels' eyes were dazzled; they chittered with pain. I leaped over them and ran through the garden, dodging bolts of magic from the house that incinerated trees.

At the far end of the garden, between a compost heap and a motorized lawnmower, I vaulted the wall. I tore through the blue latticework of magical nodes, leaving a boy-shaped hole. Instantly alarm bells began ringing all over the grounds.

I hit the pavement outside, the Amulet bouncing and banging off my chest. On the other side of the wall I heard the sound of galloping hooves. It was high time I made a change.

Peregrine falcons are the fastest birds on record. They can attain a speed of two hundred kilometres an hour in diving flight. Rarely has one achieved this horizontally over the roofs of North London. Some would even doubt that this was possible, particularly while carrying a weighty amulet around its neck. Suffice it to say, however, that when Faquarl and Jabor landed in the Hampstead backstreet, creating an invisible obstruction that was immediately hit by a speeding removal van, I was nowhere to be seen.

I was long gone.

Nathaniel

5

'Above all,' said his master, 'there is one fact that we must drive into your wretched little skull now so that you never afterwards forget. Can you guess what that fact is?'

'No, sir,' the boy said.

'No?' The bristling eyebrows shot up in mock surprise. Mesmerized, the boy watched them disappear under the hanging white thatch of hair. There, almost coyly, they remained just out of sight for a moment, before suddenly descending with a terrible finality and weight. '*No.* Well then . . .' The magician bent forward in his chair. 'I shall tell you.'

With a slow, deliberate motion, he placed his hands together so that the fingertips formed a steepled arch, which he pointed at the boy.

'Remember *this*,' he said in a soft voice. 'Demons are very wicked. They will hurt you if they can. Do you understand this?'

The boy was still watching the eyebrows. He could not wrench his gaze away from them. Now they were furrowed sternly downwards, two sharp arrowheads meeting. They moved with a quite remarkable agility – up, down, tilting, arching, sometimes together, sometimes singly. With their parody of independent life they exerted a strange fascination on the boy. Besides, he found studying them infinitely preferable to meeting his master's gaze.

The magician coughed dangerously. 'Do you understand?'

'Oh – yes, sir.'

'Well now, you say yes, and I am sure you mean yes – and yet . . .' One eyebrow inched skywards musingly. 'And yet I do not feel convinced that you really, truly *understand*.'

'Oh, yes, sir; yes I do, sir. Demons are wicked and they are hurtful and they will hurt you if you let them, sir.' The boy fidgeted anxiously on his cushion. He was eager to prove that he had been listening well. Outside, the summer sun was beating on the grass and the hot pavements; an ice-cream van had passed merrily under the window five minutes before. But only a bright rim of pure daylight skirted the heavy red curtains of the magician's room; the air within was stuffy and thick. The boy wished for the lesson to be over, to be allowed to go.

'I have listened very carefully, sir,' he said.

His master nodded. 'Have you ever seen a demon?' he asked.

'No, sir. I mean, only in books.'

'Stand up.'

The boy stood quickly, one foot almost slipping on his cushion. He waited awkwardly, hands at his sides. His master indicated a door behind him with a casual finger. 'You know what's through there?'

'Your study, sir.'

'Good. Go down the steps and cross the room. At the far end you'll find my desk. On the desk is a box. In the box is a pair of spectacles. Put them on and come back to me. Got that?'

'Yes, sir.'

'Very well then. Off you go.'

Under his master's watchful eye, the boy crossed to the door, which was made of a dark, unpainted wood with many whorls and grains. He had to struggle to turn the heavy brass knob, but the coolness of its touch pleased him. The door swung open soundlessly on oiled hinges and the boy stepped through to find himself at the top of a carpeted staircase. The walls were elegantly papered with a flowery pattern. A small window halfway down let in a friendly stream of sunlight.

The boy descended carefully, one step at a time. The silence and sunlight reassured him and quelled some of his fears. Never having been beyond this point before, he had nothing but nursery stories to furnish his ideas of what might be waiting in his master's study. Terrible images of stuffed crocodiles and bottled eyeballs sprang garishly into his mind. Furiously he drove them out again. He would not be afraid.

At the foot of the staircase was another door, similar to the first, but smaller and decorated, in its centre, with a five-sided star painted in red. The boy turned the knob and pushed: the door opened reluctantly, sticking on the thick carpet. When the gap was wide enough the boy passed through into the study.

Subconsciously he had held his breath as he entered; now he let it out again, almost with a sense of disappointment. It was all so *ordinary*. A long room lined with books on either side. At the far end a great wooden desk with a padded leather chair set behind it. Pens on the table, a few papers, an old computer, a small metal box. The window beyond looked out towards a horse chestnut tree adorned with the full splendour of summer. The light in the room had a sweet greenish tint.

The boy made for the table.

Halfway there, he stopped and looked behind him.

Nothing. Yet he'd had the strangest feeling . . . For some reason the slightly open door, through which he had entered only a moment before, now gave him an unsettled sensation. He wished that he had thought to close it after him.

He shook his head. No need. He was going back through it in a matter of seconds.

Four hasty steps took him to the edge of the table. He looked round again. Surely there had been a noise . . .

The room was empty. The boy listened as intently as a rabbit in a covert. No, there was nothing to hear except faint sounds of distant traffic.

Wide-eyed, breathing hard, the boy turned to the table. The metal box glinted in the sun. He reached for it across the leather surface of the desk. This was not strictly necessary – he could have walked round to the other side of the desk and picked the box up easily – but somehow he wanted to save time, grab what he'd come for and get out. He leaned over the table and stretched out his hand, but the box remained obstinately just out of reach. The boy rocked forwards, swung his fingertips out wildly. They missed the box, but his flailing arm knocked over a small pot of pens. The pens sprayed across the leather.

The boy felt a bead of sweat trickle under his arm. Frantically, he began to collect up the pens and stuff them back into the pot.

There was a throaty chuckle, right behind him, in the room.

He wheeled round, stifling his yell. But there was nothing there.

For a moment the boy remained leaning with his back against the desk, paralysed with fear. Then something reasserted itself in him. 'Forget the pens,' it seemed to say. 'The box is what you came for.' Slowly, imperceptibly, he began to inch his way round the side of the desk, his back to the window, his eyes on the room.

Something tapped the window, urgently, three times. He spun round. Nothing there; only the horse chestnut beyond the garden, waving gently in the summer breeze.

Nothing there.

At that moment one of the pens he had spilled rolled off the desk onto the carpet. It made no sound, but he caught sight of it out of the corner of his eye. Another pen began to rock back and forth – first slowly, then faster and faster. Suddenly it spun away, bounced off the base of the computer and dropped over the edge onto the floor. Another did the same. Then another. Suddenly, all the pens were rolling, in several directions at once, accelerating off the edges of the desk, colliding, falling, lying still.

The boy watched. The last one fell.

He did not move.

Something laughed softly, right in his ear.

With a cry he lashed out with his left arm, but made no contact. The momentum of his swing turned him round to face the desk. The box was directly in front of him. He snatched it up and dropped it instantly – the metal had been sitting in the sun and its heat seared his palm. The box struck the desktop and lost its lid. A pair of horn-rimmed spectacles fell out. A moment later, he had them in his hand and was running for the door.

Something came behind him. He heard it hopping at his back.

He was almost at the door; he could see the stairs beyond that led up to his master.

And the door slammed shut.

The boy wrenched at the doorknob, beat at the wood, hammered, called to his master in a choking sob, but all to no avail. Something was whispering in his ear and he could not hear the words. In mortal panic, he kicked at the door, succeeding only in jarring his toe through his small black boot.

He turned then and faced the empty room.

Small rustlings sounded all about him, delicate taps and little flitterings, as if the carpet, the books, the shelves, even the ceiling was being brushed against by invisible, moving things. One of the light shades above his head swung slightly in a non-existent breeze.

Through his tears, through his terror, the boy found words to speak.

'Stop!' he shouted. 'Begone!'

The rustling, tapping and flittering stopped dead. The light shade's swing slowed, diminished and came to a halt.

The room was very still.

Gulping for breath, the boy waited with his back against the door, watching the room. Not a sound came.

Then he remembered the spectacles that he was still holding in his hand. Out of the clinging fog of fear he recalled that his master had told him to put them on before returning. Perhaps if he did so, the door would open and he would be allowed to climb the stairs to safety.

With trembling fingers he raised the spectacles and put them on.

And saw the truth about the study.

A hundred small demons filled every inch of the space in front of him. They were stacked one on top of the other all over the room, like seeds in a melon or nuts in a bag, with feet squishing faces and elbows jabbed into bellies. So tightly were they clustered that the very carpet was blocked out. Leering obscenely, they squatted on the desk, hung from the lights and bookcases and hovered in mid-air. Some balanced on the protruding noses of others or were suspended from their limbs. A few had huge bodies with heads the size of oranges; several displayed the reverse. There were tails and wings and horns and warts and extra hands, mouths, feet and eyes. There were too many scales and too much hair and other things in impossible places. Some had beaks, others had suckers, most had teeth. They were every conceivable colour, often in inappropriate combinations. And they were all doing their best to keep very, very still so as to convince the boy that nobody was there. They were trying extremely hard to remain frozen, despite the repressed shaking and trembling of tails and wings and the uncontrollable twitching of their extremely mobile mouths.

But at the very moment the boy put on the spectacles and saw them, they realized that he could see them too.

Then, with a cry of glee, they leaped at him.

The boy screamed, fell back against the door and sideways

onto the floor. He raised his hands to protect himself, dashing the spectacles from his nose. Blindly he rolled over onto his face and curled himself up into a ball, smothered by the terrible noise of wings and scales and small sharp claws on top, around, beside him.

The boy was still there twenty minutes later, when his master came to fetch him and dismiss the company of imps. He was carried to his room. For a day and a night he did not eat. For a further week he remained mute and unresponsive, but at length he regained his speech and was able to resume his studies.

His master never referred to the incident again, but he was satisfied with the outcome of the lesson – with the well of hate and fear that had been dug for his apprentice in that sunny room.

This was one of Nathaniel's earliest experiences. He did not speak of it to anyone, but the shadow of it never left his heart. He was six years old at the time.

Bartimaeus

6

The problem with a highly magical artefact such as the Amulet of Samarkand is that it has a distinctive pulsating aura[1] that attracts attention like a naked man at a funeral. I knew that no sooner had Simon Lovelace been informed of my escapade than he would send out searchers looking for the telltale pulse, and that the longer I remained in one place, the more chance there was of something pinpointing it. The boy would not summon me until

---

[1] All living things have auras too. They take the form of a coloured nimbus surrounding the individual's body and are in fact the closest a visual phenomenon gets to becoming a smell. Auras do exist on the first plane but are invisible to most humans. Many animals, such as cats, can see them; djinn and a few exceptional persons likewise. Auras change colour depending on mood and are a useful indication of fear, hatred, sorrow, etc. This is why it is very hard to deceive a cat (or a djinni) when you wish it ill.

dawn,[2] so I had several restless hours to survive first.

What might the magician send after me? He was unlikely to command many other djinn of Faquarl and Jabor's strength, but he would certainly be able to whip up a host of weaker servants to join in the hunt. Ordinarily I can dispose of foliots and the like with one claw tied behind my back, but if they arrived in large numbers, and I was weary, things might become difficult.[3]

I flew from Hampstead at top speed and took shelter under the eaves of a deserted house beside the Thames, where I preened my feathers and watched the sky. After a time seven small spheres of red light passed across the heavens at low altitude. When they reached the middle of the river they split forces: three continued south, two went west, two east. I pressed myself deep into the shadows of the roof, but couldn't help notice the Amulet giving an extra-vibrant throb as the nearest questing spheres disappeared downriver. This unnerved me; shortly afterwards I departed to a girder halfway up a

---

[2] It would have been a lot more agreeable to return to the urchin immediately to rid myself of the Amulet. But magicians almost always insist on specific summons at specific times. It removes the possibility of us catching them at a (potentially fatal) disadvantage.

[3] Even magicians are confused by our infinite varieties, which are as different one from the other as elephants are from insects, or eagles from amoebae. However, broadly speaking, there are five basic ranks that you are likely to find working in a magician's service. These are, in descending order of power and general awe: marids, afrits, djinn, foliots, imps. (There are legions of lowly sprites that are weaker than the imps, but magicians rarely bother summoning these. Likewise, far above the marids exist great entities of terrible power; they are seldom seen on Earth, since few magicians dare even uncover their names.) A detailed knowledge of this hierarchy is vitally important for both magicians and for us, since survival frequently depends on knowing exactly where you stand. For example, as a particularly fine specimen of a djinni, I treat other djinn and anything above my rank with a certain degree of courtesy, but give foliots and imps short shrift.

crane on the opposite bank, where they were erecting a swish riverside condo for the magical gentry.

Five silent minutes passed. The river sucked and swirled round the muddy posts of the wharf. Clouds passed over the moon. A sudden green and sickly light flared in all the windows of the deserted house on the other side of the river. Hunched shadows moved within it, searching. They found nothing; the light congealed and became a glowing mist that drifted from the windows and was blown away. Darkness shrouded the house again. I flew south at once, darting and swooping from street to street.

For half the night I continued my frantic, fugitive dance across London. The spheres[4] were out in even greater numbers than I had feared (evidently more than one magician had summoned them) and appeared above me at regular intervals. To keep safe I had to keep moving, and even then I was nearly caught twice. Once I flew around an office block and nearly collided with a sphere coming the other way; another came upon me as, overcome with exhaustion, I huddled in a birch tree in Green Park. On both occasions I managed to escape before reinforcements arrived.

Before long I was on my last wings. The constant drag of supporting my physical form was wearing me down and using up precious energy. So I decided to adopt a different plan – to find a place where the Amulet's pulse would be drowned out by other magical emissions. It was time to mingle with the

---

[4] Search spheres like these are a kind of sturdy imp. They possess giant scaly ears and a single bristled nostril, which make them particularly sensitive to magical pulsation and extremely irritable when exposed to any loud noise or pungent smell. For some of the night I was consequently forced to bunker down in the middle of Rotherhithe Sewage Works.

Many-headed Multitude, the Great Unwashed: in other words, with people. I was that desperate.

I flew back to the centre of the city. Even at this late hour, the tourists in Trafalgar Square still flowed around the base of Nelson's Column in a gaudy tide, buying cut-price charms from the official vending booths wedged between the lions. A cacophony of magical pulses rose up from the square. It was as good a place as anywhere to hide.

A bolt of feathered lightning plunged down out of the night and disappeared into the narrow space between two stalls. Presently a young sad-eyed Egyptian boy emerged and elbowed his way into the throng. He wore new blue jeans and a padded black bomber jacket over a white T-shirt; also a pair of big white trainers with laces that were constantly coming loose. He mingled with the crowd.

I felt the Amulet burning against my chest. At regular intervals it sent out little waves of intense heat in double bursts, like heartbeats. I fervently hoped that this signal would now be swallowed by the auras all around.

Much of the magic here was all show, no substance. The plaza was littered with licensed quacks selling minor charms and trinkets that had been approved by the authorities for common use.[5] Wide-eyed tourists from North America and

---

[5] Particularly popular were shards of crystal that were purported to exude life-enhancing auras. People hung them round their necks for good luck. The shards had no magical properties whatsoever, but I suppose in one way they *did* have a protective function: anybody wearing one immediately advertised themselves as a magical ignoramus, and as a result they were ignored by the many factions of feuding magicians. In London it was dangerous for a person to have had even the slightest magical training: then one became useful and/or dangerous — and as a result fair game for other magicians.

Japan eagerly probed the stacks of multicoloured stones and gimcrack jewellery, trying to recall the birth-signs of their relatives back home while being patiently prompted by the cheery Cockney vendors. If it wasn't for the camera bulbs flashing I might have been back in Karnak. Bargains were being struck, happy cries rang out, everyone was smiling. It was a timeless tableau of gullibility and greed.

But not everything in the square was trivial. Here and there rather more sober-faced men stood at the entrances to small closed tents. Visitors were admitted to these one by one. Evidently there were artefacts of genuine value inside, since without exception small watchers loitered near each booth. They came in various unobtrusive forms – pigeons mostly; I avoided going too close in case they were more perceptive than they looked.

A few magicians wandered about amid the crowd. They were unlikely to be buying anything here; more probably they were doing the night shift in the government offices in Whitehall and had come out for a breather. One (in a good suit) had an accompanying second-plane imp hopping at his heel; the others (more shabbily attired) simply trailed the tell-tale odour of incense, dried sweat and candle wax.

The police were present too – several ordinary constables and a couple of hairy, hatchet-faced men from the Night Police keeping themselves just visible enough to prevent trouble.

And all around the square the car lights swirled, carrying ministers and other magicians from their offices in Parliament to their clubs at St James's. I was near the hub of a great wheel of power that extended over an empire, and here, with luck, I would remain undetected until I was finally summoned.

Or possibly not.

I had sauntered over to a particularly tatty-looking stall and was examining its fare when I had the uneasy feeling that I was being watched. I turned my head a little and scanned the crowd. An amorphous mass. I checked the planes. No hidden dangers: a bovine herd, all of it dull and human. I turned back to the stall and absently picked up a My Magic Mirror™, a piece of cheap glass glued into a frame of pink plastic and feebly decorated with wands, cats and wizards' hats.

There it was again! I turned my body sharply. Through a gap in the crowd directly behind me I could see a short, plump female magician, a bunch of kids clustered round a stand, a policeman eyeing them suspiciously. No one seemed to have the slightest interest in me. But I knew what I'd felt. Next time I'd be ready. I made a big show of considering the mirror. 'ANOTHER GREAT GIFT FROM LONDON, MAGIC CAPITAL OF THE WORLD!' screamed the label on its back. 'MADE IN TAIW—'

Then the feeling came again. I swivelled quicker than a cat and – success! I caught the starers eyeball to eyeball. Two of them, a boy and a girl, from within the gaggle of kids. They didn't have time to drop their gaze. The boy was mid-teens; acne was laying siege to his face with some success. The girl was younger, but her eyes were cold and hard. I gazed back. What did I care? They were human, they couldn't see what I was. Let them stare.

After a few seconds they couldn't handle it; they looked away. I shrugged and made to move off. There was a loud cough from the man on the stand. I replaced My Magic Mirror™ carefully on his tray, gave him a cheesy smile and went my way.

The children followed me.

I caught sight of them at the next booth, watching from behind a candyfloss stand. They were moving in a huddle – maybe five or six of them, I couldn't be sure. What did they want? A mugging? If so, why pick me out? There were dozens of better, fatter, richer candidates here. To test this I cosied up to a very small, wealthy-looking tourist with a giant camera and thick spectacles. If I'd wanted to mug someone he'd have been top of my list. But when I left him and went on a loop through the crowd, the children followed right along too.

Weird. And annoying. I didn't want to make a change and fly off; I was too weary. All I wanted was to be left in peace. I still had many hours to go before the dawn.

I speeded up; the children did so too. Long before we'd done three circuits of the square, I'd had enough. A couple of policemen had watched us beetling around and they were likely to halt us soon, if only to stop themselves getting dizzy. It was time to go. Whatever the kids were after, I did not want any more attention drawn to me.

There was a subway close by. I hotfooted it down the steps, ignored the entrance to the Underground and came up again on the other side of the road, opposite the central square. The kids had vanished – maybe they were in the subway. Now was my chance. I slipped round a street corner, along past a book-shop and ducked down an alley. I waited a little there, in the shadows among the dumper bins.

A couple of cars drove past the end of the alley. No one came after me.

I allowed myself a brief smile. I thought I'd lost them.

I was wrong.

7

The Egyptian boy wandered off along the alley, made a couple of right-angle turns and came out in one of the many roads that radiate from Trafalgar Square. I was revising my plans as I went.

Forget the square. Too many irritating children around. But perhaps if I found a shelter close by, the Amulet's pulse would still be hard for the spheres to locate. I could hole up behind some dustbins until the morning came. It was the only option. I was too weary to take to the skies again.

And I wanted to do some thinking.

The old pain had started up again, throbbing in my chest, stomach, bones. It wasn't healthy to be encased in a body for so long. How humans can stand it without going completely mad, I'll never know.[1]

I stumped down the dark, cold street, looking at my reflection as it flitted across the blank squares of the windows alongside. The boy's shoulders were hunched against the wind, his hands deep in his jacket pockets. His trainers scuffed the concrete. His posture perfectly expressed the annoyance I was feeling. The Amulet beat against my chest with every step. If it had been in my power I would have ripped it off and lobbed it into the nearest bin before dematerializing in high dudgeon.

---

[1] Then again . . . maybe that explains a lot.

But I was bound by the orders of the child's command.[2] I had to keep it with me.

I took a side road away from the traffic. The massed darkness of high buildings closed in on either side, oppressing me. Cities get me down, almost as if I am underground. London is particularly bad – cold, grey, heavy with odours and rain. It makes me long for the south, for the deserts and the blank blue sky.

Another alley led off to the left, choked with wet cardboard and newspapers. Automatically I scanned through the planes, saw nothing. It would do. I rejected the first two doorways for reasons of hygiene. The third was dry. I sat there.

It was high time I thought through the events of the night so far. It had been a busy one. There was the pale-faced boy, Simon Lovelace, the Amulet, Jabor, Faquarl . . . A pretty hellish brew all round. Still, what did it matter? At dawn I would hand over the Amulet and escape this sorry mess for good.

Except for my business with the boy. He'd pay for it, big time. You didn't reduce Bartimaeus of Uruk to dossing in a West End alley-back and expect to get away with it. First I'd find out his name, then—

---

[2] There have been cases where a spirit has attempted to refuse a command. On one notable occasion, Asmoral the Resolute was instructed by his master to destroy the djinni Ianna. But Ianna had long been Asmoral's closest ally and there was great love between them. Despite his master's increasingly severe injunctions, Asmoral refused to act. Sadly, though his willpower was equal to the challenge, his essence was tied to the irresistible tug of the magician's command. Before long, because he did not give way, he was literally torn in two. The resulting matter explosion destroyed the magician, his palace and an outlying suburb of Baghdad. After this tragic event, magicians learned to be cautious of ordering direct attacks on opposing spirits (opposing magicians were a different matter). For our part, we learned to avoid conflicts of principle. As a result, loyalties amongst us are temporary and liable to shift. Friendship is essentially a matter of strategy.

Wait . . .

Footsteps in the alley . . . Several pairs of boots approaching.

Perhaps it was just coincidence. London's a city. People use it. People use alleys. Whoever was coming was probably just taking a shortcut home.

Up the very alley that I happened to be hiding in.

I don't believe in coincidences.

I shrank back into the doorway's shallow well of darkness and cast a Concealment upon myself. A layer of tightly laced black threads covered me where I sat in the shadows, blending me into the murk. I waited.

The boots drew nearer. Who might it be? A Night Police patrol? A phalanx of magicians sent by Simon Lovelace? Perhaps the spheres *had* spotted me after all.

It was neither police nor magicians. It was the children from Trafalgar Square.

Five boys, with the girl at their head. They were dawdling along, looking casually from side to side. I relaxed a little. I was well hidden, and even if I hadn't been, there was nothing to fear from them now that we were out of the public gaze. Admittedly, the boys were big and loutish looking, but they were still just boys, dressed in jeans and leathers. The girl wore a black leather jacket and trousers that flared wildly from the knees down. There was enough spare material there to make a second pair for a midget. Down the alley they came, scuffling through the litter. I realized suddenly how unnaturally silent they were.

In doubt, I checked the other planes again. On each, everything was just as it should be. Six children.

Hidden behind my barrier, I waited for them to go past.

The girl was in the lead. She drew level with me.

Safe behind my barrier, I yawned.

One of the boys tapped the girl's shoulder.

'It's there,' he said, pointing.

'Get it,' the girl said.

Before I had a chance to get over my surprise, three of the burliest boys leaped into the doorway and crashed down upon me. As they touched the Concealment wisps, the threads tore and dissolved away into nothingness. For an instant I was overwhelmed by a tidal wave of distressed leather, cheap aftershave and body odour. I was sat upon, punched and smacked about the head. I was bundled unceremoniously to my feet.

Then I reasserted myself. I am Bartimaeus, after all.

The alley was illuminated by a brief discharge of heat and light. The bricks of the doorway looked as if they had been seared on a griddle.

To my surprise the boys were still holding on. Two of them gripped my wrists like a manacle twin-set, while the third had both arms tight round my waist.

I repeated the effect with greater emphasis. Car alarms in the next street started ringing. This time, I confess, I expected to be left in the charcoaly grip of three charred corpses.[3]

But the boys were still there, breathing hard and holding on like grim death.

Something was not quite right here.

'Hold it steady,' the girl said.

I looked at her, she looked at me. She was a little bit taller

---

[3] Despite what some would say on the subject, many of us have no particular interest in harming ordinary humans. There are exceptions, of course, of which Jabor is one. However, even for mild-tempered djinn such as me, there is such a thing as being pushed too far.

than my current manifestation, with dark eyes, long dark hair. The other two boys stood on either side of her like an acned guard of honour. I grew impatient.

'What do you want?' I said.

'You have something round your neck.' The girl had a remarkably level and authoritative voice for someone so young. I guessed she was about thirteen.

'Says who?'

'It's been in full view for the last two minutes, you cretin. It fell out of your T-shirt when we jumped you.'

'Oh. Fair enough.'

'Hand it over.'

'No.'

She shrugged. 'Then we'll take it. It's your funeral.'

'You don't really know who I am, do you?' I made it sound damn casual, with a side helping of menace. 'You're not a magician.'

'Too right I'm not.' She spat the words out.

'A magician would know better than to trifle with one such as me.' I was busy cranking up the awe-factor again, although this is always fairly tricky when you have a brawny half-wit clasping you round your waist.

The girl grinned coldly. 'Would a magician do so well against your wickedness?'

She had a point there. For a start a magician wouldn't have wanted to come within a dog's bark of me without being protected up to the hilt with charms and pentacles. Next he would have needed the help of imps to find me under my Concealment and finally he would have had to conjure up a fairly heavyweight djinni to subdue me. If he dared. But this girl and her boyfriends had done it

46

all on their own, without seeming particularly fussed.

I should have let fly a full-strength Detonation or something, but I was too tired for anything fancy. I fell back on empty bluster.

I laughed eerily. 'Hah! I'm toying with you.'

'That's empty bluster.'

I tried another tack. 'Despite myself,' I said, 'I confess I'm intrigued. I applaud your bravery in daring to accost me. If you tell me your name and purpose I will spare you. In fact, I might well be able to help you. I have many abilities at my command.'

To my disappointment, the girl clamped her hands over her ears. 'Don't give me your weasel words, demon!' she said. 'I won't be tempted.'

'Surely you do not want my enmity,' I went on, soothingly. 'My friendship is greatly to be preferred.'

'I don't care about either,' the girl said, lowering her hands. 'I want whatever it is you have round your neck.'

'You can't have it. But you can have a fight if you like. Apart from the damage it'll do you, I'll make sure I let off a signal that'll bring the Night Police down on us like gorgons from hell. You don't want *their* attention, do you?'

That made her flinch a bit. I built on my advantage.

'Don't be naive,' I said. 'Think about it. You're trying to rob me of a very powerful object. It belongs to a terrible magician. If you so much as touch it, he'll find you and nail your skin to his door.'

Whether it was this threat or the accusation of naiveté that got to her, the girl was rattled. I could tell by the direction of her pout.

Experimentally I shifted one elbow a little. The corresponding boy grunted and tightened his grip on my arm.

A siren sounded a few roads away. The girl and her body-guards looked uneasily down the alley into the darkness. A few drops of rain began to fall from the hidden sky.

'Enough of this,' the girl said. She stepped towards me.

'Careful,' I said.

She stretched out a hand. As she did so, I opened my mouth, very, very slowly. Then she reached for the chain round my neck.

In an instant I was a Nile crocodile with jaws agape. I snapped down at her fingers. The girl shrieked and jerked her arm backwards faster than I would have believed possible. My snaggleteeth clashed just short of her retreating fingernails. I snapped at her again, thrashing from side to side in my captors' grasp. The girl squawked, slipped and fell into a pile of litter, knocking over one of her two guards. My sudden trans-formation took my three boys by surprise, particularly the one who was clutching me around my wide scaly midriff. His grip had loosened, but the other two were still hanging on. My long hard tail scythed left, then right, making satisfyingly crisp contact with two thick skulls. Their brains, if they had any, were nicely addled; their jaws slackened and so did their grasps.

One of the girl's two guards had been only momentarily shocked. He recovered himself, reached inside his jacket, emerged with something shiny in his hand.

As he threw it, I changed again.

The quick shift from big (the croc) to small (a fox) was nicely judged, if I say so myself. The six hands that had been struggling to cope with large-scale scales suddenly found themselves clenching thin air as a tiny red bundle of fur and whirling claws dropped through their flailing fingers to the floor. At the same moment a missile of flashing silver passed through the point where the croc's throat had recently been and embedded itself in the metal door beyond.

The fox ran up the alley, paws skittering on the slippery cobbles.

A piercing whistle sounded ahead. The fox pulled up. Searchlights dipped and spun against the doors and brickwork. Running feet followed the lights.

That was all I needed. The Night Police were coming.

As a beam swung towards me, I leaped fluidly into the open mouth of a plastic bin. Head, body, brush – gone; the light passed over the bin and went on down the alley.

Men came now, shouting, blowing whistles, racing towards where I'd left the girl and her companions. Then a growling, an acrid smell; and something that might have been a big dog rushing after them into the night.

The sounds echoed away. Curled snugly between a seeping bin bag and a vinegary crate of empty bottles, the fox listened, his ears pricked forwards. The shouts and whistles grew distant and confused, and to the fox it seemed as if they merged and became an agitated howling.

Then the noise faded altogether. The alleyway was silent.

Alone in the foulness, the fox lay low.

Nathaniel

8

Arthur Underwood was a middle-ranking magician who worked for the Ministry of Internal Affairs. A solitary man, of a somewhat cantankerous nature, he lived with his wife Martha in a tall Georgian house in Highgate.

Mr Underwood had never had an apprentice, and nor did he want one. He was quite happy working on his own. But he knew that sooner or later, like all other magicians, he would have to take his turn and accept a child into his house.

Sure enough, the inevitable happened: one day a letter arrived from the Employment Ministry, containing the dreaded request. With grim resignation, Mr Underwood carried out his duty. On the appointed afternoon, he travelled to the ministry to collect his nameless charge.

He ascended the marbled steps between two granite pillars and entered the echoing foyer. It was a vast, featureless space;

office workers passed quietly back and forth between wooden doors on either side, their shoes making respectful pattering noises on the floor. Across the hall, two statues of past Employment ministers had been built on a heroic scale, and sandwiched between them was a desk, piled high with papers. Mr Underwood approached. It was only when he actually reached the desk that he was able to glimpse, behind the bristling rampart of bulging files, the face of a small, smiling clerk.

'Hello, sir,' said the clerk.

'Junior Minister Underwood. I'm here to collect my new apprentice.'

'Ah – yes, sir. I was expecting you. If you'll just sign a few documents . . .' The clerk rummaged in a nearby stack. 'Won't take a minute. Then you can pick him up from the day room.'

' "Him"? It's a boy, then?'

'A boy, five years old. Very bright, if the tests are anything to go by. Obviously a little upset at the moment . . .' The clerk located a wodge of papers and withdrew a pen from behind his ear. 'If you could initial each page and sign on the dotted lines . . .'

Mr Underwood flourished the pen. 'His parents – they've left, I take it?'

'Yes, sir. They couldn't get away fast enough. The usual sort: take the money and run, if you get my meaning, sir. Barely stopped to say goodbye to him.'

'And all the normal safety procedures—?'

'His birth records have been removed and destroyed, sir, and he has been strictly instructed to forget his birth-name and not reveal it to anyone. He is now officially unformed. You can start with him from scratch.'

'Very well.' With a sigh, Mr Underwood completed his last spidery signature and passed the documents back. 'If that's all, I suppose I had better collect him.'

He passed down a series of silent corridors and through a heavy, panelled door to a brightly painted room that had been filled with toys for the entertainment of unhappy children. There, between a grimacing rocking horse and a plastic wizard doll wearing a comedy conical hat, he found a small, pale-faced boy. It had been crying in the recent past, but had now fortunately desisted. Two red-rimmed eyes looked up at him blankly. Mr Underwood cleared his throat.

'I'm Underwood, your master. Your true life begins now. Come with me.'

The child gave a loud sniff. Mr Underwood noticed its chin wobbling dangerously. With some distaste, he took the boy by the hand, pulled it to its feet and led it out down echoing corridors to his waiting car.

On the journey back to Highgate, the magician once or twice tried to engage the child in conversation, but was met with teary silence. This did not please him; with a snort of frustration, he gave it up and turned on the radio to catch the cricket scores. The child sat stock still in the back seat, gazing at its knees.

His wife met them at the door. She carried a tray of biscuits and a steaming mug of hot chocolate, and straight away bustled the boy into a cosy sitting room, where a fire leaped in the grate.

'You won't get any sense out of him, Martha,' Mr Underwood grunted. 'Hasn't said a word.'

'Do you wonder? He's terrified, poor thing. Leave him to me.' Mrs Underwood was a diminutive, roundish woman with very white hair cropped short. She sat the boy in a chair by the fire and offered him a biscuit. He didn't acknowledge her at all.

Half an hour passed. Mrs Underwood chatted pleasantly about anything that came into her head. The boy drank some chocolate and nibbled a biscuit, but otherwise stared silently into the fire. Finally, Mrs Underwood made a decision. She sat beside him and put her arm round his shoulders.

'Now dear,' she said, 'let's make a deal. I know that you've been told not to tell anyone your name, but you can make an exception with me. I can't get to know you properly just calling you "boy"; can I? So, if you tell me your name, I'll tell you mine – in strictest confidence. What do you think? Was that a nod? Very well, then. I'm Martha. And you are . . . ?'

A small snuffle, a smaller voice. '*Nathaniel.*'

'That's a lovely name, dear, and don't worry, I won't tell a soul. Don't you feel better already? Now have another biscuit, Nathaniel, and I'll show you to your bedroom.'

With the child fed and bathed and finally put to bed, Mrs Underwood reported back to her husband, who was working in his study.

'He's asleep at last,' she said. 'It wouldn't surprise me if he was in shock – and no wonder, his parents leaving him like that. I think it's disgraceful, ripping a child from his home so young.'

'That's how it's always been done, Martha. Apprentices have to come from somewhere.' The magician kept his head bent meaningfully towards his book.

His wife did not take the hint. 'He should be allowed to stay with his family,' she went on. 'Or at least *see* them sometimes.'

Wearily, Mr Underwood placed the book on the table. 'You know very well that is quite impossible. His birth-name must be forgotten, or else future enemies will use it to harm him. How can it be forgotten if his family keeps in contact? Besides, no one has *forced* his parents to part with their brat. They didn't want him, that's the truth of it, Martha, or they wouldn't have answered the advertisements. It's quite straight-forward. They get a considerable amount of money as compensation, he gets a chance to serve his country at the highest level, and the State gets a new apprentice. Simple. Everyone wins. No one loses out.'

'All the same . . .'

'It didn't do *me* any harm, Martha.' Mr Underwood reached for his book.

'It would be a lot less cruel if magicians were allowed their *own* children.'

'That road leads to competing dynasties, family alliances . . . it all ends in blood feuds. Read your history books, Martha: see what happened in Italy. So, don't worry about the boy. He's young. He'll forget soon enough. Now, what about making me some supper?'

The magician Underwood's house was the kind of building that presented a slender, simple, dignified countenance to the street, but which extended back for a remarkable distance in a confusion of stairs, corridors and slightly varying levels. There were five main floors altogether: a cellar, filled with wine racks, mushroom boxes and cases of drying fruit; the ground floor, containing reception room, dining hall, kitchen and conservatory; two upper floors, mainly consisting of bath-rooms, bedrooms and workrooms; and, at the very top, an attic.

It was here that Nathaniel slept, under a steeply sloping ceiling of whitewashed rafters.

Each morning, at dawn, he was woken by the fluting clamour of pigeons on the roof above. A small skylight was set in the ceiling. Through it, if he stood on a chair, he could see out over the grey rain-washed London horizon. The house stood on a hill and the view was good; on clear days he could see the Crystal Palace radio mast far away on the other side of the city.

His bedroom was furnished with a cheap plywood wardrobe, a small chest of drawers, a desk and chair and a bed-side bookcase. Every week Mrs Underwood placed a new cutting of garden flowers in a vase on the desk.

From that first miserable day, the magician's wife had taken Nathaniel under her wing. She liked the boy and was kind to him. In the privacy of the house, she often addressed the apprentice by his birth-name, despite the stern displeasure of her husband.

'We shouldn't even *know* the brat's name,' he told her. 'It's forbidden! He could be compromised. When he is twelve, at his coming of age, he will be given his new name, by which he will be known, as magician and man, for the rest of his life. In the meantime, it is quite wrong—'

'Who's going to notice?' she protested. 'No one. It gives the poor lad comfort.'

She was the only person to use his name. His tutors called him 'Underwood', after his master. His master himself just addressed him as 'boy'.

In return for her affection, Nathaniel rewarded Mrs Underwood with open devotion. He hung on her every word, and followed her directions in everything.

At the end of his first week at the house, she brought a present to his room. 'This is for you,' she said. 'It's a bit old and dreary, but I thought you might like it.'

It was a painting of boats sailing up a creek, surrounded by mudflats and low countryside. The varnish was so dark with age that the details could hardly be made out, but Nathaniel loved it instantly. He watched Mrs Underwood hang it on the wall above his desk.

'You're to be a magician, Nathaniel,' she said, 'and that is the greatest privilege that any boy or girl could have. Your parents have made the ultimate sacrifice by giving you up for this noble destiny. No, don't cry, dear. So in turn you must be strong, strive as hard as you can, and learn everything your tutors ask of you. By doing that you will honour both your parents and yourself. Come over to the window. Stand on that chair. Now – look over there; do you see that little tower in the distance?'

'That one?'

'No, that's an office block, dear. The little brown one, over on the left? That's it. That's the Houses of Parliament, my dear, where all the finest magicians go, to rule Britain and our empire. Mr Underwood goes there all the time. And if you work hard and do everything your master tells you, one day you will go there too, and I will be as proud of you as can be.'

'Yes, Mrs Underwood.' He stared at the tower until his eyes ached, fixing its position firmly in his mind. To go to Parliament . . . One day it would be so. He would indeed work hard and make her proud.

With time, and the constant ministrations of Mrs Underwood, Nathaniel's homesickness began to fade. Memory of his distant parents dimmed and the pain inside him grew ever less, until he had almost forgotten its existence. A strict routine of work and study helped with this process: it took up nearly all his time and left him little space to brood. On weekdays, the routine began with Mrs Underwood rousing him with a double rap on his bedroom door.

'Tea outside, on the step. Mouth, not toes.'

This call was a ritual stemming from one morning when, on his way downstairs to the bathroom, Nathaniel had charged out of his bedroom in a befuddled state, made precise contact between foot and mug and sent a tidal wave of hot tea crashing against the landing wall. The stain was still visible years later, like the imprint of a gout of blood. Fortunately his master had not discovered this disaster. He never ascended to the attic.

After washing in the bathroom on the level below, Nathaniel would dress himself in shirt, grey trousers, long grey socks, smart black shoes and, if it was winter and the house was cold, a thick Arran jumper that Mrs Underwood had bought for him. He would brush his hair carefully in front of a tall mirror in the bathroom, running his eyes over the thin, neat figure with the pale face gazing back at him. Then he descended by the back stairs to the kitchen, carrying his schoolwork. While Mrs Underwood fixed the cornflakes and toast, he would try to finish the homework left over from the night before. Mrs Underwood frequently did her best to help him.

'Azerbaijan? The capital's Baku, I think.'

'Bakoo?'

'Yes. Look in your atlas. What are you learning that for?'

'Mr Purcell says I have to master the Middle East this week

– learn the countries and stuff.'

'Don't look so down. Toast's ready. Well, it is important you learn all that "stuff" – you have to know the background before you can get to the interesting bits.'

'But it's so *boring*.'

'That's all you know. I've been to Azerbaijan. Baku's a bit of a dump, but it is an important centre for researching afrits.'

'What are they?'

'Demons of fire. The second most powerful form of spirit. The fiery element is very strong in the mountains of Azerbaijan. That's where the Zoroastrian faith began too; they venerate the divine fire found in all living things. If you're looking for the chocolate spread it's behind the cereal.'

'Did you see a djinni when you were there, Mrs Underwood?'

'You don't need to go to Baku to find a djinni, Nathaniel – and don't speak with your mouth full. You're spraying crumbs all over my tablecloth. No, djinn will come to you, especially if you're here in London.'

'When will I see a freet?'

'An *afrit*. Not for a long time, if you know what's good for you. Now finish up quickly – Mr Purcell will be waiting.'

After breakfast, Nathaniel would gather his school books and head upstairs to the first-floor workroom where Mr Purcell would indeed be waiting for him. His teacher was a young man with thinning blond hair, which he frequently smoothed down in a vain effort to hide his scalp. He wore a grey suit that was slightly too big for him and an alternating sequence of horrible ties. His first name was Walter. Many things made him nervous, and speaking to Mr Underwood (which he had to, on occasions) made him downright twitchy.

As a result of his nerves he took his frustrations out on Nathaniel. He was too honest a man to be really brutal with the boy, who was a competent worker; instead he tended to snap tetchily at his mistakes, yipping like a small dog.

Nathaniel learned no magic with Mr Purcell. His teacher did not know any. Instead he had to apply himself to other subjects, primarily mathematics, modern languages (French, Czech), geography and history. Politics was also important.

'Now then, young Underwood,' Mr Purcell would say. 'What is the chief purpose of our noble government?' Nathaniel looked blank. 'Come on! Come on!'

'To rule us, sir?'

'To *protect* us. Do not forget that our country is at war. Prague still commands the plains east of Bohemia, and we are struggling to keep her armies out of Italy. These are dangerous times. Agitators and spies are loose in London. If the Empire is to be kept whole, a strong government must be in place, and strong means magicians. Imagine the country without them! It would be unthinkable: *commoners* would be in charge! We would slip into chaos and invasion would quickly follow. All that stands between us and anarchy is our leaders. This is what you should aspire to, boy. To be a part of the Government and rule honourably. Remember that.'

'Yes, sir.'

'Honour is the most important quality for a magician,' Mr Purcell went on. 'He or she has great power, and must use it with discretion. In the past, rogue magicians have attempted to overthrow the State: they have always been defeated. Why? Because true magicians fight with virtue and justice on their side.'

'Mr Purcell, are *you* a magician?'

His teacher smoothed back his hair and sighed. 'No, Underwood. I was . . . not selected. But I still serve as best I can. Now—'

'Then you're a commoner?'

Mr Purcell slapped the table with his palm. 'If you please! *I'm* asking the questions! Take up your protractor. We shall move on to geometry.'

Shortly after his eighth birthday Nathaniel's curriculum was expanded. He began to study chemistry and physics on the one hand, and the history of religion on the other. He also began several other key languages, including Latin, Aramaic and Hebrew.

These activities occupied Nathaniel from nine in the morning until lunch at one, at which time he would descend to the kitchen to devour in solitude the sandwiches that Mrs Underwood had left out for him under a moist clingfilm wrapper.

In the afternoons the timetable was varied. On two days of the week, Nathaniel continued work with Mr Purcell. On two other afternoons he was escorted down the road to a public baths, where a burly man with a moustache shaped like a mudguard supervised a punishing regimen. Along with a bedraggled posse of other small children, Nathaniel had to swim countless lengths using every conceivable style of stroke. He was always too shy and exhausted to talk much to his fellow swimmers and they, sensing him for what he was, kept their distance from him. Already, by the age of eight, he was avoided and left alone.

The other two afternoon activities were music (Thursday) and drawing (Saturday). Nathaniel dreaded music even more than swimming. His tutor, Mr Sindra, was an obese, short-tempered man whose chins quivered as he walked. Nathaniel kept a close eye on those chins: if their trembling increased it was a sure sign of a coming rage. Rages came with depressing regularity. Mr Sindra could barely contain his fury whenever Nathaniel rushed his scales, misread his notes or fluffed his sight-reading, and these things happened often.

'How,' Mr Sindra yelled, 'do you propose to summon a lamia with plucking like this? How? The mind boggles! Give me that!' He snatched the lyre from Nathaniel's hand and held it against his ample chest. Then, his eyes closed in rapture, he began to play. A sweet melody filled the workroom. The short, fat fingers moved like dancing sausages across the strings; outside, birds stopped in the tree to listen. Nathaniel's eyes filled with tears. Memories from the distant past drifted ghost-like before him . . .

'Now you!' The music broke off with a jarring screech. The lyre was thrust back at him. Nathaniel began to pluck at the strings. His fingers tripped and stumbled; outside, several birds dropped from the tree in a stupor. Mr Sindra's jowls shook like cold tapioca.

'You idiot! Stop! Do you want the lamia to eat you? She must be charmed, not roused to fury! Put down that poor instrument. We shall try the pipes.'

Pipes or lyre, choral voice or sistrum rattle – whatever Nathaniel tried, his faltering attempts met with bellows of outrage and despair. It was a far cry from his drawing lessons, which proceeded peacefully and well under his tutor Ms Lutyens. Willowy and sweet-tempered, she was the only one of his teachers to whom Nathaniel could talk freely. Like Mrs Underwood, she had little time for his 'nameless' status. In confidence, she had asked him to tell her his name, and he had done so without a second thought.

'Why,' he asked her one spring afternoon, as they sat in the workroom with a fresh breeze drifting through the open window, 'why do I spend all my time copying this pattern? It is both difficult *and* dull. I would much rather be drawing the garden, or this room – or *you*, Ms Lutyens.'

She laughed at him. 'Sketching is all very well for artists, Nathaniel, or for rich young women with nothing else to do. You are not going to become an artist or a rich young woman and the purpose for you picking up your pencil is very different. You are to be a craftsman, a technical draughtsman – you must be able to reproduce any pattern you wish, quickly, confidently and above all *accurately*.'

He looked dismally at the paper resting on the table between them. It showed a complex design of branching leaves, flowers and foliage, with abstract shapes fitted snugly in between. He was recreating the image in his sketchbook and had been working on it for two hours without a break. He was about halfway finished.

'It just seems pointless, that's all,' he said in a small voice.

'Pointless it is not,' Ms Lutyens replied. 'Let me see your work. Well, it's not bad, Nathaniel, not bad at all, but look – do you not think that this cupola is rather bigger than the original? See here? And you've left a hole in this stem – that's rather a bad mistake.'

'It's only a *small* mistake. The rest's OK, isn't it?'

'That's not the issue. If you were copying out a pentacle and you left a hole in it, what would happen? It would cost you your life. You don't want to die just yet, do you, Nathaniel?'

'No.'

'Well then. You simply mustn't make mistakes. They'll have

you, else.' Ms Lutyens sat back in her chair. 'By rights I should get you to start again with this.'

'Ms Lutyens!'

'Mr Underwood would expect no less.' She paused, pondering. 'But from your cry of anguish I suppose it would be useless to expect you to do any better the second time round. We will stop for today. Why don't you go out into the garden? You look like you could do with some fresh air.'

For Nathaniel, the garden of the house was a place of temporary solitude and retreat. No lessons took place there. It had no unpleasant memories. It was long and thin and surrounded by a high wall of red brick. Climbing roses grew against this in the summer and six apple trees shed white blossom over the lawn. Two rhododendron bushes sprawled widthways halfway down the garden – beyond them was a sheltered area largely concealed from the many gaping windows of the house. Here the grass grew long and wet. A horse chestnut tree in a neighbouring garden towered above, and a stone seat, green with lichen, rested in the shadows of the wall. Beside the seat was a marble statue of a man holding a fork of lightning in his hand. He wore a Victorian-style jacket and had a gigantic pair of sideburns that protruded from his cheeks like the pincers of a beetle. The statue was weather-worn and coated with a thin mantle of moss, but still gave an impression of great energy and power. Nathaniel was fascinated by it and had even gone so far as to ask Mrs Underwood who it was, but she had only smiled.

'Ask your master,' she said. 'He knows everything.'

But Nathaniel had not dared ask.

NATHANIEL

This restful spot, with its solitude, its stone seat and its statue of an unknown magician, was where Nathaniel came whenever he needed to compose himself before a lesson with his cold, forbidding master.

9

Between the ages of six and eight, Nathaniel visited his master only once a week. These occasions, on Friday afternoons, were subjects of great ritual. After lunch, Nathaniel had to go upstairs to wash and change his shirt. Then, at precisely 2.30, he presented himself at the door of his master's reading room on the first floor. He would knock three times, at which a voice would call on him to enter.

His master reclined in a wicker chair in front of a window overlooking the street. His face was often in shadow. Light from the window spilled round him in a nebulous haze. As Nathaniel entered, a long thin hand would gesture towards the cushions piled high on the oriental couch on the opposite wall. Nathaniel would take a cushion and place it on the floor. Then he sat, heart pounding, straining to catch every nuance of his master's voice, terrified of missing a thing.

In the early years, the magician usually contented himself with questioning the boy about his studies, inviting him to discuss vectors, algebra or the principles of probability; asking him to describe briefly the history of Prague or recount, in French, the key events of the Crusades. The replies satisfied him almost always – Nathaniel was a very quick learner.

On rare occasions, the master would motion the boy to be silent in the middle of an answer and would himself speak about the objectives and limitations of magic.

'A magician,' he said, 'is a wielder of power. A magician exerts his will and effects change. He can do it from selfish motives or virtuous ones. The results of his actions can be good or evil, but the only *bad* magician is an incompetent one. What is the definition of incompetence, boy?'

Nathaniel twitched on his cushion. 'Loss of control.'

'Correct. Providing the magician remains in control of the forces he has set to work he remains – what does he remain?'

Nathaniel rocked back and forth. 'Er . . .'

'The three Ss boy, the three Ss. Use your head.'

'Safe, secret, strong, sir.'

'Correct. What is the great secret?'

'Spirits, sir.'

'Demons, boy. Call 'em as they are. What must one never forget?'

'Demons are very wicked and will hurt you if they can, sir.' His voice shook as he said this.

'Good, good. What an excellent memory you have, to be sure. Be careful how you pronounce your words – I fancy your tongue tripped over itself there. Mispronouncing a syllable at the wrong time may give a demon just the opportunity it has been seeking.'

'Yes, sir.'

'So, demons are the great secret. Common people know of their existence and know that we can commune with them – that is why they fear us so! But they do not realize the full truth, which is that *all* our power derives from demons. Without their aid we are nothing but cheap conjurors and charlatans. Our single great ability is to summon them and bend them to our will. If we do it correctly they must obey us. If we make but the slightest error, they fall upon us and tear us to shreds. It is a fine line that we walk, boy. How old are you now?'

'Eight, sir. Nine next week.'

'Nine? Good. Then next week we shall start your magical studies proper. Mr Purcell is busy giving you a sufficient grounding in the basic knowledge. Henceforward we shall meet twice weekly, and I shall start introducing you to the central tenets of our order. However, for today we shall finish with you reciting the Hebrew alphabet and its first dozen numbers. Proceed.'

Under the eyes of his master and his tutors, Nathaniel's education progressed rapidly. He delighted in reporting his daily achievements to Mrs Underwood and basking in the warmth of her praise. In the evenings, he would gaze out of his window towards the distant yellow glow that marked the tower of the Parliament buildings, and dream of the day when he would go there as a magician, as one of the ministers of the noble Government.

Two days after his ninth birthday, his master appeared in the kitchen while he was eating breakfast.

'Leave that and come with me,' the magician said.

Nathaniel followed him along the hall and into the room that served as his master's library. Mr Underwood stood next to a broad bookcase filled with volumes of every size and colour, ranging from heavy leather-bound lexicons of great antiquity to battered yellow paperbacks with mystic signs scrawled on the spines.

'This is your reading-matter for the next three years,' his master said, tapping the top of the case. 'By the time you're twelve, you must have familiarized yourself with everything it contains. The books are written in Middle English, Latin, Czech and Hebrew for the most part, although you'll find some Coptic works on the Egyptian rituals of the dead too. There's a Coptic dictionary to help you with those. It's up to you to read through all this; I haven't time to coddle you. Mr Purcell will keep your languages up to speed. Understand?'

'Yes, sir. Sir?'

'What, boy?'

'When I've read through all this, sir, will I know everything I need? To be a magician, I mean, sir. It seems such an awful lot.'

His master snorted; his eyebrows ascended to the skies. 'Look behind you,' he said.

Nathaniel turned. Behind the door was a bookcase that climbed from floor to ceiling; it overflowed with hundreds of books, each one fatter and more dusty than the last, the sort of books that, one could tell without even opening them, were printed in minute script in double columns on every page. Nathaniel gave a small gulp.

'Work your way through that lot,' his master said drily, 'and you might be getting somewhere. That case contains the rites and incantations you'd need to summon significant demons and you won't even begin to use them till you're in your teens, so cast it out of your mind. *Your* case —' he tapped the wood again — 'gives you the preparatory knowledge and is more than enough for the moment. Right, follow me.'

They proceeded to a workroom that Nathaniel had never visited before. A large number of bottles and vials clustered there on stained and dirty shelves, filled with liquids of varying colour. Some of the bottles had floating objects in them. Nathaniel couldn't tell whether it was the thick, curved glass of the bottles that made the objects look so distorted and strange.

His master sat on a stool at a simple wooden worktable and indicated for Nathaniel to sit alongside. He pushed a narrow box across. Nathaniel opened it. Inside was a small pair of spectacles. A distant memory made him shudder sharply.

'Well, take them out, boy; they won't bite you. Right. Now look at me. Look at my eyes; what do you see?'

Unwillingly, Nathaniel looked. He found it very difficult to peer into the fierce, fiery brown eyes of the old man and as a result his brain froze. He saw nothing.

'Well?'

'Um, um . . . I'm sorry, I don't . . .'

'Look around my irises – see anything there?'

'Um . . .'

'Oh, you dolt!' His master gave a cry of frustration and pulled down the skin below one eye, revealing its red under-belly. 'Can't you see it? A *lens*, boy! A contact lens! Around the middle of my eye! See it?'

Desperately, Nathaniel looked again, and this time he did see a faint circular rim, thin as a pencil line around the iris, sealing it in.

'Yes, sir,' he said eagerly. 'Yes, I see it.'

'About time. Right.' His master sat back on the stool. 'When you are twelve years old two important things will happen. First, you will be given a new name, which you shall take as your own. Why?'

'To prevent demons getting power over me by discovering my birth-name, sir.'

'Correct. Enemy magicians are equally perilous, of course. Secondly, you will get your first pair of lenses, which you can wear at all times. They will allow you to see through a little of the trickery of demons. Until that time you will use these glasses, but only when instructed, and on no account are they to be removed from this workroom. Understand?'

'Yes, sir. How do they help see through things, sir?'

'When demons materialize, they can adopt all manner of false shapes, not just in this material realm, but on other planes of perception too – I shall teach you of these planes anon; do not question me on them now. Some demons of the higher sort can even become invisible; there is no end to the wickedness of their deceptions. The lenses, and to a lesser extent the glasses, allow you to see on several planes at once, giving you a better chance of piercing their illusions. Observe . . .'

Nathaniel's master reached over to a crowded shelf behind him and selected a large glass bottle that was sealed with cork and wax. It contained a greenish briny liquid and a dead rat, all brownish bristles and pale flesh. Nathaniel made a face. His master considered him.

'What would you say this was, boy?' he asked.

'A rat, sir.'

'What kind?'

'A brown one. *Rattus norvegicus*, sir.'

'Good. Latin tag too, eh? Very good. Completely wrong, but good nevertheless. It isn't a rat at all. Put on your glasses and look again.'

Nathaniel did as he was told. The spectacles felt cold and heavy on his nose. He peered through the filmy pebble-glass, taking a moment or two to focus. When the bottle swam into view he gasped. The rat was gone. In its place was a small black and red creature with a spongy face, beetle's wings and a concertina-shaped underside. The creature's eyes were open and bore an aggrieved expression. Nathaniel took the spectacles off and looked again. The brown rat floated in the pickling fluid.

'Gosh,' he said.

His master grunted. 'A Scarlet Vexation, caught and bottled by the Medical Institute of Lincoln's Inn. A minor imp, but a notable spreader of pestilence. It can only create the illusion of the rat on the material plane. On the others its true essence is revealed.'

'Is it dead, sir?' Nathaniel asked.

'Hmm? Dead? I should think so. If not, it'll certainly be angry. It's been in that jar for at least fifty years – I inherited it from my old master.'

He returned the bottle to the shelf. 'You see, boy,' he went on, 'even the least powerful demons are vicious, dangerous and evasive. One cannot withdraw one's guard for a moment. Observe this.'

From behind a Bunsen burner he drew a rectangular glass box that seemed to have no lid. Six minute creatures buzzed within it, ceaselessly butting against the walls of their prison. From a distance they seemed like insects; as they drew closer, Nathaniel observed that they had rather too many legs for this to be so.

'These mites,' his master said, 'are possibly the lowest form of demon. Scarcely any intelligence to speak of. You do not require your spectacles to see their true form. Yet even these are a menace unless properly controlled. Notice those orange stings beneath their tails? They create exquisitely painful swellings on the victim's body; far worse than bees or hornets. An admirable method of chastising someone, be it annoying rival . . . or disobedient pupil.'

Nathaniel watched the furious little mites bunting their

heads against the glass. He nodded vigorously. 'Yes, sir.'

'Vicious little things.' His master pushed the box away. 'Yet all they need are the proper words of command and they will obey any instruction. They thus demonstrate, on the smallest scale, the principles of our craft. We have dangerous tools that we must control. We shall now begin learning how to protect ourselves.'

Nathaniel soon found that it would be a long time before he was allowed to wield the tools himself. He had lessons with his master in the workroom twice a week, and for months he did nothing except take notes. He was taught the principles of pentacles and the art of runes. He learned the appropriate rites of purification that magicians had to observe before summoning could take place. He was set to work with mortar and pestle to pound out mixtures of incense that would encourage demons or keep unwanted ones away. He cut candles into varying sizes and arranged them in a host of different patterns. And not once did his master summon anything.

Impatient for progress, in his spare time Nathaniel devoured the books in the library case. He impressed Mr Purcell with his omnivorous appetite for knowledge. He worked with great vigour in Ms Lutyens's drawing lessons, applying his skill to the pentacles he now traced under the beady eye of his master. And all this time, the spectacles gathered dust on the workroom shelf.

Ms Lutyens was the only person to whom he confided his frustrations.

'Patience,' she told him. 'Patience is the prime virtue. If you hurry, you will fail. And failure is painful. You must always relax and concentrate on the task in hand. Now, if you're ready I want you to sketch that again, but this time with a blindfold.'

Six months into his training, Nathaniel observed a summoning for the first time. To his deep annoyance, he took no active part. His master drew the pentacles, including a secondary one for Nathaniel to stand in. Nathaniel was not even allowed to light the candles and, what was worse, he was told to leave the spectacles behind.

'How will I see anything?' he asked, rather more pettishly than was his habit with his master; a narrow-eyed stare instantly reduced him to silence.

The summoning began as a deep disappointment. After the incantations, which Nathaniel was pleased to find he largely understood, nothing seemed to happen. A slight breeze blew through the workroom; otherwise all was still. The empty pentacle stayed empty. His master stood close by, eyes shut, seemingly asleep. Nathaniel grew very bored. His legs began to ache. Evidently this particular demon had decided not to come. All at once, he noticed with horror that several of the candles in one corner of the workroom had toppled over. A pile of papers was alight and the fire was spreading. Nathaniel gave a cry of alarm and stepped—

'Stay where you are!'

Nathaniel's heart nearly stopped in fright. He froze with one foot lifted. His master's eyes had opened and were gazing at him with an awful anger. With a voice of thunder, his master uttered the seven Words of Dismissal. The fire in the corner of the room vanished, the pile of papers with them; the candles were once again upright and burning quietly. Nathaniel's heart quailed in his breast.

'Step outside the circle, would you?' Never had he heard his master's voice so scathing. 'I told you that some remain invisible. They are masters of illusion and know a thousand ways to distract and tempt you. One step more and you'd have been on fire yourself. Think of that while you go hungry tonight. Get up to your room!'

Further summonings were less distressing. Guided only by his ordinary senses, Nathaniel observed demons in a host of beguiling shapes. Some appeared as familiar animals – mewling cats, wide-eyed dogs, forlorn, limping hamsters that Nathaniel ached to hold. Sweet little birds hopped and pecked at the margins of their circles. Once, a shower of apple blossom cascaded from the air, filling the room with heady scent that made him drowsy.

He learned to withstand inducements of all kinds. Some invisible spirits assailed him with foul smells that made him retch; others charmed him with perfume that reminded him of Ms Lutyens's or Mrs Underwood's. Some attempted to frighten him with hideous sounds – with squelchy rendings, whisperings and gibbering cries. He heard strange voices calling out beseechingly, first high-pitched, then plummeting deeper and deeper until they rang like a funeral bell. But he closed his mind to all these things and never came close to leaving the circle.

A year passed before Nathaniel was allowed to wear his spectacles during each summoning. Now he could observe many of the demons as they really were. Others, slightly more powerful ones, maintained their illusions even on the other observable planes. To all these disorientating shifts in perception Nathaniel acclimatized calmly and confidently. His lessons were progressing well, his self-possession likewise. He grew harder, more resilient, more determined to progress.

He spent all his spare waking hours poring through new manuscripts.

His master was satisfied with his pupil's progress and Nathaniel, despite his impatience with the pace of his education, was delighted with what he learned. It was a productive relationship, if not a close one, and might well have continued to be so, but for the terrible incident that occurred in the summer before Nathaniel's eleventh birthday.

Bartimaeus

10

In the end, dawn came.

The first grudging rays flickered in the eastern sky. A halo of light slowly emerged over the Docklands horizon. I cheered it on. It couldn't come fast enough.

The whole night had been a wearisome and often humiliating business. I had repeatedly lurked, loitered and fled, in that order, through half the postal districts of London. I had been manhandled by a thirteen-year-old girl. I had taken shelter in a bin. And now, to cap it all, I was crouching on the roof of Westminster Abbey, pretending to be a gargoyle. Things don't get much worse than that.

A rising shaft of sunlight caught the edge of the Amulet, which was suspended round my lichen-covered neck. It flashed, bright as glass. Automatically I raised a claw to cup it, just in case sharp eyes were on the lookout, but I wasn't too worried by then.

I had remained in that bin in the alley for a couple of hours, long enough to rest and become thoroughly ingrained with the odour of rotting vegetables. Then I'd had the bright idea of taking up stony residence on the abbey. I was protected there by the profusion of magical ornaments within the build-ing – they masked the Amulet's signal.[1] From my new vantage point I'd seen a few spheres in the distance, but none of them came near. At last the night had ebbed away and the magicians had become weary. The spheres in the sky winked out. The heat was off.

As the sun rose, I waited impatiently for the expected summons. The boy had said he would call me at dawn, but he was no doubt sleeping in like the layabout adolescent he was.

In the meantime I ordered my thoughts. One thing that was crystal clear was that the boy was the patsy of an adult magician, some shadowy influence who sought to deflect blame for the theft onto the kid. It wasn't hard to guess this – no child of his age would summon me for so great a task on his own. Presumably the unknown magician wished to deal a blow to Lovelace and gain control over the Amulet's powers. If so, he was risking everything. Judging by the scale of the hunt I had just evaded, several powerful people were greatly

---

[1] Many great magicians of the nineteenth and twentieth centuries were entombed at Westminster Abbey after (and on one or two occasions shortly before) their death. Almost all took at least one powerful artefact with them to their grave. This was little more than a self-conscious flaunting of their wealth and power and a complete waste of the object in question. It was also a way of spitefully denying their successors any chance of inheriting the object – other mages were justly wary of retrieving the grave goods for fear of supernatural reprisals.

concerned by its loss.

Even alone, Simon Lovelace was a formidable proposition. The fact that he was able to employ (and restrain) both Faquarl and Jabor proved as much. I did not relish the urchin's chances when the magician caught up with him.

Then there was the girl, that non-magician whose friends withstood my magic and saw through my illusions. Several centuries had gone by since I had last encountered humans of their sort, so to find them here in London was intriguing. Whether or not they understood the implications of their power was difficult to say. The girl didn't even seem to know exactly what the Amulet was; only that it was a prize worth having. She certainly wasn't allied to Lovelace or the boy. Strange . . . I couldn't see where she fitted into this at all.

Oh well, it wasn't going to be my problem. Sunlight hit the roof of the abbey. I allowed myself a short, luxurious flex of my wings.

At that moment, the summons came.

A thousand fish-hooks seemed to embed themselves in me. I was pulled in several directions at once. Resisting too long risked tearing my essence, but I had no interest in delay. I wished to hand over the Amulet and be done.

With this eager hope in mind I submitted to the summons, vanishing from the rooftop . . .

. . . and reappearing instantaneously in the child's room. I looked around.

'All right, what's this?'

'I order you, Bartimaeus, to reveal whether you have diligently and wholly carried out your charge—'

'Of course I have – what do you think this is, costume

79

jewellery?' I pointed with my gargoyle's claw at the Amulet dangling on my chest. It waved and winked in the shuddering light of the candles. 'The Amulet of Samarkand. It was Simon Lovelace's. Now it is yours. Soon it will be Simon Lovelace's again. Take it and enjoy the consequences. I'm asking about this pentacle you've drawn here: what are these runes? This extra line?'

The kid puffed out his chest. 'Adelbrand's Pentacle.' If I didn't know better I'd have sworn he smirked, an unseemly facial posture for one so young.

Adelbrand's Pentacle. That meant trouble. I made a big show of checking the lines of the star and circle, looking for minute breaks or wiggles in the chalk. Then I perused the runes and symbols themselves.

'Aha!' I roared. 'You've spelled this wrong! And you know what that means, don't you . . . ?' I drew myself up like a cat ready to pounce.

The kid's face went an interesting mix of white and red, his lower lip wobbled, his eyes bulged from their sockets. He looked very much like he wanted to run for it, but he didn't, so my plan was foiled.[2] Hastily he scanned the letters on the floor.

'Recreant demon! The pentacle is sound – it binds you still!'

'OK, so I lied.' I reduced in size. My stone wings folded back under my hump. 'Do you want this amulet or not?'

'P-place it in the vessel.'

---

[2] If a magician leaves his circle during a summons his power over his victim is broken. I was hoping I would thus be able to leave. Incidentally, it would also have left me free to step out of my own pentacle and nobble him.

A small soapstone bowl sat on the floor midway between the outermost arcs of the two circles. I removed the Amulet and with a certain amount of inner relief tossed it casually into the bowl. The boy bent towards it. Out of the corner of my eyes I watched him closely – if one foot, one finger fell outside his circle I would be on him faster than a praying mantis.

But the kid was wise to this. He produced a stick from the pocket of his tatty coat. Jammed into the tip was a hooked piece of wire that looked suspiciously like a twisted paperclip. With a couple of cautious prods and jerks he caught the lip of the bowl with the hook and drew it into his circle. Then he picked up the Amulet's chain, wrinkling his nose as he did so.

'Euch, this is disgusting!'

'Nothing to do with me. Blame Rotherhithe Sewage Works. No, on second thoughts blame yourself. I've spent the whole night trying to evade capture on your account. You're lucky I didn't immerse myself completely.'

'You were pursued?' He sounded almost eager. Wrong emotion, kid – try fear.

'By half the demonic hordes of London.' I rolled my stony eyes and clashed my horny beak. 'Make no mistake about it, boy, they are coming here, yellow-eyed and ravening, ready to seize you. You will be helpless, defenceless against their power. You have one chance only; release me from this circle and I will help you evade their clutches.'[3]

'Do you take me for a fool?'

'The Amulet in your hands answers that. Well, no matter. I have carried out my charge, my task is done. For the remainder of your short life, fare well!' My form shimmered,

---

[3] Yep, by destroying him myself before they got there.

began to fade. A rippling pillar of steam issued up from the floor as if to swallow me and spirit me away. It was wishful thinking – Adelbrand's Pentacle would see to that.

'You cannot depart! I have other work for thee.'

More than the renewed captivity, it was these occasional archaisms that annoyed me so much. '*Thee*', '*recreant demon*': I ask you! No one used language like that any more, hadn't done for two hundred years. Anyone would think he had learned his trade entirely out of some old book.

But extraneous thees or not, he was quite right. Most ordinary pentacles bind you to one service only. Carry it out and you are free to go. If the magician requires you again he must repeat the whole draining rigmarole of summoning from the beginning. But Adelbrand's Pentacle countermanded this: its extra lines and incantations double-locked the door and forced you to remain for further orders. It was a complex magical formula that required adult stamina and concentration, and this gave me ammunition for my next attack.

I allowed the steam to ebb away. 'So where is he, then?'

The boy was busy turning the Amulet over and over in his pale hands. He looked up absently. 'Where is who?'

'The boss, your master, the *éminence grise*, the power behind the throne. The man who has put you up to this little theft, who's told you what to say and what to draw. The man who'll still be standing unharmed in the shadows when Lovelace's djinn are tossing your ragged corpse around the London rooftops. He's playing some game that you know nothing of, appealing to your ignorance and youthful vanity.'

That stung him. His lips curled back a little.

'What did he say to you, I wonder?' I adopted a patronizing singsong voice: ' "Well *done*, young fellow, you're the best little magician I've seen in a long while. Tell me, would you like to raise a powerful djinni? You would? Well, why don't we do just that! We can play a prank on someone too – steal an amulet—" '

The boy laughed. Unexpected, that. I was anticipating a furious outburst or some anxiety. But no, he laughed.

He turned the Amulet over a final time, then bent and replaced it in the pot. Also unexpected. Using the stick with the hook, he pushed the pot back through the circle to its original position on the floor.

'What are you doing?'

'Giving it back.'

'I don't want it.'

'Pick it up.'

I wasn't about to get into a prissy slanging match with a twelve-year-old, particularly one who could impose his will on me, so I reached out through my circle and hefted the Amulet.

'Now what? When Simon Lovelace comes I won't be hanging onto this, you know. I'll be giving it right back to him with a smile and a wave. And pointing out which curtain you're shivering behind.'

'Wait.'

The kid produced something shiny from one of the inner pockets of his voluminous coat. Did I mention that this coat was about three sizes too big for him? It had evidently once belonged to a very careless magician, since although heavily patched, it still displayed the unmistakable ravages of fire, blood and talon. I wished the boy similar fortune.

Now he was holding in his left hand a burnished disc – a scrying glass of highly polished brass. He passed his right hand over it a few times and began to gaze into the reflective metal with passive concentration. Whatever captive imp dwelt within the disc soon responded. A murky picture formed; the boy observed it closely. I was too far off to see the image, but while he was distracted I did a bit of looking of my own.

His room . . . I wanted a clue to his identity. Some letter addressed to him, perhaps, or a nametag in his coat. Both of those had worked before. I wasn't after his birth-name, of course – that would be too much to hope for, but his official name would do for a start.[4] But I was out of luck. The most private, intimate, telltale place in the room – his desk – had been carefully covered with a thick black cloth. A wardrobe in the corner was shut; ditto a chest of drawers. There was a cracked glass vase with fresh flowers amongst the mess of candles – an odd touch, this. He hadn't put it there himself, I reckoned; so somebody liked him.

The kid waved his hand over the scrying glass and the surface went dull. He replaced the disc in his pocket, then looked up at me suddenly. Uh-oh. Here it came.

'Bartimaeus,' he began, 'I charge you to take the Amulet of Samarkand and hide it in the magical repository of the magician Arthur Underwood, concealing it so that he cannot observe it, and achieving this so stealthily that no one, neither

---

[4] All magicians have two names, their official name and their birth-name. Their birth-name is that given to them by their parents, and because it is intimately bound up with their true nature and being, it is a source of great strength and weakness. They seek to keep it secret from everyone, for if an enemy learns it, he or she can use it to gain power over them, rather in the same way that a magician can only summon a djinni if he knows their true name. Magicians thus conceal their birth-names with great care, replacing them with official names at the time of their coming of age. It is always useful to know a magician's official name – but far, far better to learn his secret one.

human nor spirit, on this plane or any other, shall see you enter or depart; I further charge you to return to me immediately, silent and unseen, to await further instructions.'

He was blue in the face when he finished this, having completed it all in one straight breath.[5]

I glowered under my stony brows. 'Very well. Where does this unfortunate magician reside?'

The boy smiled thinly. 'Downstairs.'

---

[5] Strictly advisable when dealing with subtle, intelligent entities such as myself. It is often possible to interpret a pause for breath as a full stop, which either changes the meaning of the instructions or turns them into gobbledegook. If we can misinterpret something to our advantage, we most certainly will.

II

Downstairs . . . Well, that *was* surprising.

'Framing your master, are you? Nasty.'

'I'm not framing him. I just want it safe, behind whatever security he's got. No one's going to find it there.' He paused. 'But if they do . . .'

'You'll be in the clear. Typical magician's trick. You're learning faster than most.'

'No one's going to find it.'

'You think so? We'll see.'

Still, I couldn't float there gossiping all day. I encased the Amulet with a Charm, rendering it temporarily small and giving it the appearance of a drifting cobweb. Then I sank through a knothole in the nearest plank, snaked as a vapour through the empty floor space and in spider guise crawled cautiously out of a crack in the ceiling of the room below.

I was in a deserted bathroom. Its door was open; I scurried towards it along the plaster as fast as eight legs could carry me. As I went I shook my mandibles at the effrontery of the boy.

Framing another magician: that wasn't unusual. That was part and parcel, it came with the territory.[1] Framing your own master, though, now that *was* out of the ordinary – in fact

---

[1] Magicians are the most conniving, jealous, duplicitous group of people on earth, even including lawyers and academics. They worship power and the wielding thereof, and seek every chance they can to undercut their rivals. At a rough guess, about eighty per cent of all summonings have to do with carrying out some skulduggery against a fellow magician, or with defence against the same. By contrast,

possibly unique in a wizardling of twelve. Sure, as adults, magicians fell out with ridiculous regularity, but not when they were starting off; not when they were just being taught the rules.

How was I sure the magician in question was his master? Well, unless age-old practices were now being dropped and apprentices were being bussed off to boarding school together (hardly likely), there was no other explanation. Magicians hold their knowledge close to their shrivelled little hearts, coveting its power the way a miser covets gold, and they will only pass it on with caution. Since the days of the Median Magi students have always lived alone in their mentors' houses – one master to one pupil, conducting their lessons with secrecy and stealth. From ziggurat to pyramid, from sacred oak to sky-scraper, four thousands of years pass and things don't change.

To sum up then: it seemed that to guard his own skin this ungrateful child was risking bringing the wrath of a powerful magician down upon his innocent master's head. I was very impressed. Even though he had to be in cahoots with an adult – some enemy of his master presumably – it was an admirably twisted plan for one so young.

I did an eight-fold tiptoe out of the door. Then I saw the master.

I had not heard of this magician, this Mr Arthur Underwood. I assumed him therefore to be a minor conjuror, a dabbler in fakery and mumbo jumbo who never dared

---

most confrontations between spirits aren't personal at all, simply because they do not occur of our own free will. At that moment, for instance, I did not dislike Faquarl particularly; well, actually that's a lie – I loathed him, but no more than I had before. Anyway, our mutual hatred had taken many centuries, indeed millennia, to build up. Magicians squabble for fun. We'd really had to work at it.

disturb the rest of higher beings such as me. Certainly, as he passed underneath me into the bathroom (I had evidently exited just in time), he fitted the bill of second-rater. A sure sign of this was that he had all the time-honoured attributes that other humans associate with great and powerful magic: a mane of unkempt hair the colour of tobacco ash, a long whitish beard that jutted outwards like the prow of a ship, and a pair of particularly bristly eyebrows.[2] I could imagine him stalking through the streets of London in a black velveteen suit, hair billowing behind him in a sorcerous sort of way. He probably flourished a gold-tipped cane, maybe even a swanky cape. Yes, he'd look the part then, all right: very impressive. As opposed to now, stumbling along in his pyjama bottoms, scratching his unmentionables and sporting a folded news-paper under his arm.

'Martha!' He called this just before closing the bathroom door.

A small, spherical female emerged from a bedroom. Thankfully, she was fully dressed. 'Yes, dear?'

'I thought you said that woman cleaned yesterday.'

'Yes, she did, dear. Why?'

'Because there's a grubby cobweb dangling from the middle of the ceiling, with a repellent spider skulking in it. Loathsome. She should be sacked.'

'Oh, I see it. How foul. Don't worry, I'll speak to her. And I'll get the duster to it shortly.'

The great magician humphed and shut the door. The woman shook her head in a forgiving manner and, humming

---

[2] Minor magicians take pains to fit this traditional wizardly bill. By contrast, the really powerful magicians take pleasure in looking like accountants.

a light-hearted ditty, disappeared downstairs. The 'loathsome' spider made a rude sign with two of its legs and set off along the ceiling, trailing its cobweb behind it.

It took several minutes' scuttering before I located the entrance to the study at the bottom of a short flight of stairs. And here I halted. The door was protected against interlopers by a hex in the form of a five-pointed star. It was a simple device. The star appeared to consist of flaking red paint; however, if an unwary trespasser opened the door the trap would be triggered and the 'paint' would revert to its original state – a ricocheting bolt of fire.

Sounds good, I know, but it was pretty basic stuff actually. A curious housemaid might be frazzled, but not Bartimaeus. I erected a Shield around me and, touching the base of the door with a tiny claw, instantly sprang back a metre.

Thin orange streaks appeared within the red lines of the five-pointed star. For a second the lines coursed like liquid, racing round and round the shape. Then a jet of flame burst from the star's uppermost point, rebounded off the ceiling and speared down towards me.

I was ready for the impact on my Shield, but it never took place. The flame bypassed me altogether and hit the cobweb I was trailing. And the cobweb sucked it up, drawing the fire from the star like juice through a straw. In an instant it was over. The flame was gone. It had disappeared into the cobweb, which remained as cool as ever.

In some surprise, I looked around. A charcoal-black star was seared into the wood of the study door. As I watched, the hex began to redden slowly – it was reassembling its charge for the next intruder.

I suddenly realized what had happened. It was obvious. The

Amulet of Samarkand had done what amulets are supposed to do — it had protected its wearer.[3] Very nicely, too. It had absorbed the hex without any trouble whatsoever. That was fine by me. I removed my Shield and squeezed myself beneath the door and into Underwood's study.

Beyond the door I found no further traps on any of the planes, another sign that the magician was of a fairly low order. (I recalled the extensive network of defences that Simon Lovelace had rigged up and which I'd broached with such easy panache. If the boy thought that the Amulet would be safe behind his master's 'security' he had another think coming.) The room was tidy, if dusty, and contained among other things a locked cupboard that I guessed housed his treasures. I entered via the keyhole, tugging the cobweb in my wake.

Once inside I performed a small Illumination. A pitiful array of magical gimcracks were arranged with loving care on three glass shelves. Some of them, such as the Tinker's Purse, with its secret pocket for making coins 'vanish', were frankly not magical at all. It made my estimate of second-rater seem overly generous. I almost felt sorry for the old duffer. For his sake I hoped Simon Lovelace never came to call.

There was a Javanese bird totem at the back of the cupboard, its beak and plumes grey with dust. Underwood obviously never touched it. I pulled the cobweb between the purse and an Edwardian rabbit's foot and tucked it behind the totem. Good. No one would find it there unless they were

---

[3] *Amulets* are protective charms; they fend off evil. They are passive objects and although they can absorb or deflect all manner of dangerous magic they cannot be actively controlled by their owner. They are thus the opposite of *talismans*, which have active magical powers that can be used at their owner's discretion. A horse-shoe is a (primitive) amulet; seven-league boots are a form of talisman.

really hunting. Finally I removed the Charm on it, restoring it to its normal amulety size and shape.

With that, my assignment was complete. All that remained was to return to the boy. I exited cupboard and study without any hiccups and set off back upstairs.

This was where it got interesting.

I was heading up to the attic room again, of course, using the sloping ceiling above the stairs, when unexpectedly the boy passed me coming down. He was trailing in the wake of the magician's wife, looking thoroughly fed up. Evidently he had just been summoned from his room.

I perked up at once. This was bad for him and I could see from his face that he realized it too. He knew I was loose, somewhere nearby. He knew I would be coming back, that my charge had been to '*return to him* immediately, silent and unseen, to await further instructions'. He knew that I might therefore be following him now, listening and watching, learning more about him, and that he couldn't do anything about it until he got back to his room and stood again within the pentacle.

In short, he had lost control of the situation, a dangerous state of affairs for any magician.

I swivelled and followed eagerly in their wake. True to my charge, no one saw or heard me as I crept along behind.

The woman led the boy to a door on the ground floor. 'He's in there, dear,' she said.

'OK,' the boy said. His voice was nice and despondent, just how I like it.

They went in, woman first, boy second. The door shut so fast that I had to do a couple of quick-fire shots of web to trapeze myself through the crack before it closed. It was a great stunt – I wish someone had seen it. But no. 'Silent and unseen', that's me.

We were in a gloomy dining room. The magician, Arthur Underwood, was seated alone at the head of a dark and shiny dining table, with cup, saucer and silver coffee pot close to hand. He was still occupied with his newspaper, which lay folded in half on the table. As the woman and the boy entered, he picked up the paper, unfolded it, turned the page crisply and smacked the whole thing in half again. He didn't look up.

The woman hovered near the table. 'Arthur, Nathaniel's here,' she said.

The spider had backed its way into a dark corner above the door. On hearing these words it remained motionless, as spiders do. But inwardly it thrilled.

Nathaniel! Good. That was a start.

I had the pleasure of seeing the boy wince. His eyes flitted to and fro, no doubt wondering if I was there.

The magician gave no sign that he had heard, but remained engrossed in the paper. His wife began rearranging a rather sorry display of dried flowers over the mantelpiece. I guessed then who was responsible for the vase in the boy's room. Dead flowers for the husband, fresh ones for the apprentice – that was intriguing.

Again Underwood unfolded, turned, smacked the paper, resumed his reading. The boy stood silently waiting. Now that I was free of the circle and thus not under his direct control, I had a chance to assess him more clinically. He had (of course) removed his raggedy coat and was soberly dressed in grey trousers and jumper. His hair had been wetted and was slicked back. A sheaf of papers was under his arm. He was a picture of quiet deference.

He had no obviously defining features – no moles, no oddities, no scars. His hair was dark and straight, his face tended towards the pinched. His skin was very pale. To a casual observer, he was an unremarkable boy. But to my wiser and more jaundiced gaze there were other things to note: shrewd and calculating eyes; fingers that tapped impatiently on the papers he held; most of all a very careful face that by subtle shifts took on whatever expression was expected of it. For the moment he had adopted a submissive but attentive look that would flatter an old man's vanity. Yet continually he cast his eye around the room, searching for me.

I made it easy for him. When he was looking in my direction, I gave a couple of small scuttles on the wall, waved a few arms, wiggled my abdomen in a cheery fashion. He saw me straight off, went paler than ever, bit his lip. Couldn't do anything about me though, without giving his game away.

In the middle of my dance, Underwood suddenly grunted dismissively and slapped the back of his hand against his paper. 'See here, Martha,' he said. 'Makepeace is filling the theatres again with his eastern piffle. *Swans of Araby* . . . I ask you, did you ever hear of such sentimental claptrap? And yet it's advance booked until the end of January! Quite bizarre.'

'It's all booked up? Oh Arthur, I'd rather wanted to go—'

'And I quote: ". . . in which a sweet-limbed missionary lass from Chiswick falls in love with a tawny djinni . . ." – it's not just romantic tushery, it's damnably dangerous too. Spreads misinformation to the people.'

'Oh, Arthur—'

'You've seen djinn, Martha. Have you seen one "with dusky eyes that will melt your heart"? Melt your face, maybe.'

'I'm sure you're right, Arthur.'

'Makepeace should know better. Disgraceful. I'd do something about it, but he's in too deep with the PM.'

'Yes, dear. Would you like more coffee, dear?'

'No. The PM should be helping out my Internal Affairs Department rather than socializing his time away. *Four more thefts*, Martha, four in the last week. Valuable items they were, too. I tell you, we're going to the dogs.' So saying, Underwood lifted his moustache with one hand and expertly passed the lip of his cup beneath. He drank long and loudly. 'Martha, this is cold. Fetch more coffee, will you?'

With good grace the wife bustled off on her errand. As she exited, the magician tossed his paper to one side and deigned to notice his pupil at last.

The old man grunted. 'So. You're here, are you?'

Despite his anxiety, the boy's voice was steady. 'Yes, sir. You sent for me, sir.'

'I did indeed. Now, I have been speaking to your teachers, and with the exception of Mr Sindra, all have satisfactory reports to make on you.' He held up his hand to silence the boy's prompt articulations of thanks. 'Heaven knows, you don't deserve it after what you did last year. However, despite certain deficiencies, to which I have repeatedly drawn your attention, you have made some progress with the central tenets. Thus –' a dramatic pause – 'I feel that the time is right for you to conduct your first summons.'

He uttered this last sentence in slow resounding tones that were evidently designed to fill the boy with awe. But *Nathaniel*, as I was now so delighted to call him, was distracted. He had a spider on his mind.

His unease was not lost on Underwood. The magician rapped the table peremptorily to attract his pupil's attention.

'Listen to me, boy!' he said. 'If you fret at the very prospect of a summons you will never make a magician, even now. A well-prepared magician fears nothing. Do you understand?'

The boy gathered himself, fixed his attention on his master. 'Yes, sir; of course, sir.'

'Besides, I shall be with you at all times during the summoning, in an adjoining circle. I shall have a dozen protective charms to hand and plenty of powdered rosemary. We shall start with a lowly demon, a natterjack impling.[4] If that proves successful, we shall move on to a mouler.'[5]

It was a measure of how unobservant this magician was that he quite failed to notice the flame of contempt that flickered in the boy's eyes. He only heard the blandly eager voice. 'Yes, sir. I'm looking forward to it very much, sir.'

'Excellent. You have your lenses?'

'Yes, sir. They arrived last week.'

'Good. Then there is only one other arrangement we need to make, and that is—'

'Was that the door, sir?'

'Don't interrupt me, boy. How dare you? The other arrangement, which I will withhold if you are insolent again, is the choosing of your official name. We shall turn our attention to that this afternoon. Bring *Loew's Nominative Almanac* to me in the library after luncheon and we shall choose one for you together.'

'Yes, sir.'

The boy's shoulders had slumped; his voice was barely

---

[4] *Natterjack impling*: an unadventurous creature that affects the semblance and habits of a dull sort of toad.

[5] *Mouler*: even less exciting than a natterjack impling, were that possible.

audible. He did not need to see me capering on my web to know that I had heard and understood.

Nathaniel wasn't just his official name! It was his real name! The fool had summoned me before consigning his birth-name to oblivion. And now I knew it! Underwood shifted in his chair. 'Well, what are you waiting for, boy? This is no time for slacking – you've got hours yet to study before lunch. Get on your way.'

'Yes, sir; thank you, sir.'

The boy moved listlessly to the door. Gnashing my mandibles with glee, I followed him through with an extra-special reverse somersault with octal hitch-kick.

I had a chance at him now. Things were a bit more even. He knew my name, I knew his. He had six years' experience, I had five thousand and ten. That was the kind of odds you could do something with.

I accompanied him up the stairs. He was dawdling now, dragging each step out.

Come on, come on! Get back to your pentacle. I was racing ahead, eager for the contest to begin.

Oh, the boots were on the other eight feet now, all right.

Nathaniel

12

One summer's day, when Nathaniel was ten years old, he sat with his tutor on the stone seat in the garden, sketching the horse chestnut tree beyond the wall. The sun beat upon the red bricks. A grey and white cat lolled on the top of the wall, idly swishing its tail from side to side. A gentle breeze shifted the leaves of the tree and carried a faint scent across from the rhododendron bushes. The moss on the statue of the man with the lightning fork gleamed richly in the yellow sunlight. Insects hummed.

It was the day that everything changed.

'Patience, Nathaniel.'

'You've said that so many times, Ms Lutyens.'

'And I'll say it again, I have no doubt. You are too restless. It's your biggest fault.'

Nathaniel irritably cross-hatched a patch of shade.

'But it's so frustrating,' he exclaimed. 'He never lets me *try* anything! All I'm allowed to do is set up the candles and the incense and other stuff that I could do in my sleep standing on my head! I'm not even allowed to talk to them.'

'Quite right too,' Ms Lutyens said firmly. 'Remember, I just want subtleties of shading. No hard lines.'

'It's ridiculous.' Nathaniel made a face. 'He doesn't realize what I can do. I've read all his books, and—'

'*All* of them?'

'Well, all the ones in his little bookcase, and he said they'd keep me going till I was twelve. I'm not even eleven yet, Ms Lutyens. I mean, I've already mastered the Words of Direction and Control, most of them; I could give a djinni an order, if he summoned it for me. But he won't even let me try.'

'I don't know which is less attractive, Nathaniel – your boasting or your petulance. You should stop worrying about what you don't yet have and enjoy what you have now. This garden, for instance. I'm very pleased you thought of having our lesson out here today.'

'I always come here when I can. It helps me think.'

'I'm not surprised. It's peaceful, solitary . . . and there are precious few parts of London like that, so be grateful.'

'He keeps me company.' Nathaniel indicated the statue. 'I like him, even though I don't know who he is.'

'Him?' Ms Lutyens glanced up from her sketchbook, but went on drawing. 'Oh, that's easy. That's Gladstone.'

'Who?'

'Gladstone. Surely you know. Doesn't Mr Purcell teach you recent history?'

'We've done contemporary politics.'

'Too recent. Gladstone died more than a hundred years ago.

He was a great hero of the time. There must have been thousands of statues made of him, put up all over the country. Rightly so, from your point of view. You owe him a lot.'

Nathaniel was puzzled. 'Why?'

'He was the most powerful magician ever to become Prime Minister. He dominated the Victorian Age for thirty years and brought the feuding factions of magicians under government control. You must have heard of his duel with the sorcerer Disraeli on Westminster Green? No? You should go and see. The scorch marks are still on show. Gladstone was famous for his supreme energy and his implacable defiance when the chips were down. He never gave up his cause, even when things looked bad.'

'Gosh.' Nathaniel gazed at the stern face staring from beneath its covering of moss. The stone hand gripped its lightning bolt loosely, confidently, ready to throw.

'Why did he have that duel, Ms Lutyens?'

'I believe Disraeli made a rude remark about a female friend of Gladstone's. That was a big mistake. Gladstone never let anyone insult his honour, or that of his friends. He was very powerful and quite prepared to challenge anyone who had wronged him.' She blew charcoal from her sketch and held it up to the light critically.

'Gladstone did more than anyone else to help London ascend to magical prominence. In those days Prague was still the most powerful city in the world, but its time had long gone; it was old and decadent and its magicians bickered amongst the slums of the Ghetto. Gladstone provided new ideals, new projects. He attracted many foreign magicians here by acquiring certain relics. London became the place to be. As it still is, for better or for worse. Like I say, you ought to be grateful.'

Nathaniel looked at her. 'What do you mean, "For better or for worse?" What's worse about it?'

Ms Lutyens pursed her lips. 'The current system is very beneficial for magicians and for a few lucky others who cluster all about them. Less so for everyone else. Now – let me see how your sketch is going.'

Something in her tone aroused Nathaniel's indignation. His lessons with Mr Purcell came flooding into his mind. 'You shouldn't speak of the Government like that,' he said. 'Without magicians, the country would be defenceless! Commoners would rule and the country would fall apart. Magicians give their lives to keep the country safe! You should remember that, Ms Lutyens.' Even to his own ears, his voice sounded rather shrill.

'I'm sure that when you have grown up you will make many telling sacrifices, Nathaniel.' She spoke rather more sharply than was usual. 'But in fact not all countries have magicians. Plenty do very well without them.'

'You seem to know a lot about it all.'

'For a humble drawing tutor? Do I detect surprise in your voice?'

'Well, you're only a commoner—' He stopped short, flushed. 'Sorry, I didn't mean—'

'Quite right,' Ms Lutyens said shortly, 'I *am* a commoner. But magicians don't have a complete monopoly on knowledge, you know. Far from it. And anyway, knowledge and intelligence are very different things. As you'll one day discover.'

For a few minutes they busied themselves with their paper and pens and did not speak. The cat on the wall flicked a lazy paw at a circling wasp. At length Nathaniel broke the silence.

'Did you not want to become a magician, Ms Lutyens?' he asked, in a small voice.

She gave a small dry laugh. 'I didn't have that privilege,' she said. 'No, I'm just an art teacher and happy to be one.'

Nathaniel tried again. 'What do you do when you're not here? With me, I mean.'

'I'm with other pupils, of course. What did you think – that I'd go home and mope? Mr Underwood doesn't pay me enough for moping, I'm afraid. I have to work.'

'Oh.' It had never occurred to Nathaniel that Ms Lutyens might have other pupils. Somehow the knowledge gave him a slightly knotty feeling in the pit of his stomach.

Perhaps Ms Lutyens sensed this; after a short pause she spoke again in a less frosty manner. 'Anyway,' she said, 'I look forward to my lessons here very much. One of the highlights of my working week. You're good company, even if you're still prone to rushing things and think you know it all. So cheer up and let me see how you've got on with that tree.'

Following a few minutes of calm discussion about art-related issues, the conversation resumed its usual peaceful course, but it was not long afterwards that the lesson was suspended by the unexpected arrival of Mrs Underwood, all in a fluster.

'Nathaniel!' she cried. 'There you are!'

Ms Lutyens and Nathaniel both stood up respectfully. 'I've looked all over for you, dear,' Mrs Underwood said, breathing hard. 'I thought you'd be in the schoolroom . . .'

'I'm so sorry, Mrs Underwood,' Ms Lutyens began. 'It was such a nice day—'

'Oh, that doesn't matter. That's quite all right. It's just that my husband needs Nathaniel straight away. He has guests over, and wishes to present him.'

'There you are, then,' Ms Lutyens said quietly, as they hurried back up the garden. 'Mr Underwood isn't overlooking you at all. He must be very pleased with you to introduce you to other magicians. He's going to show you off!'

Nathaniel smiled weakly, but said nothing. The thought of meeting other magicians made him feel quite queasy. Through all his years in the house he had never once been allowed to meet his master's professional colleagues, who appeared there intermittently. He was always packed off to his bedroom, or kept out of harm's way with his tutors upstairs. This was a new and exciting development, if a rather frightening one. He imagined a room stuffed full of tall, brooding men of power, glowering at him over their bristling beards and swirling robes. His knees shook in anticipation.

'They're in the reception room,' Mrs Underwood said as they entered the kitchen. 'Let's look at you . . .' She wet her finger and hurriedly removed a pencil-lead smudge from the side of his forehead. 'Very presentable. All right, in you go.'

The room *was* full; he'd got that part right. It was warm with bodies, the smell of tea and the effort of polite conversation. But by the time Nathaniel had closed the door and edged across to occupy the only space available, in the lee of an ornamental dresser, his magnificent visions of a company of great men had already evaporated.

They just didn't look the part.

There wasn't a cape to be seen. There were precious few beards on display, and none half as impressive as that of his own master. Most of the men wore drab suits with drabber ties; only a few sported daring additions, such as a grey waistcoat or a visible breast-pocket handkerchief. All wore shiny black shoes. It felt to Nathaniel as if he had strayed upon an undertaker's office party. None of them seemed like Gladstone, in strength or in demeanour. Some were short, others were crabbed and old, more than one was prone to podge. They talked amongst themselves earnestly, sipping tea and nibbling dry biscuits, and not one of them raised his voice above the consensus murmuring.

Nathaniel was deeply disappointed. He stuck his hands in his pockets and breathed deeply.

His master was inching himself through the throng, shaking hands and uttering the odd short, barking laugh whenever a guest said something that he thought was intended to be funny. Catching sight of Nathaniel, he beckoned him over; Nathaniel squeezed between a tea plate and someone's protruding belly and approached.

'This is the boy,' the magician said gruffly, clapping Nathaniel on the shoulder in an awkward gesture. Three men looked down at him. One was old, white-haired, with a florid sun-dried-tomato face, covered in tiny creases. Another was a doughy, watery-eyed individual in middle age; his skin looked cold and clammy, like a fish on a slab. The third was much younger and more handsome, with slicked-back hair, round glasses and a xylophone-sized array of gleaming white teeth. Nathaniel stared back at them in silence.

'Doesn't look like much,' the clammy man said. He sniffed and swallowed something.

'He's learning slowly,' Nathaniel's master said, his hand still patting Nathaniel on the shoulder in an aimless manner that suggested he was ill at ease.

'Slow, is he?' said the old man. He spoke with an accent so

thick that Nathaniel could barely understand the words. 'Yes, some boys are. You must persevere.'

'Do you beat him?' the clammy man said.

'Rarely.'

'Unwise. It stimulates the memory.'

'How old are you, boy?' the younger man asked.

'Ten, sir.' Nathaniel said politely. 'Eleven in Nov—'

'Still a couple of years before he'll be any use to you, Underwood.' The young man cut over Nathaniel as if he did not exist. 'Costs a fortune, I suppose.'

'What, bed and board? Of course.'

'I'll bet he eats like a ferret, too.'

'Greedy, is he?' said the old man. He nodded regretfully. 'Yes, some boys are.'

Nathaniel listened with barely suppressed indignation. 'I'm not greedy, sir,' he said in his politest voice. The old man's eyes flickered towards him, then drifted away again as if he had not heard; but his master's hand clamped down on his shoulder with some force.

'Well, boy; you must get back to your studies,' he said. 'Run along.'

Nathaniel was only too happy to leave, but as he began to sidle off the young man in the glasses raised a hand.

'You've got a tongue in your head, I see,' he said. 'Not afraid of your elders.'

Nathaniel said nothing.

'Perhaps you don't think we're your betters too?'

The man spoke lightly, but the sharpness in his voice was clear. Nathaniel could tell at once that he himself was not the point at issue and that the young man was challenging his master through him. He felt as if he ought to answer, but was so confused by the question that he did not know whether to say yes or no.

The young man misinterpreted his silence. 'He thinks he's too good to talk to us at all now!' he said to his companions and grinned.

The clammy man tittered wetly into his hand and the old, red-faced man shook his head. 'Tcha,' he said.

'Run along, boy,' Nathaniel's master said again.

'Hold on, Underwood,' the young man said, smiling broadly. 'Before he goes, let's see what you've taught this whippet of yours. It'll be amusing. Come here, lad.'

Nathaniel glanced across at his master, who did not meet his eye. Slowly and unwillingly he drew near to the group again. The young man snapped his fingers with a flourish and spoke at top speed.

'How many classified types of spirit are there?'

Nathaniel replied without a pause. 'Thirteen thousand and forty-six, sir.'

'And unclassified?'

'Petronius postulates forty-five thousand; Zavattini forty-eight thousand, sir.'

'What is the *modus apparendi* of the Carthaginian subgroup?'

'They appear as crying infants, sir, or as doppelgängers of the magician in his youth.'

'How should one chastise them?'

'Make them drink a vat of asses' milk.'

'Hmmph. If summoning a cockatrice, what precautions should one take?'

'Wear mirrored glasses, sir. And surround the pentacle with mirrors on two other sides also, to force the cockatrice to gaze in the remaining direction, where its written instructions will be waiting.'

Nathaniel was gaining in confidence. He had committed simple details such as these to memory long ago and he was pleased to note that his unerringly correct answers were exasperating the young man. His success had also stopped the clammy man's snickering, and the old magician, who was listening with his head cocked to one side, had even nodded grudgingly once or twice. He noticed his master smiling, rather smugly. Not that any of this is down to you, Nathaniel thought witheringly. I *read* all this. You've taught me next to nothing.

For the first time there was a pause in the barrage of the young man's questions. He appeared to be thinking. 'All right,' he said at last, speaking much more slowly now and rolling the words luxuriantly over his tongue, 'what are the six Words of Direction? Any language.'

Arthur Underwood uttered a startled protest – 'Be fair, Simon! He can't know that yet!' – but even as he spoke, Nathaniel was opening his mouth. This was a formula contained in several of the books in his master's large book-case, where Nathaniel was already browsing.

'*Appare; Mane; Ausculta; Se Dede; Pare; Redi* – Appear; Remain; Listen; Submit; Obey; Return.' He looked into the young magician's eyes as he finished, conscious of his triumph.

Their audience murmured their approval – his master now wore an unconcealed grin, the clammy man raised his eyebrows and the old man made a wry face, quietly mouthing, 'Bravo.' But his interrogator just shrugged dismissively, as if the incident was of no account. He looked so supercilious that Nathaniel felt his self-satisfaction turn into a fiery anger.

'Standards must have dropped,' said the young man, taking

a handkerchief from his pocket and wiping at an imaginary spot on his sleeve, 'if a backward apprentice can be congratulated for spouting something we all learned at our mothers' teats.'

'You're just a sore loser,' Nathaniel said.

There was a moment's hush. Then the young man barked a word and Nathaniel felt something small and compact land heavily upon his shoulders. Invisible hands clenched into his hair and jerked it backwards with vicious strength, so that his face stared at the ceiling and he cried out with pain. He tried to raise his arms, but found them pinioned to his sides by a hideously muscular coil that wrapped itself around him like a giant tongue. He could see nothing except the ceiling; delicate fingers tickled his exposed neck with horrible finesse. In panic, he cried out for his master.

Someone came close, but it was not his master. It was the young man.

'You cocksure guttersnipe,' the young man said softly. 'What will you do now? Can you get free? No. How surprising: you're helpless. You know a few words, but you're capable of nothing. Perhaps this will teach you the dangers of insolence when you're too weak to fight back. Now get out of my sight.'

Something sniggered in his ear and with a kick of powerful legs removed itself from Nathaniel's shoulders. At the same moment, his arms were freed. His head drooped forward; tears welled from his eyes. They were caused by the injury to his hair, but Nathaniel feared that they would seem the weeping of a cowardly boy. He wiped them away with his cuff.

The room was still. All the magicians had dropped their conversations and were staring at him. Nathaniel looked at his master, silently appealing for support or aid, but Arthur

THE AMULET OF SAMARKAND

Underwood's eyes were bright with rage — rage that appeared to be directed at him. Nathaniel returned the look blankly, then he turned and walked along the silent passage that parted for him across the room, reached the door, opened it and walked through.

He shut the door carefully and quietly behind him.

White-faced and expressionless, he climbed the stairs.

On the way up he met Mrs Underwood coming down.

'How did it go, dear?' she asked him. 'Did you shine? Is anything wrong?'

Nathaniel could not look at her for grief and shame. He started to go past her without answering, but at the last moment stopped short. 'It was fine,' he said. 'Tell me, do you know who the magician is with the little glasses and the wide, white teeth?'

Mrs Underwood frowned. 'That would be Simon Lovelace, I expect. The Junior Minister for Trade. He *does* have quite a set of gnashers, doesn't he? A rising star, I'm told. Did you meet him?'

'Yes. I did.'

You're capable of nothing.

'Are you sure you're all right? You look so pale.'

'Yes, thank you, Mrs Underwood. I'll go up now.'

'Ms Lutyens is waiting for you in the schoolroom.'

You're helpless.

'I'll go right along, Mrs Underwood.'

Nathaniel did not go to the schoolroom. With slow, steady tread, he made his way to his master's workroom, where the dust on the dirty bottles gleamed in the sunlight, obscuring their pickled contents.

Nathaniel walked along the pitted worktable, which was

strewn with diagrams that he had been working on the day before.

You're too weak to fight back.

He stopped and reached out for a small glass box, in which six objects buzzed and whirred.

We'll see.

With slow, steady tread, Nathaniel crossed to a wall-cupboard and pulled at a drawer. It was so warped that it stuck halfway and he had to place the glass box carefully on the work surface before wrenching it open with a couple of forceful tugs. Inside the drawer, amongst a host of other tools, was a small steel hammer. Nathaniel took it out, picked up the box again and, leaving the drawer hanging open, left the sunny workroom.

He stood in the cool shadows of the landing, silently rehearsing the Words of Direction and Control. In the glass box, the six mites tore back and forth with added zest; the box vibrated in his hands.

You're capable of nothing.

The party was breaking up. The door opened and the first few magicians emerged in dribs and drabs. Mr Underwood escorted them to the front door. Polite words were exchanged, farewells said. None of them noticed the pale-faced boy watching from beyond the stairs.

You had to say the name *after* the first three commands, but *before* the last. It was not too difficult, providing you didn't trip over the quicker syllables. He ran it through his head again. Yes, he had it down fine.

More magicians departed. Nathaniel's fingers were cold. There was a thin film of sweat between them and the box they held.

The young magician and his two companions sauntered from the reception room. They were talking animatedly, chuckling over a remark made by the one with clammy skin. At a leisurely pace they approached Nathaniel's master, waiting by the door.

Nathaniel gripped the hammer firmly.

He held the glass box out in front of him. It shook from within.

The old man was clasping Mr Underwood's hand. The young magician was next in line, looking out into the street as if eager to be gone.

In a loud voice Nathaniel spoke the first three commands, uttered the name of Simon Lovelace and followed it with the final word.

Then he smashed the box.

A brittle cracking, a frenzied droning. Glass splinters cascaded towards the carpet. The six mites burst from their prison and rocketed down the stairs, their eager stings jutting forward.

The magicians barely had time to look up before the mites were upon them. Three made a beeline for Simon Lovelace's face; raising his hand, he made a rapid sign. Instantly, each mite erupted into a ball of flame and careered off at an angle to explode against the wall. The three other mites disobeyed their command. Two darted towards the clammy, doughy-faced magician; with a cry, he stumbled back, tripped over the door-sill and fell out onto the garden path. The mites bobbed and dived above him, seeking exposed flesh. His arms thrashed back and forth in front of his face, but to no avail. Several successful jabs were made, each one accompanied by a howl of agony. The sixth mite approached the old man at speed. He appeared to do nothing, but when it was just inches from his face, the mite suddenly pulled to a halt and reversed frantically, cartwheeling in mid-air. It spun out of control and landed near Simon Lovelace, who trod it into the carpet.

Arthur Underwood had been watching this in horror; now he pulled himself together. He stepped over the threshold to where his guest was writhing in the flowerbed and clapped his hands sharply. The two vengeful mites dropped to the ground as if stunned.

At this point Nathaniel thought to make a judicious retreat.

He slipped away to the schoolroom, where Ms Lutyens was sitting by the table reading a magazine. She smiled as he entered.

'How did you get on? Sounds like a boisterous party for this time of day. I'm sure I heard someone's glass smashing.'

Nathaniel said nothing. In his mind's eye he saw the three mites exploding harmlessly into the wall. He began to shake – whether from fear or disappointed rage, he did not know.

Ms Lutyens was on her feet in a trice. 'Nathaniel, come here. What's the matter? You look ill! You're shaking!' She put her arm round him and let his head rest gently against her side. He closed his eyes. His face was on fire; he felt cold and hot all at the same time. She was still talking to him, but he could not answer her . . .

At that moment the schoolroom door blew open.

Simon Lovelace stood there, his glasses flashing in the light from the window. He issued a command; Nathaniel was ripped bodily from Ms Lutyens's grasp and carried through the air. For a moment, he hung suspended midway between ceiling and floor, time enough to catch a glimpse of the other two magicians crowding in behind their leader, and also, relegated to the back almost out of sight, his master.

Nathaniel heard Ms Lutyens shouting something, but then he was upended, the blood rushed to his ears and everything else was drowned out.

He hung with his head, arms and legs dangling towards the carpet and his bottom aloft. Then an invisible hand, or an invisible stick, struck him on his rump. He yelled, wriggled, kicked in all directions. The hand descended again, harder than before. And then again . . .

Long before the tireless hand ceased its work, Nathaniel stopped kicking. He hung limply, aware only of the stinging pain and the ignominy of his punishment. The fact that Ms Lutyens was witness to it made it far more brutal than he could bear. Fervently he wished he were dead. And when at last a darkness welled up and began to carry him away, he welcomed it with all his heart.

The hands released him, but he was already unconscious before he hit the floor.

Nathaniel was confined to his room for a month and subjected to a great number of further punishments and deprivations. After the initial series of penalties his master chose not to speak to him, and contact with everyone else – with the exception of Mrs Underwood, who brought him his meals and dealt with his chamber pot – ceased forthwith. Nathaniel had no lessons and was allowed no books. He sat in his room from dawn until dusk looking out across the roofscapes of London towards the distant Houses of Parliament.

Such solitude might have driven him mad had he not discovered a discarded biro under his bed. With this and a few old sheets of paper he managed to while away some of the time with a series of sketches of the world beyond the window.

When these became tedious, Nathaniel devoted himself instead to compiling a large number of minutely detailed lists and notes, drawn over his sketches, which he concealed under his mattress whenever he heard footsteps on the stair. These notes contained the beginnings of his revenge.

To Nathaniel's great distress, Mrs Underwood had been forbidden to talk to him. Although he detected some sympathy in her manner, her silence gave him cold comfort. He withdrew into himself and did not speak when she entered.

It was thus only when his month's isolation came to an end and his lessons started up once more that he discovered that Ms Lutyens had been dismissed.

13

Throughout the long, wet autumn, Nathaniel retreated to the garden whenever he could. When the weather was fine, he brought with him books from his master's shelves and devoured their contents with a remorseless hunger while the leaves rained down upon the stone seat and the lawn. On drizzly days, he sat and watched the dripping bushes, his thoughts circling to and fro on familiar paths of bitterness and revenge.

He made swift progress with his studies, for his mind was fired with hate. All the rites of summoning, all the incantations that a magician could bind around himself to prevent attack, all the words of power that smote the disobedient demon or dismissed it in a trice — Nathaniel read and committed these to memory. If he met with a difficult passage — perhaps written in Samarian or Coptic, or hidden within a tortuous runic cipher — and he felt his heart quail, he had only to glance up at the grey-green statue of Gladstone to recover his determination.

Gladstone had avenged himself on anyone who wronged him: he had upheld his honour and was praised for it. Nathaniel planned to do the same, but he was no longer mastered by his impatience; from now on he used it only to spur himself on. If he had learned one painful lesson, it was not to act until he was truly ready, and through many long, solitary months, he worked tirelessly towards his first aim: the humiliation of Simon Lovelace.

The history books that Nathaniel studied were full of countless episodes in which rival magicians had fought each other. Sometimes the most powerful mages had won, yet often they had been defeated by stealth or guile. Nathaniel had no intention of challenging his formidable enemy head on – at least not until he had grown in strength. He would bring him down by other means.

His proper lessons at this time were a tedious distraction. As soon as they had resumed, Nathaniel had immediately adopted a mask of obedience and contrition, designed to convince Arthur Underwood that his wicked act was now, for him, a matter of the utmost shame. This mask never slipped, even when he was put to the most wearisome and banal jobs in the workroom. If his master harangued him for some trifling error, Nathaniel did not allow so much as a flicker of discontent to cross his face. He simply bowed his head and hastened to repair the fault. He was outwardly the perfect apprentice, deferring to his master in every way and certainly never expressing any impatience with the snail's pace at which his studies now progressed.

In truth, this was because Nathaniel did not regard Arthur Underwood as his true master any longer. His masters were the magicians of old, who spoke to him through their books, allowing him to learn at his own pace and offering ever-multiplying marvels for his mind. They did not patronize or betray him.

Arthur Underwood had forfeited his right to Nathaniel's obedience and respect the moment he failed to shield him from Simon Lovelace's jibes and physical assaults. This, Nathaniel knew, simply was not done. Every apprentice was taught that their master was effectively their parent. He or she protected them until they were old enough to stand up for themselves. Arthur Underwood had failed to do this. He had stood by and watched Nathaniel's unjust humiliation – first at the party, then in the schoolroom. Why? Because he was a coward and feared Lovelace's power.

Worse than this, he had sacked Ms Lutyens.

From brief conversations with Mrs Underwood, Nathaniel learned that while he had been suspended upside-down, being beaten by Lovelace's imp, Ms Lutyens had done her best to help him. Officially she had been handed her notice for 'insolence and impertinence', but it was hinted that she had actually tried to hit Mr Lovelace and had only been restrained from doing so by his companions. When he thought about this, Nathaniel's blood boiled even more forcefully than when he considered his own humiliation. She had tried to protect him, and for doing this, for doing exactly what Mr Underwood *should* have done, his master had dismissed her.

This was something that Nathaniel could never forgive.

With Ms Lutyens gone, Mrs Underwood was now the only person whose company gave Nathaniel any pleasure. Her fondness punctuated his days of studying and brought relief from his master's cold detachment and the indifference of his tutors. But he could not confide his plans to her: they were too dangerous. To be safe and strong, you had to be secret. A true magician kept his own counsel.

After several months Nathaniel set himself his first real test – the task of summoning a minor imp. There were risks involved, for although he was confident enough about the incantations, he neither owned a pair of contact lenses for observing the first three planes, nor had received his new official name. Both of these were due to appear on Underwood's say-so, at the beginning of his coming of age, but Nathaniel could not wait for this far-off day. The spectacles from the workroom would help his vision. As for his name, he would not give the demon any opportunity to learn it.

Nathaniel stole an old piece of bronze sheeting from his master's workroom and cut it, with great difficulty, into a rough disc. Over several weeks, he polished the disc and buffed it and polished it again until it sparkled in the candlelight and reflected his image without defect.

Next, he waited until one weekend when both his master and Mrs Underwood were away. No sooner had their car vanished down the road than Nathaniel set to work. He rolled back the carpet in his bedroom and on the bare floorboards chalked two simple pentacles. Sweating profusely despite the chill in the room, he drew the curtains and lit the candles. A single bowl of rowan wood and hazel was placed between the circles (only one was required, since the imp concerned was weak and timorous). When all was ready, Nathaniel took the polished bronze disc and set it in the centre of the circle in which the demon was to appear. Then he placed the spectacles on his nose, put on a tattered lab coat he had found on the workroom door, and stepped into his circle to begin the incantation.

Dry-mouthed, he spoke the six syllables of the summoning and called out the creature's name. His voice cracked a little as he spoke and he wished that he had had the foresight to enclose a glass of water within his circle. He could not afford to mispronounce a word.

He waited, counting under his breath the nine seconds that

it would take for his voice to carry across the void to the Other Place. Then he counted the seven seconds that it would take for the creature to awaken to its name. Finally he counted the three seconds that it would take for—

— a naked baby floated above the circle, moving its arms and legs as if it were swimming on the spot. It looked at him with sullen yellow eyes. Its small red lips pursed and blew an insolent bubble of spit.

Nathaniel spoke the words of Confinement.

The baby gurgled with rage, frantically flapping its pudgy arms as its legs were drawn downwards towards the shining bronze disc. The command was too strong: as if sucked suddenly down a plughole, the baby elongated into a flow of colour, which spiralled down into the disc. For an instant its angry face could be seen squashing its nose up against the metal surface from below; then a misty sheen obscured it and the disc was clear once more.

Nathaniel uttered several charms to secure the disc and check for snares, but all was well. With shaking legs, he stepped from his circle.

His first summons had been successful.

The imprisoned imp was surly and impudent, but by applying a small spell that amounted to a brisk electric shock, Nathaniel could induce it to reveal true glimpses of things happening far away. It was able to report conversations it overheard as well as reveal them visually in the disc. Nathaniel kept his crude but effective scrying glass hidden under the roof tiles outside the skylight, and with its aid learned many things.

As a trial, he directed the imp to reveal what went on in his master's study. After a morning's observation, he discovered that Underwood spent most of his time on the telephone, attempting to keep abreast of political developments. He seemed to be paranoid that his enemies in Parliament were seeking his downfall. Nathaniel found this interesting in principle but dull in the details, and soon left off spying on his master.

Next he observed Ms Lutyens from afar. The mist swirled across the disc, cleared – and with a quickening heart, Nathaniel glimpsed her again as he remembered her so well: smiling, working . . . and teaching. The disc's image shifted across to reveal a small, gap-toothed boy apprentice, drawing furiously in a sketchpad and evidently hanging on Ms Lutyens's every word. Nathaniel's eyes burned hot with jealousy and grief. In a choked voice, he ordered the image to vanish, grinding his teeth at the laughter that bubbled up from the delighted imp.

Nathaniel then turned his attention to his main objective. Late one evening, he ordered the imp to spy on Simon Lovelace, but was disconcerted to see the baby's face appear in the burnished bronze instead.

'What are you doing?' Nathaniel cried. 'I've given you the order – now obey!'

The baby wrinkled its nose and spoke in a disconcertingly deep voice. 'Trouble is, this one's tricky, innit?' it said. 'He's got barriers up. Not sure I can pass 'em. Might set off a spot of bother, if you know what I mean.'

Nathaniel raised a hand and waved it menacingly. 'Are you saying it's impossible?'

The baby winced and extended a pointed tongue gingerly out of the side of its mouth, as if licking old wounds. 'Not *impossible*, no. Just difficult.'

'Well then.'

The baby sighed heavily and vanished. After a short pause, a flickering image began to form in the disc. It blurred and leaped like a badly tuned television. Nathaniel cursed. He was about to speak the words of the Punitive Jab when he considered that this was probably the best the imp could do. He bent close to the disc and gazed into it, focusing on the scene within . . .

A man was sitting at a table, typing rapidly into a laptop computer.

Nathaniel's eyes narrowed. It was Simon Lovelace all right.

The imp's vantage point was from the ceiling and Nathaniel had a good view of the room behind the magician, although it was a little distorted, as if seen through a fish-eye lens. The room was in shadow; the only light came from a lamp on Lovelace's desk. In the background was a set of dark curtains, stretching from ceiling to floor.

The magician typed. He wore a dinner jacket, with the tie hanging loose. Once or twice he scratched his nose.

Suddenly the baby's face cut in. 'Can't take much more of this,' it sniffed. 'I'm bored, innit, and like I say, if we stick around too long there could be trouble.'

'You'll stick with it till I say so,' Nathaniel snarled. He spoke a syllable and the baby scrunched up its eyes with pain.

'All right, all right! How could you do that to a wee babe, you monster!' The face flicked out and the scene reappeared. Lovelace was still seated, still typing. Nathaniel wished he could get a closer look at the papers on his desk, but magicians often had sensors on their person to detect unexpected magic in their vicinity. It would not be wise to stray too near. This was as good a view as he was going to—

Nathaniel jumped.

Someone else was in Simon Lovelace's room, standing in the shadows by the curtains. Nathaniel had not seen him enter, and nor for that matter had the magician, who was still typing away with his back to the intruder. The figure was a tall, massively built man, swathed in a long leather travelling cape that extended almost to the bottom of his boots. Both cape and boots were heavily stained with mud and wear. A thick black beard covered most of the man's face; above it, his eyes glinted in the darkness. Something about the look of them made Nathaniel's skin crawl.

Evidently the figure now spoke or made a noise, for Simon Lovelace suddenly started and wheeled round in his chair.

The image flickered, faded, reappeared again. Nathaniel cursed and pressed his face closer to the disc. It was as if the picture had jumped forward a moment or two in time. The two men were closer now – the intruder had moved to stand beside the desk. Simon Lovelace was talking to him eagerly. He held out his hand, but the stranger merely inclined his head towards the desk. The magician nodded, opened a drawer and, pulling out a cloth bag, emptied it upon the desktop. Bundles of banknotes spilled forth.

The bronze disc emitted a throaty voice, which spoke urgently. 'Just thought I'd warn you and please don't jab me again, but there's some kinda watcher coming. Two rooms away, heading in our direction. We need to pull out, boss, and do it swiftish.'

Nathaniel bit his lip. 'Stay where you are until the very last moment. I want to see what he's paying for. And memorize the conversation.'

'It's your funeral, boss.'

The stranger had extended a gloved hand from under his cape and was slowly replacing the banknotes inside the bag. Nathaniel was nearly hopping with frustration – at any moment the imp would leave the scene and he would be none the wiser.

Fortunately, his impatience was shared by Simon Lovelace, who held out his hand again, more decisively this time. The stranger nodded. He reached inside his cape and drew forth a small packet. The magician snatched it and feverishly tore the wrapping apart.

The imp's voice sounded. 'It's at the door! We're pulling out.'

Nathaniel just had time to see his enemy reach into the wrapping and draw forth something that sparkled in the lamp-light – then the disc was wiped clean.

He uttered a terse command and the baby's face reluctantly appeared.

'Ain't that all? I need a bit of shut-eye now, I can tell you. Whoof, that was a close one. We *so* nearly got fried.'

'What did they say?'

'Well now, what *did* they say? I might have heard snatches, won't say I didn't, but my hearing's not what it was, what with my long confinement—'

'Just tell me!'

'Big fella didn't say much. Did you see those red stains on his cape, incidentally? Ve-rrry suspicious. Not ketchup, let's put it that way. Fresh too, I could smell it. What did he say now? "I have it." That was one thing. And, "I want my payment first." Man of few words, I'd call him.'

'Was he a demon?'

'By that crude remark I assume you mean a noble entity from the Other Place? Nope. Man.'

'And what did the magician say?'

'He was a bit more forthcoming. Quite voluble in fact. "Do you have it?" That's how he began. Then he said, "How did you—? No, I don't want to know the details. Just give it to me." He was all breathless and eager. Then he got the cash out.'

'Was that it? What was the object? Did either of them say?'

'Don't know that I recall – no, wait! Wait! You don't need to get nasty with me – I'm doing what you asked, ain't I? When the big guy handed over the package, he said something . . .'

'What?'

'So quiet, almost didn't catch it . . .'

'*What did he say?*'

'He said: "The Amulet of Samarkand is yours, Lovelace." That's what he said.'

It took Nathaniel almost another six months before he felt himself to be ready. He mastered new areas of his craft, learned new and greater Commands, and took himself swimming every morning before lessons to increase his stamina. By these means he grew strong in body and mind.

Never again was he able to spy directly on his enemy. Whether or not its presence had been detected, the imp was unable to get close again.

No matter. Nathaniel had the information that he needed.

He sat in the garden as spring turned into summer, devising and refining his plan. It pleased him. It had the merit of simplicity and an even greater one in that nobody in all the world guessed at his power. His master was only just ordering his lenses now; he had spoken absently of perhaps trying out a basic summons in the winter. To his master, his tutors, even to

Mrs Underwood, he was an apprentice of no great talent. This would remain the case while he stole Simon Lovelace's amulet.

The theft was only the beginning, a test of his own power. After that, if all went well, he would set his trap.

All that remained was to find himself a servant who could do what he required. Something powerful and resourceful enough to carry out his plan, but not so potent that it would threaten Nathaniel himself. The time for mastering the great entities was not yet here.

He read through his master's works of demonology. He studied track records through the ages. He read about the lesser servants of Solomon and Ptolemy.

Finally, he chose:

Bartimaeus.

Bartimaeus

14

I knew there was going to be a decent scrap when we got back to the attic, so this time I prepared for it properly. First, I had to decide what shape to take. I wanted something that would really goad him – make him totally lose his cool – and, strange as it may seem, that ruled out most of my more scary forms. In fact, it meant appearing as a person of some kind. It's odd, but being insulted by a flickering spectre or being called names by a fiery winged serpent isn't half as *annoying* for a hardened magician as hearing it from the mouth of something that seems to be human. Don't ask me why. It's just something to do with the way people's minds work.

I figured that the best I could do was appear as another boy of about the same age – someone who would rouse all the kid's feelings of direct competition and rivalry. That was no problem. Ptolemy was fourteen when I knew him best. Ptolemy it would be.

After that, all that remained was to revise my best counter-spells and look forward with pleasure to being able to return home shortly.

Perceptive readers might have noticed a new optimism in my attitude towards the kid. They would not be wrong. Why? Because I knew his birth-name.[1]

Give him his due, however: he came out fighting. No sooner had he got up to his room than he put on his coat, hopped into his circle and summoned me in a loud voice. He didn't have to shout so; I was right beside him, scuttling along the floor.

An instant later, the small Egyptian boy appeared in the circle opposite, wearing his London gear. I flashed a grin.

'Nathaniel, eh? Very posh. Doesn't really suit you. I'd have guessed something a bit more down-market – Bert or Chuck, maybe.'

The boy was white with rage and fear; I could see panic in his eyes. He controlled himself with an effort and put on a lying face.

'That's not my true name. Even my master doesn't know it.'

'Yeah, *right*. Who are you trying to kid?'

'You can think what you want. I charge you now—'

I couldn't believe it – he was trying to send me off again! I laughed in his face, adopted a puckish pose with hands on hips and interrupted in sophisticated style.

---

[1] Armed with this, I would be able to combat the whippersnapper's most vicious attacks. Knowledge of the name redresses the power balance a little, you see, acting as a kind of defensive shield for djinn inside the circle. It's a simple and very ancient kind of talisman and— Well, what are you hanging around reading this for? Read on quickly and see for yourself.

'Go boil your head.'

'I charge you now—'

'Yah, boo, sucks!'

The boy was almost frothing at the mouth he was so angry.[2] He stamped his foot like a toddler in the playground. Then – as I hoped – he forgot himself and went for the obvious attack. It was the Systematic Vice again, the bully's favourite.

He spat out the incantation and I felt the bands drawing in.[3]

'*Nathaniel.*' Under my breath I spoke his name and then the words of the appropriate counter-spell.

The bands immediately reversed their loop. They expanded outwards, away from me, out of the circle like ripples in a pond. Through his lenses, the boy saw them heading in his direction. He gave a yelp and, after a moment's panic, found the words of cancellation. He gabbled them out; the bands vanished.

I flicked a non-existent piece of dust from the sleeve of my jacket and winked at him. 'Whoops,' I said. 'Nearly took your own head off there.'

If the boy had paused, he would have realized what had happened, but his rage was too great. He probably thought he had made some error, spoken something out of turn. Breathing deeply, he searched through his repertoire of nasty tricks. Then he clapped his hands, spoke again.

---

[2] Old or young, small or fat, the besetting weakness of all magicians is their pride. They can't bear to be laughed at. They hate it so much even the cleverest ones can lose control and make silly mistakes.

[3] The Systematic Vice consists of a number of concentric bands of force that squeeze round you, tight as a mummy's bandage-cloth. As the magician repeats the incantation, the bands grow tighter and tighter until the helpless djinni trapped inside begs for mercy.

I wasn't expecting anything as potent as the Stimulating Compass. From each of the five points of the pentacle I was in, a glowing column of electricity shot up, jarring and crackling. It was as if five lightning bolts had been momentarily trapped; in another instant, each column had discharged into a horizontal beam that pierced me with the force of a javelin. Arcs of electricity coursed around my body; I screamed and jerked, carried off the floor by the force of the charge.

Through gritted teeth I spoke it – '*Nathaniel!*' – then a counter-spell as before. The effect was immediate. The charge left me, I slumped to the ground. Small lightning bolts shot off in all directions. The boy dived just in time – an electric charge that would have killed him beautifully speared straight through his flailing coat as he hit the floor. Other bolts collided with his bed and desk; one zapped into his vase of flowers, slicing the glass cleanly in two. The rest vanished into the walls, peppering them with small, asterisk-shaped burn marks. It was a delightful sight.

The kid's coat had fallen over his face. Slowly he raised his head and peered out from under it. I gave him a friendly thumbs-up.

'Keep going,' I grinned. 'One day, if you work hard and stop all these stupid mistakes, you might make a real grown-up wizard.'

The kid said nothing. He got painfully to his feet. By pure fluke, he had dived pretty much straight down and so was still safe within his pentacle. I didn't mind. I was looking forward to whatever mistake he would make next.

But his brain was working again. He stood still for a minute and took stock.

'Better get shot of me quickly,' I said, in a helpful sort of way. 'Old man Underwood will be coming to see what all the noise is about.'

'No, he won't. We're too high up.'

'Only two floors.'

'And he's deaf in one ear. He never hears anything.'

'His missus—'

'Shut up. I'm thinking. You did something then, both times . . . What was it . . . ?'

He snapped his fingers. 'My name! That's it! You used it to deflect my spells, curse you.'

I studied my fingernails, eyebrows raised. 'Might have, might not. It's for me to know and you to find out.'

The kid stamped his foot again. 'Stop it! Don't speak to me like that!'

'Like what?'

'Like you just did! You're speaking like a child.'

'Takes one to know one, bud.'

This was fun. I was really riling him. The loss of his name had made him lose his rag. He was seconds away from another attack, I could tell – he had the stance and everything. I adopted a similar, but defensive pose, like a sumo wrestler. Ptolemy had been exactly this boy's height, dark hair and everything,[4] so it was nice and symmetrical.

With an effort, the kid controlled himself. You could see him flicking through all his lessons, trying to remember what he should do. He had realized that an ordinary quick-fire punishment was out of the question now: I'd just send it back at him.

'I'll find another way,' he muttered darkly. 'Wait and see.'

----

[4] Better looking by far, of course.

'Ooh, I'm really scared,' I said. 'Watch me shiver.'

The kid was thinking hard. There were big grey bags under his eyes. Every time he made an incantation he wore himself out further, which suited me just fine. Some magicians have been known to drop dead simply from over-exertion. It's a high-stress lifestyle, they have, poor things.

His thinking went on for a long time. I gave an ostentatious yawn and made a watch appear on my wrist so that I could glance at it wearily.

'Why not ask the boss?' I suggested. 'He'll help you out.'

'My master? You must be joking.'

'Not that old fool. The one who's directing you against Lovelace.'

The boy wrinkled his brow. 'There's no one. I don't have a boss.'

Now it was my turn to look blank.

'I'm acting on my own.'

I whistled. 'You mean you really summoned me on your lonesome? Not bad . . . for a kid.' I tried to sound suitably sycophantic. 'Well then, let me give you a tip. The best thing now is for you to let me go. You need a rest. Have you looked in a mirror recently? One without an imp inside, I mean? There's worry lines there. Not good at your age. It'll be grey hairs next. What will you do then when you meet your first succubus?[5] Put her right off, it will.'

I was talking too much, I knew, but I couldn't help it. I was worried. The kid was looking at me with a calculating expression that I didn't like.

---

[5] *Succubus:* a seductively shaped djinni in female form. Oddly popular with male magicians.

'Besides,' I said, 'with me gone, no one will know you have the Amulet. You'll be able to use it in complete secrecy. It's a precious commodity – everybody seems to want it. I didn't tell you before, but some girl tried to jump me for it when I was hanging around in town.'

The boy frowned. 'What girl?'

'Search me.' I neglected to mention that this was pretty much what the girl had succeeded in doing.

He shrugged. 'It's Simon Lovelace I'm interested in,' he said, almost to himself. 'Not the Amulet. He humiliated me and I'm going to destroy him for it.'

'Too much hate is bad for you,' I ventured.

'Why?'

'Um . . .'

'I shall tell you a secret, demon,' he went on. 'By dint of my magic,[6] I saw how Simon Lovelace came by the Amulet of Samarkand. Some months ago, a stranger – swarthy, black-bearded and cloaked – came to him at night. He brought him the Amulet. Money was exchanged. It was a furtive meeting.'

I snorted. 'What's surprising there? It's how all magicians trade. You should know that. They thrive on unnecessary secrecy.'

'It was more than that. I saw it in Lovelace's eyes and in the eyes of the stranger. There was something illegal, underhand about it . . . The man's cloak was stained with fresh blood.'

'I'm still not impressed. Murder's part of the game for you lot. I mean, you're obsessed with revenge already and you're only about six.'

---

[6] Typical magician's guff this. It was the unfortunate imp inside the bronze disc that did all the work.

'Twelve.'

'Same difference. No, there's nothing unusual in it. That bloke with the bloodstains probably runs a well-known service. He'll be in the *Yellow Pages*, if you let your fingers do the walking.'

'I want to find out who he is.'

'Hmm. Black-bearded and cloaked, eh? That narrows our suspects down to about fifty-five per cent of the magicians in London. Doesn't even exclude all the female ones.'

'Stop talking!' The kid seemed to have had enough.

'What's the matter? I thought we were getting along well.'

'I *know* that the Amulet was stolen. Someone was killed to get it. When I find out who, I shall expose Lovelace and see him destroyed. I will plant the Amulet, lure him to it and alert the police at the same time. They will catch him red-handed. But first, I want to know all about him and what he gets up to. I want to know his secrets, how he does business, who his friends are, everything! I need to discover who had the Amulet before and exactly what it does. And I must know *why* Lovelace stole it. To this end, I charge you, Bartimaeus—'

'Wait just a minute. Aren't you forgetting something?'

'What?'

'I know your true name, *Natty boy*. That means I have some power over you. It's not all one way any more, is it?'

The kid paused to consider.

'You can't hurt me so easily now,' I went on. 'And that limits your room for manoeuvre in my book. Throw something at me and I'll throw it right back.'

'I can still bind you to my will. You still have to obey my commands.'

'That's true. Your commands are the terms on which I'm in

this world at all. I can't break out of them without you unleashing the Shrivelling Fire.[7] But I can sure as hell make life difficult for you when I carry out your orders. For example, while I'm spying on Simon Lovelace, why shouldn't I grass you up to some other magician? The only thing that stopped me doing that before was fear of the consequences. But I'm not so worried about them now. And even if you explicitly forbid me to grass you up, I'll find some other way to do you a nasty. Let slip your birth-name, maybe, to acquaintances of mine. You won't be able to sleep in your bed for terror of what I might do.'

He was rattled, I could see that much. His eyes flicked from side to side, as if hunting for a flaw in my reasoning. But I was quietly confident: entrusting a mission to a djinni who knows your name is like tossing lit matches into a firework factory. Sooner or later you're going to have *consequences*. The best he could do was let me go and hope no one else called me up while he was alive.

Or so I thought. But he was an unusually clever and resourceful child.

'No,' he said slowly, 'I can't stop you if you want to betray me. All I can do is make sure you suffer along with me. Let's see . . .'

He rummaged through the pockets of his shabby coat. 'There must be something in here somewhere . . . Aha!' His hand emerged holding a small, battered metal tin, on which the words OLD CHOKEY were ornately inscribed.

---

[7] A complicated penalty made up of fifteen curses in five different languages. Magicians can only use it on one of us who *deliberately* disobeys or refuses to carry out a given command. It causes immediate incineration. Only applied in extreme cases, since it is tiring for the magician and robs them of a slave.

'That's a tobacco tin!' I exclaimed. 'Don't you know smoking kills?'

'It doesn't contain tobacco any more,' the boy said. 'It's one of my master's incense pots. It's full of rosemary now.' He lifted the lid a fraction; sure enough, an instant later, a waft of the hellish scent reached me and made the hairs rise on the back of my neck. Some herbs are very bad for our essence and rosemary is one of these. In consequence, magicians can't get enough of it.[8]

'I'd turf that out and fill it up with some honest baccy,' I advised. 'Far healthier.'

The boy closed the lid. 'I am going to send you on a mission,' he said. 'The moment you've gone, I shall cast the spell of Indefinite Confinement, binding you into this tin. The spell will not take effect immediately; in fact I shall make it start up a month from today. If for any reason I am not around to cancel this spell before a month is up, you shall find yourself drawn into this tin and trapped there, until such time as it is opened again. How'd you like the idea of that? A few hundred years encased in a small tin of rosemary. That will do wonders for your complexion.'

'You've got a scheming little mind, haven't you?' I said glumly.

'And in case you're tempted to risk the penalty, I shall bind this tin with bricks and throw it into the Thames before the day is out. So don't go expecting anyone to release you early.'

---

[8] There's big business in protective herbal aftershaves and underarm deodorants for magicians. Simon Lovelace, for instance, positively reeked of Rowan-tree Rub-on.

'I won't.' Too right – I'm not insanely optimistic.[9]

The kid's face now bore a horribly triumphant look. He looked like an unpleasant boy in a playground who'd just won my best marble.

'So, Bartimaeus,' he said, sneering. 'What do you say to *that*?'

I gave him a beaming smile. 'How about you forget all that silly tin business and just trust me instead?'

'Not a chance.'

My shoulders sagged. That's the trouble, you see. No matter how hard you try, magicians always find a way to clobber you in the end.

'All right, Nathaniel,' I said. 'What exactly is it that you want me to do?'

---

[9] The Indefinite Confinement spell is a bad 'un, and one of the worst threats magicians can make. You can be trapped for centuries in horrid minute spaces and, to cap it all, some of them are just plain daft. Matchboxes, bottles, handbags . . . I even knew a djinni once who was imprisoned in a dirty old lamp.

Part
Two

Nathaniel

15

No sooner had the djinni transformed itself into a pigeon and flown from his window than Nathaniel closed the fastener, drew the curtains, and sank down upon the floor. His face was corpse-white and his body shook with exhaustion. For almost an hour, he remained slumped against the wall, staring at nothing.

He had done it; yes, he had done it all right – the demon was bested, was under his control again. He only had to work the binding spell on the tin, and Bartimaeus would be forced to serve him for as long as he desired. It was all going to be fine. He had nothing to worry about. Nothing at all.

So he told himself. But his hands trembled in his lap and his heart pounded painfully against his chest and the confident assertions he tried to conjure fell from his mind. Angrily, he forced himself to breathe deeply and clasped his hands together tightly to suppress the shaking. Of course, this fear was only natural. He had ducked the Stimulating Compass by a fraction of a second. It was the first time he had come near death. That sort of thing was bound to cause a reaction. In a few minutes he would be back to normal; he could work the spell, take the bus to the Thames . . .

The djinni knew his birth-name.

It knew his birth-name.

Bartimaeus of Uruk, Sakhr al-Jinni of Al-Arish . . . He had allowed it to uncover his name. Mrs Underwood had spoken and the djinni had heard and in that moment the cardinal rule had been broken. And now Nathaniel was compromised, perhaps for ever.

He felt the panic welling up in his throat; the force of it practically made him gag. For the first time he could remember, his eyes stung with tears. The cardinal rule . . . If you broke that, you gave yourself up for lost. Demons always found a way. Give them any power at all and sooner or later they would have you. Sometimes it took years, but they would always . . .

He remembered famous case studies from the books. Werner of Prague: he had allowed his birth-name to be uncovered by a harmless imp in his employ; in due course the imp had told a foliot and the foliot had told a djinni and the djinni had told an afrit. And three years later, when Werner had been crossing Wenceslas Square to buy a smoked sausage, a whirlwind had swept him into the air. For several hours his howls from above had deafened the townspeople going about their business, until the disruption had finished with pieces of the magician raining down upon on the weathercocks and chimneys. And this fate was hardly the most horrible that had befallen careless magicians. There was Paulo of Turin, Septimus Manning, Johann Faust . . .

A sob broke from Nathaniel's mouth and the small, pathetic sound shocked him out of his despair and self-pity. Enough of this. He wasn't dead yet and the demon was still under his command. Or it would be once he had disposed of the tobacco tin properly. He would pull himself together.

Nathaniel struggled to his feet, his limbs awash with weakness. With a great effort, he drove his fears to the back of his mind and began his preparations. The pentacle was redrawn, the incense changed. New candles were lit. He stole down to his master's library and double-checked the incantations. Then he added more rosemary to the tobacco tin, placed it in the centre of its circle and began the spell of Indefinite Confinement. After five long minutes his mouth was dry and his voice cracked, but a steel-grey aura began to gleam across the surface of the tin. It flared and faded. Nathaniel uttered the name of Bartimaeus, added an astrological date on which the confinement would begin, and finished. The tin was as before. Nathaniel put it in the pocket of his jacket, snuffed out the candles and drew the rug over the markings on the floor. Then he collapsed upon the bed.

When Mrs Underwood brought her husband his lunch an hour later, she confided an anxiety with him.

'I'm worried about the boy,' she said. 'He's barely touched his sandwich. He's flopped himself down at the table, white as a sheet. Like he's been up all night. Something's scared him, or he's sickening for something.' She paused. 'Dear?'

Mr Underwood was inspecting the array of food upon his

plate. 'No mango chutney, Martha. You know I like it with my ham and salad.'

'We've run out, dear. So what do you think we should do?'

'Buy some more. That's obvious, isn't it? Heavens above, woman—'

'About the boy.'

'Mmm? Oh, *he's* all right. The brat's just nervous about the Naming. And about summoning his first impling. I remember how terrified I got – my master practically had to whip me into the circle.' Mr Underwood shovelled a forkful of ham into his mouth. 'Tell him to meet me in the library in an hour and a half's time and not to forget the Almanac. No – make it an hour. I'll need to ring Duvall about those thefts afterwards, curse him.'

In the kitchen, Nathaniel had still only managed half a sandwich. Mrs Underwood ruffled his hair.

'Buck up,' she said. 'Is it the Naming that's unsettled you? You mustn't worry about it at all. Nathaniel's nice, but there are lots of other good names out there. Just think, you can choose *whatever* name you like, within reason. As long as no other current magician has it. Commoners don't have that privilege, you know. They have to stick with what they're given.' She bustled about, filling the teapot and finding the milk and all the while talking, talking, talking. Nathaniel felt the tin weighing down his pocket.

'I'd like to go out for a bit, Mrs Underwood,' he said. 'I need some fresh air.'

She looked at him blankly. 'But you can't, dear, can you? Not before your Naming. Your master wants you in the library in an hour. And don't forget the *Nominative Almanac*, he says.

Though having said that, you *do* look rather peaky. Fresh air would do you good, I suppose . . . I'm sure he won't notice if you nip out for five minutes.'

'It's all right, Mrs Underwood. I'll stay in.' Five minutes? He needed two hours, maybe more. He would have to dispose of the tin later, and hope Bartimaeus didn't try anything beforehand.

She poured a cup of tea and plonked it on the table before him. 'That'll put colour in your cheeks. It's a big day for you, Nathaniel. When I see you again, you'll be someone else. This will probably be the last time I call you by your old name. I suppose I shall have to start forgetting it now.'

Why couldn't you have started forgetting it this morning? he thought. A small, malicious part of him wished to blame her for her careless affection, but he knew that this was totally unjust. It was his fault the demon had been on hand to hear her. *Safe, secret, strong.* He was none of these things now. He took a gulp of tea and burned his mouth.

'Come in, boy, come in.' His master, seated in a tall upright chair beside the library desk, seemed almost genial. He eyed Nathaniel as he approached and indicated a stool beside him. 'Sit, sit. Well, you're looking smarter than usual. Even wearing a jacket, eh? I'm pleased to see that you register the importance of the occasion.'

'Yes, sir.'

'Right. Where's the Almanac? Good, let's have it . . .' The book was bound in shiny green leather, with an ox-hair ribbon bookmark. It had been delivered by Jaroslav's only the day before and had not yet been read. Mr Underwood opened the cover delicately and glanced at the title page. '*Loew's*

Nominative Almanac, three hundred and ninety-fifth edition . . .
How time flies. I chose my name from the three hundred and
fiftieth, would you believe? I remember it as if it were
yesterday.'

'Yes, sir.' Nathaniel stifled a yawn. His exertions of the
morning were catching up with him, but he had to concentrate on the task in hand. He watched as his master flipped
the pages, talking all the while.

'The Almanac, boy, lists all official names used by magicians
between Prague's golden age and the present. Many have been
used more than once. Beside each is a register that indicates
whether the name is currently being occupied. If not, the
name is free to be taken. Or you can invent one of your own.
See here – "Underwood, Arthur; London" . . . I am the second
of that name, boy. The first was a prominent Jacobean; a close
associate of King James the First, I believe. Now, I have been
giving the matter some consideration, and I think you would
do well to follow in the footsteps of one of the great
magicians.'

'Yes, sir.'

'I thought Theophilus Throckmorton, perhaps – he was a
notable alchemist. And . . . yes, I see that combination *is* free.
No? That doesn't appeal? What about Balthazar Jones? You're
not convinced? Well, perhaps he is a hard act to follow. Yes,
boy? You have a suggestion?'

'Is William Gladstone free, sir? I admire him.'

'Gladstone!' His master's eyes bulged. 'The very idea . . . There
are some names, boy, that are too great and too recent to touch.
No one would dare! It would be the height of arrogance to
assume his mantle.' The eyebrows bristled. 'If you aren't capable
of a sensible suggestion, I shall do the choosing for you.'

'Sorry, sir. I didn't think.'

'Ambition is all very well, my lad, but you must cloak it. If it is too obvious, you will find yourself brought down in flames before you reach your twenties. A magician must not draw attention to himself too soon; certainly not before he has summoned his first mouler. Well, we shall browse together from the beginning . . .'

It took an hour and twenty-five minutes for the choice to be made, and a harrowing time Nathaniel had of it. His master seemed to have a great deal of affection for obscure magicians with obscurer names, and Fitzgibbon, Treacle, Hooms and Gallimaufry were avoided only with difficulty. Likewise, Nathaniel's preferences always seemed too arrogant or ostentatious to Mr Underwood. But in the end the choice was made. Wearily, Mr Underwood brought out the official form and entered in the new name and signed it. Nathaniel had to sign too, in a large box at the bottom of the page. His signature was spiky and ill-formed, but then it was the first time he had used it. He read it back to himself under his breath:

John Mandrake.

He was the third magician of that name. Neither of his predecessors had achieved much of significance, but by this time Nathaniel didn't care. Anything was better than Treacle. It would do.

His master folded the paper, placed it in a brown envelope and sat back in his chair.

'Well, John,' he said. 'It is done. I shall get that stamped at the ministry directly and you will then officially exist. However, don't go getting above yourself. You still know almost nothing, as you will see when you attempt to summon the natterjack impling tomorrow. Still, the first stage of your education is completed, thanks to me.'

'Yes, sir; thank you, sir.'

'Heaven knows, it has been six long and tedious years. I often doubted you would get this far. Most masters would have turned you out onto the streets after that little affair last year. But I persevered . . . No matter. From now on you may wear your lenses.'

'Thank you, sir.' Nathaniel couldn't help blinking. He was already wearing them.

Mr Underwood's voice took on a complacent tone. 'All being well, in a few years we will have you in a worthy job: perhaps as an under-secretary in one of the lesser ministries. It won't be glamorous, but it will suit your modest capabilities perfectly. Not every magician can aspire to become an important minister like me, John, but that shouldn't stop you making a contribution of your own, however meagre. In the meantime, as my apprentice, you will be able to assist me in trivial conjurations, and pay me back a little for all the effort I have spent on you.'

'It would be an honour, sir.'

His master waved a hand of dismissal, allowing Nathaniel to turn away and assume a sour expression. He was halfway to the door when his master remembered something.

'One thing more,' he said. 'Your Naming has happened just in time. In three days, I shall be attending Parliament to hear the State Address given by the Prime Minister to all senior members of his government. It is a largely ceremonial occasion, but he will be outlining his intended policies at home and abroad. Named apprentices are invited too, along with spouses. Providing you do not displease me beforehand, I shall take you with me. It will be an eye-opening experience for you to see us master magicians all together!'

'Yes, sir; thank you very much, sir!' For the first time almost in living memory when talking to his master, Nathaniel's enthusiasm was actually genuine. Parliament! The Prime Minister! He left the library and ran up the staircase to his room and the skylight, through which the distant Houses of Parliament were barely visible beneath the grey November sky. To Nathaniel, the matchstick tower seemed bathed in sunshine.

A little later, he remembered the tobacco tin in his pocket.

There were still two hours till dinner. Mrs Underwood was in the kitchen, while his master was on the telephone in his study. Stealthily, Nathaniel left the house by the front door, taking five pounds from the tradesmen's jar that Mrs Underwood kept on a shelf in the hall. At the main road, he caught a bus heading south.

Magicians were not known for catching public transport. He sat on the back seat, as far away from the other passengers as possible, watching them get on and off out of the corner of his eye. Men, women, old, young; youths dressed in drab colours, girls with flashes of jewellery at their throats. They bickered, laughed or sat quietly, read newspapers, books and glossy magazines. Human, yes, but it was easy to see they had no power. To Nathaniel, whose experience of people was very limited, this made them oddly two-dimensional. Their conversations seemed about nothing; the books they read looked trivial. Aside from feeling that most of them were faintly vulgar, he could make nothing of them.

After half an hour the bus arrived at Blackfriars Bridge and the river Thames.

Nathaniel alighted and walked to the very centre of the bridge, where he leaned out over the wrought-iron balustrade. The river was at high tide; its fast grey waters raced beneath him, its uneven surface swirling ceaselessly. Along both sides, blank-eyed office blocks clustered above the Embankment roads, where car lights and streetlamps were just beginning to come on. The Houses of Parliament, Nathaniel knew, stood just around a bend in the river. He had never been so close to them before. The very thought made his heart quicken.

Time enough for that another day. First he had a vital task to accomplish. From one pocket he drew a plastic bag and a half-brick found in his master's garden. From another he took the tobacco tin. Brick and tin went into the bag, the head of which was tied with a double knot.

Nathaniel gave a quick glance both ways along the bridge. Other pedestrians hurried past him, heads down, shoulders hunched. No one glanced in his direction. Without any more ado, he tossed the package over the balustrade and watched it fall.

Down . . . down . . . By the end it was nothing but a white speck. He could barely see the splash.

Gone. Sunk like a stone.

Nathaniel pulled up the collar of his jacket, shielding his neck from the wind gusting along the river. He was safe. Well, safe as he could be for the moment. He had carried out his threat. If Bartimaeus dared betray him now . . .

It began to rain as he made his way back along the bridge to the bus stop. He walked slowly, lost in thought, almost colliding with several hurrying commuters coming in the opposite direction. They cursed him as they passed, but he barely noticed. Safe . . . That was all that mattered . . .

A great weariness descended upon him with every step.

Bartimaeus

16

When I set out from the boy's attic window, my head was so full of competing plans and complex stratagems that I didn't look where I was going and flew straight into a chimney.

Something symbolic in that. It's what fake freedom does for you.

Off I went, flying through the air, one of a million pigeons in the great metropolis. The sun was on my wings, the cold air ruffled my handsome feathers. The endless rows of grey-brown roofs stretched below me and away to the dim horizon like the furrows of a giant autumn field. How that great space called to me. I wanted to fly until I had left the cursed city far behind, never looking back. I could have done so. No one would have stopped me. I would not be summoned back.

But I could not follow this desire. The boy had made quite clear what would happen if I failed to spy on Simon Lovelace and dish the dirt on him. Sure, I could go anywhere I wanted right now. Sure, I could use any methods I chose to acquire my info (bearing in mind that anything I did that harmed Nathaniel would in due course harm me too). Sure, the boy would not summon me for a while at least. (He was weary and needed rest.[1]) Sure, I had a month to do the job. But I still had to obey his orders to his satisfaction. If not, I had an appointment with Old Chokey, which at that moment was probably settling softly into the thick, dark ooze at the bottom of the Thames.

Freedom is an illusion. It always comes at a price.

Thinking things through, I decided that I had the meagre choice between starting with a known place or with a known fact. The *place* was Simon Lovelace's villa in Hampstead, where much of his secret business presumably occurred. I did not wish to enter it again, but perhaps I could mount a watch outside and see who went in and who went out. The *fact* was that the magician had seemingly come into possession of the Amulet of Samarkand by ill means. Perhaps I could find someone who knew more about the object's recent history – such as who had owned it last.

Of the two starting points, visiting Hampstead seemed the best way to begin. At least I knew how to get there.

This time I kept as far away as possible. Finding a house on the opposite side of the road that afforded a decent view of the villa's front drive and gate, I alighted upon it and perched on the gutter. Then I surveyed the terrain. A few changes had been made to Lovelace's pad since the night before. The

---

[1] He wasn't the only one, believe me.

defence nexus had been repaired and strengthened with an extra layer, while the most badly scorched trees had been cut up and taken away. More ominously, several tall, thin, reddish creatures were now prowling the lawns on the fourth and fifth planes.

There was no sign of Lovelace, Faquarl or Jabor, but then I didn't expect anything right away. I was bound to have to wait for an hour or so. Fluffing up my feathers against the wind, I settled down to my surveillance.

Three days I stayed on that gutter. Three whole days. It did me good to rest myself, I'm sure, but the ache that grew up within my manifestation made me fretful. Moreover, I was very bored. Nothing significant happened.

Each morning, an elderly gardener toddled around the estate scattering fertilizer on the stretches of lawn where Jabor's Detonations had landed. In the afternoons, he snipped at token stems and raked the drive before pottering in for a cup of tea. He was oblivious to the red things, three of which stalked him at all times, like giant yearning birds of prey. No doubt only the strict terms of their summoning prevented them from devouring him.

Each evening, a flotilla of search spheres emerged to resume their hunt across the city. The magician himself remained inside, doubtless orchestrating other attempts to locate his amulet. I wondered idly whether Faquarl and Jabor had suffered for letting me escape. One could only hope.

On the morning of the third day, a soft coo of approval broke my concentration. A small, well-presented pigeon had appeared on the guttering to my right and was looking at me with a distinctly interested tilt of the head. Something about it made me suspect it was female. I gave what I hoped was a haughty and dismissive coo and looked away. The pigeon gave a coquettish hop along the guttering. Just what I needed: an amorous bird. I edged away. She hopped a little closer. I edged away again. Now I was right at the end of the gutter, perched above the opening to the drainpipe.

It was tempting to turn into an alley cat and frighten her out of her feathers, but it was too risky to make a change so close to the villa. I was just about to fly elsewhere, when at long last I spotted something leaving Simon Lovelace's compound.

A small circular hole widened in the shimmering blue nexus and a bottle-green imp with bat's wings and the snout of a pig issued through it. The hole closed up; the imp beat his wings and flew down the road at streetlamp height.

He carried a pair of letters in one paw.

At that moment, a purring coo sounded directly in my ear. I half turned my head – and looked directly into the beak of that benighted she-pigeon. With devious feminine cunning she'd seized the opportunity to snuggle right up close.

My response was eloquent and brief. She got a wingtip in the eye and a kick in the plumage. And with that I was air-borne, following the imp.

It was clear to me that he was a messenger of some kind, probably entrusted with something too dangerous or secret for telephone or mail. I had seen creatures of his kind before.[2] Whatever he was carrying now, this was my

---

[2] Some societies I had known made great use of messenger imps. The rooftops and date palms of old Baghdad (which had neither telephone nor e-mail) used to swarm with the things after breakfast and shortly before sundown, which were the two traditional times for messages to be sent.

first opportunity to spy on Lovelace's doings.

The imp drifted over some gardens, soaring on an updraught. I followed, labouring somewhat on my stubby wings. As I went I considered the situation carefully. The safest and most sensible thing to do was to ignore the envelopes he was carrying and concentrate instead on making friends with him. I could, for instance, adopt the semblance of another messenger imp and start up a conversation, perhaps winning his confidence during the course of several 'chance' meetings. If I were patient, friendly and casual enough, he would no doubt eventually spill some beans . . .

Or I could just beat him up instead. This was a quicker and more direct approach and all in all I favoured it. So I followed the imp at a discreet distance and jumped him over Hampstead Heath.

When we were in a remote enough area, I made the change from pigeon to gargoyle; then I swooped down upon the unlucky imp and bundled us to earth among some scrubby trees. This done, I held him by a foot and gave him a decent shaking.

'Leggo!' he squealed, flailing back and forth with his four clawed paws. 'I'll have you! I'll cut you to ribbons, I will!'

'Will you, my lad?' I dragged him into a thicket and fixed him nicely under a small boulder. Only his snout and paws protruded.

'Right,' I said, sitting myself cross-legged on top of the stone and plucking the envelopes from a paw. 'First I'm going to read these, then we can talk. You can tell me what and all you know about Simon Lovelace.'

Affecting not to notice the frankly shocking curses that sounded up from below, I considered the envelopes. They were very different. One was plain and completely blank: it bore no name or mark and had been sealed with a small blob of red wax. The other was more showy; made of soft yellowish vellum, its seal had been pressed with the shape of the magician's monogram, SL. It was addressed to someone named R. Devereaux Esq.

'First question,' I said. 'Who's R. Devereaux?'

The imp's voice was muffled but insolent. 'You're kidding! You don't know who Rupert Devereaux is? You stupid or something?'

'A small piece of advice,' I said. 'Generally speaking, it isn't wise to be rude to someone bigger than you, especially when they've just trapped you under a boulder.'

'You can stick your advice up—'

★★★[3]

'I'll ask again. Who is Rupert Devereaux?'

'He's the British Prime Minister, O Most Bounteous and Merciful One.'

'Is he?[4] Lovelace *does* move in high circles. Let's see what he's got to say to the Prime Minister then . . .'

Extending the sharpest of my claws I carefully prised the sealing wax off the envelope with minimum damage and

---

[3] These polite asterisks replace a short, censored episode characterized by bad language and some sadly necessary violence. When we pick up the story again, everything is as before, except that I am perspiring slightly and the contrite imp is the model of co-operation.

[4] On the night I stole the Amulet, I'd heard Lovelace being sceptical about the Prime Minister's abilities and this gap in my knowledge suggested he was right. If Devereaux had been a prominent magician, chances are I would have heard his name. Word spreads quickly about the powerful ones, who are always the most trouble.

placed it on the boulder beside me for safekeeping. Then I opened the envelope.

It wasn't the most thrilling letter I've ever intercepted.

Dear Rupert,

Please accept my deepest, most humble apologies, but I may be slightly late arriving at Parliament this evening. Something urgent has come up in relation to next week's big event and I simply must try to resolve it today. I would not wish for any of the preparations to get badly behind schedule. I do hope you will see fit to forgive me if I am delayed.

May I take this opportunity to say again how eternally grateful we are to have the opportunity of hosting the conference?

Amanda has already renovated the Hall and is now in the process of fitting new soft furnishings (in the Nouveau Persian style) in your suite. She has also ordered a large number of your favourite delicacies, including fresh larks' tongues.

Apologies again. I will certainly be present for your Address.

Your faithful and unfailingly obedient servant,
Simon

Just your typical grovelling magician-speak; the kind of sycophantic twaddle that leaves an oily sensation on the tongue. And isn't greatly informative either. Still, at least I had no difficulty in guessing what 'something extremely urgent' was – that could only be the missing Amulet, surely. Also, it was noticeable that he needed to sort it out before a 'big event' next week – a conference of some kind. Perhaps that was worth investigating. As for 'Amanda': she could only be the woman I had seen with Lovelace on my first trip to the villa. It would be useful to learn more about her.

I replaced the letter carefully in the envelope, took up the sealing wax and, by judiciously applying a tiny burst of heat, melted its underside. Then I stuck the seal down again and – presto! Good as new.

Next, I opened the second envelope. Inside was a small slip of paper, inscribed with a brief message.

The tickets remain lost. We may have to cancel the performance.

Please consider our options. Will see you at P. tonight.

Now this was more like it! *Much* more suspicious: no addressee, no signature at the bottom, everything nice and vague. And, like all the best secret messages, its true meaning was concealed. Or at least, it would have been for any human numbskull who'd chanced to read it. I, on the other hand, instantly saw through all the tripe about lost 'tickets'. Lovelace was quietly discussing his missing amulet again. It looked as if the kid was right: perhaps the magician *did* have something to hide. It was time to ask my friend the imp a few straight questions.

'Right,' I said, 'this blank envelope. Where are you taking it?'

'To the residence of Mr Schyler, O Most Awful One. He lives in Greenwich.'

'And who is Mr Schyler?'

'I believe, O Light of All Djinn, that he is Mr Lovelace's old master. I regularly take correspondence between them. They are both ministers in the Government.'

'I see.' This was something to go on, if not much. What were they up to? What was this 'performance' that might have to be cancelled? From the clues in both letters, it seemed that Lovelace and Schyler would meet to discuss their affairs this evening at Parliament. It would be well worth being there to hear what they had to say.

In the meantime, I resumed my enquiries. 'Simon Lovelace. What do you know about him? What's this conference he's organizing?'

The imp gave a forlorn cry. 'O Brilliant Ray of Starlight, it grieves me, but I do not know! May I be toasted for my ignorance! I simply carry messages, worthless as I am. I go where I'm directed and bring replies by return, never deviating from my course and never pausing – unless I am so fortunate as to be waylaid by your good grace and squashed under a stone.'

'Indeed. Well, who is Lovelace closest to? Who do you carry messages to most often?'

'O Most Glorious Person of High Repute, perhaps Mr Schyler is his most frequent correspondent. Otherwise, no one stands out. They are mainly politicians and people of stature in London society. All magicians, of course, but they vary greatly. Only the other day, for instance, I carried messages to Tim Hildick, Minister for the Regions, to Sholto Pinn of Pinn's Accoutrements, and to and from Quentin Makepeace, the theatrical impresario. That is a typical cross-section.'

'Pinn's Accoutrements – what's that?'

'If anyone else asked that question, O He Who Is Terrible and Great, I would have said they were an ignorant fool; in you it is a sign of that disarming simplicity which is the fount of all virtue. Pinn's Accoutrements is the most prestigious supplier of magical artefacts in London. It is situated on Piccadilly. Sholto Pinn is the proprietor.'

'Interesting. So if a magician wanted to buy an artefact he would go to Pinn's?'

'Yes.'

'What?'

'I'm sorry, Miraculous One, it's difficult to think of new titles for you when you ask short questions.'

'We'll let it pass this time. So, other than Schyler, no one stands out amongst all his contacts? You're sure?'

'Yes, Exalted Being. He has many friends. I cannot single one out.'

'Who's Amanda?'

'I could not say, O Ace One. Perhaps she is his wife. I have never taken messages to her.'

'"*O Ace One.*" You really are struggling, aren't you? All right. Two last questions coming up. First: have you ever seen or delivered messages to a tall, dark-bearded man wearing a travel-stained cloak and gloves? Glowering, mysterious. Second: what servants does Simon Lovelace employ? I don't mean squirts like yourself, but potent ones like me. Look sharp and I might remove this pebble before I go.'

The imp's voice was doleful. 'I wish I could satisfy your every whim, Lord of All You Survey, but first: I fear I have never set eyes on such a bearded person, and second: I do not have access to any of the magician's inner chambers. There are formidable entities within; I sense their power, but fortunately I have never met them. All I know is that this morning the master installed thirteen ravenous krels in his grounds. Thirteen! One would be bad enough. They always go for my leg when I arrive with a letter.'

I debated for a moment. My biggest lead was the Schyler connection. He and Lovelace were up to something, no doubt about it, and if I eavesdropped at Parliament that evening, I might very well find out what. But that meeting was hours away; in the meantime, I thought I would call in on Pinn's Accoutrements of Piccadilly. For sure, Lovelace hadn't got his Amulet there, but I might learn something about the bauble's recent past if I checked the place out.

There was a slight wriggling under the stone.

'If you are finished, O Lenient One, might I be allowed to proceed on my way? I suffer the Red-hot Stipples if I am late delivering my messages.'

'Very well.' It is not uncommon to swallow lesser imps that fall into one's power, but that wasn't really my style.[5] I removed myself from the boulder and tossed it to one side. A paper-thin messenger folded himself in a couple of places and got painfully to his feet.

'Here're your letters. Don't worry, I haven't doctored them.'

'Nothing to do with me if you had, O Glorious Meteor of the East. I simply carry the envelopes. Don't know nuffin' about what's in 'em, do I?' The crisis over, the imp was already reverting to its obnoxious type.

'Tell no one about our meeting, or I'll be waiting for you next time you set out.'

'What, d'you think I'd go looking for trouble? No way. Well, if my drubbing's over, I'm out of here.'

With a few weary beats of his leathery wings, the imp rose into the air and disappeared over the trees. I gave him a few minutes to get clear, then I turned into a pigeon again and flew off myself, heading southwards over the lonely heath to distant Piccadilly.

-----

[5] Besides, it would have given me a stitch when flying.

17

Pinn's Accoutrements was the sort of shop that only the very rich or brave dare enter. Occupying an advantageous position at the corner of Duke Street and Piccadilly, it gave the impression that a palace of some kind had been dropped there by a gang of knackered djinn, and then been soldered onto the drabber buildings alongside. Its illuminated windows and fluted golden pillars stood out amongst the magicians' bookshops and the caviar-and-pâté houses that lined the wide, grey boulevard; even when seen from the air, its aura of refined elegance stood out almost a mile away.

I had to be careful when landing – many of the ledges had been spiked or painted with sticky lime to deter no-good pigeons such as me – but I finally settled on the top of a road sign with a good view of Pinn's and proceeded to case the joint.

Each window was a monument to the pretension and vulgarity to which all magicians secretly aspired: jewelled staffs rotated on stands; giant magnifying glasses were trained on sparkling arrays of rings and bracelets; automated mannequins jerked back and forth wearing swanky Italian suits with diamond pins in the lapels. On the pavement outside, common-or-garden magicians trolled along in their shabby work attire, gazed longingly at the displays and went away dreaming of wealth and fame. There were very few non-magicians to be seen. It wasn't a commoner part of town.

Through one of the windows I could see a high counter of

polished wood at which sat an immensely fat man dressed all in white. Perched precariously on a stool, he was busy issuing orders to a pile of boxes that wobbled and teetered beside him. A final command was given, the fat man looked away and the pile of boxes set off uncertainly across the room. A moment later they turned and I glimpsed a small stumpy foliot[1] labouring beneath them. When he arrived at a set of shelves in one corner of the shop, he extended a particularly long tail and, with a series of deft movements, scooped the boxes one by one from the top of the pile and set them carefully on the shelf.

The fat man I took to be Sholto Pinn himself, the owner of the shop. The messenger imp had said he was a magician, and I noticed that he had a gold-rimmed monocle stuffed against one eye. No doubt it was this that enabled him to observe his servant's true shape, since on the first plane the foliot wore the semblance of a youth to prevent startling non-magical passers-by. As humans went, Sholto looked a formidable fellow; for all his size, his movements were fluid and powerful, and his eyes were quick and piercing. Something told me he would be difficult to fool, so I abandoned my first plan of adopting a human disguise and trying to draw information out of him.

The small foliot looked a better bet. I waited patiently for my chance.

When lunch time came, the trickle of well-heeled customers entering Pinn's swelled a little. Sholto fawned and scraped; at his command the foliot scampered to and fro about the shop, gathering boxes, capes, umbrellas or any other item that was required.

-----

[1] *Foliot*: a cut-price djinni.

A few sales were made, then the lunch hour drew to a close and the customers departed. Now Sholto's thoughts turned to his belly. He gave the foliot a few instructions, put on a thick black overcoat and left his shop. I watched him hail a cab and be driven off into the traffic. This was good. He was going to be some time.

Behind him, the foliot had put up a CLOSED sign on the door and had retired to the stool beside the counter, where in mimicry of Sholto he puffed himself out importantly.

Now was my chance. I changed my guise. Gone was the pigeon; instead a humble messenger imp, modelled on the one I'd beaten up at Hampstead, came a-knocking on Pinn's door. The foliot looked up in surprise, gave me a glare and signalled for me to be gone. I knocked again, only louder. With a cry of exasperation, the foliot hopped off the stool, trotted across to the door and opened it a crack. The shop bell tinkled.

'We're closed.'

'Message here for Mr Sholto.'

'He's out. Come back later.'

'It can't wait, guv'nor. Urgent. When's he due back?'

'In an hour or so. The master has gone for lunch.'

'Where's he gone?'

'He did not furnish me with that information.' This foliot had a haughty, superior sort of manner; he evidently considered himself too good to talk to imps such as me.

'Don't matter. I'll wait.' And with a wriggle and a slide I rounded the door, ducked under his arm and entered the shop.

'Coo, this is posh, innit?'

The foliot hurried after me in a panic. 'Get out! Get out! Mr Pinn has given me strict instructions not to allow anyone—'

'Don't get so steamed up, matey. I won't nick nuffin'.'

The foliot positioned himself between me and the nearest rack of silver pocket watches. 'I should think not! With one stamp of my foot I can call up a horla to devour any thief or intruder! Now please leave!'

'All right, all right.' My shoulders slumped as I turned for the door. 'You're too powerful for me. And too highly favoured. It's not everyone gets to run a posh place like this.'

'You're right there.' The foliot was prickly, but also vain and weak.

'Bet you don't get any beatings, or the Red-hot Stipples neither.'

'I certainly do not! I am a model of efficiency and the master is very gracious to me.'

I knew then what sort I was dealing with. He was a collaborator of the worst kind. I wanted to bite him.[2] However, it did give me an angle to work on.

'Cor!' I said. 'I should think he *is* gracious and all. Why? 'Cos he knows how lucky he is to have your help. Reckon he can't do without you. I bet you're good at lugging heavy stuff around. And you can reach high shelves with that tail of yours, or use it to sweep the floor—'

The foliot drew himself up. 'You cheeky fungus! The master values me for a great deal more than that! I'll have you know he refers to me (in company, mark you) as his *assistant*! I mind

---

[2] Most of us enact our duties only under sufferance, simply because we are hurt if we do not co-operate. But a few, typically ones in cushy jobs like Sholto's servant, grow to enjoy their servile status, and no longer resent their situation. Often they do not even have to be summoned, but are happy to engage in prolonged work for their masters, heedless of the pain they suffer from being continually trapped in a physical body. The rest of us generally regard them with hatred and contempt.

the shop for him while he takes his lunch. I keep the accounts, I help research the items that are offered, I have many contacts—'

'Hold on – "the items"?' I gave a low whistle. 'You mean to say he lets you handle the merchandise – all his magical stuff, amulets and the like? Never!'

At this, the repellent creature actually simpered. 'He does indeed! Mr Pinn trusts me implicitly.'

'What – real powerful things, or just the bog-end of the market: you know – hands of glory, mouler glasses and such?'

'Of *course* powerful things! Items that are most dangerous and rare! The master has to be sure of their powers, you see, and check they aren't forgeries – and he needs my assistance for that.'

'No! What sort of stuff, then? Not anything famous?' I was nicely settled in now, leaning on the wall. The traitorous slave's head was swelling so much[3] he had completely forgotten about turfing me out.

'Huh, you've probably not have heard of any of them. Well, let me see . . . The highlight last year was Nefertiti's ankle bracelet! That was a sensation! One of Mr Pinn's agents dug it up in Egypt and brought it over by special plane. I was allowed to clean it – actually clean it! Think of *that* when you're next flying about in the rain. The Duke of Westminster snapped it up at auction for a considerable sum. They say –' here he leaned closer, dropped his voice – 'that it was a present for his wife, who is distressingly plain. The anklet confers great glamour and beauty on the wearer, which was how Nefertiti

---

[3] Literally swelling, I mean. Like a lime-green balloon slowly inflated by a foot-pump. Some foliots (the simple sort) change size and shape to express their mood.

won the pharaoh, of course. But then, you wouldn't know anything about that.'[4]

'Nah.'

'What else did we have? The wolf pelt of Romulus, the flute of Chartres, Friar Bacon's skull . . . I could go on, but I'd only bore you.'

'All a bit above my head, guv'nor. Here, listen, I'll tell you something I've heard of. The Amulet of Samarkand. My master's mentioned that a few times. Bet you never cleaned that.'

But this casual comment had struck some sort of nerve. The foliot's eyes narrowed and his tail gave a quiver. 'Who *is* your master, then?' he said abruptly. 'And where's your message? I don't see you carrying any.'

'Of course you don't. It's in here, ain't it?' I tapped my head with a claw. 'As for my master, there ain't no secret about that. Simon Lovelace's the name. Perhaps you've seen him about.'

This was a bit of a gamble, bringing the magician into the equation. But the foliot's manner had changed at the mention of the Amulet, and I didn't want to increase his suspicions by evading the question. Fortunately, he seemed impressed.

'Oh, it's Mr Lovelace, is it? You're a new one for him, aren't you? Where's Nittles?'

'He lost a message last night. The master stippled him permanently.'

'Did he? Always thought Nittles was too frivolous. Serve

---

[4] How wrong can you get? I brought the anklet to Nefertiti in the first place. And I might add that she was a stunner *before* she put it on. (By the way, these modern magicians were mistaken. The anklet doesn't improve a woman's looks; it forces her husband to obey her every whim. I half wondered how the poor old Duke was getting on.)

him right.' This pleasant thought seemed to relax the foliot; a dreamy look came into his eye. 'Real gent, Mr Lovelace is, a perfect customer. Always dresses nice, asks for things politely. Good friend of Mr Pinn, of course . . . So he was on about the Amulet, was he? Of course, that's not surprising, considering what happened. That was a nasty business and they've still not found the murderer, six months on.'

This made me prick up my ears, but I didn't show it. I scratched my nose casually.

'Yeah, Mr Lovelace said something bad had happened. Didn't say what, though.'

'Well, he wouldn't to a speck like you, would he? Some people reckon it was the "Resistance" what did it, whatever that is. Or a renegade magician – that's more likely, perhaps. I don't know, you'd think with all the resources the State's got—'

'So what did happen to the Amulet? It got nicked, did it?'

'It got stolen, yes. And there was murder involved too. Grisly. Dear me, it was most upsetting. Poor, *poor* Mr Beecham.' And so saying, this travesty of a foliot wiped a tear from his eye.[5] 'You asked me if we'd had the Amulet here? Well, of course not. It was far too valuable to be presented on the open market. It's been government property for years, and for the last thirty of them it was kept under guard at Mr Beecham's estate in Surrey. High security, portals and all. Mr Beecham used to mention it occasionally to Mr Pinn when he came to see us. He was a fine man – hard but fair, very admirable. Ah me.'

---

[5] You could see how far he'd gone over to the enemy by the way he described the death of a magician as 'murder'. And was upset! Honestly, it almost makes you long for the simple aggression of Jabor.

'And somebody stole the Amulet from Beecham?'

'Yes, six months ago. Not one portal was triggered, the guards were none the wiser, but late one evening it was gone. Vanished! And there was poor Mr Beecham, lying beside its empty case in a pool of blood. Quite dead! He must have been in the room with the Amulet at the time the thieves entered and before he could summon help they'd cut his throat. What a tragedy! Mr Pinn was most upset.'

'I'm sure he was. That's terrible, guv'nor, a most terrible thing.' I looked as mournful as an imp can be, but hidden inside I was crowing with triumph. This was just the tasty bit of information I had been searching for. So Simon Lovelace had indeed had the Amulet stolen – and he'd had murder committed to get it. The black-bearded man that Nathaniel had seen in Lovelace's study must have gone there fresh from killing Beecham. Moreover, whether he was working on his own, or as part of some secret group, Lovelace had stolen the Amulet from the Government itself, and was thus engaged in treason. Well, if this didn't please the kid, I was a mouler.

One thing was for sure: the boy Nathaniel had got himself into deep waters when he'd ordered me to pinch the Amulet, far deeper than he knew. It stood to reason that Simon Lovelace would stop at nothing to get the thing back – and silence anyone who knew that he'd had it in the first place.

But why had he stolen it from Beecham? What made him risk the wrath of the State? I knew the Amulet by reputation – but not the exact nature of its power. Perhaps this foliot could help me on the matter. 'That Amulet must be quite something,' I said. 'Useful piece, is it?'

'So my master informs me. It is said to contain a most powerful being – something from the deepest areas of the

Other Place, where chaos rules. It protects the wearer against attack by—'

The foliot's eyes strayed behind me and he broke off with a sudden gasp. A shadow enveloped him, a broad one that swelled as it extended out across the polished floor. The tinkling bell sounded as the door to Pinn's Accoutrements opened, briefly allowing the din of Piccadilly traffic into the shop's comfortable hush. I turned round slowly.

'Well, well, Simpkin,' Sholto Pinn said, as he pushed shut the door with an ivory cane. 'Entertaining a friend while I'm out, are we? While the cat's away . . .'

'N-n-no, master, not at all.' The snivelling wretch was touching his forelock and bowing and retreating as best he could. His swollen head was visibly shrivelling. What an exhibition. I stayed where I was, cool as a cucumber, leaning against the wall.

'Not a friend?' Sholto's voice was low, rich and rumbling; it somehow made you think of sunlight shining on age-blackened wood, of jars of beeswax polish and bottles of fine red port.[6] It was a good-humoured voice, seemingly always on the cusp of breaking into a throaty chuckle. A smile played on his thin, wide lips, but the eyes above were cold and hard. Close up he was even larger than I'd expected, a great white wall of a man. With his fur coat on, he might have been mistaken in bad light for a mammoth's backside.

Simpkin had edged away against the front of the counter. 'No, master. H–he is a messenger for you. H-h-he brings a message.'

'You stagger me, Simpkin! A messenger with a message!

---

[6] No? Oh, well. It's the poet in me, I think.

Extraordinary. So why didn't you take the message and send it on its way? I left you with plenty of work to do.'

'You did, master, you did. He has only just arrived!'

'More extraordinary than ever! With my scrying glass, I have been watching you chattering away with it like a fishwife for the last ten minutes! What explanation can there be? Perhaps my eyesight is fading at last in my advanced old age.' The magician drew his monocle out of a waistcoat pocket, screwed it into position over his left eye[7] and took a couple of steps forward, idly swinging his cane. Simpkin flinched but made no answer.

'Well then.' The cane suddenly swung in my direction. 'Your message, imp, where is it?'

I touched my forelock respectfully. 'I entrusted it to my memory, sir. My master considered it too important to be inscribed on paper.'

'Is that so?' The eye behind the monocle looked me up and down. 'And your master is . . .'

'Simon Lovelace, sir!' I gave a smart salute and stood to attention. 'And if you'll give me leave, sir, I shall relay his message now, then depart. I do not wish to take up any more of your time.'

'Quite so.' Sholto Pinn drew closer and fixed me keenly with both eyes. 'Your message – please proceed.'

'Simply this, sir. "Dear Sholto, Have you been invited along to Parliament tonight? I've not – the Prime Minister seems to have forgotten me and I feel rather snubbed. Please respond

---

[7] With the aid of their lenses, magicians can see clearly onto the second and third planes and blearily onto the fourth. Sholto was no doubt checking me out on these. Fortunately my imp-form extended to the fourth, so I was safe.

with advice a.s.a.p. All the best for now, Simon." Word for word, that is, sir, word for word.' This sounded plausible enough to me, but I didn't want to push my luck. I saluted again and set off for the door.

'Snubbed, eh? Poor Simon. Mmm.' The magician considered a moment. 'Before you go, what is your name, imp?'

'Erm – Bodmin, sir.'

'Bodmin. Mmm.' Sholto Pinn rubbed one of his chins with a thick, jewelled finger. 'You're doubtless keen to get back to your master, Bodmin, but before you go I have two questions.'

Reluctantly I drew to a halt. 'Oh – yes, sir.'

'What a polite imp you are, to be sure. Well, firstly – why would Simon not *write down* such a harmless note? It is hardly seditious and might well become mangled in the memory of a lesser demon such as yourself.'

'I have a very fine memory, sir. Renowned for it, I am.'

'Even so, it is out of character . . . No matter. My other question . . .' And here Sholto moved a step or two closer and sort of loomed. He loomed very effectively. In my current shape I didn't half feel small. 'My other question is this: why did Simon not ask my advice in person fifteen minutes ago, *when I met him for a prearranged lunch*?'

Ah. Time to leave.

I made a leap for the exit, but quick as I was, Sholto Pinn was quicker. He banged his cane on the floor and tilted it forward. A yellow ray of light shot from the end and collided with the door, sending out globular plasms that froze instantly against anything they touched. I somersaulted over them through a cloud of icy vapour and landed on the top of a display stand chock-full of satin undergarments. The staff let out another beam; before it hit I was already in mid-air, leaping over the head of the magician and landing hard on the top of his counter, scattering papers in every direction.

Then I spun and fired off a Detonation – it collided directly with the magician's back, propelling him forwards straight into the frozen display stand. He had a protective field around him – I could see it as pretty yellow sparkles when I flipped through the planes – but though there wasn't the hole in him I wanted, he was badly winded. He subsided gasping into a mess of icy boxer shorts. I set off for the nearest window, intending to bust my way out into the street.

I had forgotten Simpkin. Stepping smartly from behind a rack of cloaks, he swung a giant staff (with a tag marked EXTRA-LARGE) directly at my head. I ducked; the staff smashed into the glass front of the counter. Simpkin drew back to repeat the blow; I leaped at him, wrested the staff from his claws and gave him a clout that reversed the topography of his features. With a grunt he fell back into a pile of silly hats and I proceeded on my way.

Between two mannequins, I spied a nice open stretch of window, made of clear, curved glass that refracted the incoming sunlight into gentle rainbow colours. It looked very pretty and expensive. I fired a Detonation through it, sending a cloud of powdered glass shards pluming out into the street, and dived for the hole.

Too late. As the window broke, a trap was triggered.

The mannequins turned round.

They were made of dark polished wood – the kind of shop dummy that has no human features, just a slender smooth oval where the face should be. The barest suggestion of a nose perhaps, but no mouth, no eyes. They were modelling the latest fashionable wizard gear: his-'n'-hers black suits with slim

THE AMULET OF SAMARKAND

white pinstripes and razor-sharp lapels; lemon-white shirts with high, well-starched collars; daringly colourful ties. They wore no shoes: from each trouser leg projected only a simple nub of wood.

As I leaped between them, their arms shot out to bar the way. From the depths of each sleeve a silver blade extended and clicked into place in their fingerless hands. I was going too fast to stop, but I was still holding the extra-large staff. The blades swung towards me in two synchronized arcs. I raised the staff in front of my face just in time: the blades sank deep into it, almost cutting right through and jerking me to a sudden painful halt.

For a moment I felt the cold aura of the silver against my skin,[8] then I let go of the staff and flung myself back. The mannequins shook their blades; my staff fell to the floor in two halves. They bent their knees and sprang—

I back-flipped over the counter.

The silver blades bit into the parquet flooring where I had just stood.

I needed to change, and fast – the falcon form would probably do – but I also needed to defend myself. Before I could make up my mind quite how, they were upon me again, whistling through the air, wind ruffling their oversized collars. I dived to one side, crashing into a pile of empty gift boxes. One mannequin landed on the counter top, the other behind it, their smooth heads turning towards me.

I could feel my energy getting low. Too many changes, too

---

[8] Silver hurts us badly; it burns our essence with its searing cold. Which is why Sholto had installed it in his security system. What it did to the djinn imprisoned within the mannequins I dread to think.

many spells in too short a time. But I wasn't helpless yet. I cast an Inferno on the nearer mannequin – the one creeping along the counter. A burst of blue fire erupted from its crisp, white shirtfront and began to spread quickly across the fabric. Its tie shrivelled, its jacket smouldered. The mannequin ignored this, as it was bound to do;[9] it raised its blade again. I edged back. The mannequin bent its legs, ready to spring. Fire was licking across the torso; now the varnished timber body was itself ablaze.

The mannequin jumped high into the air and looped down onto me, the flames dancing behind it like an outstretched cloak. At the last moment I jumped aside. It hit the ground heavily. There was a painful crack: the weakened, burning wood had splintered in the impact. The mannequin gave a lopsided stride towards me, its body swaying at a grotesque angle – then its legs gave way. It collapsed in a fiery mess of blackening limbs.

I was about to do the same to its companion, which had hopped over the bonfire and was fast approaching, when a slight sound behind alerted me to the partial recovery of Sholto Pinn. I glanced back. Sholto was half sitting up, looking as if he'd been hit by a herd of buffalo. A pair of Y-fronts draped his forehead at a fetching angle. But he was still dangerous. He groped for his staff, found it, stabbed it in my direction. The yellow ray of light shot out once more – but I was already gone from the spot and the plasms enveloped the second mannequin in mid-bound. Its limbs helplessly frozen,

---

[9] The djinni within was forced to obey its instruction – the defence of the shop – no matter what the consequence to itself. This was where I held a slight advantage, since my only current obligation was to save my skin.

it crashed to the floor, shattering a leg into a dozen pieces.

Sholto cursed, looked around wildly. He really didn't have to look far for little me. I was right above him, balanced on the top of a free-standing set of shelves. The whole stack was filled with meticulously indexed files and beautifully arranged displays of shields, statuary and antique boxes that had all no doubt been filched from their proper owners across the world. It must have been worth a fortune. I leaned my back against the wall, set my feet firmly on the shelf-top and pushed hard.

The shelves groaned and teetered.

Sholto heard the sound. He looked up. I saw his eyes widen in horror.

I gave an extra-hard push, putting a bit of venom into it. I was thinking of the helpless djinn trapped inside the ruined mannequins.

The shelves hung suspended for an instant. A small Egyptian Canopic jar was the first to fall, closely followed by a teak incense chest. Then the centre of gravity shifted, the shelves shuddered, and the whole edifice toppled down with wondrous swiftness upon the sprawling magician.

Sholto had time for maybe half a cry before his accoutrements hit him.

At the sound of the impact cars on Piccadilly swerved, collided. A cloud of incense and funeral dust boiled up from the strewn remnants of Sholto's fine display.

I was satisfied with my performance so far, but it is always best to quit while you're ahead. I eyed the shelving cautiously, but nothing stirred beneath it. Whether his defensive Shield had been enough to save him I couldn't tell. No matter. Surely *now* I was free to leave.

Once more, I made for the hole in the window. Once more, a figure rose to block my way.

Simpkin.

I paused in mid-air. '*Please*,' I said, 'don't waste my time. I've already rearranged your face once for you.' Rather like the finger of an inside-out glove, his previously protruding nose was still squished back deep into his head. He looked testy.

He gave a nasal whisper. 'You've hurt the master.'

'Yes, and you should be dancing with joy!' I sneered. 'If I was in your place I'd be going in to finish him off, not whingeing on the sidelines like *you*, you miserable turncoat.'

'It took me weeks to set up that display.'

I lost patience. 'You've got one second to split, traitor.'

'It's too late, Bodmin! I've sounded the alarm. The authorities have sent an af—'

'Yeah, yeah.' Summoning the last of my remaining energy, I changed into the falcon. Simpkin didn't expect such a transformation from a humble messenger imp. He stumbled back; I shot over his head, depositing a farewell dropping on his scalp as I did so, and burst out at last into the freedom of the air!

Upon which, a net of silver threads descended, dragging me down against the Piccadilly pavement.

The threads were a Snare of the most resilient kind: they bound me on every plane, adhering to my struggling feathers, my kicking legs and snapping beak. I fought back with all my strength, but the threads clung to me, heavy with earth, the element that is most alien to me, and with the agonizing touch of silver. I could not change, I could not work any magic, great or small. My essence was wounded by the barest contact with the threads – the more I flailed about, the worse it felt.

After a few seconds, I gave up. I lay there huddled under the net, a small, still, feathered mound. One of my eyes peeped out under the crook of my wing. I looked beyond the deadly lattice of threads to the grey pavement, still wet after the last rain and thinly covered with a sprinkling of glass shards. And somewhere or other, I could hear Simpkin laughing, long and shrill.

Then the paving slabs grew dark under a descending shadow.

Two great, cloven hooves landed with a soft clink upon the slabs. The concrete bubbled and popped where each hoof touched.

A vapour rose around the net, heavy with the noxious fumes of garlic and rosemary. My mind was poisoned; my head swam, my muscles sagged . . .

Then darkness swathed the falcon and, like a guttering candle, snuffed its intelligence out.

Nathaniel

18

The two days following his Naming were uncomfortable ones for Nathaniel. Physically, he was at a low ebb: the summoning of Bartimaeus and their magical duel had seen to that. By the time he arrived back from his trip to the Thames, he was already sniffing slightly; at nightfall he was snuffling like a hog, and by the following morning he had a full-blown, taps-running head cold. When he appeared wraith-like in her kitchen, Mrs Underwood took one look at him, spun him on his heels and sent him back to bed. She followed him up shortly afterwards with a hot-water bottle, a pile of chocolate spread sandwiches and a steaming mug of honey and lemon. From the depths of his blankets, Nathaniel coughed his thanks.

'Don't mention it, John,' she said. 'I don't want to hear another peep out of you this morning. We have to get you better for the State Address, don't we?' She glanced around the room, frowning. 'There's a very strong smell of candles up here,' she said. '*And* incense. You haven't been practising here, have you?'

'No, Mrs Underwood.' Inwardly Nathaniel cursed his carelessness. He had been meaning to open the window to let the stench out, but he had felt so weary the evening before it had slipped his mind. 'That happens sometimes. Smells rise to the top of the house from Mr Underwood's workroom.'

'Odd. I've never noticed it before.'

She sniffed again. Nathaniel's eyes were drawn as if by a magnet to one edge of his rug, where to his horror he saw the perimeter of an incriminating pentacle peeping out. With a great effort of will he tore his gaze away and broke into a vigorous fit of coughing. Mrs Underwood was distracted. She passed him the honey and lemon.

'Drink that, dear. Then sleep,' she said. 'I'll come up again at lunch time.'

Long before she did so the window had been opened and the room well and truly aired. The floorboards beneath the rug had been scrubbed clean.

Nathaniel lay in bed. His new name, which Mrs Underwood had seemed determined to break in for him, rang strangely in his ears. It sounded fake, even a little foolish. *John Mandrake.* Appropriate perhaps for a magician from the history books; less so for a dribbly, cold-ridden boy. He would find it hard to get used to this new identity, harder still to forget his old name . . .

Not that he'd be allowed to forget it, with Bartimaeus around. Even with his safeguard – the tobacco tin washing about at the bottom of the river – Nathaniel did not feel quite secure. Try as he might to eject it from his mind, the anxiety came back: it was like a guilty conscience, prodding him, reminding him, never letting him rest easy. Maybe he had forgotten something vital that the demon would spot . . . maybe even now it was hatching its plan, instead of spying on Lovelace as he had directed.

A multitude of unpleasant possibilities spun endlessly through his mind as he sprawled amid the debris of orange peel and crumpled tissues. He was sorely tempted to bring out the scrying glass from its hiding place under the roof tiles, and with its help check up on Bartimaeus. But he knew this was unwise – his head was fogged, his voice a feeble croak and his body didn't have strength enough to sit upright, let alone control a small, belligerent imp. For the moment, the djinni would have to be left to its own dubious devices. All would no doubt be well.

Mrs Underwood's attentions saw Nathaniel back on his feet by the third morning.

'And not a moment too soon,' she said. 'It's our big outing this evening.'

'Who will be there?' Nathaniel asked. He was sitting cross-legged in the corner of the kitchen, polishing his shoes.

'The three hundred ministers of the Government, their husbands and wives, some very lucky named apprentices . . . and a few hangers-on – the lesser magicians from the civil service or military, who are close to being promoted, but don't yet know the right people. It's a good opportunity to see who's in and who's out, John, not to mention what everyone's wearing. At the summer gathering in June, several of the female ministers experimented with caftans in the Samarkand style. It caused quite a stir, but it didn't catch on, of course. Oh, please *concentrate*, John.' He had dropped his brush.

'Sorry, it slipped, that's all. Why Samarkand, Mrs Underwood? What's so trendy about it?'

'I'm sure I haven't the faintest idea. If you've finished your shoes, you'd better get on with brushing your jacket.'

It was a Saturday and there were no lessons to distract Nathaniel from the thrill of what was to come, so as the day wore on he became possessed by a wildly mounting excitement. By three o'clock, several hours before it was necessary, he was already dressed in his smartest clothes and prowling back and forth about the house – a state of affairs that continued until his master put his head out of his bedroom and abruptly ordered him to stop.

'Cease your tramping, boy! You're making my head throb! Or would you prefer to remain behind this evening?'

Nathaniel shook his head numbly and descended on tiptoe to the library, where he kept himself out of trouble researching new Constraining spells for middle-ranking djinn. Time passed agreeably, and he was still busy learning the difficult incantation for the Jagged Pendulum, when Mr Underwood strode into the room, his best overcoat flowing behind him.

'There you are, you idiot! I've been calling for you, up and down the house! Another minute and you'd have found us gone.'

'Sorry, sir – I was reading—'

'Not that book you weren't, you dozy fool. It's fourth level, written in Coptic – you'd never have a hope. You were asleep and don't deny it. Right, snap to sharpish, or I really will leave you behind.'

Nathaniel's eyes *had* been closed at the moment his master walked in: he found it easier to memorize things that way. All things considered, this was perhaps fortunate, since he didn't have to come up with any further explanations. In an instant the book was lying discarded on the chair and he was out of the library at his master's heels and following him in a wide-eyed, heart-pounding flurry down the hall, through the front door and out into the night, where Mrs Underwood, in a shiny green dress and with something like a furry anaconda wound loosely round her neck, waited smiling beside the big black car.

Nathaniel had only been in his master's car once before, and he did not remember it. He climbed into the back, marvelling at the feel of the shiny leather seat and the odd, fake smell of the pine-tree odorizer dangling from the rear-view mirror.

'Sit back and don't touch the windows.' Mr Underwood's eyebrows glowered at him in the mirror. Nathaniel sat back, his hands contentedly in his lap, and the journey to Parliament began.

Nathaniel stared out of the window as the car cruised south. The countless glowing lights of London – headlamps, street-lamps, shop fronts, windows, vigilance spheres – flashed in quick succession across his face. He gazed wide-eyed, blinking hardly at all, drinking everything in. Travelling across the city was a special occasion in itself – it rarely happened to Nathaniel, whose experience of the world was confined mainly to books. Now and then, Mrs Underwood took him on necessary bus trips to clothes and shoe stores, and once, when Mr Underwood was away on business, he had been taken to the zoo. But he had seldom gone beyond the outskirts of Highgate, and certainly never at night.

As usual, it was the sheer *scale* that took his breath away; the profusion of streets and side roads, the ribbons of lights curving off on all sides. Most of the houses seemed very different from the ones in his master's street: much smaller, meaner, more tightly packed. Often they seemed to congregate around large, windowless buildings with flat roofs and tall chimneys, presumably factories where commoners assembled for some dull purpose. As such they didn't really interest him.

The commoners themselves were in evidence too. Nathaniel was always amazed by how many of them there were. Despite the dark and the evening drizzle, they were out in surprising numbers, heads down, hurrying along like ants in his garden, ducking in and out of shops, or sometimes disappearing into ramshackle inns on street corners, where warm, orange light shone through frosted windows. Every house like this had its own vigilance sphere floating prominently in the air above the door; whenever someone walked below, it bobbed and pulsed with a deeper red.

The car had just passed one of these inns – a particularly large example opposite a tube station – when Mr Underwood banged his fist down on the dashboard hard enough to make Nathaniel jump.

'That's one, Martha!' he exclaimed. 'That's one of the worst of them! If it was up to me the Night Police would move in tomorrow and carry off everyone they found inside.'

'Oh, not the Night Police, Arthur,' his wife said, in a pained voice. 'Surely there are better ways of re-educating them.'

'You don't know what you're talking about, Martha. Show me a London inn, and I'll show you a commoners' meeting house hidden inside. In the attic, in the cellar, in a secret room behind the bar . . . I've seen it all – Internal Affairs have raided them often enough. But there's never any evidence and none of the goods we're after – just empty rooms, a few chairs and tables . . . Take it from me – it's filthy dives and pits like that where all this trouble's starting. The PM'll have to act soon, but by then who knows what kind of outrage they'll have committed. Vigilance spheres aren't enough! We need to burn the places to the ground – that's what I told Duvall this afternoon. But of course no one listens to me.'

Nathaniel had long ago learned never to ask questions, no matter how interested he was in something. He craned his head and watched the orange lights of the inn dwindle and vanish behind them.

Now they were entering central London, where the buildings became ever bigger and more grand, as befitted the capital of the Empire. The number of private cars on the roads increased, while the shop fronts grew wide and gaudy, and magicians as well as commoners became visible strolling on the pavements.

'How are you doing in the back, dear?' Mrs Underwood asked.

'Very well, Mrs Underwood. Are we nearly there yet?'

'Another couple of minutes, John.'

His master took a glance in the rear-view mirror. 'Time enough then to give you a warning,' he said. 'Tonight you're representing *me*. We're going to be in the same room as all the major magicians in the country and that means men and women whose power you can't even begin to guess at. Put a foot out of line and it'll ruin my reputation. Do you know what happened to Disraeli's apprentice?'

'No, sir.'

'It was a State Address much like this one. The apprentice tripped on Westminster steps while Disraeli was being introduced to the assembly. He knocked against his master and sent him tumbling head over heels down the stairs. Disraeli's fall was broken by the Duchess of Argyll – fortunately a well-padded lady.'

'Yes, sir.'

'Disraeli stood up and apologized to the Duchess with great courtesy. Then he turned to where his apprentice was trembling and weeping at the top of the steps and clapped his hands. The apprentice fell to his knees, his hands outstretched, but to no avail. A darkness fell across the hall for approximately fifteen seconds. When it cleared the apprentice had gone and in his place was a solid iron statue, in exactly the wretched boy's shape. In its supplicating hands was a boot scraper, on which everyone entering the hall for the last hundred and fifty years has been able to clean their shoes.'

'*Really*, sir? Will I see it?'

'*The point being*, boy, that if you embarrass me in any way I shall ensure that there's a matching hat stand there too. Do you understand?'

'I do indeed, sir.' Nathaniel made a mental note to check the formulae for Petrifaction. He had a feeling it involved summoning an afrit of considerable power. From what he knew of his master's ability, he doubted he would have the slightest chance of accomplishing this. He smiled slightly in the darkness.

'Stay beside me at all times,' Mr Underwood went on. 'Do

not speak unless I give you leave and do not stare at any of the magicians, no matter what deformities they may possess. And now, be quiet – we're there, and I need to concentrate.'

The car slowed; it joined a procession of similar black vehicles that moved along the broad grey span of Whitehall. They passed a succession of granite monuments to the conquering magicians of the late Victorian age and the fallen heroes of the Great War, then a few monolithic sculptures representing Ideal Virtues (Patriotism, Respect for Authority, the Dutiful Wife). Behind soared the flat-fronted, many-windowed office blocks that housed the Imperial Government.

The pace slowed to a crawl. Nathaniel began to notice groups of silent onlookers standing on the pavements, watching the cars go by. As best he could judge, their mood seemed sullen, even hostile. Most of the faces were thin and drawn. Large men in grey uniforms stood casually further off, keeping an eye upon the crowds. Everyone – policemen and commoners alike – looked very cold.

Sitting by himself in the insulated comfort of the car, a glow of self-satisfaction began to steal over Nathaniel. He was part of things now; he was an insider on his way to Parliament at last. He was important, set apart from the rest – and it felt good. For the first time in his life he knew the lazy exhilaration of easy power.

Presently the car entered Parliament Square and they turned left through some wrought-iron gates. Mr Underwood flashed a pass, someone signalled them to go on, then the car was crossing a cobbled yard and descending a ramp into an underground car park lit by neon striplights. Mr Underwood pulled into a free bay and switched off the ignition.

In the back, Nathaniel's fingers dug into the leather seat. He was shaking with suppressed excitement.

They had arrived.

19

They walked beside an endless row of glittering black cars towards a pair of metal doors. By this time, Nathaniel's anticipation was such that he could hardly focus on anything at all. He was so distracted that he scarcely took in the two slim guards who stopped them beside the doors, or noticed his master produce three plastic passes, which were inspected and returned. He barely registered the oak-panelled lift that they entered, or the tiny red sphere observing them from the ceiling. And it was only when the lift doors opened and they stepped out into the splendour of Westminster Hall that, with a rush, his senses returned to him.

It was a vast space, wide and open under a steeply pitched ceiling of age-black beams. The walls and floors were made of giant, smoothed blocks of stone; the windows were ornate arches filled with intricate stained glass. At the far end a multitude of doors and windows opened onto a terrace overlooking the river. Yellow lanterns hung from the roof and projected from the walls on metal braziers. Perhaps two hundred people already stood or strolled about the hall, but they were so engulfed by the great expanse it seemed the place was almost empty. Nathaniel swallowed hard. He felt himself reduced to sudden insignificance.

He stood beside Mr and Mrs Underwood at the top of a flight of steps that swept down into the hall. A black-suited servant glided forward and retreated with his master's coat. Another gestured politely and they set off down the stairs.

An object to the side caught his eye. A dull-grey statue – a crouching boy dressed in strange clothes, looking up with wide eyes and holding a boot scraper in his hands. Although age had long since worn away the finer details of the face, it still had a curiously imploring look that made Nathaniel's skin crawl. He hurried onwards, careful not to get too close to his master's heels.

At the foot of the steps they paused. Servants approached bearing glasses of champagne (which Nathaniel wanted), and lime cordial (which he didn't, but received). Mr Underwood took a long swig from his glass and flicked his eyes anxiously to and fro. Mrs Underwood gazed about her with a vague, dreamy smile. Nathaniel drank some cordial and looked around.

Magicians of every age milled about, talking and laughing. The hall was a blur of black suits and elegant dresses, of white teeth flashing and jewels sparkling under the lantern light. A few hard-faced men wearing identical grey jackets lounged near each exit. Nathaniel guessed they were police, or magicians on security duty, ready to call up djinn at the slightest hint of trouble – but even through his lenses, he could spot no magical entities currently present in the room.

He did, however, notice several strutting youths and straight-backed girls who were evidently apprentices like himself. Without exception they were chatting confidently to other guests, all very much at ease. Nathaniel suddenly became acutely conscious of how awkwardly his master and Mrs Underwood were standing, isolated and alone.

'Oughtn't we to talk to someone?' he ventured.

Mr Underwood flashed him a venomous look. 'I thought I told you—' He broke off and hailed a fat man who had just come down the steps. 'Grigori!'

Grigori didn't seem particularly thrilled. 'Oh. Hullo, Underwood.'

'How delightful to see you!' Mr Underwood stepped across to the man, practically pouncing on him in his eagerness to start a conversation. Mrs Underwood and Nathaniel were left on their own.

'Isn't he going to introduce us?' Nathaniel asked peevishly.

'Don't worry, dear. It's important for your master to talk to the top people. *We* don't need to talk to anyone, do we? But we can still watch, which is always a pleasure . . .' She tutted a little. 'I must say the styles this year are *so* conservative.'

'Is the Prime Minister here, Mrs Underwood?'

She craned her neck. 'I don't think so, dear, no. Not yet. But that's Mr Duvall, the Chief of Police . . .' A short distance away a burly man in grey uniform stood listening patiently to two young women, who both seemed to be talking animatedly to him at the same time. 'I met him once – such a charming gentleman. And very powerful, of course. Let me see, who else? Goodness, yes . . . you see that lady there?' Nathaniel did. She was startlingly thin, with cropped white hair; her fingers clasped the stem of her glass like the clenched talons of a bird. 'Jessica Whitwell. She's something to do with Security: a very celebrated magician. She was the one who caught the Czech infiltrators ten years ago. They raised a marid and set it on her, but she created a Void and sucked it in. All on her own she did that, and with minimum loss of life. So – don't cross *her* when you're older, John.'

She laughed and drained her glass. Instantly, a servant appeared at her shoulder and refilled it almost to the brim. Nathaniel laughed too. As often happened in her company, he found some of Mrs Underwood's serenity rubbing off on him. He relaxed a little.

'Excuse me, excuse me! The Duke and Duchess of Westminster.' A pair of liveried servants hustled past. Nathaniel was pushed unceremoniously to one side. A small, shrewish woman wearing a frumpy black dress, a gold anklet and an imperious expression elbowed her way through the throng. An exhausted-looking man followed in her wake. Mrs Underwood looked after them, marvelling.

'What a *hideous* woman she is; I can't *think* what the Duke sees in her.' She took another sip of champagne. 'And that there – Good Heavens! What has befallen him? – is the merchant Sholto Pinn.' Nathaniel observed a great, fat man wearing a white linen suit come hobbling down the steps, supporting himself on a pair of crutches. He moved as if it gave him great pain to do so. His face was covered with bruises; one eye was black and closed. Two menservants hovered about him, clearing his way towards some chairs set against the wall.

'He doesn't look too well,' Nathaniel said.

'No indeed. Some dreadful accident. Perhaps some artefact went wrong, poor man . . .' Bolstered by her champagne, Mrs Underwood continued to give Nathaniel a running guide to many of the great men and women arriving in the hall. It was the cream of Government and society; the most influential people in London (and that, of course, meant the world). As she expanded on their most famous feats, Nathaniel became ever more glumly aware how peripheral he was to all this glamour and power. The self-satisfied feeling that had warmed him briefly in the car was now forgotten, replaced instead by a gnawing frustration. He caught sight of his master again several times, always standing on the fringes of a group, always barely tolerated or ignored. Ever since the Lovelace incident he had known how ineffectual Underwood was. Here was yet more proof. All his colleagues *knew* the man was weak. Nathaniel ground his teeth with anger. To be the despised apprentice of a despised magician! This wasn't the start in life that he wanted or deserved . . .

Mrs Underwood jerked his arm urgently. 'There! John – do you see him? That's him! That's him!'

'Who?'

'Rupert Devereaux. The Prime Minister.'

Where he had come from, Nathaniel had no idea. But there suddenly he was: a small, slim man with light brown hair, standing at the centre of a scrummage of competing dinner jackets and cocktail dresses, yet miraculously occupying a solitary point of grace and calm. He was listening to someone, nodding his head and smiling slightly. The Prime Minister! The most powerful man in Britain, perhaps the world . . . Even at a distance, Nathaniel experienced a warm glow of admiration; he wanted nothing more than to get close and watch him, to listen to him speak. He sensed that the whole room felt as he did; that behind the surface of each conversation, everyone's senses were angled in that one direction. But even as he began to stare, the scrum closed in and the slender, dapper figure was hidden from his view.

Reluctantly, Nathaniel turned away. He took a resigned sip of his cordial – and froze.

Near the foot of the staircase, two magicians stood. Almost alone of all the guests in that vicinity they were taking no interest in the Prime Ministerial throng; they talked animatedly, heads close together. Nathaniel took a deep breath. He knew them both – indeed, their faces had been imprinted on his memory since his humiliation the year before. The old man with the florid, wrinkled skin, more withered and bent than ever; the younger man with the clammy complexion, his lank hair draping down over his collar. Lovelace's friends. And if they were present, would Lovelace himself be far away?

An uncomfortable prickling broke out in Nathaniel's stomach, a feeling of weakness that annoyed him greatly. He licked his dry lips. Calm down. There was nothing to fear. Lovelace had no way of tracing the Amulet to him, even if they met face to face. His searchers would actually have to enter Underwood's house before they could detect its aura. He was safe enough. No, he should seize this opportunity, like any good magician. If he drew close to his enemies, he might overhear what they had to say.

He glanced round; Mrs Underwood's attention had been diverted. She was in conversation with a short, squat gentleman and had just broken into peals of laughter. Nathaniel began to sidle through the crowd on a trajectory that would bring him round to the shadows of the staircase, not far from where the two magicians stood.

Halfway across, he saw the old man break off in mid-sentence and look up towards the entrance gallery. Nathaniel followed his gaze. His heart jolted.

There he was: Simon Lovelace, red-faced and out of breath. Evidently he had only just arrived. He removed his overcoat in a flurry and tossed it to a servant, before adjusting the lapels of his jacket and hurrying for the stairs. His appearance was just how Nathaniel remembered it: the glasses, the hair slicked back, the energy of movement, the broad mouth flicking a smile on-off at everyone he passed. He trotted down the steps briskly, spurning the champagne that was offered him, making for his friends.

Nathaniel speeded up. In a few seconds, he had reached an empty patch of floor beside one sweeping banister of the staircase. He was now not far from the foot of the stairs, close to where the end of the banister curled round to form an ornate plinth, topped with a stone vase. Behind one side of the vase, he glimpsed the back of the clammy magician's head; behind the other, part of the old man's jacket. Lovelace himself had now descended the staircase to join them and was out of view.

The vase shielded Nathaniel from their sight. He eased himself against the rear of the plinth and leaned against it in what he hoped was a debonair fashion. Then he strained to distinguish their voices from the hubbub all around.

Success. Lovelace himself was speaking, his voice harsh and irritable. '. . . no luck whatsoever. I've tried every inducement possible. Nothing I've summoned can tell me who controls it.'

'Tcha, you have been wasting your time.' It was the thick accent of the older man. 'How should the other demons know?'

'It's not my habit to leave any possibility untried. But no – you're right. And the spheres have been useless, too. So perhaps we have to change our plans. You got my message? I think we should cancel.'

'Cancel?' A third voice, presumably the clammy man's.

'I can always blame the girl.'

'I don't think that would be wise.' The old man spoke softly; Nathaniel could barely hear the words. 'Devereaux would be down on you even more if you cancelled. He's looking forward to all the little luxuries you've promised to provide. No,

Simon, we have to put a brave face on it. Keep searching. We've got a few days. It may yet turn up.'

'It'll ruin me if it's all for nothing! Do you know how much that room's cost?'

'Calm down. You're raising your voice.'

'All right. But you know what I can't stand? Whoever did it is *here*, somewhere. Watching me, laughing . . . When I discover who it is, I'll—'

'Keep your voice down, Lovelace!' The clammy man again.

'Perhaps, Simon, we *should* go somewhere a little more discreet . . .' Behind the plinth, Nathaniel jerked himself backwards as if propelled by an electric charge. They were moving off. It would not do to come face to face with them here. Without pausing, he sidestepped away from the shadow of the staircase and took a few steps into the crowd. Once he had got far enough away to be safe, he looked back. Lovelace and his companions had scarcely moved: an elderly magician had imposed herself on their company and was jabbering away – to their vast impatience.

Nathaniel took a sip of his drink and composed himself. He had not understood all he had heard, but Lovelace's fury was pleasingly evident. To find out more, he would have to summon Bartimaeus. Perhaps his slave was even here right now, trailing Lovelace . . . Nothing showed up in his lenses, admittedly, but the djinni would have changed its form on each of the first four planes. Any one of these seemingly solid people might be a shell, concealing the demon within.

He stood, lost in thought for a time, at the edge of a small group of magicians. Gradually, their conversation broke in on him.

'. . . so handsome. Is he attached?'

'Simon Lovelace? Some woman. I don't recall her name.'

'You want to stick clear of him, Devina. He's no longer the golden boy.'

'He's holding the conference next week, isn't he? And he's *so* good looking . . .'

'He had to suck up to Devereaux long and hard for that. No, his career's going nowhere fast. The PM's sidelined him – Lovelace tried for the Home Office a year ago, but Duvall blocked it. Hates him, can't recall why.'

'That's old Schyler with Lovelace, isn't it? Whatever did he summon to get a face like that? I've seen better-looking imps.'

'Lovelace chooses curious company for a minister, I'll say that much. Who's that greasy one?'

'Lime, I think. Agriculture.'

'He's a queer fish . . .'

'Where's this conference taking place, anyway?'

'Some godforsaken place – out of London.'

'Oh no, *really*? How desperately tedious. We'll probably all be pitchforked by men in smocks.'

'Well, if that's what the PM wants . . .'

'Dreadful.'

'*So* handsome, though . . .'

'John—'

'You *are* shallow, Devina; mind you, I'd like to know where he got that suit.'

'*John!*'

Mrs Underwood, her face flushed – perhaps with the heat of the room – materialized in front of Nathaniel. She grabbed his arm. 'John, I've been calling and calling! Mr Devereaux is about to make his speech. We need to go to the back; ministers only at the front. Hurry up.'

They slipped to the side as, with a clopping of heels and a shuffling of gowns, a vigorous herd instinct moved the guests towards a small stage, draped with purple cloth, that had been wheeled in from a side room. Nathaniel and Mrs Underwood were buffeted uncomfortably in the general rush, and ended up at the back and to the side of the assembled audience, near the doors that opened out onto the river terrace. The number of guests had swelled considerably since they had arrived; Nathaniel estimated there were now several hundred contained within the hall.

With a youthful spring, Rupert Devereaux bounded up onto the stage.

'Ladies, gentlemen, ministers – how glad I am to see you here this evening . . .' He had an attractive voice, deep but lilting, full of casual command. A spontaneous round of cheers and clapping broke out. Mrs Underwood nearly dropped her champagne glass in her excitement. By her side, Nathaniel applauded enthusiastically.

'Giving a State Address is always a particularly *pleasant* task for me,' Devereaux continued. 'Requiring as it does that I be surrounded by so many *wonderful* people . . .' More whoops and cheers erupted, fairly shaking the rafters of the ancient hall. 'Thank you. Today I am pleased to be able to report success on all fronts, both at home and abroad. I shall go into more detail in a moment, but I can announce that our armies have fought the Italian rebels to a stalemate near Turin and have bunkered down for the winter. In addition, our alpine battalions have annihilated a Czech expeditionary force—' For a moment, his voice was drowned out in the general applause. 'And destroyed a number of their djinn.'

He paused. 'On the home front, concern has been expressed

again about another outbreak of petty pilfering in London: a number of magical artefacts have been reported stolen in the last few weeks alone. Now, we all know these are the actions of a handful of traitors, small-time ne'er-do-wells of no consequence. However, if we do not stamp it out, other commoners may follow their lead like the brainless cattle they are. We will therefore take draconian measures to halt this vandalism. All suspected subversives will be detained without trial. I feel sure that with this extra power, Internal Affairs will soon have the ringleaders safely in custody.'

The State Address continued for many minutes, liberally punctuated with explosions of joy from the assembled crowd. What little substance it contained soon degenerated into a mass of repetitive platitudes about the virtues of the Government and the wickedness of its enemies. After a time, Nathaniel grew bored: he could almost feel his brain turning to jelly as he strove to listen. Finally he gave up trying altogether, and looked about him.

By half turning, he could see through an open door onto the terrace. The black waters of the Thames stretched beyond the marble balustrade, picked out here and there by reflections of the yellow lights from the south side. The river was at its height, flowing away to the left under Westminster Bridge towards the Docklands and the sea.

Someone else had evidently decided the speech was too tedious to bear and had actually stepped out onto the terrace. Nathaniel could see him standing just beyond the well of light that spilled out from the hall. It was a reckless guest indeed who so blatantly ignored the Prime Minister ... more probably it was just a security official.

Nathaniel's mind wandered. He imagined the ooze at the

bottom of the Thames. Bartimaeus's tin would be half buried now; lost for ever in the rushing darkness.

Out of the corner of his eye he noticed the man on the terrace make a sudden, decisive movement, as if he had drawn something large out from under his coat or jacket.

Nathaniel tried to focus, but the figure was shrouded in darkness. Behind him, he could hear the Prime Minister's mellifluous voice still sounding. '. . . this is an age of consolidation, my friends. We are the greatest magical elite on earth; nothing is beyond us . . .'

The figure stepped forward towards the door.

Nathaniel's lenses logged a flash of colour within the darkness; something not entirely on one plane . . .

'. . . we must follow the example of our ancestors, and strive . . .'

In doubt, Nathaniel tried to speak, but his tongue was furred to the roof of his mouth.

The figure leaped through into the hall. A youth with wild, dark eyes; he wore black jeans, a black anorak; his face was smeared with some dark oil or paste. In his hands was a bright blue sphere, the size of a large grapefruit. It pulsated with light. Nathaniel could see tiny white objects swirling within it, round and round and round.

'. . . for further domination. Our enemies are wilting . . .'

The youth raised his arm. The sphere glinted in the lantern light.

A gasp from within the crowd. Someone noticing—

'. . . Yes, I say to you again . . .'

Nathaniel's mouth opened in a soundless cry.

The arm jerked forward; the sphere left the hand.

'. . . they are *wilting* . . .'

The blue sphere arced into the air, over Nathaniel's head, over the heads of the crowd. To Nathaniel, transfixed by its movement like a mouse mazed by the swaying of a snake, its trajectory seemed to take for ever. All sounds ceased in the hall, except for a barely discernible fizzing from the sphere – and from the crowd, the gulped, high-pitched beginnings of a woman's scream.

The sphere disappeared over the heads of the crowd. Then came the tinkle of breaking glass.

And, a split second later, the explosion.

20

The shattering of an elemental sphere in an enclosed space is always a frightening and destructive act: the smaller the space, or the bigger the sphere, the worse the consequences are. It was fortunate for Nathaniel and for the majority of the magicians with him that Westminster Hall was extremely large and the tossed sphere relatively small. Even so, the effects were noteworthy.

As the glass broke, the trapped elementals, which had been compressed within it for many years, loathing each other's essences and limited conversation, recoiled from each other with savage force. Air, earth, fire and water: all four kinds exploded from their minute prison at top speed, unleashing chaos in all directions. Many people standing nearby were at one and the same time blown backwards, pelted with rocks, lacerated with fire and deluged with horizontal columns of water. Almost all the company of magicians fell to the ground, scattered like skittles around the epicentre of the explosion. Standing at the edge of the crowd, Nathaniel was shielded from the brunt of the blast, but even so found himself propelled into the air and sent careering back against the door that led onto the river terrace.

The major magicians escaped largely unscathed. They had safety mechanisms in place, mainly captive djinn charged to materialize the instant any aggressive magic drew near their masters' persons. Protective Shields absorbed or deflected the ballooning gobbets of fire, earth and water, and sent the gusts of wind screeching off towards the rafters. A few of the lesser magicians and their guests were not so fortunate. Some were sent ricocheting between existing defensive barriers, bludgeoned into unconsciousness by the competing elements; others were swept along the flagstones by small tidal waves of steaming water and deposited in sodden humps halfway across the hall.

The Prime Minister was already gone. Even as the sphere crashed onto the stones three metres from the stage, a dark-green afrit had stepped from the air and swathed him in a Hermetic Mantle, which it promptly carried into the air and out through a skylight in the roof.

Half dazed by his impact with the door, Nathaniel was struggling to rise when he saw two of the men in grey jackets running towards him at frightening speed. He fell back; they leaped over him, out of the door and onto the terrace. As the second one passed above with a prodigious bound, he let out a peculiarly guttural snarl that raised the hairs on Nathaniel's neck. He heard scuffling on the river terrace; a scrabbling noise like claws on stone; two distant splashes.

He raised his head cautiously. The terrace was empty. In the hall the pent-up energy of the released elementals had run its course. Water sluiced along cracks between the flagstones; clods of earth and mud were spattered across the walls and the faces of the guests; a few flames still licked at the edges of the purple drape upon the stage. Many of the magicians were stirring now, levering themselves to their feet, or helping others to rise. A few remained sprawled upon the floor. Servants were running down the staircase and in from adjoining rooms. Slowly people began to find their voices; there was shouting, weeping, a few belated and rather redundant screams.

Nathaniel got to his feet, ignoring a sharp pain in his shoulder where he had collided with the wall, and set off in anxious search of Mrs Underwood. His boots slipped in the mess on the floor.

The fat man in the white suit was leaning on his crutches, talking to Simon Lovelace and the old, wrinkled magician. None of them seemed to have suffered much in the attack, although Lovelace's forehead was bruised and his glasses slightly cracked. As Nathaniel passed them, they turned together and evidently muttered a joint spell of summoning, for six tall, slender djinn wearing silver cloaks suddenly materialized in front of them. Orders were given. The demons rose into the air and floated at speed onto the terrace and away.

Mrs Underwood sat on her backside with a bewildered look on her face. Nathaniel crouched next to her. 'Are you all right?'

Her chin was caked in mud and the hair round one ear was slightly singed; otherwise she seemed unharmed. Nathaniel felt a little teary with relief. 'Yes, yes, I think so, John. You don't need to hug me so. I am glad you are not hurt. Where is Arthur?'

'I don't know.' Nathaniel scanned the bedraggled crowd. 'Oh, there he is.'

His master had evidently not had time to mount an effective defence – if his beard, which now resembled the split halves of a lightning-struck tree, was anything to go by. His smart shirt and jacket front had been blown away, leaving only a blackened vest and a slightly smoking tie. His trousers had not escaped either; they now started too late and ended too soon. Mr Underwood stood near a group of others in a similar predicament, with a look of goggling outrage on his red and soot-stained face.

'I think he'll live,' Nathaniel said.

'Go and help him, John. Go on. I'm fine, really I am. I just need to sit down a little.'

Nathaniel approached his master with some caution. He would not have put it past Underwood to blame him some-how for the disaster.

'Sir? Are you—?'

His master did not seem to register his presence. A bright light of fury shone beneath his blackened eyebrows. With a magisterial effort, he drew the tattered remnants of his jacket together and joined them at the one remaining button. He flattened down his tie, wincing a little at the heat. Then he strode over towards the nearest straggling group of guests. Unsure what to do, Nathaniel trailed along behind.

'Who was it? Did you see?' Underwood spoke abruptly.

A woman whose evening gown hung like damp tissue from her shoulders shook her head. 'It happened too fast.' Several of the others nodded.

'Some object, came from behind . . .'

'Through a portal, perhaps, a renegade magician—'

A white-haired man with a whining voice cut in. 'They say someone entered by the terrace . . .'

'Surely not – what about security?'

'Excuse me, sir . . .'

'This "Resistance", do you think they—?'

'Lovelace, Schyler and Pinn have sent tracker demons downriver.'

'Sir—'

'The villain must have jumped into the Thames and been swept away.'

'Sir! I saw him!'

Underwood turned to Nathaniel at last. 'What? What did you say?'

'I saw him, sir. The boy on the terrace—'

'By heaven, if you're lying . . .'

'No, sir, it was just before he threw it, sir. He had a blue orb in his hand. He ran in through the doors and chucked it, sir. He was dark-haired, a boy, a little older than me, sir. Thin, with dark clothes on; he had a coat, I think; I didn't see what happened to him after he threw it. It was an elemental sphere, I'm sure, sir, a small one; so he didn't need to be a magician to break it . . .'

Nathaniel paused for breath, suddenly conscious that in his enthusiasm he had revealed a far greater knowledge of magic than was appropriate in an apprentice who had yet to summon his first mouler. But neither Underwood nor any of the other magicians seemed to notice this. They took a moment to absorb his words, then turned away from him and began chattering away at breakneck speed, each talking over the others in their eagerness to proclaim their theories.

'It has to be the Resistance – but are they magicians or not? I've always said—'

'Underwood, Internal Affairs is your department. Have any elemental spheres been registered stolen? If so, what the hell's being done about it?'

'I can't say; confidential information . . .'

'Don't mutter into what's left of your beard, man. We've a right to know!'

'Ladies, gentlemen . . .' The voice was soft, but its effect was immediate. The clamour ceased, all heads turned. Simon Lovelace had appeared on the fringes of the group. His hair was back in place. Despite his broken glasses and bruised forehead, he was as elegant as ever. Nathaniel's mouth felt dry.

Lovelace looked around the group with his quick, dark eyes. 'Don't bully poor Arthur, please,' he said. For an instant, the smile flicked across the face. 'He isn't responsible for this outrage, poor fellow. The assailant appears to have entered from the river.'

A black-bearded man indicated Nathaniel. 'That's what the boy said.'

The dark eyes fixed on Nathaniel and widened slightly with recognition. 'Young Underwood. You saw him, did you?'

Nathaniel nodded dumbly.

'So. Sharp as ever, I see. Does he have a name yet, Underwood?'

'Erm, yes – John Mandrake. I've filed it officially.'

'Well, *John*.' The dark eyes fastened upon him. 'You're to be congratulated; no one else I've spoken to so far got much of a look at him. The police may want a statement from you in due course.'

Nathaniel prised his tongue free. 'Yes, sir.'

Lovelace turned back to the others. 'The assailant left a boat below the terrace, then climbed up the river-wall and cut the throat of the guard. There's no body, but a fair bit of blood, so he presumably lowered the corpse into the Thames. He too seems to have jumped into the water after the attack and allowed himself to be swept away. He may have drowned.'

The black-bearded man tutted. 'It's unheard of! What was Duvall thinking? The police should have prevented this.'

Lovelace held up a hand. 'I quite agree. However, two

officers were speedily on the trail; they may find something, though water won't help the scent. I've sent djinn out along the banks too. I'm afraid I can't tell you anything more at this point. We must all be grateful that the Prime Minister is safe and that no one important was killed. Might I humbly suggest that you all head home to recuperate – and perhaps treat yourselves to a change of clothes? More information will no doubt come your way at a later time. Now, if you'll forgive me . . .'

With a smile he detached himself and walked away to another knot of guests. The group looked after him, openmouthed.

'Of all the arrogant—' The black-bearded magician stopped himself with a snort. 'You wouldn't think he was only Deputy Minister for Trade. He's going to find an afrit waiting for him one of these days . . . Well, I'm not hanging around, even if you lot are.'

He stomped away; one by one, the others followed suit. Mr Underwood silently collected his wife, who was busily comparing bruises with a couple from the Foreign Office, and with Nathaniel trotting along behind, left the breathless confusion of Westminster Hall.

'All I can hope,' his master said, 'is that this will encourage them to give me more funds. If they don't, what can they expect? With a measly department of six magicians! I'm not a miracle worker!'

For the first half of the journey, the car had been heavy with silence and the smell of singed beard. As they left central London, however, Underwood suddenly became talkative. Something seemed to be preying on his mind.

'It's not your fault, dear,' Mrs Underwood said, soothingly.

'No, but they'll blame me! You heard them in there, boy – accusing me, because of all the thefts!'

Nathaniel ventured a rare question. 'What thefts, sir?'

Underwood slapped the steering wheel with frustration. 'The ones carried out by the so-called "Resistance", of course! Magical objects thieved from careless magicians all over London. Objects like the elemental sphere – a few of them were taken back in January from a warehouse, if I remember rightly. In the last couple of years, crimes like this have become more and more common, and *I'm* meant to tackle it – with just six other magicians in Internal Affairs!'

Nathaniel was emboldened; he leaned forward on the back seat. 'Sorry, sir, but who are the Resistance?'

Underwood turned a corner too fast, narrowly avoided an old lady and startled her into the gutter by slamming his fist down on the horn. 'A bunch of traitors who don't like us being in control,' he snarled. 'As if we hadn't given this country all its wealth and greatness. No one knows who they are, but they certainly aren't numerous. A handful of commoners drumming up support in meeting houses; a few half-wit fire-brands who resent magic and what it does for 'em.'

'They're not magicians, then, sir?'

'Of course not, you fool, that's the point! They're common as muck! They hate us and everything magical, and want to bring the Government down! As if that were possible.' He accelerated through a red light, waving his arm impatiently at the pedestrians diving back to the safety of the pavement.

'But why would they steal magical objects, sir? If they hate magical things, I mean.'

'Who knows? Their thinking's all wrong-headed, of course; they're only commoners. Perhaps they hope it'll reduce our power – as if losing a few artefacts would make a blind bit of difference! But some devices can be used by non-magicians, as you saw today. They may be stockpiling weapons for some future assault, perhaps at the behest of a foreign government . . . It's impossible to tell – until we find them and snuff them out.'

'But this was their first actual attack, sir?'

'The first on this scale. There have been a few ridiculous incidents . . . mouler glasses tossed at official cars: that sort of thing. Magicians have been hurt. In one case the driver crashed; while he was unconscious, his briefcase, with several magical items, was stolen from his car . . . It was highly embarrassing for him, the idiot. But now the Resistance has gone too far. You say the assailant was young?'

'Yes, sir.'

'Interesting . . . Youths have been reported at the scene of the other crimes too. Still, young or old, these thieves will rue the day they're caught. After tonight, anyone in possession of a magician's stolen property will suffer the severest penalties our government can devise. They won't die easily, you can be sure of that. Did you say something, boy?'

Nathaniel had uttered an involuntary noise, something between a choke and a squeak. A sudden vision of the very stolen Amulet of Samarkand, which even now was hidden somewhere in Underwood's study, had passed before his eyes. He shook his head dumbly.

The car turned the final corner and hummed down the dark and silent road. Underwood swept into the parking space in front of the house. 'Mark my words, boy,' he said, 'the Government will have to act now. I shall request more personnel for my department first thing in the morning. Then perhaps we'll start catching these thieves. And when we do, we'll tear them limb from limb.'

He got out of the car and slammed the door, leaving a fresh waft of burnt hair behind him. Mrs Underwood turned her head towards the back seat. Nathaniel was sitting bolt upright, neck rigid, looking into space.

'Hot chocolate before bed, dear?' she said.

Bartimaeus

21

The darkness cloaking my mind lifted. Instantly, I was as alert as ever, crystal-sharp in all my perceptions, a coiled spring ready to explode into action. It was time to escape!

Except it wasn't.

My mind works on several levels at once.[1] I've been known to make pleasant small talk while framing the words of a spell and assessing various escape routes at the same time. This sort of thing regularly comes in useful. But right then I didn't need more than one cognitive level to tell me that escape was wholly out of the question. I was in big trouble.

But first things first. One thing I *could* do was look good.

---

[1] Several *conscious* levels, that is. By and large, humans can only manage one conscious level, with a couple of more or less unconscious ones muddling along underneath. Think of it this way: I could read a book with four different stories typed one on top of the other, and take them all in with the same sweep of my eyes. The best I can do for you is *footnotes*.

The moment I awoke I realized that my form had slipped while I had been out. My falcon form had deteriorated into a thick, oily vapour that sloshed back and forth in mid-air, as if pulled by a miniature tide. This substance was in fact the nearest I could get to revealing my pure essence[2] while enslaved on earth, but despite its noble nature, it wasn't wholly fetching.[3] I thus quickly changed myself into the semblance of a slender human female, draped in a simple tunic, before adding a couple of small horns on her scalp for the heck of it.

With this done, I appraised my surroundings with a jaundiced eye.

I was standing on top of a small stone plinth or pillar, which rose about two metres high from the middle of a flagstoned floor. On the first plane my view was clear in all directions, but on the second to seventh, it was blocked by something nasty: a small energy sphere of considerable power. This was made up of thin, white, crisscrossing lines of force that expanded out from the top of the pillar beside my slender feet and met again over my delicate head. I didn't have to touch the lines to know that if I did so they would cause me unbearable pain and hurl me back.

There was no opening, no weak spot in my prison. I could not get out. I was stuck inside the sphere like some dumb goldfish in a bowl.

But unlike a goldfish, I had a good memory. I could remember what had happened after I bust out of Sholto's shop. The silver Snare falling on me; the afrit's red-hot hooves

---

[2] *Essence*: the fundamental, essential being of a spirit such as myself, wherein my identity and nature are contained. In your world, we are forced to incorporate our essences into some sort of physical form; in the Other Place, where we come from, our essences intermingle freely and chaotically.

[3] In fact it had the appearance and odour of dirty washing-up water.

melting the pavement stones; the smell of rosemary and garlic throttling me fast as a murderer's hands until my consciousness fled. The outrage of it – me, Bartimaeus, spark out on a London street! But there was time for anger later. Now I had to keep calm, look for a chance.

Beyond the surface of my sphere was a sizeable chamber of some antiquity. It was built of grey stone blocks and roofed with heavy wooden beams. A single window high up on one wall let in a shaft of weak and ailing light, which barely managed to push through the swirling motes of dust to reach the floor. The window was fitted with a magical barrier similar to my prison. Elsewhere in the room were several other pillars similar to the one on which I stood. Most were desolate and empty, but one had a small, bright and very dense blue sphere balanced upon it. It was hard to be sure, but I thought I could see a contorted something pressed inside.

There were no doors in the walls, though that meant little. Temporary portals were common enough in magicians' prisons. Access to the next chamber out (or in) would be impossible except through gateways opened to order by combinations of trusted magician-warders. It would be tiresomely difficult to bypass these, even if I could escape my prison sphere.

The guards didn't help matters either. They were two size-able utukku,[4] stolidly marching around the perimeter of the

---

[4] A type of djinni much favoured by the Assyrian magicians for their unintelligent devotion to violence. I first fought these at the battle of Al-Arish, when the pharaoh drove back the Assyrian army from Egyptian soil. The utukku looked good – four metres high, heads of beasts and birds of prey, crystal breastplates, flashing scimitars. But they could all be caught by the old 'He's behind you' trick. Recipe for success: 1. Take a stone. 2. Chuck behind utukku so that it makes a diverting sound. 3. Watch utukku swivel, eyes popping. 4. Run him through the back with gusto. 5. Gloat to taste. Oddly, my exploits that day made me a few enemies amongst the surviving utukku.

room. One of them had the face and crest of a desert eagle, all cruel curving beak and bristling plumes. The other was a bull-head, blowing clouds of spittle out of his nostrils. Both walked like men on massive legs; their great, veined hands clasping silver-tipped spears. Feathered wings lay folded heavily on their muscled backs. Their eyes rolled ceaselessly back and forth, covering every inch of the room with their stupid, baleful glare.

I gave a light, rather maidenly sigh. Things really didn't seem too promising.

Still, I wasn't beaten yet. Judging by the impressive scale of the prison, I was probably in the hands of the Government, but it was best to be sure. The first thing to do was grill my warders for as much information as they had.[5]

I gave a slightly insolent whistle. The nearest utukku (the eagle-headed one) looked across, jerking his spear in my direction.

I smiled winsomely. 'Hello there.'

The utukku hissed like a serpent, showing his sharp, red bird's tongue. He approached, still feinting toughly with the spear.

'Steady with that thing,' I said. 'It's always more impressive to hold a weapon still. You look as if you're trying to skewer a marshmallow with a toasting fork.'

---

[5] Which was unlikely to be much. As a rough rule of thumb, you can gauge a djinni's intelligence by the number of guises he or she likes to wear. Sprightly entities such as me have no limit to the forms we take. The more the merrier, in fact; it makes our existence slightly less weary. Conversely, the true dullards (viz. Jabor, utukku, etc.) favour only one, and it's usually one that is millennia out of date. The forms these utukku wore were fashionable in the streets of Nineveh back in 700 BC. Who goes round as a bull-headed spirit nowadays? Exactly. It's so passé.

Eagle-beak came close. His feet were on the ground, two metres below me, but even so he was easily tall enough to look me in the eye. He was careful not to get too near to the glowing wall of my sphere.

'Speak out of turn again,' the utukku said, 'and I'll prick you full of holes.' He pointed to the tip of his spear. 'Silver, this is. It can pass through your sphere easy and prick you good, if you don't shut up.'

'Point already taken.' I brushed a loop of hair back from my brow. 'I can see I'm at your mercy.'

'That's right.' The utukku made to go off, but a lonely thought had somehow made it into the wasteland of his mind. 'Here,' he added, 'my colleague –' he indicated Bull-head, who was watching us from a distance with his little red eyes – 'he says he's seen you somewhere before.'

'I don't think so.'

'Long time ago. Only you looked different. He says he's *smelt* you certain. Only he can't think when.'

'He may be right. I've been around a fair time. I have a bad memory for faces, I'm afraid. Can't help him. Where are we now, exactly?' I was trying to change the subject here, uncomfortably aware that the conversation might shortly get round to the battle of Al-Arish. If Bull-head was a survivor, and he learned my name . . .

The utukku's head-crest tipped back a little as he considered my question. 'No harm you knowing that,' he said at last. 'We're in the Tower. *The Tower of London.*' He spoke with considerable relish, banging the base of his spear on the flagstones to emphasize each word.

'Oh. That's good, is it?'

'Not for you.'

Several flippant remarks were queuing up to be spoken here, but I forced them back with difficulty and remained silent. I didn't want to be pricked. The utukku marched away to resume his patrol, but now I spied Bull-head coming closer, snuffling and sniffling all the while with his vile, wet nose.

When he was so close to the edge of my sphere that the gouts of froth he breathed out fizzed and foamed against the charged white threads, he let out a tormented growl. 'I *know* you,' he said. 'I *know* your scent. Long ago, yes, but I never forget. I know your name.'

'A friend of a friend, perhaps?' I eyed his spear-tip nervously. Unlike Eagle-beak he didn't wave it about at all.

'No . . . an enemy . . .'

'Terrible when you can't remember something that's right on the tip of your tongue,' I observed. '*Isn't* it, though? And you try so hard to recall it, but often as not you can't because some fool's interrupting you, prattling away so you can't concentrate, and—'

Bull-head gave a bellow of rage. 'Shut up! I almost had it then!'

A tremor ran through the room, vibrating along the floor and up the pillar. Instantly, Bull-head spun on his heels and trotted across to take up a sentry position against a nondescript bit of wall. A few metres away, Eagle-beak did the same. Between them an oval seam appeared in the air; it widened at the base, becoming a broad arch. Within the arch was a blackness, and from this two figures emerged, slowly gathering colour and dimension as they forced their way out of the treacly nothingness of the portal. Both were human, though their shapes were so different that this was hard to believe.

One of them was Sholto.

He was as round as ever, but hobbling nicely, as if every muscle pained him. I was pleased to see too that his plasm-firing walking stick had been swapped for a pair of very ordinary crutches. His face looked as though an elephant had just got up from it and I swear his monocle had sticky tape on its rim. One eye was black and closed. I allowed myself a smile. Despite my predicament, there were still a few things left in life to enjoy.

Sholto's bruised immensity made the woman alongside him seem even thinner than she actually was. A stooping heron of a creature, she was dressed in a grey top and a long black skirt, with straight white hair chopped short abruptly behind her ears. Her face was all cheekbones and eyes, and entirely colourless — even her eyes were washed out, two dull marbles the colour of rainwater sitting in her head. Long, nailed fingers like scalpels jutted from her frilly sleeves. She carried the odour of authority and danger: the utukku clicked their heels and saluted as she passed and, with a snap of her too-sharp nails, the portal behind her closed into nothing.

Trapped in my sphere I watched them approach — thin and fat, stooped and limping. All the while, behind its monocle, Sholto's good eye was fixed on me.

They stopped a few metres off. The woman snapped her fingers again, and to my slight surprise, the flagstones on which they stood rose slowly into the air. The captive imps beneath the stones gave occasional grunts as they shouldered the burden, but otherwise it was a pretty smooth move. Hardly any wobbling. Soon the stones stopped rising and the two magicians stood regarding me at my level. I stared back, impassive.

'Woken up, have you?' the woman said. Her voice was like

broken glass in an ice bucket.[6] 'Good. Then perhaps you can help us. Firstly, your name. I won't waste time calling you Bodmin; the records have been checked and we know that's a false identity. The only djinni with that name perished in the Thirty Years War.'

I shrugged, said nothing.

'We want your name, your purpose in coming to Mr Pinn's shop and everything you know about the Amulet of Samarkand. Above all, we want to know the identity of your master.'

I brushed my hair out of my eye and smoothed it back. My gaze wandered round the room in a bored sort of way.

The woman did not become angry or impatient; her tone remained level. 'Are you going to be sensible?' she said. 'You can tell us straight away or tell us later on. It is entirely up to you. Mr Pinn, by the way, does *not* think you will be sensible. That is why he has come. He wishes to see your pain.'

I gave the battered Sholto a wink. 'Go on,' I prompted him (with rather more cheer than I actually felt), 'give me a wink back. It's good exercise for a bruised eye.' The magician bared his teeth, but did not speak.

The woman made a motion and her flagstone slid forward. 'You are not in a position to be impudent, demon. Let me clarify the situation for you. This is the Tower of London, where all enemies of the Government are brought for punishment. Perhaps you have heard of this place? For a hundred and fifty years magicians and spirits of all kinds have found their way here; none have left it, save at our pleasure. This chamber is protected by three layers of hex-locks. Between each layer

---

[6] Unexpectedly sharp. And cold. No one can say I don't work hard describing things for you.

are vigilant battalions of horlas and utukku, patrolling constantly. But even to reach *them* you would have to leave your sphere, which is impossible. You are in a Mournful Orb. It will tear your essence if you touch it. At a word of my command –' she uttered a word and the force-lines on the sphere seemed to shudder and grow – 'the orb will shrink a little. You can shrink too, I'm sure, so to start with you will be able to avoid being burned and blistered. But the orb can shrink to nothing – and that you cannot do.'

I couldn't help glancing across at the neighbouring pillar, with its densely packed blue sphere. Something had been inside that orb and its remains were in there still. The orb had shrunk until it had run out of room. It was like glimpsing a dead spider at the bottom of a dark glass bottle.

The woman had followed my gaze. '*Exactly*,' she said. 'Need I say more?'

'If I *do* talk,' I said, addressing her for the first time, 'what happens to me then? What's to stop you squeezing the juice out of me anyway?'

'If you co-operate we will let you go,' she said. 'We have no interest in killing slaves.'

She sounded so brutally forthright I almost believed her. But not quite.

Before I could react, Sholto Pinn gave a wheezing cough to draw the woman's attention. He spoke with difficulty, as if his ribs were hurting him. 'The attack,' he whispered. 'The Resistance . . .'

'Ah, yes.' The woman turned back to me. 'You will gain even more chance of a reprieve if you can give us information about an incident that happened yesterday evening, after your capture—'

'Hold on,' I said. 'How long have you kept me knocked out?'

'For a little under twenty-four hours. We would have interrogated you last night, but as I say, this incident . . . We didn't get round to removing the silver net until about thirty minutes ago. I am impressed at the speed of your recovery.'

'Don't mention it. I've had practice.[7] So, this incident . . . Tell me what happened.'

'It was an attack by terrorists, styling themselves the "Resistance". They claim to loathe all forms of magic, but notwithstanding that, we believe they may have some magical connections. Djinn such as yourself, perhaps; conjured by enemy magicians. It's possible.'

This 'Resistance' again. Simpkin had mentioned them too. He'd guessed they'd stolen the Amulet. But Lovelace was responsible for that – perhaps he was behind this latest outrage too.

'What sort of attack was it?'

'An elemental sphere. Futile, haphazard.'

Didn't sound quite Lovelace's cup of tea. I saw him as more of a stealth and intrigue man, the kind who authorizes murders while nibbling cucumber sandwiches at garden parties. Also, his note to Schyler had suggested they were planning something a little further ahead.

My musings were rudely disrupted by a guttural snarl from my old friend Sholto.

'Enough of this! It will not tell you of its own free will. Reduce the orb, dear Jessica, so that it squirms and

---

[7] Too right. I've been knocked out at various times by various people in places as far afield as Persepolis, the Kalahari and Chesapeake Bay.

speaks! We are both far too busy to loiter in this cell all day.'

For the first time, the thin-lipped slash that was the woman's mouth extended outwards in a kind of smile. 'Mr Pinn is impatient, demon,' she said. 'He does not care whether you speak or not, as long as the orb is put to work. But I always prefer to follow the proper procedure. I have told you what we require – now is the time for you to talk.'

A pause followed. I'd like to say it was pregnant with suspense. I'd like to say that I was wrestling with my conscience about whether to spill the beans about Nathaniel and my mission; that waves of doubt poured dramatically across my delicate features, while my captors waited on tenterhooks to know what my decision would be. I'd like to say that, but it would be a lie.[8] So it was in fact a rather more leaden, dreary and desolate kind of pause, during which I tried to reconcile myself to the pain that I knew would be forthcoming.

Nothing would have given me greater pleasure than to stitch Nathaniel up good and proper. I'd have given them everything: name, address, shoe size – I'd even have hazarded a guess about his inside-leg measurement if they'd wanted it. I'd have told them about Lovelace and Faquarl too, and precisely where the Amulet of Samarkand was to be found. I'd have sung like a canary – there was so much to tell. But . . . if I did so, I doomed myself. Why? Because: 1) there was a good chance they'd just squish me in the orb anyway, and 2) even if they did let me go, Nathaniel would then be killed or otherwise inconvenienced and I'd be bound for Old Chokey at the bottom of the Thames. And just the

---

[8] And I'm scrupulously honest, as you know.

thought of all that rosemary made my nose run.[9]

Better a quick extinction in the orb than an infinity of misery. So I rubbed my delicate chin and waited for the inevitable to begin.

Sholto grunted and looked at the woman. She tapped her watch.

'Time's up,' she said. 'Well?'

And then, as if written by the hand of a bad novelist, an incredible thing happened. I was just about to give them a last tirade of impassioned (yet clever) abuse, when I felt a familiarly painful sensation in my bowels. A multitude of red-hot pincers were plucking at me, tugging at my essence . . .

I was being summoned!

---

[9] Thoughtful persons might at this point object that since Lovelace had stolen the Amulet and was thus working against the Government, it might have been worth a gamble to tell them about his crimes. Perhaps both Nathaniel and I might have then been let off for services rendered. True, but unfortunately there was no knowing who *else* was involved with Lovelace's plot, and since Sholto Pinn himself had been lunching with Lovelace the previous day, there was certainly no trusting *him*. All in all, the risks of coming clean far outweighed the possible benefits.

22

For the first time ever I felt grateful to the boy. What perfect timing! What a remarkable coincidence! I could now disappear from under their noses, dematerialized by the summons, while they gawped and gulped like startled fish. If I was quick, there would just be time to cock a quick snook before departure.

I gave a rueful shake of the head. '*So* sorry,' I smiled. 'I'd *love* to help you, really I would. But I have to go. Maybe we can pick up the torture and captivity again sometime soon. Only with a small alteration. I'll be out there and it'll be you two cuddling up inside the orb. So you'd better start dieting big time, Sholto. Meanwhile, you can both – ouch! – go boil your heads and— Ahh! . . . Oooh!' It wasn't my most fluent repartee, I'll admit, but the pain of the summoning was getting to me. It felt worse than normal, somehow – sharper, less healthy . . .

Also, it was taking longer.

I abandoned all pretence of a cheekily insolent posture, and writhed about on the top of the column, willing the boy to get on with it. What was his problem? Didn't he know I was in agony? It wasn't like I could writhe properly either – the orb's force-lines were far too close for comfort.

After two deeply unpleasant minutes, the vicious tug of the summoning lessened and died away. It left me in an un-dignified posture – crouched in a ball, head between my knees, arms over my head. With the slow stiffness of accumulated agony, I raised my face a little and gingerly brushed the hair back from my eyes.

I was still inside the orb. The two magicians were right there, grinning at me from beyond the walls of my prison.

No way to make this look good. Grimly, with a thousand residual aches, I straightened, stood up, stared back at them implacably. Sholto was chuckling quietly to himself. 'That was worth the price of admission on its own, dear Jessica,' he said. 'The look on its face was simply exquisite.'

The woman nodded. '*Such* good timing,' she said. 'I'm so glad we were here to see that. Don't you understand yet, you stupid creature?' Her flagstone shifted a little nearer. 'I told you; it is impossible to leave a Mournful Orb, and that includes by summoning. Your essence is locked inside it. Even your master cannot call you from it.'

'She'll find a way,' I said, then bit my lip as if I regretted saying it.

'*She?*' The woman's eyes narrowed. 'Your master is a woman?'

'It lies.' Sholto Pinn shook his head. 'An obvious bluff. Jessica, I am weary; also I am overdue for my morning's massage at the Byzantine Baths. I should be in the steam room this moment. Might I suggest that the creature needs further encouragement, and that we leave him to it?'

'An admirable idea, dear Sholto.' She clicked her nails five times. A hum, a shudder. Time to downsize pronto! I poured what remained of my energy into a hasty transformation, and as the flickering lines of the orb closed in on me, shrank myself into a new form. An elegant cat, hunched and sinuous, shying away from the lowering walls of the orb.

In a matter of seconds, the orb shrank to about a third of its former dimensions. The humming of its obscene energy was loud in my feline ears, but there was still a healthy gap between me and the walls. The woman snapped her nails and the rate of shrinking slowed dramatically.

'Fascinating . . .' She spoke to Sholto. 'In a time of crisis, it becomes a desert cat. *Very* Egyptian. This one's had a long career, I think.' Now she turned back to me. 'The orb will continue to shrink, demon,' she said. 'Sometimes fast, sometimes slow. Eventually it will reach a single point. You will be observed continually, so if at any time you wish to speak, you need only to say so. Otherwise, farewell.'

In reply, the cat hissed and spat. That was as articulate as I could get right then.

The flagstones turned and descended to their original positions. Sholto and the woman returned to the arch and were swallowed by the portal. The seam closed up and the wall was as before. Eagle-beak and Bull-head resumed their marching. The deathly white lines of the orb hummed and glowed and closed in imperceptibly.

The cat curled on the top of the column and wrapped its tail around itself, tight as it would go.

Over the next few hours, my situation grew ever less comfortable. The cat lasted me well at first, but eventually the orb had shrunk so much my ears were down beneath my whiskers and I could feel the tip of my tail beginning to fry. A succession of changes ensued. I knew I was being watched, so I didn't do the obvious thing and just become a flea straight off – that would only result in the orb shrinking really fast to catch up with me. Instead, I went through a series of furry and scaly variations, keeping just ahead of the shimmering prison bars each time. First a jack-rabbit, then a marmoset, then an undistinguished vole . . . Put all my forms together and you'd have a pretty decent pet shop, I suppose, but it wasn't exactly becoming.

Try as I might, I couldn't come up with any great plan of escape either. I could gain a reprieve by spinning some long, complex lie to the woman, but she'd soon find out I was fibbing and finish me off all the quicker. That was no good.

To make matters even worse, the wretched boy tried summoning me twice more. He didn't give up easily, probably reckoning he'd made some kind of mistake the first time, and ended up causing me so much discomfort I nearly decided to turn him in.

Nearly, but not quite; no point giving up just yet. There was always the chance something might happen.

'Were you at Angkor Thom?' Bull-head again, still trying to place me.

'What?' I was the vole at this point; I did my best to sound grandly dismissive, but voles can only do peeved.

'You know, the Khmer Empire. I worked for the imperial magicians, me, when they conquered Thailand. Were you something to do with that? Some rebel?'

'No.'[1]

'Sure about that?'

'Yes! Of course I'm sure! You're confusing me with someone else. But forget about that for a minute. Listen . . .' The vole dropped its voice nice and quiet, spoke from under a

---

[1] True, as it happens. That would be 800 years ago. In those days I was mostly in North America.

raised paw. 'You're obviously a clever fellow, you've been around the block a few times, worked for a lot of the most vicious empires. Look – I've got powerful friends. If you can get me out of here, they'll kill your master for you, free you from your bond.'

If Bull-head had possessed more brains, I'd have sworn he was looking at me sceptically. Nevertheless, I ploughed on regardless. 'How long have you been cooped up here on guard duty?' I said. 'Fifty years? A hundred? That's no life for an utukku, is it? You might as well be in an orb like this.'

The head came close to the bars. A shower of nose-steam jetted all over me, leaving sticky droplets in my fur. '*What* friends?'

'Erm, a marid – a big one – and four afrits, very powerful, much stronger than me . . . You can join us . . .'

The head retreated with a contemptuous growl. 'You must think I'm stupid!'

'No, no . . .' The vole gave a shrug. 'That's what Eagle-beak over there thinks. He *said* you wouldn't join our plan. Still, if you're not interested . . .' With a wriggle and a half-hop, the vole turned its back.

'What?' Bull-head hastened round to the other side of the column, holding his spear close to the orb. 'Don't you turn your back on me! What did Xerxes say?'

'Oi!' Eagle-beak came hurrying from the far corner of the room. 'I heard my name! Stop talking to the prisoner!'

Bull-head looked at him resentfully. 'I can talk if I want to. So, you think I'm stupid, do you? Well, I'm not, see? What's this plan of yours?'

'Don't tell him, Xerxes!' I whispered loudly. 'Don't tell him *anything*.'

Eagle-beak made a rasping noise with his beak. 'Plan? I know of no plan. The prisoner's lying to you, Baztuk. What's it been saying?'

'It's all right, Xerxes,' I called brightly. 'I haven't mentioned . . . *you know.*'

Bull-head brandished his spear. 'I think it's me who should be asking the questions, Xerxes,' he said. 'You've been plotting with the captive!'

'No, you idiot—'

'Idiot, am I?'

Then they were off: muzzle to beak, all posturing muscles and flaring crest feathers, shouting and landing punches on each other's armoured chests. Ho hum. Utukku always were easy to fool. In their excitement, I had been quite forgotten, which suited me fine. Ordinarily, I would have enjoyed seeing them at each other's throats, but right now it was scant consolation for the mess I was in.

The orb had become uncomfortably tight once more, so I downsized again, this time to a scarab beetle. Not that there was a great deal of point in this; but it delayed the inevitable and gave me room to scurry back and forth on the top of the pillar, flashing my wing-cases in rage and something like despair. That boy, Nathaniel! If ever I got out, I'd wreak such revenge on him that it would enter the legends and nightmares of his people! That I, Bartimaeus, who spoke with Solomon and Hiawatha, should go out like this – as a beetle crushed by an enemy too arrogant to even watch it done! No! Even now, I'd find a way . . .

I scurried back and forth, back and forth, thinking, thinking . . .

Impossible. I could not escape. Death was closing in steadily on every side. It was hard to see how the situation could possibly get any worse.

A froth of steam, a roar, a mad, red eye lowered to my level. 'Bartimaeus!'

Well, that was one way. Bull-head was no longer squabbling. He had suddenly remembered who I was. 'I know you now!' he cried. 'Your voice! Yes, it *is* you – the destroyer of my people! At last! I have waited twenty-seven centuries for this moment!'

When you're faced with a comment like that, it's hard to think of anything to say.

The utukku raised his silver spear and howled out the triumphant battle cry that his kind always deliver with the death stroke.

I settled for whirring my wings. You know, in a forlorn, defiant sort of way.

Nathaniel

23

What was to become the worst day of Nathaniel's life started out much as it meant to go on. Despite returning from Parliament at such a late hour, he had found it almost impossible to get to sleep. His master's final words rang endlessly through his mind, instilling in him a growing unease: 'Anyone in possession of stolen property will suffer the severest penalties...' *The severest penalties* ... And what was the Amulet of Samarkand if not stolen property?

True, on the one hand, he was certain Lovelace had already stolen the Amulet: it was to get proof of this that he had sent Bartimaeus on his mission. But on the other hand, he – or, strictly speaking, Underwood – currently had the stolen goods instead. If Lovelace, or the police, or anyone from the Government should find it in the house ... indeed, if Underwood himself should discover it in his collection,

Nathaniel dreaded to think what catastrophes might occur. What had started out as a personal strike against his enemy now seemed suddenly a far riskier business. It wasn't just Lovelace he was up against now, but the long arm of the Government too. He had heard about the glass prisms, containing the remains of traitors, which hung from the battlements of the Tower of London. They made an eloquent point. It was never wise to risk official wrath.

By the time the ghostly light that precedes the dawn began to glow around the skylight, Nathaniel was sure of one thing only. Whether the djinni had gathered proof or not, he ought to get rid of the Amulet fast. He would return it to Lovelace and alert the authorities in some way. But for that, he needed Bartimaeus.

And Bartimaeus refused to come to him.

Despite his bone-aching weariness, Nathaniel performed the summoning three times that morning and three times the djinni did not appear. By the third try, he was practically sobbing with panic, gabbling out the words with hardly a care that a mispronounced syllable might endanger him. When he finished, he waited, breathing fast, watching the circle. *Come on, come on.*

No smoke, no smell, no demon.

With a curse, Nathaniel cancelled the summons, kicked a pot of incense across the room and flung himself upon his bed. What was going on? If Bartimaeus had found some way to break free of his charge . . . But surely that was impossible – no demon had ever managed such a thing as far as Nathaniel knew. He beat his fist uselessly against the blankets. When he got the djinni back again, he'd make it pay for this delay – he'd subject it to the Jagged Pendulum and watch it squirm!

But in the meantime, what to do?

Use the scrying glass? No, that could come later: the three summonings had worn him out and first he had to rest. Instead, there was his master's library. That was the place to begin. Maybe there were other, more advanced methods of summoning he could try. Perhaps there was information on tricks djinn used to avoid returning.

He got up and kicked the rug over the chalk circles on the floor. No time to clear it up now. In a couple of hours he was due to meet his master, to finally try the long-awaited summoning of the natterjack impling. Nathaniel groaned with frustration – that was the last thing he needed! He could summon the impling in his sleep, but his master would ensure he checked and double-checked every line and phrase until the process took several hours. It was a waste of energy he could well do without. What a fool his master was!

Nathaniel set off for the library. He clattered down the attic stairs.

And ran headlong into his master coming up.

Underwood fell back against the wall, clutching the most expansive part of his waistcoat, which had connected sharply with one of Nathaniel's elbows. He gave a cry of rage and aimed a glancing slap at his apprentice's head.

'You little ruffian! You could have killed me!'

'Sir! I'm sorry, sir. I didn't expect—'

'Careering down stairs like some brainless oik, some commoner! A magician keeps his deportment strictly under control at all times. What are you playing at?'

'I'm dreadfully sorry, sir . . .' Nathaniel was recovering from the shock; he spoke meekly. 'I was just going down to the library, to double-check a few things before our summoning this afternoon. I'm sorry if I was too eager.'

His humble manner had its effect. Underwood breathed hard, but his expression relaxed. 'Well, if the intention was good, I suppose I can hardly blame you. In fact I was coming to say that unfortunately I shall not be in this afternoon. Something serious has happened and I must—' He stopped; the eyebrows flickered and melted into a frown. 'What's that I smell?'

'Sir?'

'That odour . . . it clings to you, boy.' He bent closer and sniffed loudly.

'I – I'm sorry, sir, I forgot to wash this morning. Mrs Underwood's mentioned this to me before.'

'I'm not talking about your own scent, boy, unpleasant though it is. No, it's more like . . . rosemary . . . Yes! And laurel . . . and St John's wort . . .' His eyes suddenly widened and flashed in the half-light of the staircase. 'This is general summoning incense hanging about your person!'

'No, sir—'

'Don't you dare contradict me, boy! How has it . . . ?' A suspicion dawned in his eyes. 'John Mandrake, I wish to see your room! Lead the way.'

'I'd rather not, sir – it's a terrible mess; I'd feel embarrassed . . .'

His master raised himself to his full height, his eyes flashing, his singed beard bristling. He seemed somehow to grow taller than Nathaniel had ever seen him, although the fact that he was standing on the step above probably helped a bit. Nathaniel felt himself shrink back, cowering.

Underwood flourished a finger and pointed up the stairs. 'Go!'

Helplessly, Nathaniel obeyed. In silence, he led the way to his chamber, his master's heavy boots treading close behind him. As he opened the door, an unmistakable stench of incense and candle wax gusted up into his face. Nathaniel stood glumly to one side as, stooping under the low ceiling, his master entered the attic room.

For a few seconds, Underwood surveyed the scene. It was an incriminating picture: an upturned pot, with a trail of multicoloured incense extending from it across the floor; several dozen summoning candles, still smouldering, arranged against the walls and upon the desk; two heavy books on magic, taken from Underwood's own personal shelves, lying open on the bed. The only things that weren't visible were the summoning circles themselves. They lay hidden under the rug. Nathaniel thought this gave him a possible way out. He cleared his throat.

'If I might explain, sir.'

His master ignored him. He strode forwards and kicked at a corner of the rug, which fell back on itself to reveal the corner of a circle and several outer runes. Underwood stooped, took hold of the rug and flung it bodily aside so that the whole diagram was revealed. For a moment, he scanned the inscriptions, then, with grim intention in his eyes, turned to his apprentice.

'Well?'

Nathaniel swallowed. He knew that no excuse would save him, but he had to try. 'I was just practising making the marks, sir,' he began in an uncertain voice. 'Getting the feel for it. I didn't actually *summon* anything, of course, sir. I wouldn't dare . . .'

He faltered, stopped. With one hand, his master was

pointing to the centre of the bigger circle, where a prominent scorch-mark had been left by Bartimaeus's first appearance. With the other, he indicated the numerous burns left on the walls by the explosion of the Stimulating Compass. Nathaniel's shoulders sagged.

'Um . . .'

For an instant, it seemed as though Mr Underwood's deportment was going to fail him. His face mottled with rage, he took two quick steps in Nathaniel's direction, his hand raised to strike. Nathaniel flinched, but the blow did not fall.

The hand lowered. 'No,' his master said, panting hard. 'No. I must consider how to deal with you. You have disobeyed me in a hundred ways, and in so doing have risked your own life and that of the people in this house. You have dabbled with works of magic that you cannot hope to comprehend – I see *Faust's Compendium* there, and *The Mouth of Ptolemy!* You have summoned, or attempted to summon, a djinni of at least the fourteenth level, and even tried to bind it with Adelbrand's Pentacle, a feat that *I* would balk at. The fact that you undoubtedly failed in no way mitigates your crime. Stupid child! Have you no concept of what such a being might *do* to you, if you made even the slightest slip? Have all my lessons over the years meant nothing? I should have known you were not to be trusted last year, when your wilful act of violence against the guests of my house nearly ruined my career. I should have disposed of you then, when you were nameless. No one would have given it a second thought! But now that you are named and will be in the next edition of the Almanac, I cannot get rid of you so easily! Questions will be asked, forms will have to be filled, and my judgement will once again be called into doubt. No, I must consider what to do with you, though my hand itches to call up a Reviler on the spot and leave you in its tender care.'

He paused for breath. Nathaniel had slumped back to sit on the edge of his bed, all energy crushed from him.

'Take it from me,' his master said, 'that no apprentice of mine disobeys me in the fashion you have done. If I didn't have to go to the ministry urgently, I would deal with you now. As it is, you are confined to your room until my return. But first –' here he strode across to Nathaniel's wardrobe and flung wide the door – 'we must see that you have no other surprises hidden away.'

For the next ten minutes, Nathaniel could only sit dull-eyed while his master searched the room. The wardrobe and the chest of drawers were turned out and rifled, his meagre quantity of clothes strewn upon the floor. Several plastic bags of incense were found, a small supply of coloured chalk and one or two sheaves of notes that Nathaniel had made during his extra-curricular studies. Only the scrying glass, secure in its hiding place beneath the eaves, remained undiscovered.

Mr Underwood gathered up the incense, books, chalk and notes. 'I shall read through your scrawlings upon my return from the ministry,' he said, 'in case I need to question you further about your activities before you receive your punishment. In the meantime, remain here and reflect upon your sins and the ruin of your career.'

Without another word, he swept from the attic and locked the door behind him.

Nathaniel's heart was a stone plummeting to the bottom of a deep, dark well. He sat motionless on the bed, listening to the rain tapping on the skylight and, far below, his master banging from room to room in his fury. Eventually a distant slam assured him that Mr Underwood had left the house.

An unknown time later, he was startled out of his misery by the sound of the key turning in the lock. His heart jolted with fear. Surely not his master back already . . . ?

But it was Mrs Underwood who entered, bringing a small bowl of tomato soup on a tray. She placed it on the table and stood regarding him. Nathaniel could not bring himself to look at her.

'*Well*,' she said, in a level voice, 'I hope you're satisfied with yourself. From what Arthur tells me, you have been very bad indeed.'

If his master's torrent of anger had merely numbed him, these few words from Mrs Underwood, laced as they were simply with quiet disappointment, pierced Nathaniel to the marrow. His last vestiges of self-control failed him. He raised his eyes to her, feeling tears prickle against the corners.

'Oh, Nath— John!' He had never heard her so exasperated. 'Why couldn't you be *patient*? Ms Lutyens used to say that this was your abiding fault and she was right! Now you've tried to run before you can walk, and I don't know if your master will ever forgive you.'

'He'll *never* forgive me. He said so.' Nathaniel's voice was faint; he was holding back the tears.

'He's extremely angry, John, and rightly.'

'He said my – my career was ruined.'

'I shouldn't be surprised if that wasn't exactly what you deserved.'

'Mrs Underwood—!'

'But perhaps, if you are open and honest with him about

what you've done, there is a chance that he will listen to you when he returns. A very small chance.'

'He won't; he's too angry.'

Mrs Underwood sat down on the bed beside Nathaniel and put her arm round his shoulder. 'You don't think it's unheard of, do you, for apprentices to try too much, too soon? It often marks out those with the most talent. Arthur is livid, but he is also impressed, I can tell. I think you should confide fully in him; throw yourself on his mercy. He will like that.'

Nathaniel gave a sniff. 'You think so, Mrs Underwood?' As always, the comfort of her presence and her calm common sense reached past his defences and soothed his pride. Maybe she was right. Maybe he *should* tell the truth about everything . . .

'I will do my best to appease him too,' she went on. 'Heaven knows, you don't deserve it. Look at the state of this room!'

'I'll clean it right away, Mrs Underwood; right away.' He felt a little comforted. Perhaps he *would* tell his master, own up to his suspicions about Lovelace and the Amulet. Things would be painful, but simpler that way.

'Drink your soup first.' She got up. 'Make sure you have everything ready to tell your master when he comes back.'

'Why's Mr Underwood gone to the ministry? It's a Sunday.' Nathaniel was already picking up some of the garments and stuffing them back into the drawers.

'Some emergency, dear. A rogue djinni has been caught in central London.'

A slight shiver ran down Nathaniel's spine. 'A djinni?'

'Yes. I don't know the details, but apparently it was masquerading as one of Mr Lovelace's imps. It broke into Mr Pinn's shop and caused no end of damage. But they sent an afrit and caught it soon enough. It's being interrogated now. Your master thinks the magician that sent the djinni may have some link to these artefact thefts that have been so bothering him – and perhaps to the Resistance too. He wants to be there when they force the information out. But that's not really your prime concern now – is it, John? You need to be deciding what to say to your master. And scrub this floor till it shines!'

'Yes, Mrs Underwood.'

'Good boy. I'll look in for your tray later.'

No sooner had the door been locked than Nathaniel was running to the skylight, throwing it open and reaching under the cold wet tiles for the bronze disc. He drew it in and shut the window against the lancing rain. The disc was cold; it took several minutes of escalating inducements before the imp's face reluctantly appeared.

'Blimey,' it said. 'It's been a while. Thought you'd forgotten me. You ready to let me out yet?'

'No.' Nathaniel was in no mood to play around. 'Bartimaeus. Find him. I want to see where he is and what he's doing. Now. Or I'll bury this disc in the earth.'

'Who's got out the wrong side of bed today? There's such a thing as asking nicely! Well, I'll have a go, but I've had easier requests in my time, even from you . . .' Muttering and grimacing with strain, the baby's face faded out, only to reappear again, faintly, as if from afar. 'Bartimaeus, you say? Of Uruk?'

'Yes! How many of them can there be?'

'You'd be surprised, Mr Tetchy. Well, don't hold your breath. This may take some time.'

The disc went blank. Nathaniel hurled it onto the bed, then thought better of it and stowed it away under the mattress, out

242

of sight. In great agitation, he proceeded to tidy his room, scrubbing the floor till all traces of the pentacles were gone and even the marks of candle grease had been improved. He stowed his clothes away tidily and returned everything to its proper place. Then he drank his soup. It was cold.

Mrs Underwood returned to reclaim the tray, and surveyed the room with approval. 'Good boy, John,' she said. 'Now tidy yourself up, and have a wash while you're about it. What was that?'

'What, Mrs Underwood?'

'I thought I heard a voice calling.'

Nathaniel had heard it too. A muffled 'Oi!' from under the bed. 'I think it was from downstairs,' he said weakly. 'Maybe someone at the door?'

'Do you think so? I'd better see, I suppose.' Somewhat uncertainly, she departed, locking the door behind her.

Nathaniel flung the mattress aside. 'Well?' he snarled.

The baby's face had big bags under the eyes and was now somehow unshaven. 'Well,' it said, 'I've done the best I could. Can't ask for no more than that.'

'Show me!'

'Here you go, then.' The face vanished, to be replaced by a long-distance view across London. A silver strip that had to be the Thames wound across the backdrop between a dark grey mess of warehouses and wharves. Rain fell, half obscuring the scene, but Nathaniel easily made out the focus of the picture: a giant castle, protected by endless loops of high, grey walls. In its centre was a tall, squared keep, with the Union Jack flying from its central roof. Black-sided police trucks moved below in the castle yard, together with troops of tiny figures, not all of them human.

Nathaniel knew what he was looking at, but he did not want to accept the truth. 'And what's this got to do with Bartimaeus?' he snapped.

The imp was weary, heavy-voiced. 'That's where he is, as far as I can reckon. I picked up his trail in the middle of London, but it was already faint and cold. It led here, and I can't get any closer to the Tower of London, as you well know. Far too many watchful eyes. Even from this distance, a few outriding spheres nearly caught me. I'm fair tuckered, I am. Anything else?' it added, as Nathaniel failed to react. 'I need a kip.'

'No, no, that's all.'

'First sensible thing you've said all day.' But the imp did not fade. 'If he's in there, this Bartimaeus is in trouble,' it observed in a rather more cheery manner. '*You* didn't send him out there, did you?'

Nathaniel made no reply.

'Oh *dear*,' said the imp. 'Then, that being the case, I'd say you was in almost as much bother as him, wouldn't you? I 'spect he's probably coughing up your name right now.' It bared its sharp, small teeth in a face-splitting grin, blew a loud raspberry and vanished.

Nathaniel sat very still, holding the disc in his hands. The daylight in the room gradually faded away.

Bartimaeus

24

Put a scarab beetle, roughly the size of a matchbox, up against a four-metre-tall, bull-headed leviathan wielding a silver spear, and you don't expect to see much of a contest, especially when the beetle is imprisoned within a small orb that will incinerate its essence if it touches so much as a stray antenna. True, I did my best to prolong the issue by hovering just off the top of the pillar, in the vague hope that I could dart to one side as the spear crashed down – but to be honest my heart wasn't really in it. I was about to be squashed by a lummox with the IQ of a flea and the sooner we got it over with the better.

So I was a little surprised when the utukku's shrieking war cry was cut off by a sudden yelled command, just as the spear was about to descend upon my head.

'Baztuk, stop!'

Eagle-beak had spoken; the urgency in his voice was clear. Once it has made its mind up to do something, an utukku finds it hard to change tack: Bull-head stopped the spear's downward swing with difficulty, but kept it raised high above the orb.

'What *now*, Xerxes?' he snarled. 'Don't try to rob me of my revenge! Twenty-seven centuries I've wanted Bartimaeus in my power—'

'Then you can wait a minute more. He'll keep. Listen – can you hear something?'

Baztuk cocked his head to one side. Within the orb, I stilled the humming of my wings and listened too. A gentle tapping sound . . . so low, so subtle, it was impossible to tell from which direction it came.

'That's nothing. Just workmen outside. Or the humans marching again. They like doing that. Now shut up, Xerxes.' Baztuk was not inclined to spare the matter another thought. The sinews along his forearms knotted as he readied the spear.

'It's not workmen. Too near.' The feathers on Xerxes' head-crest looked ruffled. He was jumpy. 'Leave Bartimaeus alone and come and listen. I want to pinpoint it.'

With a curse, Baztuk stomped away from my column. He and Xerxes ranged around the perimeter of the room, holding their ears close to the stones and muttering to each other to tread more quietly. All the while the little tapping noise continued, soft, irregular and maddeningly unlocatable.

'Can't place it.' Baztuk scraped his spear-tip against the wall. 'Could come from anywhere. Hold on . . .! Maybe *he's* doing it . . .' He looked evilly in my direction.

'Not guilty, your honour,' I said.

'Don't be stupid, Baztuk,' Eagle-beak said. 'The orb stops him using magic beyond its barrier. Something else is going on. I think we should raise the alarm.'

'But nothing's *happened*.' Bull-head looked panicked. 'They'll punish us. At least let me kill Bartimaeus first,' he pleaded. 'I mustn't lose this chance.'

'I think you should *definitely* call for help,' I advised. 'It's almost certainly something you can't handle. A deathwatch beetle, maybe. Or a disorientated woodpecker.'

Baztuk blew spume a metre into the air. 'That's the last straw, Bartimaeus! You die!' He paused. 'Mind you, it *might* be a deathwatch beetle, come to think of it . . .'

'In a solid stone building?' Xerxes sneered. 'I think not.'

'What makes you an expert all of a sudden?'

A new argument broke out. My two captors faced up to each other again, strutting and shoving, roused to blind fury by each other's stupidity and by the occasional careful prompting from me.

Underneath it all, the tap, tap, tapping went on. I had long since located the source of it as a patch of stone high up along one wall, not too far from the single window. While encouraging the squabble, I kept a constant eye on this area, and was rewarded, after several minutes, by spying a discreet shower of stone-dust come trickling out between two blocks. A moment later, a tiny hole appeared; this was rapidly enlarged as more dust and flakes dropped from it, propelled by something small, sharp and black.

To my annoyance, after working their way round the room in a flurry of girly slaps and yells, Xerxes and Baztuk had come to rest not far from the mysterious hole. It was only a matter of time before they noticed the spiralling dust-fall, so I decided I had to risk all in a final gambit.

'Hey, you pair of sand-eaters!' I shouted. 'The moon shines on the corpses of your fellows! The jackals carry home the severed heads for their pups to play with!'[1]

As I had expected, Baztuk instantly left off tugging at Xerxes' side-feathers and Xerxes prised his fingers out of Baztuk's nose. Both of them slowly turned towards me with murder in their eyes. So far, so good. I calculated that I had approximately thirty seconds before whatever was coming through the hole put in an appearance. Should it delay, I was dead – if not by the hands of Baztuk and Xerxes, then by the orb, which had now diminished to the size of a runty grapefruit.

'Baztuk,' Xerxes said politely, 'I shall allow you to strike the first blow.'

'That is good of you, Xerxes,' Baztuk replied. 'Afterwards, you may dice the remains to your heart's content.'

Both hefted their spears and strode towards me. Behind them, the tapping suddenly ceased, and from the hole in the wall, which had by now grown quite large, a shiny beak poked out, sharp as an anvil. This was followed by a tufted jet-black head, complete with beady eye. The eye flicked rapidly to and fro, taking in the scene, then silently the bird behind it began to squeeze its way through the hole, wriggling forward in a distinctly unbirdlike way.

---

[1] Well, this loses something in translation, of course. I shouted it in the language of Old Egypt, which both of them knew and hated. It was a reference to the time when the pharaoh sent his armies deep into the lands of Assyria, causing general mayhem. It is deeply impolite for djinn to bring up between themselves the memories of human wars (in which we are always forced to take sides). Reminding utukku of wars that they *lost* is both impolite and deeply unwise.

With a shake and a hop, an enormous black raven perched on the lip of the stone. As its tail feathers cleared the hole, another beak appeared behind it.

By now the utukku had reached my pillar. Baztuk flung back his arm.

I coughed. 'Look behind you?'

'That won't work on me, Bartimaeus!' Baztuk cried. His arm jerked forward, the spear began to plunge. A flash of black shot across its path, seized the spear-shaft in its beak and flew onwards, wrenching it out of the utukku's hand. Baztuk gave a yelp of astonishment and turned. Xerxes spun round too.

A raven sat on a vacant column, holding the spear neatly in its beak.

Uncertainly, Baztuk stepped towards it.

With deliberate care, the raven bit down on the steel shaft. The spear snapped in two; both halves fell to the ground.

Baztuk stopped dead.

Another raven fluttered down and came to rest on a neighbouring pillar. Both sat silently, watching the utukku with unblinking eyes.

Baztuk looked at his companion. 'Erm, Xerxes . . . ?'

Eagle-beak rattled his tongue warningly. 'Raise the alarm, Baztuk,' he said. 'I'll deal with them.' He bent his legs; leaped high into the air. With a sound like ripping cloth, his great, white wings unfolded. They beat once, twice; he soared up, up, almost to the ceiling. The feathers angled, tensed; he spun and dived, head first, wings back, one hand holding the outstretched spear; hurtling down at lightning speed.

Towards a raven, calmly waiting.

A look of doubt came into Xerxes' eyes. Now he was almost

upon the raven and still it hadn't moved. Doubt was replaced by sudden fear. His wings jerked out; desperately, he tried to bank, to avoid colliding—

The raven opened its beak wide.

Xerxes screamed.

There was a blur of movement, a snap and a gulp. A few fluttering feathers drifted slowly down upon the stones around the pillar. The raven still sat there, a dreamy look in its eyes. Xerxes was gone.

Baztuk was making for the wall where the portal would appear. He was fumbling in a pouch strapped to his waist. The second raven lazily hopped from one pillar to another, cutting him off. With a cry of woe, Baztuk hurled his spear. It missed the raven, embedding itself to the hilt in the side of the pillar. The raven shook its head sorrowfully and spread its wings. Baztuk wrenched his pouch open and removed a small bronze whistle. He set it to his lips—

Another blur, a whirlwind too swift to follow. Credit to him, Baztuk was fast; I glimpsed him lowering his head, lashing out with his horns – and then the whirlwind had engulfed him. When it ceased, so had Baztuk. He was nowhere to be seen. The raven landed awkwardly on the ground, green blood oozing from one wing.

Inside its orb, the scarab beetle skittered about. 'Well done!' I called, trying to make my voice a little less high and piping. 'I don't know who you are, but how about getting me . . .'

My voice trailed away. Thanks to the orb, I could only see the newcomers on the first plane, where up until now they'd worn their raven guise. Perhaps they realized this, because suddenly, for a split second, they displayed their true selves to me on the first plane. It was only a flash, but it was all I needed. I knew who they were.

Trapped in the orb, the beetle gave a strangled gulp.

'Oh,' I said. 'Hello.'

'Hello, Bartimaeus,' Faquarl said.

25

'And Jabor *too*,' I added. 'How nice of you both to come.'

'We thought you might be feeling lonely, Bartimaeus.' The nearest raven, the one with the bleeding wing, gave a shimmy and took on the semblance of the cook. His arm was badly gashed.

'No, no, I've had plenty of attention.'

'So I see.' The cook walked forward to inspect my orb. 'Dear me, you *are* in a tight spot.'

I chortled unconvincingly. 'Witticisms aside, old friend, perhaps you could see your way to helping me out of here. I can feel the tickle of the barriers pressing in.'

The cook stroked one of his chins. 'A difficult problem. But I *do* have a solution.'

'Good!'

'You could become a flea, or some other form of skin-mite. That would give you another precious few minutes of life before your essence is destroyed.'

'Thank you, yes, that is a useful suggestion.' I was gasping a little here. The orb was drawing very near. 'Or perhaps you could disable the orb in some way and set me free. Imagine my gratitude . . .'

The cook raised a finger. 'Another thought occurs to me. You could tell us where you have secreted the Amulet of Samarkand. If you speak rapidly, we might then have time to destroy the orb before you perish.'

'Reverse that sequence and you could have yourselves a deal.'

The cook sighed heavily. 'I don't think you're in a position to—' He broke off at the sound of a distant wailing noise; at the same time a familiar reverberation ran across the room.

'A portal's about to open,' I said hastily. 'The far wall.'

Faquarl looked at the other raven, still sitting on its pillar, examining its claws. 'Jabor, if you would be so kind . . . ?' The raven stepped forwards into space and became a tall, jackal-headed man with bright-red skin. He strode across the room and took up position against the far wall, one leg forward, one leg back, both his hands outstretched.

The cook turned back to me. 'Now, Bartimaeus—'

My cuticle was beginning to singe. 'Let's cut to the chase,' I said. 'We both know that if I tell you the location, you'll leave me to die. We also know that, with that being so, I'll obviously give you false information just to spite you. So anything I say from in here will be worthless. That means you've got to let me out.'

Faquarl tapped the edge of my pillar irritably. 'Annoying, but I see your point.'

'And that wailing sound is sure to be an alarm,' I went on. 'The magicians who put me here mentioned something about legions of horlas and utukku. I doubt even Jabor can swallow them all. So perhaps we could continue this discussion a little later?'

'Agreed.' Faquarl put his face close to the orb, which was now scarcely more than satsuma-sized. 'You will never escape the Tower without us, Bartimaeus, so do not try any tricks just yet. I must warn you that I had two orders in coming here. The first was to learn the location of the Amulet. If that is impossible, the second is to destroy you. I needn't tell you which will give me greater pleasure.'

His face withdrew. At that moment the oval seam appeared in the back wall and broadened into the portal arch. From the blackness several figures began to emerge: pale-faced horlas,[1] holding tridents and silver nets in their stick-thin arms. Once beyond the portal, the protective Shields around their bodies would become invulnerable; while passing through, however, the Shields were weak and their essences momentarily exposed. Jabor took full advantage of this, firing off three rapid Detonations in quick succession. Bright-green explosions engulfed the archway. Twittering piteously, the horlas crumpled to the ground, still half in and half out of the portal. But behind came another troop, stepping with fastidious care over the bodies of their fellows. Jabor fired again.

Faquarl, meanwhile, had not been idle. From a pocket in his coat he drew forth a ring of iron, about the size of a bracelet, fixed to the end of a long wooden rod. I viewed the ring warily.[2]

'And what do you expect me to do with that?' I asked.

'Leap through it, of course. Imagine you're a trained dog in a circus. Not hard for you, I'm sure, Bartimaeus; you've tried most jobs in your time.' Holding one end cautiously between finger and thumb, Faquarl positioned the rod so that the iron ring made contact with the surface of the orb. With a violent fizzing, the lines of the barrier diverged and arced around the edge of the ring, leaving the gap within it free.

---

[1] *Horla*: a powerful subclass of djinn. To a human, they appear as shadowy apparitions that cause madness and disease; to other djinni, they radiate a malicious aura that saps our essence.

[2] Almost as much as silver, iron does not do a djinni any good. People have been using it to ward off our influence for millennia; even horseshoes are considered 'lucky' because they are made of iron.

'Lovelace has specially strengthened the ring to enhance the magical resistance of the iron,' Faquarl went on. 'But it won't last for ever, so I suggest you jump fast.'

He was right. Already, the edges of the ring were bubbling and melting under the power of the orb. As a beetle, I didn't have room to manoeuvre, so I summoned up my remaining energy and became a fly once more. Without further ado, I did a quick circuit of the orb to build up speed and, in a flash, shot through the molten ring to freedom!

'Marvellous,' Faquarl said. 'If only we'd had a drum-roll accompaniment.'

The fly landed on the floor and became a very irritable falcon.

'It was dramatic enough for me, I assure you,' I said. 'And now?'

Faquarl tossed the remains of the ring to the floor. 'Yes, we'd better go.' A silver-headed trident shot through the air and clattered between us across the flagstones. Up by the portal, now half choked with horla corpses, Jabor was steadily retreating. A new wave of guards, utukku mainly, advanced behind a strong collective Shield, which repelled Jabor's steadily weakening Detonations and spun them away around the room. At last a horla won free of the portal and, with his armour fully formed, came creeping round the edge of the Shield. Jabor fired at him; the blast hit the horla in his spindly chest and was completely absorbed. The horla gave a wintry smile and darted forward, spinning his net like a bolas.

Faquarl became a raven and took off effortfully, one wing labouring through the air. My falcon followed him, up towards the hole. A net passed just under me; a trident buried its prongs in the wall.

'Jabor!' Faquarl shouted. 'We're leaving!'

I snatched a look below: Jabor was grappling with the horla, his strength seemingly undiminished. But countless more kept coming. I concentrated my efforts on reaching the hole. Faquarl had already vanished within it; I ducked down my beak and plunged in too. Behind me, a colossal explosion rocked the room and I heard the savage fury of the jackal's cry.

In the narrow, pitch-black tunnel, Faquarl's voice sounded muffled and strange. 'We're nearly out. Being a raven would be most appropriate from now on.'

'Why?'

'There are dozens of the things out there. We can mingle with the flock and gain time while we make for the walls.'

Loath as I was to follow Faquarl's advice about anything, I had no idea what we were up against outside. Escape from the Tower was the priority. Escape from him could come later. So I concentrated and shifted form.

'Have you changed?'

'Yep. It's not a guise I've tried before, but it doesn't seem too difficult.'

'Any sign of Jabor behind us?'

'No.'

'He'll be along. Right, the opening to the outside is just ahead of me. There's a Concealment on the exit hole, so they shouldn't have spotted it yet. Fly out fast and go straight down. You'll see a kitchen yard where the ravens congregate to gather scraps; I'll meet you there. Above all, don't be conspicuous.'

A scrabbling in the tunnel ahead, then a sudden burst of light. Faquarl was gone, revealing the outline of the exit, covered with a mesh of concealing threads. I hopped forwards until my beak hit the barrier, pressed against it and pushed my head through into the cold November air.

Without a pause, I pushed off from the hole and began to glide towards the courtyard below.

As I descended, a brief glance around confirmed how far I was from safety: the distant rooftops of London were barely visible behind a series of rounded towers and curtain walls. Guards walked upon them, and search spheres moved randomly through the sky. The alarm had already been raised. From some eyrie high above, a siren was wailing, and not far off, within this innermost courtyard, battalions of police were running towards an unseen point.

I landed in a little side yard, cut off from the general panic by two outbuildings that projected from the body of the main tower. The cobbles of the yard were covered in greasy scraps of bread and bacon rind, and by a hungry, cawing flock of ravens.

One of the ravens sidled over. 'You *idiot*, Bartimaeus.'

'What's up?'

'Your beak's bright blue. Change it.'

Well, it was my first time as a raven. *And* I'd had to alter in the dark. What did he expect? But it wasn't the time or place to argue. I changed the beak.

'They'll see through the disguise anyway,' I snapped. 'There must be a thousand sentries of one sort or another out there.'

'True, but all we need's a little time. They don't know we're ravens yet, and if we're in a flock, it'll take them a few extra seconds to pick us out and check. All we need now is for the flock to fly . . .'

One moment a hundred ravens were snapping innocently

at cold bacon rind, at peace with themselves and the world. The next, Faquarl revealed his true self to them on the first plane: he only did so for a fraction of a second, but the glimpse was enough. Four ravens dropped dead on the instant, several others lost their breakfast, and the rest took off from the court-yard in a panic-stricken mob, cawing and clawing at the air. Faquarl and I were in the heart of the flock, flapping as hard as we could, wheeling and diving when the others did so, desperately trying not to be left behind.

Up high and over the flat roof of the great keep, where a huge flag fluttered and human sentries stood gazing out across the waters of the Thames; then down low and sweeping across the grey courtyard on the other side. Around twenty perma-nent workaday pentacles had been painted in the centre of the parade ground, and as I flashed past, I caught a glimpse of a formidable company of spirits appearing within them, sum-moned at that moment by a troop of grey-uniformed magicians. The spirits were minor ones, glorified imps for the most part,[3] but en masse they would present problems. I hoped the flock of ravens would not land here.

But the birds displayed no desire to halt; fear still carried them onwards in a whirling course across the fortifications of the Tower. Several times they seemed to be heading for an outer wall; on each occasion they banked and turned back.

---

[3] The less powerful the being, the quicker and easier it is to summon. Most magical empires employ some magicians specially to rustle up whole cohorts of imps at short notice. Only the greatest empires have the strength in depth to create armies of higher entities. The most formidable such army ever seen was put together by Pharaoh Tuthmosis III in 1478 BC. It included a legion of afrits and a motley group of higher djinn, of which surely the most notable was . . . No, modesty prevents me continuing.

Once I was tempted to make a break for it alone, but was discouraged by the appearance on the battlements of an odd blue-black sentry with four spider-like legs. I didn't like its look, and was too weary after my captivity and forced changes of form to risk its unknown power.

At last we came to yet another courtyard, surrounded on three sides by castle buildings and on the other by a steep bank of green grass rising up to a high wall. The ravens alighted on the bank and began to mill about, pecking at the ground aimlessly.

Faquarl hopped over to me, one wing hanging away from his breast. It was still bleeding.

'These birds are never going to leave the grounds,' I said. 'They get fed here.'

The raven nodded. 'They've got us as far as they can, but it'll do. This is an outer wall. Over that and we're away.'

'Then let's go.'

'In a minute. I need to rest. And perhaps Jabor—'

'Jabor's dead.'

'You know him better than that, Bartimaeus.' Faquarl pecked at his wounded wing, pulling a feather away from the clotting blood. 'Just give me a moment. That utukku! I wouldn't have guessed he had it in him.'

'Imps coming,' I hissed. A battalion had scurried through an arch into the far corner of the yard and were fanning out to begin a meticulous survey of every brick and stone. We were still concealed within the flock of ravens, but not for long.

Faquarl spat another feather onto the grass, where it briefly changed into a writhing strip of jelly before melting away. 'Very well. Up, over and out. Don't stop for anything.'

I gestured politely with a wing. 'After you.'

259

'No, no, Bartimaeus – after *you*.' The raven flexed one large, clawed foot. 'I shall be right behind you *all* the time, so please be original and don't try to escape.'

'You have a horrid, suspicious mind.'

The imps were creeping nearer, sniffing the ground like dogs. I took off and shot up towards the battlements at speed. As I drew level with them, I perceived a sentry patrolling the walkway. It was a small foliot, with a battered bronze horn strapped to the side of his head. Unfortunately, he perceived me too. Before I could react, he had swivelled his lips to the mouthpiece of the horn and blown a short, sharp blast, which instantly triggered a wave of answering signals from along the wall, high and low, loud and soft, away into the distance. That did it: our cover was well and truly blown. I weaved at the sentry, talons grasping; he gave a squeak, lost his balance and tumbled backwards over the edge of the wall. I shot straight across the battlements, over a steep bank of tumbled black rocks and earth, and away from the Tower into the city.

No time to lose, no time to look back. I flapped onwards, fast as I could. Beneath me passed a broad grey thoroughfare, heavy with traffic, then a block of flat-roofed garages, a narrow road, a slab of shingle, a curve of the Thames, a wharf and steelyard, another road . . . Hey! This wasn't too bad – with my customary panache, I was getting away! The Tower of London must already be a mile back. Pretty soon, I could—

I looked up and blinked in shock. What was this? The Tower of London loomed ahead of me. Groups of flying figures were massing over the central keep. I was flying back towards it! Something had gone seriously wrong with my directions. In great perplexity I did a U-turn round a chimney and shot off again in the opposite direction. Faquarl's voice sounded behind me.

'Bartimaeus, stop!'

'Didn't you see them?' I yelled back over my wing. 'They'll be on us in moments!' I redoubled my speed, ignoring Faquarl's urgent calls. Rooftops flashed below me, then the mucky expanse of the Thames, which I crossed in record time, then—

The Tower of London, just as before. The flying figures were now shooting out in all directions, each group following a search sphere. One lot was heading my way. Every instinct told me to turn tail and flee, but I was too confused. I alighted upon a rooftop. A few moments later, Faquarl appeared beside me, panting and swearing fit to burst.

'You fool! Now we're back where we started!'

A penny dropped. 'You mean—'

'The first Tower you saw was a mirror illusion. We should have gone straight through it.[4] Lovelace warned me of it – and you wouldn't wait to listen! Curse my injured wing and curse you, Bartimaeus!'

The battalion of flying djinn was crossing the outer walls. Barely a road's distance separated us. Faquarl hunched dismally behind a chimney. 'We'll never out-fly them.'

Inspiration came. 'Then we won't fly. We passed some traffic lights back there.'

'So what?' Faquarl's normal urbanity was wearing a little thin.

---

[4] *Mirror illusion*: a particularly cunning and sophisticated spell. It forms false images of a large-scale object – e.g. an army, a mountain, or a castle. They are flat and dissolve away as you pass through them. Mirror illusions can baffle even the cleverest opponent. As demonstrated here.

'So we hitch a ride.' Keeping the building between me and the searchers, I swooped off the roof and down to a crossroads, where a line of cars was queuing up at a red light. I landed on the pavement, near the back of the queue, with Faquarl close on my heels.

'Right,' I said. 'Time to change.'

'What to?'

'Something with strong claws. Hurry up, the lights are turning.' Before Faquarl could object, I hopped off the pavement and under the nearest car, trying to ignore the repellent stench of oil and petrol fumes and the sickening vibrations that intensified as the unseen driver revved the engine. With no regret, I bade farewell to the raven and took on the form of a stygian implet, which is little more than a series of barbs on a tangle of muscle. Barbs and prongs shot out and embedded themselves in the filthy metal of the undercarriage, securing me fast as the car began to inch forward and away. I had hoped Faquarl would be too slow to follow, but no such luck: another implet was right beside me, grimly hanging on between the wheels and keeping his eyes fixed on me the whole time.

We didn't talk much during the journey. The engine was too loud. Besides, stygian implets go in for teeth, not tongues.

An endless time later, the car drew to a halt. Its driver got out and moved away. Silence. With a groan, I loosened my various intricate holds and dropped heavily to the tarmac, groggy with motion sickness and the smell of technology.[5] Faquarl was no

---

[5] Many modern products – plastics, synthesized metals, the inner workings of machines – carry so much of the *human* about them that they afflict our essence if we get too close for too long. It's probably some sort of allergy.

better off. Without speaking, we became a pair of elderly, slightly manky cats, which hobbled out from under the car and away across a stretch of lawn towards a thick clump of bushes. Once there, we finally relaxed into our preferred forms.

The cook sank down upon a tree stump. 'I'll pay you back for that, Bartimaeus,' he gasped. 'I've never had such torture.'

The Egyptian boy grinned. 'It got us away, didn't it? We're safe.'

'One of my prongs punctured the petrol tank. I'm covered with the stuff. I'll come up in a rash—'

'Quit complaining.' I squinted through the foliage: a residential road, big semis, lots of trees. There was no one in sight, except for a small girl playing with a tennis ball in a nearby drive. 'We're in some suburb,' I said. 'Outskirts of London, or beyond.' Faquarl only grunted. I cast a sly side-glance. He was re-examining the wound Baztuk had given him. Looked bad. He'd be weakened.

'Even with this gash I'm more than a match for you, Bartimaeus, so come and sit down.' The cook gestured impatiently. 'I've something important to tell you.'

With my usual obedience, I sat on the ground, cross-legged, the way Ptolemy used to do. I didn't get too close. Faquarl reeked of petrol.

'First,' he said, 'I've completed my side of the bargain: against my better judgement, I saved your skin. Now for your side. Where is the Amulet of Samarkand?'

I hesitated. Only the existence of that tin at the bottom of the Thames prevented me from giving him Nat's name and number. True, I owed Faquarl for my escape, but self-interest had to come first.

'Look,' I said. 'Don't think I'm not grateful to you for springing me just now. But it isn't easy for me to comply. My master—'

'Is considerably less powerful than mine.' Faquarl leaned forward urgently. 'I want you to apply your silly, footling brain and *think* for a moment, Bartimaeus. Lovelace badly wants his amulet back, badly enough to command Jabor and me to break *into* his government's securest prison to save the miserable life of a slave like you.'

'That *is* pretty badly,' I admitted.

'Imagine how dangerous that was – for us *and* for him. He was risking all. That alone should tell you something.'

'So what does he need the Amulet *for*?' I said, cutting to the chase.

'Ah, that I can't tell you.' The cook tapped the side of his nose and smiled knowingly. 'But what I can say is that you would find it very much in your interests, Bartimaeus, to join up with us on this one. We have a master who is going places, if you know what I mean.'

I sneered. 'All magicians say that.'

'Going places *very* soon. We're talking days here. And the Amulet is vital to his success.'

'Maybe, but will *we* share his success? I've heard all this type of guff before. The magicians use us to gain more power for themselves and then simply redouble our bondage! What do we get out of it?'

'I have plans, Bartimaeus—'

'Yes, yes, don't we all? Besides, none of this changes the fact that I'm bound to my original charge. There are severe penalties—'

'Penalties can be *endured*!' Faquarl slapped the side of his head in frustration. 'My essence is still recovering from the punishments Lovelace inflicted when you vanished with his amulet! In fact, our existence – and don't pretend to apologize, Bartimaeus; you don't care in the least – our existence here is nothing *but* a series of penalties! Only the cursed magicians themselves change, and as soon as one drops into his grave, another springs up, dusts off our names and summons us again! They pass on, we endure.'

I shrugged. 'I think we've had this conversation before. Great Zimbabwe, wasn't it?'

Faquarl's rage subsided. He nodded. 'Maybe so. But I sense change coming and if you had any sense you'd feel it too. The waning of an empire always brings unstable times: trouble rising from the streets, magicians squabbling heedlessly, their brains softened by luxury and power . . . We've both seen this often enough, you and I. Such occasions give us greater opportunities to act. Our masters get *lazy*, Bartimaeus – they give us more leverage.'

'Hardly.'

'Lovelace is one of those. Yes, he's strong, all right, but he's reckless. Ever since he first summoned me, he has been frustrated by the limitations of his ministerial role. He aches to emulate the great magicians of the past, to daunt the world with his achievements. As a result, he worries away at the strings of power like a dog with a mouldy bone. He spends all his time in intrigue and plotting, in ceaseless attempts to gain advantage over his rivals . . . he never rests at it. And he's not alone, either. There are others like him in government, some even more reckless than he. You know the type: when magicians play for the highest stakes, they rarely last long. Sooner or later they'll make mistakes and give us our chance. Sooner or later, we'll have our day.'

The cook gazed up at the sky. 'Well, time's getting on,' he said. 'Here's my final offer. Guide me to the Amulet and I promise that, whatever penalty you suffer, Lovelace will subsequently take you on. Your master, whoever it is, won't be able to stand in his way. So then we'll be partners, Bartimaeus, not enemies. That'll make a nice change, won't it?'

'Lovely,' I said.

'*Or* . . .' Faquarl placed his hands in readiness on his knees. 'You can die here and now in this patch of undistinguished suburban scrub. You know you've never beaten me before; chance has always saved your bacon.[6] It won't this time.'

As I was considering this rather weighty statement and debating how best to run, we were interrupted. With a small leafy crashing, something came down through the branches and bounced gently at our feet. A tennis ball. Faquarl leaped off the stump and I sprang to my feet – but it was too late to hide. Someone was already pushing her way into the centre of the copse.

It was the little girl I had seen playing in her drive: about six years old, freckle-faced, tousle-haired, a baggy T-shirt stretching down to her grubby knees. She stared at us, half fascinated, half alarmed.

For a couple of seconds, not one of us moved. The girl looked at us. Faquarl and I stared at the girl. Then she spoke.

'You smell of petrol,' said the girl.

We did not answer her. Faquarl moved his hand, beginning a gesture. I sensed his regretful intention.

---

[6] Chance or, as I prefer to think of it, my own quick-wittedness. But it was true that somehow I'd always managed to avoid a full-on fight.

Why did I act then? Pure self-interest. Because with Faquarl momentarily distracted, it was the perfect opportunity to escape. And if I happened to save the girl too . . . well, it was only fair. It was she who gave me the idea.

I lit a small Spark on the end of one finger and tossed it at the cook.

A soft noise, like a gas fire being ignited, and Faquarl was an orange-yellow ball of flame. As he blundered about, roaring with discomfort, setting fire to the leaves about him, the little girl squealed and ran. It was good thinking: I did the same.[7]

And in a few moments I was in the air and far away, hurtling with all speed towards Highgate and my stupid, misbegotten master.

---

[7] Only without the squeal. Obviously.

Nathaniel

26

As evening drew on, the clenching agonies of dread closed in upon Nathaniel. Pacing about his room like a panther in a cage, he felt as if he were trapped in a dozen different ways. Yes, the door was locked so he could not physically escape, but this was the least of his problems.

At that very moment, his servant Bartimaeus was imprisoned in the Tower, being subjected to whatever tortures the high magicians could devise. If it really *had* caused carnage in central London this was exactly what the demon deserved. But Nathaniel was its master. He was responsible for its crimes.

And that meant the magicians would be looking for him too.

Under torture, the threat of Perpetual Confinement would be forgotten. Bartimaeus would tell them Nathaniel's name and the police would come to call. And then . . .

With a shiver of fear, Nathaniel remembered the injuries Sholto Pinn had displayed the evening before. The consequences would not be pleasant.

Even if, by some miracle, Bartimaeus kept quiet, there was Underwood to deal with too. Already Nathaniel's master had promised to disown him – and perhaps worse. Now he only had to read the scribbled notes he had removed from Nathaniel's room to discover precisely what his apprentice had summoned. Then he would demand the full story. Nathaniel shuddered to guess what methods of persuasion he might use.

What could he do? Mrs Underwood had suggested a way out. She had advised him simply to tell the truth. But the thought of revealing his secrets to his master's spite and sarcasm made Nathaniel feel physically sick.

Thrusting the dilemma aside, Nathaniel summoned the weary imp and, ignoring its protests, sent it out to spy on the Tower of London once more. From a safe distance, he watched in awe as an angry horde of green-winged demons spiralled like locusts above the parapets, then suddenly dispersed in all directions across the darkening sky.

'Impressive, that is,' the scrying glass commented. 'Real class. You don't mess with them high-level djinn. Who knows?' it added. 'Maybe some of them are coming for *you*.'

'Find Underwood,' Nathaniel snarled. 'Where is he and what is he doing?'

'My, aren't we in a bate? Let's see, Arthur Underwood . . . Nope, sorry. He's in the Tower too. Can't get access. But we can speculate, can't we?' The imp chuckled. 'He's probably talking to your Bartimaeus pal right now.'

Further observation of the Tower was obviously useless. Nathaniel tossed the disc under the bed. It was no good. He would have to come clean about everything. He would have to tell his master – someone he had no respect for, who had failed to protect him, who had cowered and snivelled before Lovelace. Nathaniel could well imagine how Underwood's fury would be expressed – in sneers and jibes and fears for his own petty reputation . . . And as for what would happen then . . .

Perhaps an hour later, he caught the echo of a door slamming somewhere below. He froze, listening for his master's dreaded footsteps on the stair, but for a long while no one came. And when the key did turn in the lock, he knew already, from the gentle wheezing, that it was Mrs Underwood outside. She carried a small tea tray, with a glass of milk and a rather curled tomato and cucumber sandwich.

'I'm sorry this is late, John,' she said. 'Your food's been ready for ages, but your master came home before I could bring it up.' She took a deep breath. 'I mustn't stop. Things are a little hectic downstairs.'

'What . . . what's happening, Mrs Underwood?'

'Eat your sandwich, there's a good boy. It looks like you need it – you're quite pale. It won't be long before your master calls you, I'm sure.'

'But did he say anything—?'

'Heavens, John! Will you never stop asking questions? He said a great deal, but nothing that I'm going to share with you now. There's a pan of water on downstairs and I have to make him something quickly. Eat your sandwich, dear.'

'Is my master—?'

'He's locked himself in his study, with orders not to be disturbed. Apart from his food, of course. There's quite an emergency on.'

An emergency . . . In that instant Nathaniel came to a sudden decision. Mrs Underwood was the only person he could trust, the only person who truly cared. He would tell her everything: about the Amulet, about Lovelace. She would help him with Underwood, even with the police, if necessary; he didn't know how, but she would make everything all right.

'Mrs Underwood—'

She held up a hand. 'Not now, John. I haven't time.'

'But Mrs Underwood, I really need—'

'Not a word more! I have to go.'

And with a harassed smile, she went. The door shut. The key turned. Nathaniel was left staring after her. For an instant he felt as if he were about to cry, then a stubborn anger swelled inside him. Was he some naughty child, to be left moping in the attic while his punishment was prepared? No. He was a magician! He would not be ignored!

All his equipment had been taken. He had nothing left, except the scrying glass – and all that could do was look. Still, looking might lead to knowledge. And knowledge was power.

Nathaniel took a bite of the curling sandwich and instantly regretted it. Setting the plate aside, he crossed to the skylight and looked out at London's carpeting of yellow lights stretching away under the night sky. Surely if Bartimaeus had mentioned his name, Underwood or the police would have collared him by now. It was curious. And this emergency . . . Was it related to Bartimaeus or not?

Underwood was below, doubtless on the phone. The solution was simple: a little spying would swiftly clear up the matter.

Nathaniel retrieved the scrying glass. 'My master is in his study. Go close so that I see all; moreover, listen and relay

272

everything he says directly and accurately to me.'

'Who's a little sneak, then? Sorry, sorry, fair enough! Your morals are none of my business. Here we go, then . . .'

The centre of the disc cleared; in its place, a strong, clear view of his master's study. Underwood sat in his leather chair, hunched forward with both elbows on his desk. One hand was clutching the telephone receiver; the other waved and gesticulated as he talked. The imp drew closer; now the agitation on Underwood's face became clear. He was plainly shouting.

Nathaniel rapped the disc. 'What's he saying?'

The imp's voice began in the middle of a sentence. There was a slight delay between Underwood's lips moving and the sound reaching Nathaniel, but he could see the imp was reporting accurately. '. . . telling me? All three escaped? Leaving dozens of casualties? It's unheard of! Whitwell and Duvall must answer for this. Yes, well, I *do* feel strongly, Grigori. This is a significant blow to my enquiries. I was intending to interrogate it myself. Yes, me. Because I'm sure it is linked to the artefact thefts . . . it's the latest escalation. Everyone knows the finest objects are held at Pinn's; it was hoping to steal them . . . Well, yes, it would mean a magician was involved . . . Yes, I know that's unlikely . . . Even so, this was one of my best leads . . . the *only* lead, to be truthful, but what do you expect when I'm given no funding? What about their identities? No joy there *either*? This *will* be a kick in the teeth for Jessica – that's one good thing to come out of the whole sorry affair . . . Yes – I suppose so. And listen, Grigori, changing the subject for a moment, I wanted to ask your opinion on something more personal . . .'

At this, the imp's commentary stopped, though Underwood was evidently still talking, his mouth close up to the receiver.

Nathaniel applied an improving shock to the disc, at which the imp's face appeared.

'Hoi, there was no call for that!'

'The *sound*, where's the sound?'

'He's whispering, ain't he? I can't hear a thing. And it ain't safe to go any closer.'

'Let me hear it!'

'But boss, you know there's a safe limit. Magicians often have protective sensors; you know, even *this* guy—'

Nathaniel's face felt sore and puffy under the strain. He was past caution. '*Do* it. You won't want me to ask again.'

The imp did not answer. Underwood's face reappeared, so close it almost filled the centre of the disc. The hairs tufting from his nostrils were rendered in loving three-dimensional detail. The magician was nodding. 'I agree. I suppose I *should* be flattered . . . Yes, looking at it that way, the boy *is* a testimony to my hard graft and inspiration. Now, *my* old master—'

He broke off, with a wince and a shudder, as if something cold had brushed against him. '. . . Sorry, Grigori. It was just, I felt . . .' Nathaniel saw the eyes narrow, the familiar brows beetle sharply. At this the image on the disc suddenly broadened out, as if the imp were retreating hurriedly across the room. Underwood uttered a loud syllable; the imp's voice tried to copy it, but cut out midway, as if turned off like a radio. The image remained, quivering strangely.

Nathaniel couldn't suppress a catch in his voice. 'Imp, what's happening?'

Nothing. Silence from the imp.

'I order you to leave the study and return to me.'

No answer.

The image in the disc was not reassuring. Shaky though it was, Nathaniel could see Underwood putting down the telephone, then slowly rising and coming round to the front of his desk, all the while peering hard – up, down, in every direction – as if hunting for something he knew was there. The image shook still harder: the imp seemed to be redoubling its efforts to escape, but to no avail. In mounting panic, Nathaniel applied a few frantic Shocks to the disc in vain. The imp was frozen, unable to speak or move.

Underwood crossed to a cupboard at the back of the study, rummaged within it, and returned, carrying a metal cylinder. He shook it: from four small holes at its top, a white powder was emitted, which quickly spread out to fill the room. Whatever the powder did, the effect was immediate. Underwood gave a start and stared upwards – directly at Nathaniel. It was as if the disc was a window and he was looking directly through it. For a moment, Nathaniel thought his master could actually see him, then he realized it was simply the suspended imp that hung revealed.

Horror-stricken, Nathaniel watched his master bend down to the carpet and pull at a loop of ribbon. A great square section of carpet peeled up and fell away to one side. Below were two painted pentacles. His master stepped inside the smaller, never for one moment taking his eyes away from the frozen imp. He began to speak, and within seconds a tall misty apparition appeared within the larger circle. Underwood uttered a command. The apparition bowed and vanished. To Nathaniel's amazement, Underwood's body seemed to shimmer and slide away from itself. His master still stood within the pentacle, but another version of his master, ghost-like and see-through, stood alongside it.

The ghostly form lifted into the air, kicked its heels and began to float forwards – straight to where the helpless imp was still relaying the view from the study. Nathaniel screamed commands and shook the disc in fury, but could do nothing to stop his master's slow approach. Closer, closer . . . The spectral eyebrows were lowered, the glinting eyes never looked away. Now Underwood's form swelled to fill the disc – it seemed as if it would break right through . . .

Then nothing. The disc showed the study again, with Underwood's physical body still standing motionless in the pentacle.

Despite his panic, Nathaniel knew all too well what was happening. Having located the spy and safely frozen it in position, Underwood had decided to follow the imp's astral cord back to its source to learn the identity of the enemy magician. Such sources might be many miles away; perhaps his master was expecting a long journey in his djinni-controlled form. If so, he was about to get a surprise.

Too late, Nathaniel realized what he had to do. The window! If he could throw the disc out into the street, perhaps his master would not guess . . .

He had only taken two strides in the direction of the sky-light when, without a sound, the translucent head of Arthur Underwood welled up through the floorboards. It was see-through and glowing with a greenish phosphorescence; the tip of the dilapidated beard extended into the floor. Slowly, slowly, the head revolved through ninety degrees, until at last it caught sight of Nathaniel standing above it, holding the scrying glass in his hands.

At this, an expression appeared on his master's face that Nathaniel had never seen before. It was not the familiar look

276

of impatient disdain that had long characterized Underwood's tutelage. It was not even the fury he had witnessed that morning, following the discovery in his room. Instead, it was firstly a look of extreme shock, and then a sudden explosion of such malice that Nathaniel's knees gave way. The disc fell from his hands; he slumped against the wall; he tried to speak, but could not.

The ghostly head stared at him from the centre of the floor. Nathaniel stared back; unable to tear his eyes away. Then – very muffled and distant, perhaps because it was uttered by the physical body in the study far below – Underwood's voice came sounding from inside the upturned disc.

'Traitor . . .'

Nathaniel's mouth opened, but let forth only a strangled croak.

The voice spoke again. 'Traitor! You have betrayed me. I shall discover who is guiding you to spy on me.'

'No one – there's no one . . .' Nathaniel could only manage the barest whisper.

'Prepare yourself! I shall come for you.'

The voice faded. Underwood's head descended, spiralling into the floor. The phosphorescent glow vanished with it from the room. With trembling fingers, Nathaniel picked up the disc and peered into it. After a few seconds the view of the study grew misty as his master's spirit form passed back through the imp; it drifted away across the carpet to where the body waited. Coming alongside, it adopted the exact same posture and merged in with itself. A moment later, Underwood was himself again and the shadowy apparition had reappeared in the other circle. With a clap of the hands, Underwood dismissed the djinni; it bowed and vanished. He stepped out of the pentacle, eyes blazing, and strode out of shot towards his study door.

At this, the spell on the imp was lifted and the baby's face returned to fill the disc. It blew out its cheeks with relief. 'Whoof! I don't mind telling you, *that* was bad for my system,' it said. 'Having that horrible old geezer drifting straight through me and right up my cord . . . It gives me the willies just to think about it, it really does!'

'Shut up! Shut up!' Beside himself with terror, Nathaniel was trying to think.

'Look, do us a favour,' the imp said. 'You haven't got much time left. Couldn't you just free me now, before you die? Life gets so dreary in this disc; you don't know how lonely it gets. Go on, boss. I'd really appreciate it.' The baby's attempt at a winning smile was interrupted as the disc was hurled against the wall. 'Ow! Well, I hope you enjoy what's coming to you, then!'

Nathaniel ran to the attic door and rattled desperately at the handle. Somewhere below he heard his master's footsteps hastening up the stairs.

'He's *really* angry,' the imp called. 'Even his astral form practically pickled my essence as it went by. I wish I wasn't facing the floor – I'd love to watch what happens when he gets in here.'

Nathaniel sprang at the wardrobe, pushed at it frantically; he planned to push it in front of the door, to block the way in. Too heavy – he hadn't the strength. His breathing came in fits and gasps.

'What's the matter?' the imp asked. 'You're a big magician now. Call something up to save your skin. An afrit maybe – that should do the job. Or what about that Bartimaeus you're so obsessed with? Where's he when you need him?'

With a sob, Nathaniel stumbled back into the centre of the room and turned slowly to face the door.

'Nasty, ain't it?' The imp's voice dripped with satisfaction. 'Being at someone else's mercy. Now you know what it feels like. Face it, kid – you're on your own. You've got no one there to help you.'

Something tapped on the skylight window.

After an instant in which his heart nearly stopped, Nathaniel looked: a dishevelled pigeon was sitting beyond the glass, gesticulating urgently with both wings. In doubt, Nathaniel stepped closer.

'Bartimaeus . . . ?'

The pigeon rapped its beak several times against the pane. Nathaniel raised his hand to undo the catch—

A key rattled in a lock. With a bang, the bedroom door burst open. Underwood stood there, his face pink with exertion and framed by a furious white mane of hair and beard. Nathaniel's arm dropped to his side; he turned to his master. The pigeon had vanished from the window.

It took Underwood a moment to regain his breath. 'Miserable boy! Who is controlling you? Which of my enemies?'

Nathaniel could feel his whole body trembling, but he forced himself to stand stock-still and look his master in the eye.

'No one, sir. I—'

'Is it Duvall? Or Mortensen? Or Lovelace?'

Nathaniel's lip curled at the last name. 'None of those, sir.'

'Who taught you to make the glass? Who told you to spy on me?'

Despite his fear, anger flared in Nathaniel's heart. He spoke with contempt. 'Will you not take my word? I have already said. There is no one.'

'Even now you continue your lies! Very well! Take a last look at this room. You will not be returning here. We will go to my study, where you will enjoy the company of my imps until your tongue is loosened. Come!'

Nathaniel hesitated, but there was no help for it. His master's hand descended on his shoulder and clamped it like a vice. Almost bodily, he was propelled out of the door and down the attic stairs.

On the first landing, Mrs Underwood met them, in haste and out of breath. When she saw Nathaniel's hapless posture and the fury on her husband's face, her eyes widened with distress, but she did not comment.

'Arthur,' she panted, 'there is a visitor to see you.'

'I haven't time. This boy—'

'It's a matter of the greatest urgency, he says.'

'Who? Who says?'

'Simon Lovelace, Arthur. He practically showed himself in.'

27

Underwood's brows lowered. 'Lovelace?' he growled. 'What does *he* want? Typical of him to turn up at the worst moment. Very well, I will see him. As for you – stop your wriggling!' Nathaniel was making sudden feverish movements, as if attempting to escape his grip. '*You*, boy, can wait in the box room until I'm ready to deal with you.'

'Sir—'

'Not a word!' Underwood began to manhandle Nathaniel across the landing. 'Martha, put on the kettle for our visitor. I shall be down in a few minutes. I need to tidy myself up.'

'Yes, Arthur.'

'Sir – please listen! It's important! In the study—'

'Silence!' Underwood opened a narrow door and shoved Nathaniel through, into a small, cold room filled with old files and stacks of government papers. Without a backward glance, his master shut the door and turned the key. Nathaniel knocked on the wood and frantically called out after him.

'Sir! Sir!' No one answered. 'Sir!'

'You're too kind.' A large beetle with huge mandibles squeezed itself under the door. 'I actually find "sir" a bit formal for my taste, but it's better than "recreant demon".'

'Bartimaeus!' Nathaniel stepped back in shock; before his eyes, the beetle grew, distorted . . . the dark-skinned boy was standing in the room with him, hands on hips and head slightly to one side. As always, the form was a perfect replica: its hair shifted as it moved, the light glistened on the pores of its skin – it could not have been singled out as false from amongst a thousand true humans. Yet something about it – perhaps the soft, dark eyes that gazed at him – screamed out its alien otherness. Nathaniel blinked; he struggled to control himself. He felt the same disorientation he had experienced during their previous meeting.

The false boy surveyed the bare floorboards and piles of junk. 'Who's been a naughty little magician, then?' it said drily. 'Underwood's cottoned on to you at last, I see. He took his time.'

Nathaniel ignored this. 'So it *was* you at the window,' he began. 'How did you—?'

'Down a chimney, how d'you think? And before you say it, I *know* you didn't summon me, but things have been moving far too fast for me to wait. The Amulet—'

Nathaniel was struck by a sudden horrified realization. '*You* – you've brought Lovelace here!'

The boy seemed surprised. 'What?'

'Don't lie to me, demon! You've betrayed me! You've led him here.'

'Lovelace?' It looked genuinely taken aback. 'Where is he?'

'Downstairs. He's just arrived.'

'Nothing to do with me if he has. Have you been blabbing?'

'Me? It was you—'

'*I've* said nothing. *I've* got a tobacco tin to think of . . .' It frowned and appeared to be thinking. 'It *is* a slight coincidence, I must admit.'

'*Slight?*' Nathaniel was practically hopping with agitation. 'You've led him here, you fool! Now, quickly – get the Amulet! Get it away from the study, before Lovelace finds it!'

The boy laughed harshly. 'Not a chance. If Lovelace is here, he'll have stationed a dozen spheres outside. They'll home in on its aura and be on me the moment I leave the building.'

Nathaniel drew himself up. With his servant returned, he was not as helpless as before. There was still a chance to avoid disaster, providing the demon did as it was told. 'I *command* you to obey!' he began. 'Go to the study—'

'Oh, can it, Nat.' The boy waved a weary and dismissive hand. 'You're not in the pentacle now. You can't force me to obey each new order. Running off with the Amulet will be fatal, take it from me. How strong is Underwood?'

'What?' Nathaniel was nonplussed.

'How *strong*? What level? I assume from the size of that beard he's no great shakes, but I might be wrong. How good is he? Could he beat Lovelace? That's the point.'

'Oh. No. No, I don't think so . . .' Nathaniel had little actual evidence either way, but his master's past display of servility to Lovelace left him in little doubt. 'You think . . .'

'Your one chance is that if Lovelace finds the Amulet, he might want to keep the whole thing quiet. He may try to do a deal with Underwood. If he doesn't—'

Nathaniel went cold. 'You don't think he'll—?'

'Whoops! In all this excitement I nearly forgot to tell you what I came for!' The boy put on a deep and plangent voice: 'Know ye that I have devotedly carried out my charge. I have spied on Lovelace. I have sought the secrets of the Amulet. I have risked all for you, o my master. And the results are –' here it adopted a more normal, sardonic tone – 'you're an idiot. You've no idea what you've done. The Amulet is so powerful it's been in government keeping for decades – until Lovelace had it stolen, that is. His assassin murdered a senior magician for it. In those circumstances, I don't think it's likely that he'll worry about killing Underwood to retrieve it, do you?'

To Nathaniel, the room seemed to spin. He felt quite faint. This was worse than anything he had imagined. 'We can't just stand here,' he stammered. 'We've got to do something—'

'True. I'll go and watch developments. Meanwhile, you'd better stay here like a good little boy, and be ready for a quick exit if things get nasty.'

'I'm not running anywhere.' He said it in a small, small voice. His head was reeling with the implications. Mrs Underwood . . .

'I'll give you a tip born of long experience. Running's good if your skin needs saving. Better get used to the idea, bud.' The boy turned to the box-room door and set the palm of one hand against it. With a despairing crack, the door split around the lock and swung open. 'Go up to your room and wait. I'll tell you what happens soon enough. And be prepared to move fast.'

With that, the djinni was gone. When Nathaniel followed, the landing was already empty.

Bartimaeus

28

'My apologies for the intrusion, Arthur,' Simon Lovelace said.

Underwood had only just entered his long, dark dining room when I caught up with him – he'd spent a few minutes beside the lower landing mirror smoothing down his hair and adjusting his tie. It didn't make any difference: he still looked dishevelled and moth-eaten beside the younger magician, who was standing beside the mantelpiece, examining his nails, as cold and tense as a coiled spring.

Underwood waved his hand in an airy attempt at magnanimity. 'My house is yours, I'm sure. I am sorry for the delay, Lovelace. Won't you take a seat?'

Lovelace did not do so. He wore a slim, dark suit with a dark-green tie. His glasses caught the lamplight from the ceiling and flashed with every movement of his head. His eyes were invisible, but the skin below the glasses was grey, heavy, bagged. 'You seem flustered, Underwood,' he said.

'No, no. I was engaged at the top of the house. I am somewhat out of breath.'

I had entered the door as a spider and had crawled my way discreetly over the lintel and up the wall, until I reached the secluded gloom of the darkest corner. Here I spun several hasty threads across, obscuring me as fully as possible. I did so because I could see that the magician had his second-plane imp with him, prying into every nook and cranny with its hot little eyes.

Quite how Lovelace had found the house, I did not like to guess. For all my denials to the boy, it was certainly an unpleasant coincidence that he had arrived at the exact same time as me. But working that out could wait: the boy's future – and consequently mine – depended on my reacting quickly to whatever happened now.

Underwood sat himself in his customary chair and put on a forced smile. 'So . . .' he said. 'Are you sure you won't sit down?'

'No, thank you.'

'Well, at least tell that imp of yours to quit its jiggling. It's making me feel quite ill.' He spoke with sudden waspish asperity.

Simon Lovelace made a clicking sound with his tongue. The imp hovering behind his head instantly became rigid, holding its face in a deliberately unfortunate posture, midway between a gawp and a grin.

Underwood did his best to ignore it. 'I do have a few other matters to take care of today,' he said. 'Perhaps you might tell me what I can do for you?'

Simon Lovelace inclined his head gravely. 'A few nights ago,' he said, 'I suffered a theft. An item, a small piece of some power, was stolen from my house while I was absent.'

Underwood made a consoling sound. 'I'm sorry to hear that.'

'Thank you. It is a piece that I hold especially dear. Naturally, I am eager for its return.'

'Naturally. You think the Resistance—?'

'And it is in connection with this that I have called on you today, Underwood . . .' He spoke slowly, carefully, skirting round the issue. Perhaps even now he hoped he would not have to make the accusation directly. Magicians are always circumspect with words; hasty ones, even in a crisis, can lead to misfortune. But the older man was oblivious to the hint.

'You can count on my support, of course,' Underwood said equably. 'These thefts are an abomination. We have known for some time that a black market for stolen artefacts exists and I for one believe that their sale helps to fund resistance to our rule. We saw yesterday what outrages this can lead to.' Underwood's eyebrows lifted with something like amusement. 'I must say,' he went on, 'I am surprised to hear *you* have fallen victim. Most recent thefts were perpetrated on – may I be frank? – relatively *minor* magicians. The thieves are often thought to be youths, even children. I would have thought *your* defences might have coped with them.'

'Quite.' Simon Lovelace spoke through his teeth.

'Do you think it has any connection with the attack on Parliament?'

'A moment, please.' Lovelace held up his hand. 'I have reason to suspect that the theft of the— of my item, was not the work of the so-called Resistance, but that of a fellow magician.'

Underwood frowned. 'You think so? How can you be sure?'

'Because I know what carried out the raid. It goes by the unseemly name of Bartimaeus. A middle-ranking djinni of great impudence and small intelligence.[1] It is nothing special. Any half-wit might have summoned it. A half-wit *magician*, that is, not a commoner.'

'Nevertheless,' Underwood said mildly, 'this Bartimaeus got away with your item.'[2]

'It was a bungler! It allowed itself to be identified!' Lovelace controlled himself with difficulty. 'No, no – you are quite right. It got away.'

'And as to who summoned it . . .'

The glasses flashed. 'Well, Arthur, that is why I am here. To see *you*.'

There was a momentary pause while Underwood's brain cells struggled to make the connection. Finally, success. Several emotions competed for control of his face, then all were swept away by a kind of glacial smoothness. The temperature in the room grew cold.

'I'm sorry,' he said, very quietly. 'What did you say?'

Simon Lovelace leaned forward and rested his two hands on the dining table. He had very well manicured nails. 'Arthur,' he said, 'Bartimaeus has not been keeping a low profile lately. As of this morning, it was imprisoned within the Tower of London, following its attack on Pinn's of Piccadilly.'

---

[1] At this point someone with excellent hearing might have heard a spurt of webbing being shot furiously into the ceiling in the corner of the room. Fortunately, the imp was busy trying to intimidate Underwood by changing its frozen expression very, very slowly. It didn't hear a thing.

[2] I felt a sudden surge of affection for the old fool. Didn't last long. Just thought I'd mention it.

Underwood reeled with astonishment. '*That* djinni? How – how do you know this? They were unable to learn its name . . . And – and it escaped, this very afternoon . . .'

'It did indeed.' Lovelace did not explain how. 'After its escape, my agents . . . spotted it. They followed Bartimaeus across London – and back here.'[3]

Underwood shook his head in befuddlement. 'Back here? You lie!'

'Not ten minutes ago, it disappeared down your chimney in the form of a noxious cloud. Are you surprised that I came immediately to reclaim my object? And now that I am inside . . .' Lovelace raised his head as if he could smell something good. 'Yes, I sense its aura. It is close by.'

'But . . .'

'I would never have guessed it was you, Arthur. Not that I didn't think you coveted my treasures. I just thought you lacked the competence to take them.'

The old man opened and shut his mouth like a goldfish, making inarticulate sounds. Lovelace's imp contorted its face for an instant into a violently different expression, then reverted to the original. Its master tapped the table gently with a forefinger.

'I could have forced an entry to your house, Arthur. It would have been quite within my rights. But I prefer to be courteous. Also, this piece of mine – as I'm sure you are well aware – is rather . . . contentious. Neither of us would want word of its presence in our houses to get out, now would we?

---

[3] Oops. It looked as if Lovelace had guessed I might escape from Faquarl. He must have set spies watching the Tower to trail us once we broke free. And I'd led them straight back to the Amulet in double-quick time. How embarrassing.

So – if you return it to me with all speed, I am sure we could come to some . . . *arrangement* that will benefit both of us.' He stood back, one hand toying with a cuff. 'I'm waiting.'

If Underwood had comprehended one word of what Lovelace was saying, he might have saved himself.[4] If he had recalled his apprentice's misdeeds and put two and two together, all might have been well. But in his confusion he could see nothing beyond the false accusation being levelled, and in great wrath he rose from his chair.

'You pompous upstart!' he cried. 'How *dare* you accuse me of theft! I haven't got your object – I know nothing of it and want it even less. Why should *I* take it? I'm not a political lick-spittle, like you; I'm no fawning back-stabber. I don't go grubbing about after power and influence like a hog in a cesspit! Even if I did, I wouldn't bother robbing you. Everyone knows your star has waned. You're not *worth* harming. No, your agents have got it wrong – or more probably, they lie. Bartimaeus is not here! I know nothing of its crimes. And your trinket is not in my house!'

As he was speaking, Simon Lovelace's face seemed to shrink back into deep shadow, even though the lamplight still played on the surface of his glasses. He shook his head slowly. 'Don't be foolish, Arthur,' he said. 'My informants do not lie to me! They are things of power that grovel at my command.'

The old man jutted forth his beard defiantly. 'Get out of my house.'

---

[4] He could have produced the Amulet, agreed terms and seen Lovelace head off satisfied into the night. Of course, now that he knew a little of Lovelace's crimes, he would certainly have been bumped off soon afterwards, but that breathing space might have given him time to shave his beard, put on a flowery shirt, catch a flight somewhere hot and sandy and so survive.

'I need hardly tell you what resources I have at my disposal,' Simon Lovelace went on. 'But speak softly with me and we can yet avoid a scene.'

'I have nothing to say. Your accusation is false.'

'Well then . . .'

Simon Lovelace clicked his fingers. Instantly his imp sprang down from thin air and landed on the mahogany top of the dining-room table. It grimaced, strained. A bulb swelled at the end of its tail, finally growing into a prong with a serrated edge. The imp lowered its rump meditatively and twirled its tail. Then the prong stabbed down into the polished surface of the table, cutting it like a knife does butter. The imp strode across the width of the tabletop, dragging its tail through the wood, slicing it in two. Underwood's eyes bulged in his head. Lovelace smiled.

'Family heirloom, Arthur?' he said. 'Thought so.'

The imp had nearly reached the other side when there was a sudden knock at the door. Both men turned. The imp froze in its tracks. Mrs Underwood came in carrying a laden tray.

'Here's the tea,' she said. 'And some shortbread; that's Arthur's favourite, Mr Lovelace. I'll just set it down here, shall I?'

Wordlessly, magicians and imp watched as she approached the table. With great care she set the heavy tray down upon it midway between the sawn crack and the end where Underwood was standing. In the heavy silence, she unloaded a large porcelain teapot (which the invisible imp had to step back to avoid), two cups, two saucers, two plates, a display-rack of shortbread and several items of her best cutlery. The table's end shifted noticeably under their weight. There was a slight creak.

Mrs Underwood picked up the tray again and smiled at the visitor. 'Go on, help yourself, Mr Lovelace. You need some weight put on, you do.'

Under her direct gaze, Lovelace took a piece of shortbread from the display-rack. The tabletop wobbled. He smiled weakly.

'*That's* right. Yell if you want a fresh cup.' With the tray under her arm, Mrs Underwood bustled out. They watched her go.

The door closed.

As one, magicians and imp turned back to the table.

With a resounding crash the single connecting spur of wood gave way. One whole end of the table, complete with teapot, cups, saucers, plates, the display-rack of shortbread and several pieces of best cutlery, collapsed onto the floor. The imp jumped clear and landed on the mantelpiece beside the display of dead flowers.

There was a brief silence.

Simon Lovelace tossed his piece of shortbread into the mess on the floor. 'What I can do to a wooden table I can do to a blockhead, Arthur,' he said.

Arthur Underwood looked at him. He spoke strangely, as if from a great distance. 'That was my best teapot.'

He gave three whistles, shrill, high-pitched. An answering call sounded, deep and booming, and up from the tiles before the fireplace rose a sturdy goblin-imp, blue-faced and brawny. Underwood gestured, whistled once. The goblin-imp sprang, turning in mid-air. He fell upon the smaller imp that cowered behind the flower-heads, scooped it up with his fingerless paws and began to squeeze it, heedless of the flailing saw-tooth prong. The small imp's substance contorted, blurred, was moulded like putty. In a trice it had been squashed down, tail and all, into a yellowish pulpy ball. The goblin-imp smoothed down the surface of the ball, flicked it into the air, opened his mouth and swallowed it.

Underwood turned back to Lovelace, who had watched this all tight-lipped.

I confess the old buffer surprised me – he was putting up a better show than I'd expected. Nevertheless the strain of raising that tame imp was taking its toll. The back of his neck was sweaty.

Lovelace knew this too. 'One last chance,' he snapped. 'Give me my property or I'll raise the stakes. Lead me to your study.'

'Never!' Underwood was beside himself with strain and rage. He did not heed the promptings of common sense.

'Watch then.' Lovelace smoothed back his oiled hair. He spoke a few words under his breath. There was a frisson in the dining room; everything in it flickered. The wall at the far end of the room became insubstantial. It receded, moving further and further back until it could no longer be seen. In its place a corridor of uncertain dimensions stretched away. As Underwood watched, a figure appeared far off along the corridor. It began to move towards us, growing larger at great speed, but floating – for its legs were still.

Underwood gasped and stumbled back. He knocked against his chair.

He was right to gasp. I knew that figure, the bulky frame, the jackal's head.

'Stop!' Underwood's face was waxen; he gripped his chair for support.

'What was that?' Simon Lovelace held his fingers to his ear. 'I can't hear you.'[5]

'Stop! All right, you win! I'll take you to my study now! Call it off!'

The figure grew in size. Underwood was cowering. The goblin-imp made a rueful face and withdrew hastily back through the tiles. I shifted in my corner, wondering quite what I was going to do when Jabor finally entered the room.[6]

All at once Lovelace gave a sign. The infinite corridor and the approaching figure vanished. The wall was there again as before, a yellowed photograph of Underwood's smiling grandmother hanging in its centre.

Underwood was on his knees beside the ruins of his tea service. He shook so hard he could barely stand.

'Which way to your study, Arthur?' Simon Lovelace said.

---

[5] How unnecessary. What play-actors these magicians are.

[6] So Faquarl had been right. A small army of horlas and utukku had been unable to stop Jabor. This didn't bode too well.

Nathaniel

29

Nathaniel stood alone on the landing, gripping the banister as if he feared to fall. A murmur of voices came from the dining room below; it rose and fell, but he hardly registered it. The panic rushing in his head drowned out all other sounds. *The only bad magician is an incompetent one.* And what was incompetence? Loss of control. Slowly, steadily, over the last few days, everything had spiralled out of Nathaniel's control. First, Bartimaeus had learned his birth-name. He had remedied that all right with the tobacco tin, but the respite had not lasted long. Instead, disaster after disaster had struck in quick succession. Bartimaeus had been captured by the Government, Underwood had discovered his activities and his career had been ruined before it had begun. Now the demon refused to obey his orders and Lovelace himself was at the door. And all he could do was stand and watch, helpless to react. He was at the mercy of the events he had set in motion. Helpless . . .

A small noise sliced through his self-pity and jolted him upright. It was the gentle humming made by Mrs Underwood as she padded along the hall from the kitchen towards the dining room. She was bringing tea: Nathaniel heard the clinking of the china on the tray she carried. A knock upon the door followed; more clinking as she entered, then silence.

In that moment, Nathaniel quite forgot his own predicament. Mrs Underwood was in danger. The enemy was in the house. In a few moments, he would doubtless force or persuade Underwood to open his study for inspection. The Amulet would be found. And then . . . what might Lovelace do – to Mr Underwood or his wife?

Bartimaeus had told him to wait upstairs and be ready for the worst. But Nathaniel had had enough of helpless loitering. He was not done yet. The situation was desperate, but he could still act. The magicians were in the dining room. Underwood's study was empty. If he could slip inside and retrieve the Amulet, perhaps he could hide it somewhere, whatever Bartimaeus might say.

Quietly, quickly, he stole downstairs to the landing below, to the level of his master's study and workrooms. The muffled voices from the ground floor were raised now: he thought he could hear Underwood shouting. Time was short. Nathaniel hastened through the rooms to the door leading to the study stairs. Here he paused. He had not gone that way since he was six years old. Distant memories assailed him and made him shiver, but he shrugged them off. He passed onwards, down the steps . . .

And pulled up dead.

Underwood's study door stood before him, daubed with its red, five-pointed star. Nathaniel groaned aloud. He knew enough now to recognize a fire-hex when he saw it. He would be incinerated the moment he touched the door. Without protection, he could not progress, and protection required a circle, a summons, careful preparation . . .

And he had no time for that. He was helpless! Useless! He beat his fist against the wall. From far away in the house came a noise that might have been a cry of fear.

Nathaniel ran back up the stairs and through to the landing, and as he did so, he heard the dining-room door open and footsteps sounding in the hall.

They were coming.

Then from below, Mrs Underwood's voice, anxious and enquiring, spearing Nathaniel with a thrill of pain. 'Is everything all right, Arthur?'

The reply was dull, weary, almost unrecognizable. 'I am just showing Mr Lovelace something in my study. Thank you, we need nothing.'

They were climbing the stairs now. Nathaniel was in an agony of indecision. What should he do? Just as someone turned the corner, he ducked behind the nearest door and closed it almost to. Breathing hard, he pressed his eye against the small crack that gave a view onto the landing.

A slow procession passed. Mr Underwood led the way. His hair and clothes were disordered, his eyes wild, his back bent as if by a great weight. Behind walked Simon Lovelace, eyes hidden behind his glasses, his mouth a thin, grim slit. Behind *him* came a spider, scuttling in the shadows of the wall.

The procession disappeared in the direction of the study. Nathaniel sank back, head spinning, nauseous with guilt and fear. Underwood's face . . . Despite his extreme dislike of his master, to see him in that state rebelled against everything Nathaniel had been taught. Yes, he was weak; yes, he was petty; yes, he had treated Nathaniel with consistent disdain. But the man was a minister, one of the three hundred in the Government. And he had not taken the Amulet. Nathaniel had.

He bit his lip. Lovelace was a criminal. Who could tell what he might do? *Let* Underwood take the blame. He deserved it. He had never stuck up for Nathaniel, he had sacked Ms Lutyens . . . let him suffer too. Why had Nathaniel put the Amulet in the study in the first place, if not to protect himself when Lovelace came? He would stay out of the way like the djinni said. Get ready to run, if necessary . . .

Nathaniel's head sank into his hands.

He could not run. He could not hide. That was the advice of a demon, treacherous and sly. Running and hiding were not the actions of an honourable magician. If he let his master face Lovelace alone, how would he live with himself again? When his master suffered, Mrs Underwood would suffer too and that would be impossible to bear. No, there was no help for it. Now that the crisis was upon him, Nathaniel found, to his surprise and horror, that he had to act. Regardless of the consequences, he had to intervene.

Even to think of doing what he now did made him physically sick. Nevertheless he managed it, little by little, step by dragging step. Out from behind the door, across the landing, along towards the study stairs . . . Down the stairs, one at a time . . .

With every step, his common sense screamed at him to turn and flee, but he resisted. To run would be to fail Mrs

Underwood. He would go in there and tell the truth, come what may.

The door was open, the fiery hex defused. Yellow light spilled from inside.

Nathaniel paused at the threshold. His brain seemed to have shut down. He did not fully understand what he was about to do.

He pushed at the door and went in, just in time to witness the moment of discovery.

Lovelace and Underwood were standing by a wall-cupboard with their backs to him. The cupboard doors gaped wide. Even as he watched, Lovelace's head craned forwards eagerly like a hunting cat's, and his hand stretched out and knocked something aside. He gave a cry of triumph. Slowly, he turned and raised his hand before Underwood's corpse-white face.

Nathaniel's shoulders slumped.

How small it looked, the Amulet of Samarkand, how insignificant it seemed, as it hung from Lovelace's fingers on its slender gold chain. It swung gently, glinting in the study light.

Lovelace smiled. 'Well, well. What have we here?'

Underwood was shaking his head in confusion and disbelief. In those few seconds, his face had aged. 'No,' he whispered. 'A trick . . . You're framing me . . .'

Lovelace wasn't even looking at him. He gazed at his prize. 'I can't imagine what you thought you could do with this,' he said. 'Summoning Bartimaeus on its own would have been quite enough to wear you out.'

'I keep saying,' Underwood said weakly, 'I don't know anything about this Bartimaeus, and I know nothing about your object, nor how it got there.'

Nathaniel heard a new voice speaking, high and shaky. It was his own.

'He's telling the truth,' he said. '*I* took it. The person that you want is me.'

The silence that followed this statement lasted almost five seconds. Both magicians spun round on the instant, only to stare at him open-mouthed in shock. Mr Underwood's eyebrows rose high, sank low, then rose again, mirroring his utter bewilderment. Lovelace wore an uncomprehending frown.

Nathaniel took the opportunity to walk further into the room. 'It was I,' he said, his voice a little firmer now that the deed was done. '*He* knows nothing about it. You can leave him alone.'

Underwood blinked and shook his head. He seemed to doubt the evidence of his senses. Lovelace remained quite still, his hidden eyes fixed on Nathaniel. The Amulet of Samarkand swung gently between his motionless fingers.

Nathaniel cleared his throat, which was dry. What would happen now he dared not guess. He had not thought beyond his confession. Somewhere in the room his servant lurked, so he was not entirely defenceless. If necessary, he hoped Bartimaeus would come to his aid.

His master found his voice at last. 'What are you gibbering about, you fool? You can have no idea what we discuss. Leave here at once!' A thought occurred to him. 'Wait – how did you get out of the room?'

At his side, Lovelace's frown suddenly fractured into a twitching smile. He laughed quietly. 'A moment, Arthur. Perhaps you are being too hasty.'

For an instant, a fleeting glimpse of Underwood's irascibility returned. 'Don't be absurd! This stripling cannot have committed the crime! He would have had to bypass my fire-hex, for a start, not to mention your own defences.'

'And raise a djinni of the fourteenth level,' murmured Lovelace. 'That too.'

'Exactly. The notion is abs—' Underwood gasped. Sudden understanding dawned in his eyes. 'Wait . . . perhaps . . . Can it be possible? Only today, Lovelace, I caught this brat with summoning equipment, and Adelbrand's Pentacle chalked out in his room. He had sophisticated books – *The Mouth of Ptolemy*, for one. I assumed he had failed, was over-ambitious . . . But what if I was wrong?'

Simon Lovelace said nothing. He never looked away from Nathaniel.

'Just this past hour,' Underwood went on, 'I caught him spying on me in my study. He had a scrying glass, something I have never given him. If he is capable of that, who knows what other crimes he might attempt?'

'Even so,' Lovelace said softly, 'why should he steal from me?'

Nathaniel could tell from his master's behaviour that he had not recognized the Amulet for what it was, and realized that this ignorance might yet save him. Would Lovelace believe the same was true of Nathaniel, too? He spoke up quickly, trying to sound as much like a child as possible. 'It was just a trick, sir,' he said. 'A joke. I wanted to get back at you for hitting me that time. I asked the demon to take something of yours, anything at all. I was going to keep that thing till I was older, and, erm, till I could find out what it was and how to use it. I hope it wasn't valuable, sir. I'm very sorry for putting you to any trouble . . .'

He trailed off, excruciatingly aware how weak his story was. Lovelace just gazed at him; he could make out nothing from the man's expression.

But his master, for one, believed him. His full fury was unleashed. 'That is the last straw, Mandrake!' he cried. 'I will have you up before the court! Even if you escape prison, you will be stripped of your apprenticeship and turned out into the street! I will cast you out! All jobs will be closed to you! You will become a pauper among commoners!'

'Yes, sir.' *Anything*, if only Lovelace would leave.

'I can only apologize, Lovelace.' Underwood drew himself up and puffed out his chest. 'We have both been in-convenienced – he has betrayed me and from you he has stolen a most powerful treasure, this amulet—' He glanced towards the small gold oval dangling from Lovelace's hand and in that sudden, fatal instant realized what it was. A short, suppressed intake of breath sounded against his teeth. It was a small noise, but Nathaniel heard it clearly enough. Lovelace didn't move.

The colour drained from Underwood's cheeks. His eyes darted towards Lovelace's face to see if he had noticed any-thing. Nathaniel's eyes did likewise. Through the blood pounding in his head, he heard Underwood struggling to con-tinue where he had broken off: '– and . . . and we shall both see him suitably punished, yes we will; he will regret the day when he ever thought to—'

The other magician held up his hand. Instantly, Underwood was silent.

'Well, John Mandrake,' Simon Lovelace said, 'I am *almost* very impressed. Yes, I have been inconvenienced; the last few days have been difficult for me. But see – I have my prize again, and all will now be well. Please do not apologize. To summon a djinni such as Bartimaeus at your age is no mean achievement; to control him over several days is even more surprising. You left me frustrated, too, which is a rare event, and Underwood ignorant, which is somewhat less unusual. All very clever. Only at the end have you fallen down. What possessed you to own up to your action? I might have dealt quietly with Underwood and left you alone.' His voice was soft and reasonable.

Underwood urgently tried to speak, but Lovelace interrupted him. 'Quiet, man. I want to hear the boy's reasons.'

'Because it wasn't his fault,' Nathaniel said, stolidly. 'He knew nothing. Your quarrel was with me, whether you knew so or not. He should be left out of it. That's why I came down.' A sense of the utter futility of his action weighed down upon him.

Lovelace chuckled. 'Some childish concept of nobility, is it?' he said. 'I guessed as much. The honourable course of action. Heroic, but stupid. Where did you get that notion from? Not from Underwood here, I'll bet.'

'I robbed you because you wronged me,' Nathaniel continued. 'I wanted to get my own back. That's all there is to it. Punish me if you want. I don't care.' His attitude of surly resignation concealed a growing hope. Maybe Lovelace did not realize that they knew about the Amulet, maybe he would administer some token punishment and go.

Underwood was evidently hoping the same thing. He grasped Lovelace eagerly by the arm. 'As you have seen, Simon, I am entirely innocent in this affair. It was this wicked, scheming boy. You must deal with him as you wish. Whatever sentence fits the crime, you may administer it. I leave it entirely up to you.'

Gently, Lovelace disengaged himself. 'Thank you, Underwood. I shall administer his punishment shortly.'

'Good.'

'After disposing of you.'

'What—?' For a second, Underwood froze, then with a turn of speed unexpected in a man of his age, he ran for the open door. Just as he passed Nathaniel, a gust of wind from nowhere slammed the door tight shut. Underwood rattled the handle and pulled with all his strength, but it remained fast. With a snarl of fear, he spun round. He and Nathaniel stood facing Simon Lovelace across the room. Nathaniel's legs shook. He looked round wildly for Bartimaeus, but the spider was nowhere to be seen.

With fastidious care, Lovelace took the Amulet of Samarkand by its chain and hung it round his neck. 'I am not stupid, John,' he said. 'It is possible that you do not know what this object is, but frankly I cannot take that chance. And certainly, poor Arthur knows.'

At this, Underwood stretched out a clawing hand and grasped Nathaniel around the neck. His voice was cracked with panic. 'Yes, but I will say nothing! You can trust me, Lovelace! You may keep the Amulet for all eternity for all I care! But the boy is a meddling fool; he must be silenced before he blabs. Kill him now, and the matter will be finished!' His nails dug into Nathaniel's skin, he thrust him forward; Nathaniel cried out in pain.

A smirk extended across Lovelace's face. 'Such loyalty from a master to his apprentice! Very touching. You see, John, Underwood and I are giving you a final lesson in the art of being a magician, and perhaps with our help you will under-stand your error in owning up to me today. You believed in the notion of the honourable magician, who takes responsibility for his actions. Mere propaganda. Such a thing does not exist. There is no honour, no nobility, no justice. Every magician acts only for himself, seizing each opportunity he can. When he is weak, he avoids danger (which is why second-raters plod away within the system – Arthur knows all about *that*, don't you, Underwood?). But when he is strong, he strikes. How do you think Rupert Devereaux himself came to power? *His* master killed the previous Prime Minister in a coup twenty years ago and he inherited the title. That is the truth of it. That is how things are always done. When I use the Amulet next week, I will be following in a grand tradition reaching back to Gladstone.' The glasses flashed, a hand was raised, ready to begin a gesture. 'It may console you to know that even before you arrived, I was resolved to kill you and everyone in this house. I cannot leave anything to chance. So your stupidity in coming here has actually changed nothing.'

An image of Mrs Underwood, downstairs in the kitchen, flashed through Nathaniel's mind. Tears flooded his eyes. 'Please—'

'You are weak, boy. Just like your master.' Lovelace clapped his hands. The light in the study suddenly darkened. A tremor ran across the floor. Nathaniel sensed something appearing in the far corner of the room, but fear froze him in place – he dared not look to see. At his side, Underwood uttered the words of a defensive charm. A shimmering green net of protective threads rose up to enfold him. Nathaniel was excluded, defenceless.

'Master—!'

At that moment, like a shaft collapsing in a slate-mine, a terrible voice echoed through the room. 'YOUR WISH?'

Lovelace's voice: 'Destroy them both. And anything else living in the house. Burn it to the ground with all its contents.'

Underwood gave a great cry. 'Take the boy! Leave me!' He pushed Nathaniel with frantic strength. Nathaniel sprawled forwards, stumbled and fell. His eyes were blind with tears; he tried to rise, conscious only of his utter helplessness. Close by sounded a splintering noise. He opened his mouth to scream. Then claws descended and seized him round the throat.

Bartimaeus

30

I give Underwood's desk the credit. It was an old-fashioned, sturdy affair and fortunately Jabor had materialized on its far side. The three seconds it took him to smash his way straight through it gave me time to move. I had been loitering on the ceiling, in a crevice above the light shade; now I dropped straight down, transforming into a gargoyle as I did so. I landed directly on my master, grabbed him unceremoniously around the neck and, since Jabor blocked the window, bounded away in the direction of the door.

My response went almost unnoticed: the magicians were otherwise occupied. Swathed in his defensive nexus, Underwood sent a bolt of blue fire crackling towards Lovelace. The bolt hit Lovelace directly in his chest and vanished. The Amulet of Samarkand had absorbed its power.

I broke through the door with the boy under my arm and

set off up the stairs. I hadn't reached the top when a colossal explosion ripped through the passage from behind and sent us slamming against a far wall. The impact dazed me. As I lay there, momentarily stunned, a series of deafening crashes could be heard. Jabor's attack had perhaps been over-zealous: it sounded as if the entire study floor had given way beneath him.[1]

It didn't take me long to put my essence in order and get to my feet, but believe it or not, in those few moments, that benighted boy had gone. I caught sight of him on the landing, heading for the stairs. And going down.

I shook my head in disbelief. What had I told him about staying out of trouble? He'd already walked straight into Lovelace's hands and risked both our lives in the process. Now here he was, in all probability heading straight towards Jabor. It's all very well running for your little life, but at least do it in the right direction. I flapped my wings and set off in grim pursuit.

The second golden rule of escaping is: make no unnecessary sounds. As the boy reached the ground floor, I heard him breaking this in no uncertain terms with a bellow that echoed up and down the stairwell: 'Mrs Underwood! Mrs Underwood! Where are you?' His shouts sounded even above the crashing noises reverberating through the house.

I rolled my eyes to the skies and descended the final flight of stairs, to find the hall already beginning to fill with billowing coils of smoke. A dancing red light flickered from along

---

[1] Typical Jabor, this. He's just the sort who'd happily saw off a branch he was sitting on, or paint himself steadily into a corner. If he was given to DIY, that is. Which he isn't.

the passage. The boy was ahead of me – I could see him stumbling towards the fire.

'Mrs Underwood!'

There was a movement far off in the smoke. A shape, hunched in a corner behind a barrier of licking flames. The boy saw it too. He tottered towards it. I speeded up, claws outstretched.

'Mrs Underwood? Are you—?'

The shape rose, unbent itself. It had the head of a beast.

The boy opened his mouth to scream. At that precise moment I caught up with him and seized him round the middle. He settled for a choking yell.

'It's me, you idiot.' I hoicked him backwards towards the stairs. 'It's coming to kill you. Do you want to die along with your master?'

His face went blank. The words shocked him. I don't think that until that moment he had truly comprehended what was happening, despite seeing it all unfold before his eyes. But I was happy to spell it out; it was time he learned the consequences of his actions.

Out through a wall of fire strode Jabor. His skin gleamed as if it had been oiled; the dancing flames were reflected on him as he stalked along the hall.

We started up the stairs again. My limbs strained at my master's weight. His limbs dragged; he seemed incapable of movement.

'*Up*,' I snarled. 'This house is terraced. We'll try the roof.'

He managed a mumble. 'My master . . .'

'Is dead,' I said. 'Swallowed whole, most probably.' It was best to be precise.

'But Mrs Underwood . . .'

'Is no doubt with her husband. You can't help her now.'

And here, believe it or not, the fool began to struggle, flailing about with his puny fists. 'No!' he shouted. 'It's my fault! I must find her—!' He wriggled like an eel, slipping from my grasp. In another moment he would have hurled himself around the banister and straight into Jabor's welcoming arms. I let out a vivid curse[2] and, grabbing him by an earlobe, pulled him up and onwards.

'Stop struggling!' I said. 'Haven't you made enough useless gestures for one day?'

'Mrs Underwood—'

'Would not want you to die too,' I hazarded.[3] 'Yes, it *is* your fault, but, er, don't blame yourself. Life's for the living . . . and, erm . . . Oh, *whatever*.' I ran out of steam.[4]

Whether or not it was my words of wisdom, the boy stopped straining against me. I had my arm round his neck and was dragging him up and round each corner, half flying, half walking, fast as I could lift him. We reached the second landing and went on again, up the attic stairs. Directly below, the steps cracked and splintered under Jabor's feet.

By the time we reached the top, my master had recovered

---

[2] Don't worry. It was in Old Babylonian. The boy wouldn't have understood the references.

[3] Without much conviction. It seemed a perfectly reasonable desire to me.

[4] Psychology of this sort is not my strong suit. I haven't a clue what motivates most humans and care even less. With magicians it's usually pretty simple: they fall into three distinct types, motivated by ambition, greed or paranoia. Underwood, for example, now he was the paranoid type, from what I'd seen of him. Lovelace? Easy – ambition leaked from his body like a foul smell. The boy was of the ambitious kind as well, but he was still young, unformed. Hence this sudden ridiculous burst of altruism.

himself sufficiently to be stumbling along almost unaided. And so, like the hopeless pair in a three-legged race who trail in last to a round of sympathetic applause, we arrived at the attic room still alive. Which was something, I suppose.

'The window!' I said. 'We need to get onto the roof!' I bundled Nathaniel across to the skylight and punched it open. Cold air rushed in. I flew through the opening and, perching on the roof, extended a hand back down into the room. 'Come on,' I said. 'Out.'

But to my astonishment, the infernal boy hesitated. He shuffled off to a corner of the room, bent down and picked something up. It was his scrying glass. I ask you! Jackal-headed death hard on his heels, and he was dawdling for *that*? Only then did he amble over to the skylight, his face still wiped clean of expression.

One good thing about Jabor. Slow. It took him time to negotiate the tricky proposition of the stairs. If it had been Faquarl chasing, he'd have been able to overtake us, lock and bar the skylight and maybe even fit it with a nice new roller blind before we got there. Yet so lethargic was my master that I barely had him within grabbing distance when Jabor finally appeared at the top of the stairs, sparks of flame radiating from his body and igniting the fabric of the house around him. He caught sight of the boy, raised a hand and stepped forward.

And banged his head nicely on the low-slung attic door.

This gave me the instant I needed. I swung down from the skylight, holding on with my feet like a gibbon, seized the boy under an arm and swung myself back up and away from the hole. As we fell back against the tiles, a gout of flame erupted from the skylight. The whole building shook.

The boy would have lain there all night if I'd let him, staring glassy-eyed at the stars. He was in shock, I think. Maybe nobody had seriously tried to kill him before. Conversely, I had reactions born of long practice: in a trice I was up again, hoisting him with me and rattling off along the sloping roof, gripping tightly with my claws.

I made for the nearest chimney and, flinging the boy down behind it, peered back the way we had come. The heat from below was doing its work: tiles were popping out of position, small flames dancing through the cracks between them. Somewhere a mass of timber cracked and shifted.

At the skylight, a movement: a giant black bird flapping clear of the fire. It alighted on the roof crest and changed form. Jabor glared back and forth. I ducked down behind the chimney and snatched a quick look up ahead.

There was no sign of any of Lovelace's other slaves: no djinn, no watchful spheres. Perhaps, with the Amulet back in his hands, he felt he had no need of them. He was relying on Jabor.

The street was terraced: this gave us an avenue of escape stretching away along a succession of connecting houses. To the left, the roofs were a dark shelf above the lamp-lit expanse of the street. To the right, they looked over the shadowy mass of the gardens, full of overgrown trees and bushes. Some way off, a particularly large tree had been allowed to grow close to its house. That had potential.

But the boy was still sluggish. I couldn't rely on a speedy flight from him. Jabor would nail us with a Detonation before we'd gone five metres.

I risked a quick shufti around the edge of the brickwork. Jabor was approaching, head lowered a little, snuffling on our trail. Not long before he guessed our hiding place and vaporized the chimney. Now was very much the time to think of a brilliant, watertight plan.

Failing that, I improvised.

Leaving the boy lying, I rose up from behind the chimney in gargoyle form. Jabor saw me; as he fired, I closed my wings for a moment, allowing myself to drop momentarily through the air. The Detonation shot above my plummeting head and curved away over the roof to explode harmlessly[5] somewhere in the street beyond. I flapped my wings again and soared closer to Jabor, watching all the while the little sheets of flame licking up around his feet, cracking the tiles and feeding on the hidden timbers that fixed the roof in place.

I held up my claws in a submissive gesture. 'Can't we discuss this? Your master may want the boy alive.'

Jabor was never one for small talk. Another near miss almost finished the argument for me. I spiralled around him as fast as I could, keeping him as near as possible in the same spot. Every time he fired, the force of his shot weakened the section of roof on which he stood; every time this happened the roof trembled a little more violently. But I was running out of energy – my dodges grew less nimble. The edge of a Detonation clipped a wing and I tumbled to the tiles.

Jabor stepped forward.

I raised a hand and fired a return shot. It was weak and low, far too low to trouble Jabor. It struck the tiles directly in front of his feet. He didn't so much as flinch. Instead, he let out a triumphant laugh—

– which was cut short by the whole section of roof collapsing. The master beam that spanned the length of the

---

[5] To me. Which is what counts.

building split in two; the joists fell away, and timber and plaster and tile upon tile dropped into the inferno of the house, taking Jabor with them. He must have fallen a good long way from there – down four burning floors to the cellars below ground. Much of the house would have fallen on top of him.

Flames crackled through the hole. To me, as I grasped the edge of the chimney and swung myself over to the other side, it sounded rather like a round of applause.

The boy was crouching there, dull-eyed, looking out into the dark.

'I've given us a few minutes,' I said, 'but there's no time to waste. Get moving.'

Whether or not it was the friendly tone of my voice that did it, he struggled to his feet quickly enough. But then he set off, shuffling along the rooftop with all the speed and elegance of a walking corpse. At that pace it would have taken him a week to get close to the tree. An old man with two glass eyes could have caught up with him, let alone an angry djinni. I glanced back. As yet there was no sign of pursuit – only flames roaring up from the hole. Without wasting a moment, I summoned up my remaining strength and slung the boy over my shoulder. Then I ran as fast as I could along the roof.

Four houses further on, we drew abreast of the tree, an ever-green fir. The nearest branches were only four metres distant. Jumpable. But first, I needed a rest. I dumped the boy onto the tiles and checked behind us again. Nothing. Jabor was having problems. I imagined him thrashing around in the white heat of the cellar, buried under tons of burning debris, struggling to get out . . .

There was a sudden movement among the flames. It was time to go.

I didn't give the boy the option of panicking. Grasping him around the waist, I ran down the roof and leaped from the end. The boy made no sound as we arched through the air, picked out in orange by the light of the fire. My wings beat frantically, keeping us aloft just long enough, until with a whipping and stabbing and a cracking of branches, we plunged into the foliage of the evergreen tree.

I clasped the trunk, stopping us from falling. The boy steadied himself against a branch. I glanced back at the house. A black silhouette moved slowly against the fire.

Gripping the trunk loosely, I let us slide. The bark sheered away against each claw as we descended. We landed in wet grass in the darkness at the foot of the tree.

I set the boy on his feet again. 'Now − absolute silence!' I whispered. 'And keep below the trees.'

Then away we slunk, my master and I, into the dripping darkness of the garden, as the wail of fire engines grew in the street beyond and another great beam crashed into the flaming ruin of his master's house.

Part Three

Nathaniel

31

Beyond the broken glass, the sky lightened. The persistent rain that had been falling since dawn drizzled to a halt. Nathaniel sneezed.

London was waking up. For the first time, traffic appeared on the road below: grimy red buses with snarling engines carrying the first commuters towards the centre of the city; a few sporadic cars, honking their horns at anyone scurrying across their path; bicycles too, with riders hunched and labouring inside their heavy greatcoats.

Slowly, the shops opposite began to open. The owners emerged and with harsh rattling raised the metal night-grilles from their windows. Displays were adjusted: the butcher slapped down pink slabs of meat on his enamel shelving; the tobacconist hung a rack of magazines above his counter. Next door, the bakery's ovens had been hot for hours; warm air that

319

smelled of loaves and sugared doughnuts drifted across the street and reached Nathaniel, shivering and hungry in the empty room.

A street market was starting up in a side road close by. Shouts rang out, some cheery, others hoarse and guttural. Boys tramped past, rolling metal casks or wheeling barrows piled high with vegetables. A police car cruised north along the road, slowing as it passed the market, then revving ostentatiously and speeding away.

The sun hung low over the rooftops, a pale egg-yellow disc clouded by haze.

On any other morning, Mrs Underwood would have been busy cooking breakfast.

He could see her there in front of him: small, busy, resolutely cheerful, bustling round the kitchen clanging pans down on the cooker, chopping tomatoes, slinging toast into the toaster . . . Waiting for him to come down.

On any other morning that would have been so. But now the kitchen was gone. The house was gone. And Mrs Underwood, Mrs Underwood was—

He wanted to weep; his face was heavy with the desire for it. It was as if a floodtide of emotion lay dammed there, ready to pour forth. But his eyes remained dry. There was no release. He stared out over the gathering activity of the street below, seeing none of it, numb to the chill that bit into his bones. Whenever he closed his eyes, a flickering white shadow danced against the dark – the memory of flames.

Mrs Underwood was—

Nathaniel took a deep, shuddering breath. He buried his hands in his trouser pockets and felt the touch of the bronze disc there, smooth against his fingers. It made him start and pull his hand away. His whole body shook with cold. His brain seemed frozen too.

His master – he had tried his best for him. But she— He should have warned her, got her out of the house before it happened. Instead of which, he . . .

He had to think. This was no time to . . . He had to think what to do, or he was lost.

For half the night, he had run like a madman through the gardens and back roads of north London, eyes vacant, mouth agape. He remembered it only as a series of rushes in the dark, of scrambles over walls and dashes under streetlamps, of whispered commands that he had automatically obeyed. He had a sensation of pressing up against cold brick walls, then squeezing through hedges, cut and bruised and soaked to the skin. Once, before the all-clear was given, he had hidden for what seemed like hours at the base of a compost heap, his face pressed against the mouldering slime. It seemed no more real than a dream.

Throughout this flight, he had been replaying Underwood's face of terror, seeing a jackal head rising from the flames. Unreal also. Dreams within a dream.

He had no memory of the pursuit, though at times it had been close and pressing. The hum of a search sphere, a strange chemical scent carried on the wind: that was all he knew of it, until – shortly before dawn – they had stumbled down into an area of narrow, red-brick houses and back alleys, and found the boarded-up building.

Here, for the moment, he was safe. He had time to think, work out what to do . . .

But Mrs Underwood was—

'Cold, isn't it?' said a voice.

Nathaniel turned away from the window. A little way off across the ruined room, the boy that was not a boy was watching him with shiny eyes. It had given itself the semblance of thick winter gear – a spongy jacket top, new blue jeans, strong brown boots, a woolly hat. It looked very warm.

'You're shivering,' said the boy. 'But then you're hardly dressed for a winter's expedition. What have you got under that jersey? Just a shirt, I expect. And look at those flimsy shoes. They must be soaked right through.'

Nathaniel hardly heard him. His mind was far away.

'This isn't the place to be half naked,' the boy went on. 'Look at it! Cracks in the walls, a hole in the ceiling . . . We're open to the elements here. Brrrrrr! Chilly.'

They were on the upper floor of what had evidently been a public building. The room was cavernous, bare and empty, with whitewashed walls stained yellow and green with mould. All along each wall stretched row upon row of empty shelves, covered in dust, dirt and bird droppings. Disconsolate piles of wood that might once have been tables or chairs were tucked into a couple of corners. Tall windows looked out over the street and wide marbled steps led downstairs. The place smelt of damp and decay.

'Do you want me to help you with the cold?' the boy said, looking sideways at him. 'You only have to ask.'

Nathaniel did not respond. His breath frosted in front of his face.

The djinni came a bit closer. 'I could make a fire,' it said. 'A nice hot one. I've got plenty of control over that element. Look!' A tiny flame flickered in the centre of its palm. 'All this wood in here, going to waste . . . What *was* this place, do you think? A library? I think so. Don't suppose the commoners are

322

allowed to read much any more, are they? That's usually the way it goes.' The flame grew a little. 'You only have to ask, o my master. I'd do it as a favour. That's what friends are for.'

Nathaniel's teeth were chattering in his head. More than anything else – more even than the hunger that was gnawing in his belly like a dog – he needed warmth. The little flame danced and spun.

'Yes,' he said huskily. 'Make me a fire.'

The flame instantly died out. The boy's brow furrowed. 'Now *that* wasn't very polite.'

Nathaniel closed his eyes and heaved a sigh. '*Please.*'

'Much better.' A small spark leaped and ignited a pile of wood nearby. Nathaniel shuffled over and huddled beside it, his hands inches from the flames.

For a few minutes the djinni remained silent, pacing here and there about the room. The feeling slowly returned to Nathaniel's fingers, though his face stayed numb. At length he became aware that the djinni had come close again, and was sitting on its haunches, idly stirring a long sliver of wood in the fire.

'How does that feel?' it asked. 'Melting nicely, I hope.' It waited politely for an answer, but Nathaniel said nothing. 'I'll tell you one thing,' the djinni went on, in a conversational tone, 'you're an interesting specimen. I've known a fair few magicians in my time, and there aren't many who are quite as suicidal as you. Most would think that popping in to tell a powerful enemy you'd pinched his treasure wasn't a terribly bright idea. Especially when you're utterly defenceless. But you? All in a day's work.'

'I had to,' Nathaniel said shortly. He did not want to talk.

'Mm. No doubt you had a brilliant plan, which I – and

Lovelace, for that matter – completely missed. Mind telling me what it was?'

'Be silent!'

The djinni wrinkled its nose. 'That was your plan? It's a simple one, I'll say that much. Still, don't forget it was *my* life you were risking too back there, acting out your strange convulsion of conscience.' It reached into the fire suddenly and removed a burning ember, which it held musingly between finger and thumb. 'I had another master like you once. He had the same mulish obstinacy, seldom acted in his own best interests. Didn't live long.' It sighed, tossed the ember back into the flames. 'Never mind – all's well that ends well.'

Nathaniel looked at the djinni for the first time. 'All's *well*?'

'You're alive. Does that count as good?'

For an instant, Nathaniel saw Mrs Underwood's face watching him from the fire. He rubbed his eyes.

'I hate to say this,' the djinni said, 'but Lovelace was right. You were totally out of your depth last night. Magicians don't act the way you do. It was a good job I was there to rescue you. So – where are you going now? Prague?'

'What?'

'Well, Lovelace knows you've escaped. He'll be looking out for you – and you've seen what he'll do to keep you quiet. Your only hope is to vanish from the scene and leave London for good. Abroad will be safest. Prague.'

'Why should I go to Prague?'

'Magicians there might help you. Nice beer, too, I'm told.'

Nathaniel's lip curled. 'I'm no traitor.'

The boy shrugged. 'If that's not on, then you're left with getting a quiet new life here. There are plenty of possibilities.

Let's see . . . looking at you, I'd say heavy lifting's out – you're too spindly. That rules out being a labourer.'

Nathaniel frowned with indignation. 'I have no intention—'

The djinni ignored him. 'But you could turn your runt-like size to your advantage. Yes! A sweep's lad, that's the answer. They always need fresh urchins to climb the flues.'

'Wait! I'm not—'

'Or you could become apprentice to a sewer rat. You get a bristle brush, a hook and a rubber plunger, then wriggle up the tightest tunnels looking for blockages.'

'I won't—'

'There's a world of opportunities out there! And all of them better than being a dead magician.'

'Shut up!' The effort of raising his voice made Nathaniel feel his head was about to split in two. 'I don't need your suggestions!' He stumbled to his feet, eyes blazing with anger. The djinni's jibes had cut through his weariness and grief to ignite a pent-up fury that suddenly consumed him. It rose up from his guilt, his shock and his mortal anguish and used them for its fuel. Lovelace had said that there was no such thing as honour, that every magician acted only for himself. Very well. Nathaniel would take him at his word. He would not make such a mistake again.

But Lovelace had made an error of his own. He had under-estimated his enemy. He had called Nathaniel weak, then tried to kill him. And Nathaniel had survived.

'You want me to slink away?' he cried. 'I cannot! Lovelace has murdered the only person who ever cared for me—' He halted: there was a catch in his voice, but still his eyes were dry.

'Underwood? You must be joking! He loathed you! He was a man of sense!'

'His wife, I mean. I want justice for her. Vengeance for what he has done.'

The effect of these ringing words was slightly spoiled by the djinni blowing a loud raspberry. It rose, shaking its head sadly, as if weighed down by great wisdom. 'It isn't justice you're after, boy. It's oblivion. Everything you had went up in flames last night. So now you've got nothing to lose. I can read your thoughts as if they were my own: you want to go out in a blaze of glory against Lovelace.'

'No. I want justice.'

The djinni laughed. 'It'll be *so* easy, following your master and his wife into the darkness – so much easier than starting life afresh. Your pride is ruling your head, leading you to your death. Didn't last night teach you anything? You're no match for him, Nat. Give it up.'

'Never.'

'It's not even as if you're really a magician any more.' It gestured at the crumbling walls. 'Look around you. Where are we? This isn't some cushy town house, filled with books and papers. Where are the candles? Where's all the incense? Where's the *comfort*? Like it or not, Nathaniel, you've lost everything a magician needs. Wealth, security, self-respect, a master . . . Let's face it, you've got nothing.'

'I have my scrying glass,' Nathaniel said. 'And I have you.' Hurriedly, he sat himself back beside the fire. The cold of the room still pierced him through.

'Ah yes, I was coming to that.' The djinni began clearing a space among the debris of the floor with the side of its boot. 'When you've calmed down a bit, I shall bring you some chalk. Then you can draw me a circle here and set me free.'

Nathaniel stared at him.

'I've completed my charge,' the boy continued. 'And more, much more. I spied on Lovelace for you. I found out about the Amulet. I saved your life.'

Nathaniel's head felt oddly light and muzzy, as if it were stuffed with cloth.

'Please! Don't rush to thank me!' the boy went on. 'I'll only get embarrassed. All I want is to see you drawing that pentacle. That's all I need.'

'No,' Nathaniel said. 'Not yet.'

'Sorry?' the boy replied. 'My hearing must be going, on account of that dramatic rescue I pulled off last night. I thought you just said no.'

'I did. I'm not setting you free. Not yet.'

A heavy silence fell. As Nathaniel watched, his little fire began to dwindle, as if it were being sucked down through the floor. It vanished altogether. With little cracking noises, ice began to crust onto the scraps of wood that a moment before had been burning nicely. Cold blistered his skin. His breath became harsh and painful.

He staggered upright. 'Stop that!' he gasped. 'Bring back the fire.'

The djinni's eyes glittered. 'It's for your own good,' it said. 'I've just realized how inconsiderate I was being. You don't want to see another fire – not after the one you caused last night. Your conscience would hurt you too much.'

Flickering images rose before Nathaniel's eyes: flames erupting from the ruined kitchen. 'I didn't start the fire,' he whispered. 'It wasn't my fault.'

'No? *You* hid the Amulet. *You* framed Underwood.'

'No! I didn't intend Lovelace to come. It was for security—'

The boy sneered. 'Sure it was – *your* security.'

'If Underwood had been any good he'd have survived! He'd have fought Lovelace off – raised the alarm!'

'You don't believe that. Let's face it, *you* killed them both.'

Nathaniel's face twisted in fury. 'I was going to expose Lovelace! I was going to trap him with the Amulet – show the authorities!'

'Who cares? You were too late. You failed.'

'Thanks to you, demon! If you hadn't led them to the house none of this would have happened!' Nathaniel seized on this idea like a drowning man. 'It's all your fault and I'm going to pay you back! Think you're ever going to be freed? Think again! You're staying permanently. It's Perpetual Confinement for you!'

'Is that so? In that case –' the counterfeit boy stepped forward and was suddenly very close – 'I might as well kill you myself right now. What have I got to lose? I'll be in the tin either way, but I'll have the satisfaction of breaking your neck first.' Its hand descended gently on Nathaniel's shoulder.

Nathaniel's skin crawled. He resisted the overpowering temptation to shy away and run, and instead stared back into the dark, blank eyes.

For a long moment, neither said anything.

At last Nathaniel licked his dry lips. 'That won't be necessary,' he said thickly. 'I'll free you before the month is up.'

The djinni pulled him closer. 'Free me *now*.'

'No.' Nathaniel swallowed. 'We have work to do first.'

'Work?' It frowned; its hand stroked his shoulder. 'What work? What is there to do?'

Nathaniel forced himself to remain quite still. 'My master and his wife are dead. I must avenge them. Lovelace must pay for what he did.'

The whispering mouth was very near now, but Nathaniel could feel no breath against his face: 'But I've told you. Lovelace is too powerful. You haven't a hope of besting him. Forget the matter, as I do. Release me and forget your troubles.'

'I cannot.'

'Why so?'

'I – I owe it to my master. He was a good man—'

'No, he wasn't. That's not the reason at all.' The djinni whispered directly into his ear. 'It isn't justice or honour that drives you now, boy, but guilt. You can't take the consequences of your actions. You seek to drown out what you've done to your master and his wife. Well, if that's the way you humans choose to suffer, so be it. But leave me out of the equation.'

Nathaniel spoke with a firmness he did not feel. 'Until your month is up you'll obey me if you ever want your freedom.'

'Going after Lovelace practically amounts to suicide in any case – yours *and* mine.' The boy smiled nastily. 'That being so, I still don't see why I shouldn't kill you now . . .'

'There will be ways to expose him!' Nathaniel could not help himself; he was speaking far too fast. 'We just need to think it through carefully. I'll make a bargain with you. Help me avenge myself on Lovelace and I'll set you free immediately afterwards. Then there can be no doubt about our positions. It's in both our interests to succeed.'

The djinni's eyes glittered. 'As always, a laudably fair arrangement, dictated from a one-sided position of power. Very well. I have no choice. But if at any time you place either of us at undue risk, be warned – I shall get my revenge in first.'

'Agreed.'

The boy stepped back and released Nathaniel's shoulder.

Nathaniel retreated, eyes wide, breathing hard. Humming gently, the djinni wandered to the window, re-igniting the fire casually as it passed. Nathaniel struggled to calm himself, to regain control. Another wave of misery washed through him, but he did not succumb. No time for that. He must appear strong in front of his slave.

'Well then, master,' the djinni said. 'Enlighten me. Tell me what we do.'

Nathaniel kept his voice as level as he could. 'First, I need food, and perhaps new clothes. Then we must pool our information on Lovelace and the Amulet. We also need to know what the authorities think about . . . about what happened last night.'

'That last one's easy,' Bartimaeus said, pointing out of the window. 'Look out there.'

32

'*T*imes! Morning edition!'

The newspaperboy wheeled his handcart slowly along the pavement, stopping whenever passers-by thrust coins in his direction. The crowd was thick and the boy's progress was slow. He had barely made it as far as the baker's by the time Nathaniel and Bartimaeus sidled out from the alley beside the derelict library and crossed the road to meet him.

Nathaniel still had in his pocket the remnants of the money he had stolen from Mrs Underwood's jar a few days before. He glanced at the cart: it was piled high with copies of *The Times* – the Government's official paper. The newspaperboy himself wore a large, checked cloth cap, fingerless gloves and a long dark coat that reached almost to his ankles. The tips of his fingers were mauve with cold. Every now and then he roared out the same hoarse call: '*Times*! Morning edition!'

Nathaniel had little experience of dealing with commoners. He hailed the boy in his deepest, most assertive voice. '*The Times*. How much is it?'

'Forty pence, kid.' Coldly, Nathaniel handed over the change and received the newspaper in return. The paperboy glanced at him, first incuriously and then with what seemed a sudden intense interest. Nathaniel made to pass on, but the boy addressed him.

'You look rough, chum,' he said cheerily. 'Been out all night?'

'No.' Nathaniel adopted a stern expression, which he hoped would discourage further curiosity.

It didn't work. 'Course you ain't, course you ain't,' the paperboy said. 'And I wouldn't blame you for not admitting it if you had. But you ought to be careful with the curfew on. The police are sniffing about more than usual.'

'What curfew's this?' the djinni asked.

The boy's eyes widened. 'Where've you been, mate? After that disgraceful attack on Parliament, there's an eight-o'clock curfew each night this week. It won't do nothing, but the search spheres are out, and the Night Police too, so you'll want to hole up somewhere before they find you and eat you. Looks to me like you struck lucky so far. Tell you what – I could find you a good place to shelter tonight, if you need it. It's a safe gaff, and *the* spot to go –' he paused, looked up and down the street, and lowered his voice – 'if you've got anything you might want to sell.'

Nathaniel looked at him blankly. 'Thank you. I haven't.'

The boy scratched the back of his head. 'Suit yourself. Well, can't hang about chatting. Some of us have got work to do. I'm off.' He took up the poles of his handcart and moved away, but Nathaniel noticed him look back at them over his shoulder more than once.

'Strange,' Bartimaeus said. 'What was that about?'

Nathaniel shrugged. He had already dismissed it from his mind. 'Go and get me some food and warmer clothes. I'll go back to the library and read this.'

'Very well. *Do* try to keep out of trouble while I'm gone.' The djinni turned and headed off into the crowd.

The article was on page two, sandwiched between the Employment Ministry's monthly request for new apprentices and a short report from the Italian campaign. It was three columns in length. It noted with regret the deaths in a severe house fire of the Internal Affairs Minister Arthur Underwood and his wife Martha. The blaze had started at approximately 10.15 p.m. and had only been fully extinguished by fire crews and emergency service magicians three hours later, by which time the whole building had been gutted. Two neighbouring houses had been badly affected, and their occupants evacuated to safety. The cause of the fire was unknown, but police were keen to interview Mr Underwood's apprentice, John Mandrake, aged twelve, whose body had not been recovered. Some confused reports had him being observed running from the scene. Mandrake was rumoured to be of an unstable disposition; he was known to have assaulted several prominent magicians the year before and the public was told to approach him with caution. Mr Underwood's death, the article concluded, was a sad loss to the Government; he had served his ministry ably all his life and made many significant contributions, none of which the paper had space to describe.

Sitting below the windows, Nathaniel let the paper drop. His head sank against his chest; he closed his eyes. Seeing in cold, clear print the confirmation of what he already knew struck him like a fresh blow. He reeled with it, willing the tears to come, but his grief remained pent up, elusive. It was no good. He was too tired for anything. All he wanted was to sleep . . .

A boot nudged him, not softly. He started and awoke.

The djinni stood over him, grinning. It carried a paper bag from which steam curled promisingly. Raw hunger overcame Nathaniel's dignity – he snatched the bag, almost spilling the polystyrene cup of coffee on his lap. To his relief, beneath the cup were two neatly wrapped greaseproof paper parcels, each containing a hot steak and salad sandwich. It seemed to Nathaniel that he had never eaten anything half as good in his entire life. In two straight minutes, both sandwiches were gone and he sat nursing the coffee in his chilblained fingers, breathing heavily.

'*What* an exhibition,' the djinni said.

Nathaniel slurped the coffee. 'How did you get this?'

'Stole it. Got a delicatessen man to make it all up, then ran off with it while he was at the till. Nothing fancy. The police were summoned.'

Nathaniel groaned. 'That's all we need.'

'Don't worry. They'll be looking for a tall blonde woman in a fur coat. Speaking of which –' it pointed to a small mound amid the debris of the floor – 'you'll find some better clothing there. Coat, trousers, hat and gloves. I hope they'll fit you. I picked the scrawniest sizes I could find.'

A few minutes later, Nathaniel was better fed, better clothed and partially revived. He sat beside the fire and warmed himself. The djinni crouched nearby, staring into the flames.

'They think I did it.' Nathaniel indicated the newspaper.

'Well, what do you expect? Lovelace isn't going to come clean, is he? What magician would do a stupid thing like that?' Bartimaeus eyed him meaningfully. 'The whole point of starting the fire was to hide all trace of his visit. And since he couldn't kill you, he's set you up to take the rap.'

'The police are after me.'

'Yep. The police on one side, Lovelace on the other. He'll have his scouts out trying to track you down. A nice little pincer movement. That's what he wants – to keep you on the run, isolated, out of his hair.'

Nathaniel ground his teeth. 'We'll see about that. What if I go to the police myself? They could raid Lovelace's house – find the Amulet . . .'

'Think they'll listen to you? You're a wanted man. I use "man" in the broadest possible sense there, obviously. Even if you weren't, I'd be cautious about contacting the authorities. Lovelace isn't acting alone. There's his master, Schyler—'

'Schyler?' Of course – the wizened, red-faced old man. 'Schyler is his master? Yes . . . I know him. I overheard them discussing the Amulet at Parliament. There's another one, too, called Lime.'

The djinni nodded. 'That may just be the tip of the iceberg. A great many search spheres chased me when I stole the Amulet that first night – it was the work of several magicians. If it *is* a wide conspiracy, and you go to the authorities, you can't trust anyone in a position of power not to tip him off and kill you instead. For example, Sholto Pinn, the artefact merchant, may be in on it. He is one of Lovelace's closest friends, and in fact was having lunch with him only yesterday. I discovered that shortly before I was unavoidably detained at Pinn's shop.'

Nathaniel's anger flared. 'You were far too reckless! I asked you to investigate Lovelace, not endanger me!'

'Temper, temper. That's precisely what I was doing. It was at Pinn's that I found out about the Amulet. Lovelace had it taken from a government magician named Beecham, whose throat was cut by the thief. The Government badly wants it back. I would have learned more, but an afrit came calling and took me to the Tower.'

'But you escaped. How?'

'Ah, well, that was the interesting thing,' Bartimaeus went

on. 'It was Lovelace himself who broke me out. He must have heard from Pinn or someone that a djinni of incredible virtuosity had been captured and guessed at once that it was me, the stealer of his Amulet. He sent his djinn Faquarl and Jabor in on a rescue bid – an extremely risky enterprise. Why do you think he did that?'

'He wanted the Amulet, of course.'

'Exactly – and he needs to use it soon. He told us as much last night. Faquarl said the same thing: it's going to be used for something big in the next couple of days. Time is of the essence.'

A half-buried memory stirred in Nathaniel's mind. 'Someone at Parliament said that Lovelace was holding a ball, or conference, soon. At a place outside London.'

'Yep, I learned that too. Lovelace has a wife, girlfriend or acquaintance named Amanda. It is she who is hosting the conference, at some hall or other. The Prime Minister will be attending. I saw this Amanda at Lovelace's house when I first stole the Amulet. He was trying very hard to charm her – so she can't be his wife. I doubt they've known each other very long.'

Nathaniel pondered for a moment. 'I overheard Lovelace telling Schyler that he wanted to cancel the conference. That was when he didn't have the Amulet.'

'Yes. But now he's got it again.'

Another surge of cold rage made Nathaniel's head spin. 'The Amulet of Samarkand. Did you discover its properties?'

'Little more than I have always known. It has long had a reputation for being an item of great power. The shaman who made it was a potent magician indeed – far greater than any of your piffling crowd. His or her tribe had no books or parchments: their knowledge was passed down by mouth and memory alone. Anyway, the Amulet protects its wearer from magical attack – it is more or less as simple as that. It is not a talisman – it can't be used aggressively to kill your rivals. It only works protectively. All amulets—'

Nathaniel cut in sharply. 'Don't lecture me! I *know* what amulets do.'

'Just checking. Not sure what they teach kids nowadays. Well, I witnessed a little of the Amulet's powers when I was planting it in Underwood's study for you.'

Nathaniel's face contorted. 'I wasn't planting it!'

'Course you weren't. But it dealt with an admittedly fairly poor fire-hex without any trouble. Absorbed it just like that – gone. And it disposed of Underwood's lame attack last night too, as you may have seen while dangling under my arm. One of my informants stated that the Amulet is rumoured to contain an entity from the heart of the Other Place: if so, it will be powerful indeed.'

Nathaniel's eyes hurt. He rubbed them. More than anything else, he needed sleep.

'Whatever the Amulet's exact capacity,' the djinni continued, 'it's clear Lovelace is going to use it in the next few days, at that conference he arranged. How? Difficult to guess. Why? Easy. He's seizing power.' It yawned. '*That* old story.'

Nathaniel cursed. 'He's a renegade, a traitor!'

'He's a normal magician. You're just the same.'

'What? How dare you! I'll—'

'Well, not yet, maybe. Give it a few years.' The djinni looked a little bored. 'So – what do you propose to do?'

A thought crossed Nathaniel's mind. 'I wonder . . .' he said. 'Parliament was attacked two days ago. Do you think Lovelace was behind that too?'

The djinni looked dubious. 'Doubt it. Too amateur. Also, judging by Lovelace's correspondence, he and Schyler weren't expecting anything that evening.'

'My master thought it was the Resistance – people who hate magicians.'

Bartimaeus grinned. '*Much* more likely. You watch out – they may be disorganized now, but they'll get you in the end. It always happens. Look at Egypt, look at Prague . . .'

'Prague's decadent.'

'Prague's *magicians* are decadent. And they no longer rule. Look over there . . .' In one area of the library, the rotting shelves had fallen away. The walls there were muralled with layers of graffiti and certain carefully drawn hieroglyphs. 'Old Kingdom curses,' Bartimaeus said. 'You get a more informed class of delinquent round here. "*Death to the Overlords*", that big one says. That's you, Natty boy, if I'm not much mistaken.'

Nathaniel ignored this; he was trying to organize his thoughts. 'It's too dangerous to go to the authorities about Lovelace,' he said slowly. 'So there is only one alternative. I shall attend the conference myself and expose the plot there.'

The djinni coughed meaningfully. 'I thought we mentioned something about undue risk . . . Be careful – that idea sounds suicidal to me.'

'Not if we plan carefully. First we need to know where and when the conference is taking place. That is going to be tricky . . . You will have to go out and discover this information for me.' Nathaniel cursed. 'But that will take time! If only I had some books and the proper incense – I could organize a troop of imps to spy on all the ministers at once! No – they would be hard to control. Or I could—'

The djinni had picked up the newspaper and was flipping

through it. 'Or you could just read the information printed here.'

'What?'

'Here in the Parliament Circular. Listen: "Wednesday, December the second, Heddleham Hall. Amanda Cathcart hosts the Annual Parliamentary Conference and Winter Ball. In attendance, amongst others, the Right Honourable Rupert Devereaux, Angus Nash, Jessica Whitwell, Chloe Baskar, Tim Hildick, Sholto Pinn and other members of the elite level."'

Nathaniel snatched the paper and read it through. 'Amanda Cathcart — that's got to be Lovelace's girlfriend. There's no doubt about it. This must be it.'

'Pity we don't know where Heddleham Hall is.'

'My scrying glass will find it.' From his pocket, Nathaniel drew the bronze disc.

Bartimaeus eyed it askance. 'I doubt it. It's a duff piece if ever I saw one.'

'I *made* this.'

'Yes.'

Nathaniel passed his hand twice across the disc and muttered the invocation. At the third time of asking, the imp's face appeared, spinning as if on a roundabout. It raised an eyebrow in mild surprise.

'Ain't you dead?' it said.

'No.'

'Pity.'

'Stop spinning,' Nathaniel snarled. 'I have a task for you.'

'Hold on a sec,' the imp said, screeching to a halt suddenly. 'Who's that with you?'

'That's Bartimaeus, another of my slaves.'

'He'd like to think as much,' the djinni said.

The imp frowned. 'That's Bartimaeus? The one from the Tower?'

'Yes.'

'Ain't he dead?'

'No.'

'Pity.'

'He's a feisty one.' Bartimaeus stretched and yawned. 'Tell him to watch it. I pick my teeth with imps his size.'

The baby made a sceptical face. 'Yeah? I've eaten djinn like you for breakfast, mate.'

Nathaniel kicked a foot against the floor. 'Will you both just shut up and let me give my command? I'm in charge here. Right. Imp: I wish you to show me the building known as Heddleham Hall. Somewhere near London. Owned by a woman named Amanda Cathcart. So! Be gone about your errand!'

'Hope it ain't too far off, this hall. My astral cord's only so long, you know.'

The disc clouded. Nathaniel waited impatiently for it to clear.

And waited.

'That is one slow scrying glass,' Bartimaeus said. 'Are you sure it's working?'

'Of course. It's a difficult objective, that's why it's taking time. And don't think you're getting off lightly, either. When we find the Hall, I want you to go and check it out. See if anything's going on. Lovelace may be setting some kind of trap.'

'It would have to be a subtle one to fool all those magicians heading there on Wednesday. Why don't you try shaking it?'

'It works, I tell you! You see – here we go.'

The imp reappeared, huffing and wheezing as if it was

hideously out of breath. 'What is it with you?' it panted. 'Most magicians use their glasses to spy on people they fancy in the shower. But not you, oh no. That would be much too easy. I've never approached a place that's so well guarded. That Hall is almost as bad as the Tower itself. Hair-trigger nexuses, randomly materializing sentries, the lot. I had to retreat as soon as I got near. This is the best image I could get.'

A very blurry image filled the centre of the disc. It was possible to make out a smudgy brown building with several turrets or towers, surrounded by woodland, with a long drive approaching from one side. A couple of black dots could be seen moving rapidly through the sky behind the building.

'See those things?' the imp's voice remarked. 'Sentries. They sensed me as soon as I materialized. That's them coming for me. Fast, aren't they? No wonder I had to skedaddle straight away.'

The image disappeared; the baby took its place. 'How was that?'

'Useless,' Bartimaeus said. 'We still don't know where the Hall is.'

'That's where you're wrong.' The baby's face assumed an inconceivably smug expression. 'It's fifty miles due south of London and nine miles west of the Brighton railway line. A huge estate. Can't miss it. I may be slow, but I'm thorough.'

'You may depart.' Nathaniel passed his hand across the disc, wiping it clear again. '*Now* we're getting started,' he said. 'The amount of magical protection confirms that must be where the conference is taking place. Wednesday . . . We've two days to get there.'

The djinni blew out its cheeks rudely. 'Two days till we're back at the mercy of Lovelace, Faquarl, Jabor and a hundred wicked magicians who think you're an arsonist. Goody. Can't wait.'

Nathaniel's face hardened. 'We have an agreement, remember? All we need is proper planning. Go to Heddleham Hall now, get as close as you can and find a way to get in. I shall wait for you here. I need to sleep.'

'Humans really do have no stamina. Very well: I shall go.' The djinni rose.

'How long will it take you?'

'A few hours. I'll be back before nightfall. There's a curfew on and the spheres will be out, so don't leave this building.'

'Stop telling me what to do! Just leave! Wait – before you go, how do I build up the fire?'

A few minutes later, the djinni departed. Nathaniel lay down on the floor close to the crackling flames. His grief and guilt lay down with him like shadows, but his weariness was stronger than both of them combined. In under a minute, he was asleep.

33

In his dream, he sat in a summer garden with a woman at his side. A pleasant feeling of peace was upon him: she was talking and he listened, and the sound of her voice mingled with the birdsong and the sun's touch upon his face. A book lay unopened on his lap, but he ignored it: either he had not read it, or he did not wish to do so. The woman's voice rose and fell; he laughed and felt her put an arm round his shoulders. At this, a cloud passed over the sun and the air chilled. A sudden gust of wind blew open the cover of the book and riffled its pages loudly. The woman's voice grew deeper; for the first time he looked in her direction . . . Under a mop of long blonde hair, he saw the djinni's eyes, its leering mouth. The grip around his shoulders tightened, he was pulled towards his enemy. Its mouth opened—

He awoke in a twisted posture, one of his arms raised defensively across his face.

The fire had burned itself out and the light was dying in the sky. The library room was thick with shadow. Several hours must have passed since he had fallen asleep, but he did not feel refreshed, only stiff and cold. Hunger clamped his stomach; his limbs were weak when he tried to stand. His eyes were hot and dry.

In the light of the window, he consulted his watch. Three forty: the day was almost gone. Bartimaeus had not yet returned.

★ ★ ★

As dusk fell, men with hooked poles emerged from the shops opposite and pulled the night-grilles down in front of their display windows. For several minutes, the rattles and crashes echoed along the road from both directions, like portcullises being dropped at a hundred castle gates. Yellow streetlights came on, one by one, and Nathaniel saw thin curtains being drawn in the windows above the shops. Buses with lit windows rumbled past; people hurried along the pavements, anxious to get home.

Still Bartimaeus did not come. Nathaniel paced impatiently about the cold, dark room. The delay enraged him. Yet again he felt powerless, at the mercy of events. It was just as things had always been. In every crisis, from Lovelace's first attack the year before, to the murder of Mrs Underwood, Nathaniel had been unable to respond – his weakness had cost him dearly every time. But things would change now. He had nothing holding him back, nothing left to lose. When the djinni returned, he would—

'Evening edition! Latest news!'

The voice came faintly to him from along the darkening street. Pressing his head against the leftmost window, he saw a small weak light come swinging along the pavement. It hung from a long pole above a wobbling handcart. The paperboy, back again.

For a few minutes Nathaniel watched the boy's approach, deliberating with himself. In all probability, there was no point in buying another paper: little would have changed since the morning. But *The Times* was his only link with the outside world; it might give him more information – about the police search for him, or the conference. Besides, he would go mad if he didn't do something. He rummaged in a pocket and checked his change. The result decided him. Treading carefully in the half-light, he crossed to the staircase, descended to the ground floor and squeezed past the loose plank into the side alley.

'One copy, please.' He caught up with the paperboy just as he was wheeling his cart round a corner, off the main road. The boy's cap was hanging from the back of his head; a sprig of white hair spilled out onto his brow. He looked round and gave a slightly toothless grin.

'You again. Still out on the streets?'

'One copy.' It seemed to Nathaniel that the boy was staring at him. He held his coins out impatiently. 'It's all right – I've got the money.'

'Never said you hadn't, chum. Trouble is, I've just sold out.' He indicated the empty interior of his cart. 'Lucky for you, my mate will have some left. His pitch isn't so lucrative as mine.'

'It doesn't matter.' Nathaniel turned to go.

'Oh, he'll be just along here. Won't take a minute. I always meet him near the Nag's Head at the end of the day. Just round the next corner.'

'Well . . .' Nathaniel hesitated. Bartimaeus could be back at any time, and he'd been told to stay inside. *Told?* Who was the master here? It was just round the corner; it would be fine. 'All right,' he said.

'Dandy. Come on, then.' The boy set off, the wheel of his cart squeaking and shaking on the uneven stones. Nathaniel went beside him.

The side road was less frequented than the main highway and few people passed them before they arrived at the next corner. The lane beyond was quieter still. A little way along it was an inn, a squat and ugly building with a flat roof and grey pebbledash walls. An equally squat and ugly horse was depicted on a badly painted sign hanging above the door. Nathaniel was disconcerted to see a small vigilance sphere hovering unobtrusively beside it.

The paperboy seemed to sense Nathaniel's hesitation. 'Don't worry; we're not going near the spy. It only watches the door, acts as a deterrent. Doesn't work, mind. Everyone at the Nag's Head just goes in the back. Anyway, here's old Fred.'

A narrow alley ran off from the lane at an angle between two houses, and at its entrance another handcart had been parked. Behind it, in the shadows of the alley, a tall youth wearing a black leather jacket lounged against the wall. He was eating an apple methodically and regarding them from under lowered eyelids.

'Hallo, Fred,' the paperboy said heartily. 'I've brought a chum to see you.'

Fred said nothing. He took a giant bite out of the apple, chewed it slowly with his mouth slightly open, and swallowed. He eyed Nathaniel up and down.

'He's after an evening paper,' the boy explained.

'Is he?' Fred said.

'Yeah, I'd run out. And he's the one I was telling you of and all,' the paperboy added quickly. 'He's got it on him now.'

At this, Fred straightened, stretched, tossed the remains of the apple down the alley and turned to face them. His leather jacket squeaked as he moved. He stood head and shoulders taller than Nathaniel and was broad with it; a sea of spots on his chin and cheeks did nothing to detract from his slightly menacing appearance. Nathaniel felt a little uneasy, but drew himself up and spoke with as much brusque confidence as he could. 'Well, do you have one? I don't want to waste my time.'

Fred looked at him. 'I've run out of papers too,' he said.

'Don't worry. I didn't really need it.' Nathaniel was only too eager to depart.

'Hold on –' Fred stretched out a large hand and grabbed him by a sleeve. 'No need to run off so quick. It ain't curfew yet.'

'Get off me! Let me go!' Nathaniel tried to shake himself free. His voice felt tight and high.

The paperboy patted him on the back in a friendly manner. 'Don't panic. We're not looking for trouble. We don't look like magicians, do we? Well then. We just want to ask you a few questions, don't we, Fred?'

'That's right.' Fred seemed to exert no effort, but Nathaniel found himself drawn into the alley, out of sight of the inn along the street. He did his best to quell his mounting fear.

'What do you want?' he said. 'I haven't any money.'

The paperboy laughed. 'We're not trying to rob you, chum. Just a few questions, like I said. What's your name?'

Nathaniel swallowed. 'Um . . . John Lutyens.'

'Lutt-chens? Aren't we posh? So what are you doing round here, John? Where's your home?'

'Er, Highgate.' As soon as he said it, he guessed it was a mistake.

Fred whistled. The paperboy's tone of voice was politely sceptical. '*Very* nice. That's a magician's part of town, John. You a magician?'

'No.'

'What about your friend?'

Nathaniel was momentarily taken aback. 'My – my friend?'

'The good-looking dark kid you were with this morning.'

'Him? Good looking? He's just someone I met. I don't know where he's gone.'

'Where did you get your new clothes?'

This was too much for Nathaniel to take. 'What *is* this?' he snapped. 'I don't have to answer all this! Leave me alone!' A trace of imperiousness had returned to his manner. He had no intention of being interrogated by a pair of commoners – the whole situation was absurd.

'Simmer down,' the paperboy said. 'We're just interested in you – and in what you've got in your coat.'

Nathaniel blinked. All he had in his pocket was the scrying glass, and no one had seen him use that, he was sure. He'd only taken it out in the library. 'My coat? There's nothing in it.'

'But there is,' Fred said. 'Stanley knows – don't you, Stanley?'

The paperboy nodded. 'Yup.'

'He's lying if he says he's seen anything.'

'Oh, I ain't *seen* it,' the boy said.

Nathaniel frowned. 'You're talking nonsense. Let me go, please.' This was insufferable! If only Bartimaeus was to hand, he would teach these commoners the meaning of respect.

Fred squinted at his watch in the gloom of the alley. 'Must be getting on to curfew, Stanley. Want me to take it off him?'

The paperboy sighed. 'Look, John,' he said patiently. 'We just want to see what it is you've stolen, that's all. We're not cops or magicians, so you don't have to beat about the bush. And – who knows? – perhaps we can make it worth your while. What were you going to do with it, anyway? Use it? So – just show us the object you've got in your left-hand pocket. If not, I'll have to let old Fred here go to work.'

Nathaniel could see he had no choice. He put his hand in

348

his pocket, drew out the disc and wordlessly handed it over.

The paperboy examined the scrying glass in the light of his lantern, turning it over and over in his hands.

'What do you think, Stanley?' Fred asked.

'Modern,' he said at last. '*Very* crudely done. Home-made piece, I'd say. Nothing special, but it's worth having.' He passed it across to Fred to examine.

A suspicion took sudden shape in Nathaniel's mind. The recent spate of artefact thefts was a big concern to ministers. Devereaux had mentioned it in his speech, while his master had linked the crimes to the mysterious Resistance which had attacked Parliament two days before. It was thought that commoners had carried out the thefts, and that the magical objects were then made available to enemies of the Government . . . Nathaniel remembered the wild-eyed youth standing on the terrace at Westminster Hall, the elemental sphere spinning through the air. Here perhaps was first-hand evidence of the Resistance in action. His heart beat fast. He had to tread very carefully.

'Is it – is it valuable?' he said.

'Yeah,' Stanley said. 'It's useful in the right hands. How did you get hold of it?'

Nathaniel thought fast. 'You're right,' he said. 'I, er . . . I did steal it. I was in Highgate (I don't live there myself, obviously) and I passed this big house. There was an open window – and I saw something shining on the wall just inside. So I nipped in and took it. No one saw me. I just thought I could sell it maybe, that's all.'

'All things are possible, John,' the paperboy said. 'All things are possible. Do you know what it does?'

'No.'

'It's a magician's divining disc, or scrying glass – something like that.'

Nathaniel was gaining confidence now. It was going to be easy enough to fool them. His mouth gaped in what he imagined was a commoner's stupefied amazement. 'What – can you see the future in it?'

'Maybe.'

'Can you work it?'

Stanley spat violently against the wall. 'You cheeky little sod! I ought to punch you hard for that.'

Nathaniel backtracked in confusion. 'Sorry – I didn't mean . . . Well, um, if it's valuable, do you know anyone who might want to buy it? Thing is, I badly need the cash.'

Stanley glanced across at Fred, who nodded slowly. 'Your luck's in!' Stanley said, in a chipper tone. 'Fred's up for it, and I always go along with old Fred. We do know someone who might be able to give you a good price, and perhaps help you out if you're down on your luck. Come along with us and we can arrange a meeting.'

This was interesting, but inconvenient. He couldn't waltz off across London to an unknown rendezvous now – he had already been away from the library too long. Getting to Lovelace's conference was far more important. Besides, he would need Bartimaeus with him if he was to get involved with these criminals. Nathaniel shook his head. 'I can't come now,' he said. 'Tell me who it is, or where I need to go, and I'll meet you there later.'

The two youths stared at him blankly. 'Sorry,' Stanley said. 'It's not that sort of meeting – and not that sort of someone, neither. What've you got to do that's so important, anyway?'

'I've got to, um, meet my friend.' He cursed silently. Mistake.

Fred shifted; his jacket squeaked. 'You just said you didn't know where he was.'

'Er, yes – I need to find him.'

Stanley looked at his watch. 'Sorry, John. It's now or never. Your friend can wait. I thought you wanted to sell this thing.'

'I do, but not tonight. I'm really interested in what you suggest. I just can't do it now. Listen – I'll meet you here tomorrow. Same time, same place.' He was growing desperate now, speaking too fast. He could sense their mounting suspicion and disbelief; all that mattered was getting away from them as fast as possible.

'No can do.' The paperboy adjusted his cap squarely on his head. 'I don't think we're going to get any joy here, Fred. What say we head off?'

Fred nodded. With disbelief, Nathaniel saw him stow the scrying glass inside his jacket pocket. He let out a shout of rage. 'Hey! That's mine! Give it back!'

'You missed your chance, John – if that *is* your name. Beat it.' Stanley reached down for the poles of his handcart. Fred gave Nathaniel a push that sent him sprawling back against the wet stones of the wall.

At this, Nathaniel felt all restraint dissolve; with a strangled cry, he fell upon Fred, pummelling him with his fists and kicking out wildly in all directions. 'Give – me – back – my – disc!'

The toecap of one boot connected hard with Fred's shin, eliciting a bellow of pain. Fred's fist swung up and caught Nathaniel on the cheek; the next thing he knew he was lying in the muck of the alley floor, head spinning, watching Fred and Stanley disappear hurriedly along the alley with their carts bouncing and leaping behind them.

Fury overwhelmed his dizziness; it took control of his sense of caution. He struggled to his feet and set off unsteadily in pursuit.

He could not go fast. Night hung heavy in the alley; its walls were curtains of grey scarcely lighter than the inky nothingness out in front. Nathaniel felt his way step by fevered step, one hand brushing the bricks on his right, listening hard for the telltale squeaking and scraping of the handcarts up ahead. It seemed that Fred and Stanley had been forced to slow down too – the sounds of their progress never quite faded; he was able to guess their route at every junction.

Once again, his helplessness infuriated him. Curse the djinni! It was never there when he needed it! If he ever caught the thieves, they'd suffer such— Now where? He paused beside a tall, barred window, caked with grime. Distantly he made out the noise of handcart wheels banging hard on stone. The left fork. He set off down it.

A little later he became aware that the sound up ahead had changed. Muttered voices replaced the noise of movement. He went more cautiously now, pressing himself close to the wall, placing each footfall carefully to avoid splashing in the wet.

The alley drew to an end at a narrow, cobbled lane, fringed with mean little workshops, all derelict and boarded up. Shadows choked the doorways like cobwebs. A faint smell of sawdust hung in the air.

He saw the handcarts sitting in the middle of the lane. The pole with Stanley's light had been removed from its cart and could now be seen glowing faintly in a sheltered doorway. Within its wan halo, three figures talked quietly – Fred, Stanley and someone else: a slight figure, wearing black. Nathaniel could not make out his face.

Nathaniel hardly breathed: he strained to hear their words.

No good. He was too far away. He could not fight them now, but any scrap of information might be useful in the future. It was worth risking. He edged a little nearer.

Still no luck. He could tell only that Fred and Stanley were largely silent, that the other figure was holding court. He had a high voice, young and sharp.

A little closer . . .

On the next step his boot knocked against an empty wine bottle that had been placed against the wall. It teetered, clinked faintly against the bricks, righted itself. It didn't fall. But the clink was enough. The light in the doorway jerked; three faces turned towards him: Stanley's, Fred's and—

In the instant Nathaniel was allowed, he only caught a glimpse, but it imprinted itself indelibly upon his mind. A girl's face, pale and young, whipped round by straight, dark hair. Her eyes were wide, startled but not scared, fierce too. He heard her cry a command, saw Fred lunge forward, glimpsed something pale and shiny shoot towards him out of the darkness. Nathaniel ducked frantically and cracked the side of his head against the brickwork of the building. Bile rose to his throat; he saw lights before his eyes. He collapsed in the puddle at the base of the wall.

Neither fully unconscious nor awake, he lay motionless, eyes closed, body relaxed, dimly aware of his surroundings. Pattering footsteps came close, a metal scraping sounded, leather squeaked. He sensed a presence near him, something light brushing his face.

'You missed him. He's out, but alive.' A female voice.

'I can cut his throat for you, Kitty.' Fred speaking.

The pause that followed might have been of any duration;

Nathaniel could not tell. 'No . . . He's only a stupid kid. Let's go.'

Silence fell in the darkened alley. Long after his head stopped swimming, long after the water had soaked through his coat to chill his flesh, Nathaniel remained quite still. He dared not move.

Bartimaeus

34

I had been back for almost five hours when a weary scruffling sounded at the loose plank and my sad, bedraggled and extremely smelly master tumbled back into the library. Leaving a trail of what I hoped was mud in his wake, he limped his way like some giant land snail up the stairs to the first floor room, where he promptly collapsed against a wall. Out of a spirit of scientific curiosity, I lit a small Flame and inspected him closely. It's a good job I've had experience dealing with stygian implets and the like, because he wasn't a pretty sight. He seemed to have been taken bodily and rolled through a particularly pungent mire or stable yard, before being stirred head first into a vat of dirt and grass-cuttings. His hair stuck up like a porcupine's rump. His jeans were torn and bloodied at the knee. He had a large bruise on his cheek and a nasty cut above one ear. Best of all, though, his eyes were *furious*.

'Had a good evening, sir?' I said.

'A fire,' he snarled. 'Make me a fire. I'm freezing.'

This haughty master mode sounded a little out of place coming from something a jackal would have spurned, but I didn't object. I was finding it all too amusing. So I gathered sundry bits of wood, got a reviving fire going, then settled down (in Ptolemy's form) as close as I could stomach.

'Well,' I said cheerily, 'this makes a pleasant change. Usually it's the djinni who comes in worn out and covered in muck. I approve of such innovations. What made you leave the library? Did Lovelace's forces find you? Did Jabor break in?'

He spoke slowly through clenched teeth. 'I went to get a newspaper.'

This was getting better and better! I shook my head regretfully. 'You should leave such a dangerous assignment to people better qualified: next time ask an old granny, or a toddler—'

'Shut up!' His eyes blazed. 'It was that paperboy! And his friend Fred! Two *commoners*! They stole my disc – the one I made – and lured me away from here. I followed them and they tried to kill me; would have done it too, if it wasn't for the girl—'

'A girl? What girl?'

'– but even so I smashed my head open and fell in a puddle, and then, when they'd gone, I couldn't find the way back and it was after curfew and the search spheres were out and I had to keep hiding as they passed. In the end, I found a stream under a bridge and lay there in the mud for ages while the lights patrolled up and down the road above. And *then*, when they'd gone, I *still* had to find my way back. It took me hours! *And* I hurt my knee.'

Well, it wasn't exactly Shakespeare, but it was the best

bedtime story *I'd* heard in a long time. It quite cheered me up.

'They're part of the Resistance,' he went on, staring into the fire. 'I'm sure of it. They're going to sell my disc – give it to the same people who attacked Parliament! Ahh!' He clenched his fists. 'Why weren't you there to help me? I could have caught them – forced them to tell me about their leader.'

'If you recall,' I remarked coldly, 'I was off on a mission *you* gave me. Who was this girl you mentioned?'

'I don't know. I only saw her for a second. She was in charge of them. One day, though, I'll find her and make her pay!'

'I thought you said she stopped them killing you?'

'She still took my disc! She's a thief and a traitor.'

Whatever else the girl was, she sounded very familiar. A thought struck me. 'How did they know you had the disc? Did you show it to them?'

'No. Do you think I'm stupid?'

'That's beside the point. Are you sure you didn't bring it out when you were fumbling for change?'

'*No.* The paperboy just *knew*, somehow. Like he was a djinni or imp.'

'Interesting . . .' It sounded exactly like the same bunch who jumped me the night I had the Amulet of Samarkand. My girl and her cronies hadn't needed to see the Amulet to *know* I had it on me, either. And they'd later found me hidden behind my Concealment spell. Useful abilities . . . which were evidently being put to good use. If they were part of this 'Resistance' movement, it sounded like opposition to the magicians was more developed – and potentially formidable – than I'd thought. Times were moving on in London . . .

I didn't share these thoughts with the boy. He was the enemy, after all, and the last thing magicians need are any clever insights. 'Leaving your misfortunes to one side for a moment,' I said, 'perhaps you wish to hear my report?'

He grunted. 'You found Heddleham Hall?'

'I did – and if you choose I can get you there. Beside the Thames is a railway heading south, over the river and out of London. But first I should tell you about the defences Lovelace has rigged up around his girlfriend's house. They are formidable. Airborne foliots patrol the surrounding country-side, while higher-ranking entities materialize at random on the ground. There are at least two protective domes over the estate itself, which also change position. I was unable to get beyond the boundary on my foray, and it will be even harder to succeed with a deadbeat like you in tow.'

He didn't rise to the bait. He was too tired. 'However,' I continued, 'I can feel in my essence that they are hiding some-thing at the Hall. These defences are in place two days too early, which involves a colossal expenditure of power. That implies mischief going on.'

'How long will it take to get there?'

'We can reach the edge of the estate by nightfall – if we catch an early morning train. There's a long walk at the other end. But we'll need to get going now.'

'Very well.' He began to get up, squelching and oozing as he did so.

'Are you *sure* about this plan?' I said. 'I could take you to the docks instead. There's bound to be vacancies for cabin boys there. It's a hard life, but a good one. Think of all that salty air.'

There was no answer. He was on his way out. I gave a sigh, snuffed out the fire and followed him.

The route I selected was a strip of wasteland that ran south and east between the factories and warehouses, following a narrow tributary of the Thames. Although the stream itself was meagre, it meandered excessively across its mini flood plain, creating a maze of hummocks, marshes and little pools that took us the rest of the night to negotiate. Our shoes sank into mud and water, sharp reeds spiked our legs and hands, and insects whined occasionally about our heads. The boy, by contrast, whined pretty much continually. After his adventures with the Resistance, he was in a very bad temper.

'It's worse for me than it is for you,' I snapped, after a particularly petulant outburst. 'I could have flown this in five minutes, but oh, no – I have to keep you company. Writhing about in mud and slime is *your* birthright, human, not mine.'

'I can't see where I'm putting my feet,' he said. 'Create some light, can't you?'

'Yes, if you want to attract the attention of night-flying djinn. The streets are well watched – as you've already discovered – and don't forget Lovelace may still be seeking us too. The only reason I've chosen this way is *because* it's so dark and unpleasant.'

He did not seem greatly comforted by this; nevertheless, his protests ceased.[1]

As we stumbled on, I considered our situation with my usual impeccable logic. It had been six days since the

---

[1] One side benefit of this route was that its difficulties eventually took his mind off the loss of his precious scrying glass. Honestly, the way he went on about it, you'd think that imp was his blood brother, rather than a vulgar baby-impersonator trapped against its will. He did seem to have taken his misfortune personally. But after the loss of his beloved Mrs Underwood, I suppose the disc was his only friend in the world, poor thing.

kid had summoned me. Six days of discomfort building up inside my essence. And no immediate end in sight.

The kid. Where did he rate in my list of all-time human lows? He wasn't the worst master I had endured,[2] but he presented some peculiar problems of his own. All sensible magicians, well versed in clever cruelty, know when the time is right to fight. They risk themselves (and their servants) comparatively rarely. But the kid hadn't a clue. He had been overwhelmed by a disaster brought about by his own meddling, and his reaction was to lunge back at his enemy like a wounded snake. Whatever his original grudge against Lovelace, his previous discretion had now been replaced by a desperation powered by grief. Simple things like self-preservation were disregarded in his pride and fury. He was going to his death. Which would have been fine, except he was taking me along for the ride.

I had no solution to this. I was bound to my master. All I could do was try to keep him alive.

By dawn, we had followed the waste strip down from north London almost to the Thames. Here the stream widened briefly before sluicing over a series of weirs into the main river. It was time to rejoin the roads. We climbed a bank to a wire fence (in which I burned a discreet hole), stepped through it and came out on a cobbled street. The political heart of the city was on our right, the Tower district on our left; the Thames stretched ahead. Curfew was safely over, but there was no one yet about.

---

[2] A 'good master' is a contradiction in terms, of course. Even Solomon would have been insufferable – he was so prissy in his early years – but fortunately he could command 20,000 spirits with one twist of his magic ring, so with him I got plenty of days off.

'Right,' I said, halting. 'The station is close by. Before we go there, we need to solve a problem.'

'Which is?'

'To stop you looking – and smelling – like a swineherd.' The various fluids of the wasteland adhered to him in a complex splatter-pattern. He could have been framed and hung up on a fashionable wall.

He frowned. 'Yes. Clean me up first. There must be a way.'

'There is.'

Perhaps I shouldn't have seized him and dunked him in the river. The Thames isn't that much cleaner than the quagmire we'd waded through. Still, it washed off the worst of the clag. After a minute of vigorous dousing, I allowed him to come up, water spouting through his nostrils. He made a gurgling sound that was hard to identify. I had a stab, though.

'Again? You *are* thorough.'

Another good rinsing made him look as good as new. I propped him up in the shadows of a concrete embankment and dried his clothes out with discreet use of a Flame. Oddly, his temper had not improved with his smell, but you can't have everything.

With this matter resolved, we set off and arrived at the railway station in time to catch the first train of the morning south. I stole two tickets from the kiosk, and while sundry attendants were busy combing the platforms for a red-faced clergywoman with a plausible manner, settled back into my seat just as the train got under way. Nathaniel sat in a different part of the carriage – rather pointedly, I thought. His improvised makeover still seemed to rankle with him.

The first part of the journey out of the city was thus the quietest and least troublesome half-hour I had enjoyed since first being summoned. The train pottered along at an arthritic pace through the never-ending outskirts of London, a dispiriting jumbled wilderness of brick that looked like moraine left by a giant glacier. We passed a succession of rundown factories and concrete lots run to waste; beyond them stretched narrow terraced streets, with chimney smoke rising here and there. Once, high up against the bright, colourless cloud that hid the sun, I saw a troop of djinn heading west. Even at that distance, it was possible to pick out the light glinting on their breastplates.

Few people got on or off the train. I relaxed. Djinn don't doze, but I did the equivalent, drifting back through the centuries and contemplating some of my happier moments – magicians' errors, my choice acts of revenge . . .

This reverie was finally shattered by the boy throwing himself down on the seat opposite. 'I suppose we'd better plan something,' he said sulkily. 'How can we get through the defences?'

'With randomly shifting domes *and* sentries in place,' I said, 'there's no way we can break in unmolested. We'll need some kind of Trojan Horse.' He looked blank. 'You know – something which seems innocent, which they allow in past the gates. In which we're hiding. Honestly – what *do* they teach you magicians nowadays?'[3]

'So, we need to conceal ourselves in something,' he grunted. 'Any ideas?'

'Nope.'

---

[3] Obviously not classical history. This ignorance would have upset Faquarl, as it happens, who often boasted how he'd given Odysseus the idea for the Wooden Horse in the first place. I'm sure he was lying, but I can't prove it because I wasn't at Troy: I was in Egypt at the time.

Scowling, he mulled it over. You could almost hear the fleshy innards of his brain straining. 'The guests will arrive tomorrow,' he mused. 'They have to let *them* in, so there's bound to be a steady stream of traffic getting through the gates. Perhaps we can hitch a ride in someone's car.'

'Perhaps,' I said. 'But all the magicians will be cloaked to the eyeballs with protective Shields and bug-eyed imps. We'd be hard pushed to sneak anywhere near them without being spotted.'

'What about servants?' he said. 'They must get in somehow.'

Give him credit – he'd had an idea. 'Most of them will be on site already,' I said, 'but you're right – some may arrive on the day. Also there are bound to be deliveries of fresh food; and maybe entertainers will come, musicians or jugglers—'

He looked scornful. '*Jugglers?*'

'Who's got more experience of magicians – you or me? There are *always* jugglers.[4] But the point is that there will be some non-magical outsiders entering the manor. So if we get ourselves into position early enough, we might well get a chance to sneak a ride with someone. It's worth a try. Now . . . in the meantime, you should sleep. There's a long walk ahead of us when we get to the station.'

His eyelids looked as if they were made of lead. For once he didn't argue.

I've seen glaciers cover ground more quickly than that train,

---

[4] They've got the worst taste in the world, magicians. Always have done. Oh, they keep themselves all suave and sober in public, but give them a chance to relax and do they listen to chamber orchestras? No. They'd rather have a dwarf on stilts or a belly-dancing bearded lady any day. A little-known fact about Solomon the Wise: he was entertained between judgements by a enthusiastic troupe of Lebanese girners.

so in the end he got a pretty decent kip. But finally we arrived at the station closest to Heddleham Hall. I shook my master awake and we tumbled out of the carriage onto a platform that was being speedily reclaimed by the forces of nature. Several varieties of grass grew up through the concrete, while an enterprising bindweed had colonized the walls and roof of the ramshackle waiting room. Birds nested under the rusty lamps. There was no ticket office and no sign of human life.

The train limped off as if it was going to die under a hedge. Across the track a white gate led straight onto an unmetalled road. Fields stretched away on all sides. I perked up: it felt good to be free of the city's malignant clutches and surrounded by the natural contours of the trees and crops.[5]

'We follow the road,' I said. 'The Hall is at least nine miles away, so we don't have to be on our guard yet. I— What's the matter now?'

The boy was looking quite pale and unsettled. 'It's nothing. Just . . . I'm not used to so much . . . *space*. I can't see any houses.'

'No houses is good. It means no people. No magicians.'

'It makes me feel strange. It's so quiet.'

Made sense. He'd never been out of the city before now. Never even been in a big park, most likely. The emptiness terrified him.

---

[5] Even though they have been scraped and shaped by human will, fields do not have magicians' stench about them. Throughout history, magicians have been resolutely urban creatures: they flourish in cities, multiplying like plague rats, running along thickly spun threads of gossip and intrigue like fat-bellied spiders. The nearest non-urban societies get to magicians – the shamans of North America and the Asian steppes – operate so differently that they almost deserve not to be called magicians at all. But their time is past.

I crossed the track and opened the gate. 'There's a village beyond those trees. You can get food there and cuddle up to some buildings.'

It took my master some time to lose his jitters. It was almost as if he expected the empty fields or winter bushes to rise like enemies and fall on him, and his head turned constantly against surprise attack. He quaked at every bird call.

Conversely, *I* stayed relaxed for this first part of the journey, precisely *because* the countryside seemed wholly deserted. There was no magical activity of any description, even in the distant skies.

When we reached the village, we raided its solitary grocery store and pinched sufficient supplies to keep the boy's stomach happy for the rest of the day. It was a smallish place, a few cottages clustered around a ruined church, not nearly large enough to have its own resident magician. The few humans we saw ambled around quietly without so much as an imp in tow. My master was very dismissive of them.

'Don't they realize how vulnerable they are?' he sniffed, as we passed the final cottage. 'They've got no defences. Any magical attack and they'd be helpless.'

'Perhaps that's not high on their list of priorities,' I suggested. 'There are other things to worry about: making a living, for example. Not that you'll have been taught anything about that.'[6]

---

[6] How true this was. Magicians are essentially parasitic. In societies where they are dominant, they live well off the strivings of others. In those times and places when they lose power and have to earn their own bread, they are generally reduced to a sorry state, performing small conjurations for jeering ale-house crowds in return for a few brass coins.

'Oh no?' he said. 'To be a magician is the greatest calling. Our skills and sacrifices hold the country together, and those fools should be grateful we're there.'

'Grateful for people like Lovelace, you mean?'

He frowned at this, but did not answer.

It was mid-afternoon before we ran into danger. The first thing my master knew about it was me throwing myself upon him and bundling us into a shallow ditch beside the road. I pressed him low against the earth, a little harder than necessary.

He had a mouthful of mud. 'Whop you doing?'

'Keep your voice down. A patrol's flying up ahead. North–south.'

I indicated a gap in the hedge. A small flock of starlings could be seen drifting far off across the clouds.

He spat his mouth empty. 'I can't make them out.'

'On planes five onwards they're foliots.[7] Trust me. We have to go carefully from now on.'

The starlings vanished to the south. Cautiously, I got to my feet and scanned the horizon. A little way ahead a straggling band of trees marked the beginning of an area of woodland. 'We'd better get off the road,' I said. 'It's too exposed here. After nightfall we can get closer to the house.' With infinite caution, we squeezed through a gap in the hedge and, after rounding the perimeter of the field beyond, gained the relative safety of the trees. Nothing threatened on any plane.

The wood was negotiated without incident; soon afterwards, we crouched on its far fringes, surveying the land

---

[7] A variety with five eyes: two on the head, one on either flank, and one – well, let's just say it would be hard to creep up on him unawares while he was touching his toes.

ahead. Before us, the ground fell away slightly, and we had a clear view over the autumn fields, heavily ploughed and purple-brown.

About a mile distant, the fields ran themselves out against an old brick boundary wall, much weathered and tumbledown. This, and a low, dark bunching of pine trees behind it, marked the edge of the Heddleham estate. A red dome was visible (on the fifth plane) soaring up from the pines. As I watched, it disappeared; a moment later another, bluish, dome material-ized on the sixth plane, somewhat further off.

Hunched within the trees was the suggestion of a tall arch – perhaps the official entrance to the manor's grounds. From this arch a road extended, straight as a javelin thrust between the fields, until it reached a crossroads next to a clump of oak trees, half a mile from where we stood. The lane that we had recently been following also terminated at this crossroads. Two other routes led away from it elsewhere.

The sun had not quite disappeared behind the trees and the boy squinted against its glare. 'Is that a sentry?' He pointed to a distant stump halfway to the crossroads. Something unclear rested upon it: perhaps a motionless, black figure.

'Yes,' I said. 'Another's just materialized at the edge of that triangular field.'

'Oh! The first one's gone.'

'I told you – they're randomly materializing. We can't predict where they'll appear. Do you see that dome?'

'No.'

'Your lenses are worse than useless.'

The boy cursed. 'What do you expect? I don't have your sight, demon. Where is it?'

'Coarse language will get you nowhere. I'm not telling.'

'Don't be ridiculous! I need to know.'

'This demon's not saying.'

'*Where is it?*'

'Careful where you stamp your feet. You've trodden in something.'

'Just tell me!'

'I've been meaning to mention this for some time. I don't like being called a demon. Got that?'

He took a deep breath. 'Fine.'

'Just so you know.'

'All right.'

'I'm a djinni.'

'Yes, *all right*. Where's the dome?'

'It's in the wood. On the sixth plane now, but it'll shift position soon.'

'They've made it difficult for us.'

'Yes. That's what defences do.'

His face was grey with weariness, but still set and determined. 'Well, the objective's clear. The gateway is bound to mark the official entrance to the estate – the only hole in the protective domes. That's where they'll check people's identities and passes. If we can get beyond it, we'll have got inside.'

'Ready to be trussed up and killed,' I said. 'Hurrah.'

'The question,' he continued, 'is how we get in . . .'

He sat for a long time, shading his eyes with his hand, watching as the sun sank behind the trees and the fields were swathed in cold green shadow. At irregular intervals, sentries came and went without trace (we were too far away to smell the sulphur).

A distant sound drew our attention back to the roads. Along the one that led to the horizon, something that from a mile away looked like a black matchbox came roaring: a magician's car, speeding between the hedges, honking its horn imperiously at every corner. It reached the crossroads, slowed to a halt and – safely assured that nothing was coming – turned right along the road to Heddleham. As it approached the gateway, two of the sentries bounded towards it at great speed across the darkened fields, robes fluttering behind them like tattered rags. Once they reached the hedges bordering the road they went no closer, but kept pace beside the car, which presently drew near to the gateway in the trees. The shadows here were very thick and it was hard to glimpse what happened. The car pulled up in front of the gate. Something approached it. The sentries hung back at the lip of the trees. Presently, the car proceeded on its way, through the arch and out of sight. Its drone faded on the evening air. The sentries flitted back into the fields.

The boy sat back and stretched his arms. 'Well,' he said, 'that tells us what we need to do.'

35

The crossroads was the place for the ambush. Any vehicles approaching it had to slow down for fear of accident, and it was concealed from the distant Heddleham gateway by a thick clump of oaks and laurel. This also promised good cover for lurking.

Accordingly, we made our way there that night. The boy crawled along the base of the hedges beside the road. I flitted in front of him in the guise of a bat.

No sentries materialized beside us. No watchers flew overhead. The boy reached the crossroads and burrowed into the undergrowth below the biggest oak tree. I hung from a bough, keeping watch.

My master slept, or tried to. I observed the rhythms of the night: the fleeting movements of owl and rodent, the scruffles of foraging hedgehogs, the prowling of the restive djinn. In the hours before dawn, the cloud cover drifted away and the stars shone down. I wondered whether Lovelace was reading their import from the roof of the hall, and what they told him. The night grew chill. Frost sparkled across the fields.

All at once, it struck me that my master would be suffering greatly from the cold.

A pleasant hour passed. Then another thought struck me. He might actually freeze to death in his hiding place. That would be no good: I'd never escape the tin. Reluctantly, I spiralled down into the bushes and went in search of him.

To my grudging relief, he was still alive, if somewhat blue

in the face. He was huddled in his coat under a pile of leaves, which rustled perpetually with his shivering.

'Want some heat?' I whispered.

His head moved a little. It was hard to tell whether it was a shiver or a shake.

'No?'

'No.'

'Why?'

His jaw was clamped so tight it could barely unlock. 'It might draw them to us.'

'Sure it isn't pride? Not wanting help from a nasty demon? You'd better be careful with all this frost about – bits might drop off. I've seen it happen.'[1]

'L-leave me.'

'Suit yourself.' I returned to my tree. Some while later, as the eastern sky began to lighten, I heard him sneeze, but otherwise he remained stubbornly silent, locked into his self-appointed discomfort.

With the arrival of dawn, hanging about as a bat became a less convincing occupation. I took myself off under the bushes and changed into a fieldmouse. The boy was where I had left him, stiff as a board and rather dribbly about the nose. I perched on a twig nearby.

'How about a handkerchief, o my master?' I said.

With some difficulty, he raised an arm and wiped his nose on his sleeve. He sniffed. 'Has anything happened yet?'

'Still a bit under your left nostril. Otherwise clean.'

'I meant on the road.'

---

[1] Very, very nasty it was. Remind me to tell you about it some day.

'No. Too early. If you've got any food left, you should eat it now. We need to be all set when the first car comes by.'

As it transpired, we needn't have hurried. All four roads remained still and silent. The boy ate the last of his food, then crouched in the soaking grass under a bush, watching one of the lanes. He appeared to have caught a slight chill, and shivered uncontrollably inside his coat. I scurried back and forth, keeping an eye out for trouble, but finally returned to his side.

'Remember,' I said, 'the car mustn't be seen to stop for more than a few seconds, or one of the sentries might smell a rat. We've got to get on board as soon as it reaches the crossroads. You'll have to move fast.'

'I'll be ready.'

'I mean *really* fast.'

'I'll be *ready*, I said.'

'Yes, well. I've seen slugs cover ground more quickly than you. And you've made yourself ill by refusing my help last night.'

'I'm not ill.'

'Sorry, didn't catch that. Your teeth were chattering too loudly.'

'I'll be fine. Now leave me alone.'

'This cold of yours could let us down big time if we get in the house. Lovelace might follow the trail of sn— Listen!'

'What?'

'A car! Coming from behind us. Perfect. It'll slow right here. Wait for my order.'

I scampered through the long grasses to the other side of the copse and waited behind a large stone on the dirt bank above the road. The noise of the oncoming vehicle grew loud.

I scanned the sky – no watchers could be seen, and the trees hid the road from the direction of the house. I readied myself to spring . . .

Then hunched down behind the stone. No good. A black and shiny limousine: a magician's car. Too risky to try. It flashed past in a welter of dust and pebbles; all skirling brakes and shining bonnet. I caught a glimpse of its occupant: a man I did not know, broad-lipped, pasty, with slicked back hair. There was no sign of an imp or other guardian, but that meant nothing. There was no point ambushing a magician.

I returned to the boy, still motionless under the bush. 'No go,' I said. 'Magician.'

'I've got eyes.' He sniffed messily. 'I know him, too. That's Lime, one of Lovelace's cronies. Don't know why he's in on the plot; he's not very powerful. I once stung him with some mites. Swelled up like a balloon.'

'Did you?' I confess I was impressed. 'What happened?'

He shrugged. 'They beat me. Is that someone coming?'

A bicycle had appeared round the bend in front of us. Upon it was a short, fat man, his legs whirring round like helicopter blades. Above the bicycle's front wheel was an enormous basket, covered with a weighted white cloth. 'Butcher,' I said.

The boy shrugged. 'Maybe. Do we get him?'

'Could you wear his clothes?'

'No.'

'Then we let him pass. There'll be other options.'

Red-faced and perspiring freely, the cyclist arrived at the crossroads, skidded to a halt, wiped his brow and proceeded on towards the Hall. We watched him go, the boy's eyes mainly on the basket.

'We should have taken him out,' he said wistfully. 'I'm starving.'

Time passed and the bicycling butcher returned. He whistled as he pedalled, making light of his journey. His basket was now empty, but no doubt his wallet had been nicely filled. Beyond the hedge, one of the sentries trailed in his wake with great loping bounds, its body and tattered robes almost translucent in the sunlight.

The butcher freewheeled into the distance. The boy suppressed a sneeze. The sentry drifted away. I scuttled up a thorn stem that ran through the bush and peered out at the top. The skies were clear; the winter sun bathed the fields with unseasonable warmth. The roads were empty.

Twice more during the next hour, vehicles approached the crossroads. The first was a florist's van, driven by a slatternly woman smoking a cigarette. I was about to pounce on her, when out of the corner of my mouse's eye I spied a trio of blackbird sentries sailing lazily over the copse at low altitude. Their beady eyes flicked hither and thither. No chance: they would have seen everything. I hid and let the woman drive on her way.

The blackbirds flew off, but the next passer-by served me no better: an open-top magician's car, this time coming *from* the direction of the Hall. The driver's face was mostly obscured under a cap and a pair of driving goggles: I only caught a flash of reddish beard, short and clipped, as he shot by.

'Who's that?' I asked. 'Another accomplice?'

'Never seen him before. Maybe he was the one who drove in last night.'

'He's not sticking around, whoever he is.'

The boy's frustration was getting to him. He beat a fist against the grass. 'If we don't get in soon, all the other guests will start arriving. We need time in there to find out what's going on. Ahh! If I only had more power!'

'The eternal cry of all magicians,' I said wearily. 'Have patience.'

He looked up at me savagely. 'You need *time* to have patience,' he snarled. 'We *have* no time.'

But in fact it was only twenty minutes later that we got our chance.

Once again the sound of a car; once again I crossed to the other side of the copse and took a look from the top of the bank. Immediately I did so, I knew the time had come. It was a dark-green grocer's van, tall and squared, with smart black mudguards and a newly washed look. On its side, in proud black lettering, were painted the words: SQUALLS AND SON, GROCERS OF CROYDON, TASTY COMESTIBLES FOR SOCIETY — and to my great delight, it appeared as if Squalls and Son themselves were sitting in the cab. An elderly man with a bald head was at the wheel. At his side sat a chipper youth wearing a green cap. Both looked eager and well spruced up for their big day; the old man's head seemed to have been buffed until it shone.

The fieldmouse flexed its muscles behind its ambush stone.

The van drew closer, its engine rattling and growling under the bonnet. I checked the skies — no blackbirds or other dangers. All clear.

The van drew abreast of the copse, out of sight of the distant Heddleham gateway.

Both Squalls and Son had wound down their windows to catch the pleasant air. Son was humming a happy tune.

Midway past the copse, Son caught a slight rustling noise from outside the cab. He glanced to his right.

And saw a fieldmouse whistling through the air in a karate

attack position, claws out, hind legs foremost – right at him.

The mouse plopped straight through the open window. Neither Squalls nor Son had time to react. There was a whirl of inexplicable movements from within the cab; it rocked violently to and fro. The van swerved gently and ran up against the dirt bank at the side of the road, where its wheel skidded and slipped. The engine petered and cut out.

A moment's silence. The passenger door opened. A man who looked very like Squalls hopped out, reached back in and drew out the unconscious bodies of Squalls and Son. Son had lost the majority of his clothes.

It was the matter of a moment to drag the pair across the road, up the bank and into the depths of the copse. I hid them there under a bramble thicket and returned to the van.[2]

This was the worst bit for me. Djinn and vehicles just don't mix; it's an alien sensation to be trapped in a tin shroud, surrounded by the smells of petrol, oil and artificial leather, by the stench of people and their creations. It reminds you how weak and shoddy it must feel to be a human, requiring such decrepit devices to travel far.

Besides, I didn't really know how to drive.[3]

---

[2] Faquarl would have argued that it was more expedient simply to devour them, while Jabor wouldn't have argued at all, but just done it. But I find that human flesh makes my essence ache. It's like eating bad seafood – too much accumulated grime per mouthful.

[3] To date the only experience I'd had of driving had been during the Great War, when the British army had been camped thirty miles outside Prague. A Czech magician, who shall remain nameless, charged me to steal certain documents. They were well guarded and I was forced to pass the enemy djinn by driving a staff ambulance into the British camp. My driving was very bad, but at least it enabled me to complete my disguise (by filling the ambulance with each soldier I knocked down en route). When I entered the camp, the men were rushed off to hospital, while I slipped away to steal the plans of campaign.

Nevertheless, I got the engine started again and managed to reverse away from the bank into the middle of the road. Then onwards to the crossroads. All this had taken scarcely a minute, but I admit I was anxious: a sharp-eyed sentry might well wonder why the van was taking so long to clear the trees. At the crossroads I slowed, took a hasty look around and leaned towards the passenger window.

'Quick! Get in!'

A nearby bush rustled frantically, there was a wrenching at the cab door and the boy was inside, breathing like a bull elephant. The door slammed shut; an instant later, we were on our way, turning right along the Heddleham road.

'It's you, is it?' he panted, staring at me.

'Of course. Now get changed, quick as you can. The sentries will be on us in moments.'

He scrabbled around on the seat, ripping off his coat and reaching for Son's discarded shirt, green jacket and trousers. How smart this outfit had been five minutes before; now it was all crumpled.

'Hurry up! They're coming.'

Across the fields from both sides, the sentries approached, hopping and bounding, black rags flapping. The boy pawed at his shirt.

'The buttons are so tight! I can't undo them!'

'Pull it over your head!'

The sentry to my left was approaching fastest. I could see its eyes – two black ovals with pinpricks of light at their cores. I tried to accelerate, pressed the wrong pedal; the van juddered and nearly stopped. The boy's head was halfway through the shirt collar at the time. He fell forward against the dashboard.

'Ow! You did that on purpose!'

I pressed the correct pedal. We speeded up once more. 'Get that jacket on, or we're done. And the cap.'

'What about the trousers?'

'Forget them. No time.'

The boy had the jacket on and was just jamming the cap down on his tousled head when the two sentries drew along-side. They remained on the other side of the hedges, surveying us with their shining eyes.

'Remember – we shouldn't be able to see them,' I said. 'Keep looking straight ahead.'

'I am.' A thought struck him. 'Won't they realize what you are?'

'They're not powerful enough.' I devoutly hoped that this was true. I thought they were ghuls,[4] but you can never be sure these days.[5]

For a time, we drove along the road towards the bank of trees. Both of us looked straight ahead. The sentries kept pace beside the van.

Presently, the boy spoke again. 'What am I going to do about the trousers?'

'Nothing. You'll have to make do with what you've got. We'll be at the gate soon. Your top half's smart enough, anyway.'

---

[4] *Ghuls*: lesser djinn of an unsavoury cast, keen on the taste of humans. Hence efficient (if frustrated) sentries. They can only see onto five planes. I was Squalls on all but the seventh.

[5] Everything seems to aspire to be something better than it is. Mites aspire to be moulers, moulers aspire to be foliots, foliots aspire to be djinn. Some djinn aspire to be afrits or even marids. In each case it's hopeless. It is impossible to alter the limitations of one's essence. But that doesn't stop many entities waltzing around in the guise of something more powerful than they are. Of course, when you're pretty darn perfect to start with, you don't want to change anything.

'But—'

'Smooth down your jacket, get rid of any wrinkles you can see. It'll have to do. Right – I'm Squalls and you're my son. We're delivering groceries to Heddleham Hall, fresh for conference day. Which reminds me, we'd better check what it is we're actually bringing. Can you have a look?'

'But—'

'Don't worry, there's nothing odd about you peering in the back.' Between us, in the rear wall of the cab, was a metal hatch. I gestured at it. 'Have a quick peek. I would, but I'm driving.'

'Very well.' He kneeled on the seat and, opening the hatch, stuck his head through.

'It's quite dark . . . there's lots of stuff in here . . .'

'Can you make anything out?' I took a glance at him and nearly lost control of the wheel. The van swerved wildly towards the hedge; I righted it just in time.

'Your trousers! Sit back down! Where are your trousers?'

He sat back in his seat. The view to my left improved markedly. 'I took my ones off, didn't I? You told me not to put the new ones on.'

'I didn't realize you'd ditched the others! Put them on.'

'But the sentry will see—'

'The sentry's already seen, believe you me. Just put them on.'

As he fumbled with his shoes against the dashboard, I shook my shiny head. 'We'll just have to hope ghuls aren't too clever when it comes to the etiquette of human attire. Maybe they'll think it normal for you to be changing costume now. But the guards at the gate will be more perceptive, you can be sure of that.'

We were nearly at the boundary of the estate. Trees spanned the view through the windscreen. The road ahead curved into them in leisurely fashion; almost immediately the great arch came in sight. Constructed from massive blocks of yellow sandstone, it rose from the bushes at the roadside with the portentous solidity of a hundred thousand similar arches across the world.[6] What particular lordling had paid for this one, and why he had done so, I doubted anyone knew. The faces on the caryatids that held up the roof were worn away, the detail on the inscriptions likewise. Eventually, the ivy that clung to it all would destroy the stonework too.

Above and around the arch, the red dome soared into the sky and extended into the woods. Only through the arch was the way clear.

Our accompanying sentries were looking ahead expectantly.

A few metres from the arch I slowed the van to a halt, but kept the engine on. It thrummed gently. We sat in the cab waiting.

A wooden door opened in one side of the arch and a man came striding out. At my side, the boy gave a slight shiver. I glanced at him. Pale as he was, he'd just gone paler. His eyes were round as dinner plates.

'What is it?' I hissed.

'It's *him* . . . the one I saw in the disc, the one who brought the Amulet to Lovelace.'

There was no time to answer, no time to act. Strolling casually, smiling a little smile, the murderer approached the van.

---

[6] All built to celebrate one insignificant tribe's victory over another. From Rome to Beijing, Timbuktu to London, triumphal arches crop up wherever there are cities, heavy with the weight of earth and death. I've never seen one I liked.

36

So here he was – the man who had stolen the Amulet of Samarkand and vanished without a trace, the man who had cut its keeper's throat and left him lying in his blood. Lovelace's hireling.

For a human, he was sizeable, a head taller than most men and broad with it. He wore a long buttoned jacket of dark cloth and wide trousers in the eastern style that were loosely tucked into high leather boots. His beard was jet-black, his nose broad, his eyes a piercing blue beneath his heavy brows. For a big man, he moved gracefully, one hand swinging easily at his side, the other tucked into his belt.

The mercenary walked around the bonnet towards my side window, his eyes on us all the while. As he drew close, he looked away and waved dismissively; I glimpsed our escort ghuls vanishing back towards the fields.

I stuck my head part-way out of the window. 'Good morning,' I said cheerily, in what I hoped was a suitable London accent. 'Ernest Squalls and Son, with a delivery of groceries for the Hall.'

The man stopped and considered us silently for a moment.

'Squalls and Son . . .' The voice was slow, deep; the blue eyes seemed to look through me as he spoke. It was a disconcerting effect; at my side, the boy gave an involuntary gulp; I hoped he wasn't going to panic. 'Squalls and Son . . . Yes, you are expected.'

'Yes, guv'nor.'

'What have you brought?'

'Groceries, guv'nor.'

'Namely?'

'Um . . .' I hadn't a clue. 'All sorts, guv'nor. Would you like to inspect them?'

'A list will suffice.'

Drat. 'Very well, guv. Um, we've got boxes, we've got tins – lots of tins, sir – packets of things, bottles—'

The eyes narrowed. 'You don't sound very specific.'

A high voice sounded at my elbow. Nathaniel leaned across me. 'He didn't take the list, sir. I did. We've got Baltic caviare, plovers' eggs, fresh asparagus flutes, cured Bolognese salami, Syrian olives, vanilla stalks from Middle America, newly pressed pasta, larks' tongues in aspic, giant land snails marinated in their shells, tubes of freshly ground black pepper and rock salt, Wirral oysters, ostrich meat—'

The mercenary held up a hand. 'Enough. *Now* I wish to inspect them.'

'Yes, guv'nor.' Glumly I got down from the cab and led the way to the back of the van, devoutly wishing that the boy hadn't let his imagination run away with him quite so much. What would happen when some completely different groceries were revealed I did not care to think. But it could not be helped now. With the mercenary looming impassively at my side, I opened the rear door and inched it open.

He surveyed the interior for a few moments. 'Very well. You may continue up to the house.'

Almost in disbelief I considered the contents of the van. A crate of bottles in one corner caught my eye: Syrian olives. Half hidden behind them, a small box of larks' tongues, sheets of wrapped pasta . . . I shut the door and returned to the cab.

'Any directions for us, guv'nor?'

The man rested a hand on the lip of my open window: the back of the hand was crisscrossed with thin white scars. 'Follow the drive until it splits, take the right fork to the rear of the house. Someone will meet you there. Carry out your business and return. Before you go, I shall give you a warning: you are now entering the private property of a great magician. Do not stray or trespass if you value your lives. The penalties are severe and would curdle your blood.'

'Yes, guv'nor.'

With a nod, he stepped back and signalled us to pass. I revved the engine and we passed slowly under the arch. Soon afterwards we crossed beneath the protective domes; both made my essence tingle. Then we were through, and following a sandy, curving driveway between the trees.

I regarded the boy. His face was impassive, but a single bead of sweat trickled down his temple. 'How did you know all the items?' I said. 'You only had a couple of seconds looking in the back.'

He gave a thin smile. 'I've been trained. I read fast and remember accurately. So, what did you think of him?'

'Lovelace's little assassin? Intriguing. He's not a djinni, and I don't think he's a magician either – he doesn't quite have your scent of corruption.[1] But we know he was able to seize the

---

[1] I wasn't being rude here. Well, all right, I *was*, but it was accurate abuse nevertheless. I may not be a search sphere imp (all nostrils, remember), but I've got an acute sense of smell, and can nearly always identify a magician, even when they're going incognito. All those years of hanging out in smoky rooms summoning powerful entities gives their skin a distinctive odour, in which incense and the sharp pang of fear feature prominently. If after that you're still unsure, the clincher is to look 'em in the eyes: usually you can see their lenses.

THE AMULET OF SAMARKAND

Amulet, so he must have some power . . . And he exudes great confidence. Did you notice how the ghuls obeyed him?'

The boy runkled his forehead. 'If he's not a magician or a demon, what sort of power *can* he have?'

'Don't deceive yourself,' I said darkly; 'there *are* other kinds.' I was thinking of the Resistance girl and her companions.

I was spared further questioning, as the driveway suddenly straightened and we broke out of the belt of trees. And up ahead we saw Heddleham Hall.

The boy gasped.

It didn't have quite the same effect on me. When you've helped construct several of the world's most majestic buildings, and in some instances given pretty useful tips to the architects concerned,[2] a second-rate Victorian mansion in the Gothic style doesn't exactly wet your whistle. You know the kind of thing: lots of twiddly bits and turrets.[3] It was surrounded by a wide expanse of lawn, on which peacocks and wallabies were decoratively scattered.[4] A couple of striped marquees had been erected on the lawns, to which sundry servants were already carting trays of bottles and wineglasses down from the terrace. In front of the house was a massive, ancient yew; under its spreading limbs the driveway split. The

---

[2] Not that my advice was always taken: check out the Leaning Tower of Pisa.

[3] Not a good enough description for you? Well, I was only trying to move the story on. Heddleham Hall was a great rectangular pile with stubby north/south wings, plenty of tall, arched windows, two storeys, high sloping gables, a surfeit of brick chimneys, ornate tracery that amounted to the Baroque, faux-battlements above the main door, high vaulted ceilings (heavily groined), sundry gargoyles (likewise) and all constructed from a creamy-brown stone that looked attractive in moderation but en masse made everything blur like a big block of melting fudge.

[4] *So* decoratively that I wondered if their feet had been glued in position.

left-hand fork swooped elegantly round to the front of the house; the right-hand fork trundled meekly round the back. As per our orders, we took the tradesmen's route.

My master was still drinking the whole sight in with a lustful look.

'Forget your pathetic daydreams,' I said. 'If you want to end up with one of these, you've got to survive today first. So – now we're inside, we need to formulate our plan. What exactly is it?'

The boy was focused again in an instant. 'From what Lovelace told us,' he said, 'we guess that he is going to attack the ministers in some way. How, we don't know. It'll happen once they've arrived, when they're most relaxed and unawares. The Amulet is vital to his scheme, whatever it is.'

'Yes. Agreed.' I tapped the steering wheel. 'But what about *our* plan?'

'We've got two objectives: to find the Amulet and to work out what trap Lovelace is preparing. Lovelace will probably have the Amulet on his person. In any event it'll be well guarded. It would be useful to locate it, but we don't want to take it from him until everyone's arrived. We've got to show them that he has it: prove he's a traitor. And if we can show them the trap too, so much the better. We'll have all the evidence we need.'

'You make it sound so simple.' I considered Faquarl, Jabor and all the other slaves Lovelace was likely to have to hand, and sighed. 'Well, first we need to ditch this van and these disguises.'

The driveway came to a sudden end at a circular area of gravel at the back of the house. The florist's van was parked there. A set of white double doors was open nearby, with a man dressed in a dark uniform standing outside. He indicated for us to pull over.

'All right,' the boy said. 'We unload the van and seize the first chance we get. Wait for my orders.'

'Hey, do I ever do anything else?' I managed to skid the van to a halt a few millimetres away from the ornamental shrubbery and got out. The flunky approached.

'Mr Squalls?'

'That's me, guv'nor. This here's . . . my son.'

'You're late. The cook has need of your items. Please bring them to the kitchen with all speed.'

'Yes, guv'nor.' An uneasy feeling ran through my essence and rippled the bristles on the back of my neck. The cook . . . No, it wouldn't be. He'd be elsewhere, surely. I opened the van door. 'Son – snap to it, or you'll feel the back of my hand!'

I took a certain bleak pleasure in loading the boy up with as many jars of Syrian olives and giant land snails as I could, then propelled him on his way. He staggered off under his load, not unlike Simpkin in Pinn's shop.[5] I selected a small tub of larks' tongues and followed him through the doors and into a cool, whitewashed passage. Various servants of every shape, sex and size were racing about like startled hares, engaged in a hundred tasks; everywhere there was a great clattering and hubbub. A scent of baked bread and roasting meats hung in the air, emanating from a wide arch that led on to the kitchen.

I peered through the arch. Dozens of white-clothed under-cooks, chopping, basting, rinsing, slicing . . . Something turned on the spit in the fireplace. Stacks of vegetables were piled

---

[5] Don't think I'd forgotten Simpkin. On the contrary. I have a long memory and a fertile imagination. I had plans for him.

high on tables, beside open pastry cases being filled with jellied fruits. It was a hive of activity. Orchestrating it all was a sizeable head chef, who at that moment was shouting at a small boy wearing a blue uniform.

The chef's sleeves were rolled up. He had a thick white bandage wrapped round one arm.

I flipped to the seventh plane.

And ducked back out of sight. I knew those tentacles far too well for there to be any doubt.

My master had entered the kitchen, placed his precarious load on a nearby work surface and was coming out again, none the wiser. As he rounded the door I thrust the larks' tongues into his hand.

'Take those too,' I hissed. 'I can't go in.'

'Why?'

'Just do it.'

He had the sense to obey, and quickly, for the servant in the dark uniform had reappeared in the corridor, and was observing us intently. We headed back out again for the next load.

'The head cook,' I whispered, as I pulled a crate of boar pâté to the back of the van, 'is the djinni Faquarl. Don't ask me why he likes that disguise, I've no idea. But I can't go in. He'll spot me instantly.'

The boy's eyes narrowed. 'How do I know you're telling the truth?'

'You'll just have to trust me on this one. There – you can manage another sack of ostrich steaks, can't you? Oops. Perhaps not.' I helped him to his feet. 'I'll unload the van; you take the stuff in. We both think what to do.'

During the course of several round trips for the boy, we thrashed out a plan of campaign. It took a fair bit of thrashing to reach agreement. He wanted us both to slip past the kitchen to explore the house, but I was extremely reluctant to go anywhere near Faquarl. *My* idea was to unload, ditch the van in the trees somewhere and creep back to start our investigations, but the kid would have none of this. 'It's all right for you,' he said. 'You can cross the lawns like a gust of poisonous wind or something; I can't – they'll catch me before I'm half way. Now that I'm at the house, I've got to go in.'

'But you're a grocer's boy. How will you explain that when you're seen?'

He smiled an unpleasant smile. 'Don't worry. I won't be a grocer's boy for long.'

'Well, it's too risky for me to pass the kitchen,' I said. 'I was lucky just now. Faquarl can usually sense me a mile off. It's no good; I'll have to find another way in.'

'I don't like it,' he said. 'How will we meet up?'

'I'll find you. Just don't get caught in the meantime.'

He shrugged. If he was terrified out of his wits, he was doing a good job of hiding it. I piled the last baskets of plovers' eggs into his hands and watched him waddle off into the house. Then I shut the van doors, left the keys on the driver's seat and considered the position. I soon abandoned my idea of disposing of the van in the trees: that was more likely to attract attention than just quietly leaving it here. No one was worrying about the florist's van, after all.

There were too many windows in the house. Something could be watching from any of them. I walked towards the door as if I were going inside, checking the planes en route: far off, a sentry patrol passed above the trees, just inside the innermost dome; that was OK – they'd see nothing. The house itself looked clear.

As I neared the door I stepped to one side, out of view from within, and changed. Mr Squalls became a small lizard that dropped to the ground, scuttled to the nearest patch of wall and ran up it, making for the first floor. My creamy-brown skin was ideally camouflaged against the stone. The minute bristles on my feet gave me an excellent grip. My swivel-eyes looked up, around, behind. All things considered, it was another perfect choice of form. Up the wall I ran, wondering how my master was getting on with his more cumbersome disguise.

Nathaniel

37

As he set the basket of eggs down on the nearest surface, Nathaniel looked around the kitchen for his intended victim. There were so many people bustling about that at first he could see no sign of the small boy with the dark-blue uniform, and he feared that he had already gone. But then, in the shadow of a large lady pastry chef, he saw him. He was transferring a mountain of bite-sized canapés to a two-storeyed silver platter.

It was clear that the boy planned to take this dish elsewhere in the house. Nathaniel intended to be there when he did.

He skulked around the kitchen, pretending to be emptying out his baskets and crates, biding his time, and growing ever more impatient as the boy painstakingly placed each cream-cheese-and-prawn pastry on the dish.

Something hard and heavy tapped him on the shoulder. He turned.

The head cook stood there, pink-faced and glistening from the heat of the roasting spit. Two bright black eyes looked down on him. The chef was holding a meat cleaver in his podgy hand; it was with the blunt edge of this that he had tapped Nathaniel.

'And what,' asked the chef, in a gentle voice, 'are you doing in my kitchen?'

Nothing about the man, on any of the planes to which Nathaniel had access, remotely suggested he was inhuman. Nevertheless, with Bartimaeus's warning in mind, he took no chances. 'Just collecting up a couple of my father's baskets,' he said politely. 'We don't have many, you see. I'm sorry if I've got in the way.'

The chef pointed his cleaver at the door. 'Leave.'

'Yes, sir. Just going.' But only as far as the passage directly outside the door, where Nathaniel propped himself against the wall and waited. Whenever someone came out of the kitchen, he ducked down as if he were doing up his shoes. It was an edgy business and he dreaded the appearance of the chef, but otherwise he felt a strange exhilaration. After the first shock of seeing the mercenary at the gate, his fear had fallen away and been replaced with a thrill he had rarely experienced before – the thrill of action. Whatever happened, there would be no more helpless standing by while his enemies acted with impunity. *He* was taking control of events now. *He* was doing the hunting. *He* was closing in.

Light, tripping footsteps. The pageboy appeared through the arch, balancing the double dish of canapés on his head. Steadying it with one hand, he turned right, heading up the passage. Nathaniel fell in alongside him.

'*Hello* there.' He spoke in an extra-friendly fashion; as he did so, he ran his eyes up and down the boy. Perfect. Just the right size.

The lad couldn't help but notice this interest. 'Er, do you want something?'

'Yes. Is there a cloakroom near here? I've had a long journey and . . . you know how it is.'

At the foot of a broad staircase, the boy halted. He pointed along a side passage. 'Down there.'

'Can you show me? I'm afraid of getting the wrong door.'

'I'm late as it is, pal.'

'*Please.*'

With a groan of reluctance, the boy turned aside and led Nathaniel along the corridor. He walked so fast that the dish on his head began to wobble precariously. He paused, straightened it, and continued on his way. Nathaniel followed behind, pausing only to draw from his uppermost basket the hefty rolling pin that he had stolen from the kitchen. At the fourth door, the boy stopped.

'There.'

'Are you sure it's the right one? I don't want to barge in on anyone.'

'I'm telling you it is. Look.' The boy kicked out with a foot. The door swung open. Nathaniel swung the rolling pin. Boy and silver platter went crashing forwards onto the washroom floor. They hit the tiles with a sound like a rifle-crack; a rainstorm of cream-cheese-and-prawn canapés fell all around. Nathaniel stepped in smartly after them and closed and locked the door.

The boy was out cold, so Nathaniel met no resistance when he took his clothes. He had infinitely more difficulty in gathering up the canapés, which had scattered and smeared themselves in every crack and cranny of the washroom. The cheese was soft and could often be shovelled back onto the pastry, but it was not always possible to resurrect the prawns.

When he had arranged the platters as best he could, he tore his grocer's shirt into strips and bound and gagged the boy. Then he pulled him into one of the cubicles, locked the door on the inside and clambered out over the top by balancing on the cistern.

With the evidence safely hidden, Nathaniel straightened his uniform in the mirror, balanced the platter upon his head and left the washroom. Reasoning that anything worth discovering was unlikely to be in the servants' quarters, he retraced his steps and set off up the staircase.

Various servants hurried past in both directions, carrying trays and crates of bottles, but no one challenged him.

At the top of the stairs, a door opened onto a hallway, lit by a row of high, arched windows. The flooring was polished marble, covered at intervals by richly woven carpets from Persia and the East. Alabaster busts, depicting great leaders of ages past, sat in special niches along the whitewashed walls. The whole effect, even in the weak winter sunlight, was one of dazzling brightness.

Nathaniel passed along the hall, keeping his eyes peeled.

Ahead he heard loud, laughing voices raised in greeting. He thought it wisest to avoid them. An open side door showed a flash of books. He stepped through—

— into a beautiful circular library, which rose through two full storeys to a glass dome in the roof. A spiral staircase wound up to a metal walkway circling the wall far above his head. On one side, great glass doors with windows above them looked out onto the lawns and a distant ornamental lake. Every other inch of wall was covered with books: large, expensive, ancient, collected from cities all over the world. Nathaniel's heart skipped a beat in wonder. One day he too would have a library like this . . .

'What do you think you're doing?' A panel of books had swung forwards, revealing a door opposite him. A young woman stood there, dark-haired and frowning. For some reason, she reminded him of Ms Lutyens; his initiative failed him, he opened and shut his mouth aimlessly.

The woman strode forwards. She wore an elegant dress; jewels flashed at her slender throat. Nathaniel collected himself. 'Erm . . . would you like a prawn thing?'

'Who are you? I've not seen you before.' Her voice was hard as flint.

He cudgelled his brain into action. 'I'm John Squalls, ma'am. I helped my father deliver some supplies to you this morning. Only the pageboy's been taken ill, just now, ma'am, and they asked if I could help out. Didn't want you to be short-staffed on an important day like this. Looks as if I took a wrong turning, not being familiar—'

'That'll do.' She was still hostile; her narrowed eyes scanned the platter. 'Look at the state of these! How dare you bring such—'

'Amanda!' A young man had followed her into the library. '*There* you are – and thank goodness, *food*! Let me at it!' He plunged past her and seized three or four of the most forlorn canapés from Nathaniel's silver dish.

'Absolute lifesaver! *Famishing* journey from London. Mm, there's a prawn on this one.' He chewed heartily. 'Interesting flavour. Very fresh. So tell me, Amanda . . . is it *true* about you and Lovelace? Everyone's been talking . . .'

Amanda Cathcart began a tinkling little laugh, then gestured curtly at Nathaniel. 'You – get out and serve those in the entrance hall. And prepare the next ones better.'

'Yes, ma'am.' Nathaniel bowed slightly, as he had seen the parliamentary servants do, and exited the library.

It had been a close shave and his heart was beating fast, but his mind was calm. The guilt that had beset him after the fire had now hardened into a cold acceptance of his situation. Mrs Underwood had died because he had stolen the Amulet. She had died, Nathaniel had survived. So be it. Now he would destroy Lovelace in his turn. He knew the likelihood was that he would not survive the day. This did not worry him. The odds were stacked in his enemy's favour, but that was the way it should be. He would succeed, or die trying.

A certain heroism in this equation appealed to him. It was clear and simple; it helped block out the messiness of his conscience.

He followed the hubbub to the entrance hall. The guests were arriving in droves now; the marbled pillars echoed with the noise of their chattering. Ministers of State shuffled through the open door, taking off gloves and unwinding long silk scarves, their breath hanging in the cold air of the hall. The men wore dinner jackets, the women elegant dresses. Servants stood on the fringes, accepting coats and proffering champagne. Nathaniel hung back for a moment, then, with his platter held high, dived into the throng.

'Sir, madam, would you like . . . ?'

'Cheese and prawn things, madam . . .'

'Can I interest you in . . . ?'

He wheeled about, buffeted this way and that by a battery of outstretched hands that preyed on his dish like seagulls swooping on a catch. No one spoke to him or even seemed to see him: several times his head was struck by an arm or hand blindly reaching out towards the platter, or raising a canapé to an open mouth. In seconds, the uppermost dish was empty save for a few crumbs and only a few desultory morsels remained on the lower. Nathaniel found himself expelled from the group, out of breath and with collar awry.

A tall, lugubrious-looking servant was standing near him, filling glasses from a bottle. 'Like animals, ain't they?' he mouthed under his breath. 'Bloody magicians.'

'Yes.' Nathaniel was barely listening. He watched the crowd of ministers, his lenses allowing him to see the full extent of activity in the hall. Almost every man and woman present had an imp hovering behind them, and while their masters engaged in smiling social chatter, talking over one another and fingering their jewels, the servants conducted a discourse of their own. Each imp postured and preened and swelled itself to ridiculous degrees, often attempting to deflate its rivals by surreptitiously prodding them in delicate places with a spiny tail. Some changed colour, going through a rainbow selection before ending with warning scarlet or bright yellow. Others contented themselves with pulling faces, imitating the expressions or gestures of their rivals' masters. If the magicians noticed all this, they made a good show of ignoring it, but the combination of the guests' false grins and the antics of their imps made Nathaniel's head spin.

'Are you serving those, or taking them for a walk?'

A scowling woman, broad of hip and waist, with an even broader imp floating behind her. And at her side . . . Nathaniel's heart fluttered – he recognized the watery eyes, the fish-like face. Mr Lime, Lovelace's companion, with the smallest, most maladroit imp imaginable skulking behind his ear. Nathaniel remained expressionless and bowed his head, offering up the dish. 'I'm sorry, madam.'

She took two pastries, Lime took one. Nathaniel was staring at the floor meekly, but he felt the man's gaze upon him.

'Haven't I seen you somewhere before?' the clammy man said.

The woman plucked at her companion's sleeve. 'Come, Rufus; why address a commoner, when there are so many *real* people to talk to? Look – there's Amanda!'

The magician shrugged and allowed himself to be pulled away. Glancing uneasily after them, Nathaniel noticed Rufus Lime's imp still staring back at him, its head turned at ninety degrees, until it was lost in the crowd.

The servant beside him was oblivious to it all; the imps were invisible to him. 'You've finished that lot,' he said. 'Take this tray of drinks round. They're as thirsty as camels. With worse manners, most of them.'

Some guests were drifting off down the hall towards an inner gallery, and Nathaniel was pleased to have an excuse to drift off with them. He needed to get away from the crowds to explore other regions of the house. So far, he had seen no sign of Lovelace, the Amulet or any possible trap. But nothing would happen yet, since the Prime Minister had not arrived.

Halfway along the hall, the woman from the library was standing in the midst of a small group, holding court. Nathaniel loitered nearby, allowing guests to swap empty glasses for the full ones on his tray.

'. . . You'll see it in a few minutes,' she said. 'It's the most wonderful thing I've *ever* seen. Simon had it brought from Persia especially for this afternoon.'

'He's treating you very well,' a man said drily, sipping his drink.

Amanda Cathcart blushed. 'He *is*,' she said. 'He's very good to me. Oh – but it's simply the cleverest thing! I'm sure it'll set an instant trend. Mind you, it wasn't easy to install – his men have been working on it all week. I saw the room for the first time only this morning. Simon said it would take my breath away and he was right.'

'The PM's here,' someone shouted. With little cries of excitement, the guests rushed back towards the doors, Amanda Cathcart at their head. Nathaniel copied the other servants and positioned himself respectfully beside a pillar, ready to be called.

Rupert Devereaux entered, slapping his gloves together in one hand and smiling his half smile. He stood out from the adoring throng, not just for his elegant attire and personal grace (which were just as striking as Nathaniel remembered), but for his companions: a bodyguard of four sullen, grey-suited magicians and – more startlingly – a hulking two-metre-tall afrit with luminous black-green skin. The afrit stood directly behind its master, casting baleful red eyes upon the company.

All the imps chittered with fear. The guests bowed their heads respectfully.

Nathaniel realized that the Prime Minister was making a blatant show of his power to all his assembled ministers, some of whom perhaps aspired to his position. It was certainly enough to impress Nathaniel. How could Lovelace expect to overcome something as strong as that afrit? Surely the very idea was madness.

But here was Lovelace himself, bounding down the hall to

greet his leader. Nathaniel's face remained impassive; his whole body tensed with hatred.

'Welcome, Rupert!' Much hand-shaking. Lovelace seemed oblivious of the afrit's presence at his shoulder. He turned to address the crowd. 'Ladies and gentlemen! With our beloved Prime Minister here, the conference can officially begin. On behalf of Lady Amanda, may I welcome you to Heddleham Hall. Please treat the house as your own!' His eyes glanced in Nathaniel's direction. Nathaniel shrank deeper into the shadow of the pillar. Lovelace's eyes moved on. 'In a short while, we will hear the first speeches in the Grand Salon, which Lady Amanda has refurbished especially for today. In the meantime, please make your way to the annexe, where further refreshments will be available.'

He waved his hand. The guests began to move off.

Lovelace leaned forward to speak to Devereaux. From behind the pillar, Nathaniel picked out the words: 'I must just collect some props for my opening speech, sir. Would you excuse me? I'll be with you in a few minutes.'

'Of course, of course, Lovelace. Take your time.'

Devereaux's entourage left the hall, the afrit glowering at the rear. Lovelace watched them for a moment, then set off alone in the opposite direction. Nathaniel remained where he was, making a big show of collecting used glasses that had been discarded on the antique furniture and marble pedestals lining the hall. Then, when the final servant had departed, he set his tray down quietly on a table and, like a ghost in the night, padded off on Lovelace's trail.

38

Simon Lovelace strode alone through the corridors and galleries of the great house. His head was bowed as he walked, his hands loosely clasped behind his back. He paid no heed to the rows of paintings, sculptures, tapestries and other artefacts he passed; he never looked behind him.

Nathaniel flitted from pillar to pedestal, from bookcase to writing desk, concealing himself behind each one until he was satisfied the magician was far enough ahead for him to continue. His heart pounded; he had a rushing noise in his ears – it reminded him of a time when had been ill in bed with fever. He didn't feel ill now, but very much alive.

The moment was fast approaching when Lovelace would strike. He knew it as if he had planned it all himself. He didn't yet know what form the attack would take, but he could see its imminence in the tense outline of the magician's shoulders, in his stiff, distracted way of walking.

He wished Bartimaeus would find him. The djinni was his only weapon.

Lovelace ascended a narrow staircase and disappeared through an open arch. Nathaniel climbed after him, placing his feet noiselessly on the slippery marble steps.

At the arch, he peered round. It was a small library or gallery of some kind, dimly lit by windows in the roof. Lovelace was making his way along a central aisle between several rows of projecting bookcases. Here and there sat low display tables, supporting a variety of oddly shaped objects.

Nathaniel took another peek, decided that his quarry was almost at the opposite door, and tiptoed into the room.

Suddenly, Lovelace spoke. 'Maurice!'

Nathaniel shot behind the nearest bookshelf. He flattened himself against it, forcing himself to breathe quietly. He heard the far door open. Stealthily, careful not to make the slightest noise, he turned his head inch by inch, until he could look over the top of the nearest books. Other bookcases separated him from the opposite side of the gallery, but framed in a gap between two shelves he could just make out the red, wrinkled face of Schyler, the old magician. Lovelace himself was hidden from view.

'Simon – what is wrong? Why have you come?'

'I've brought you a present.' Lovelace's voice was casual, amused. 'The boy.'

Nathaniel nearly fainted with shock. His muscles tensed, ready to run—

Lovelace stepped out from behind the end of the bookshelf. 'Don't bother. You'll be dead before you can leave the room.'

Nathaniel froze. Teetering on the edge of panic, he kept quite still.

'Come round here to Maurice.' Lovelace motioned with ostentatious courtesy. Nathaniel shuffled forward. 'There's a good boy. And stop trembling like an invalid. Another lesson for you: a magician never shows his fear.'

Nathaniel entered the main aisle and halted, facing the old magician. His body was shaking with rage, not fear. He cast his eyes left and right, looking for avenues of escape, but saw none. Lovelace's hand patted him on the back; he recoiled from the touch.

'I'm afraid I haven't got time to talk,' Lovelace said. 'I will leave you in Maurice's tender care. He has an offer to make you. Pardon – was that a mumble?'

'How did you know I was here?'

'Rufus Lime recognized you. I doubted that you would try anything too hasty downstairs, given that the police are hunting you in connection with that . . . unfortunate fire. So I thought it best simply to lead you away from the crowds, before you could make trouble. Now forgive me, I have a pressing engagement. Maurice – it's time.'

Schyler's face crinkled with satisfaction. 'Rupert's arrived, has he?'

'He's arrived, and his men have conjured a formidable afrit. Do you think he suspects?'

'Tcha! No. It is the normal paranoia, sharpened by that cursed attack on Parliament. The Resistance has a lot to answer for – they have not made today's task any easier. Once in power, Simon, we must root them out, these stupid children, and hang them up in chains on Tower Hill.'

Lovelace grunted. 'The afrit will be present during the speech. Rupert's men will insist.'

'You will have to stand close to it, Simon. It must get the first full force.'

'Yes. I hope the Amulet—'

'Tcha! Stop wasting time! We have talked about this already. You know it will hold firm.' Something in the old man's voice reminded Nathaniel of his own master's cold impatience. The wrinkled face twisted unpleasantly. 'You're not fretting about the woman, are you?'

'Amanda? Of course not! She is nothing to me. So—' Lovelace took a deep breath – 'is everything set?'

'The pentacle is ready. I've a good view of the room. Rufus

has just put the horn in position, so *that's* dealt with. I shall keep watch. If any of them resist while it is happening, we shall do what we can. But I doubt if we'll be necessary.' The old man gave a little titter. 'I'm *so* looking forward to this.'

'See you shortly.' Lovelace turned and headed for the arch. He seemed to have forgotten Nathaniel's existence.

The old man suddenly spoke after him. 'The Amulet of Samarkand. Do you wear it yet?'

Lovelace didn't look back. 'No. Rufus has it. That afrit would smell it a mile off, given time. I shall put it on as I enter.'

'Well then – good luck, my boy.'

No answer. Presently, Nathaniel heard footsteps clattering away down the stairs.

Then Schyler smiled; all the wrinkles and creases of his face seemed to stem from the corners of his eyes, but the eyes themselves were blank slits. His body was so stooped with age that he was scarcely taller than Nathaniel; the skin upon his hands looked waxy, dusted with liver spots. Yet Nathaniel could sense the power in him.

'John,' Schyler said. 'That is your name, is it not? John Mandrake. We were very surprised to find you in the house. Where is your demon? Have you lost it? That is a careless thing.'

Nathaniel compressed his lips. He glanced aside at the nearest display table. It had a few strange objects on it: stone bowls, bone pipes and a large moth-eaten head-dress, perhaps once worn by a North American shaman. All useless to him.

'I was for killing you straight away,' Schyler said, 'but Simon is more far-sighted than I am. He suggested we make you a proposition.'

'Which is?' Nathaniel was looking at the next display table – it carried a few small, dull cubes of metal, wrapped in faded paper strips.

The magician followed his gaze. 'Ah – you are admiring Miss Cathcart's collection? You will find nothing of power there. It is fashionable among rich and stupid commoners to have magical items in their houses, though quite unfashionable to know anything about them. Tcha! Ignorance is bliss. Sholto Pinn is always being pestered by society fools for trinkets like these.'

Nathaniel shrugged. 'You mentioned a proposition.'

'Yes. In a few minutes the hundred most powerful and eminent ministers in the Government will be dead, along with our sainted Prime Minister. When Simon's new administration takes control, the lower magical orders will follow us unquestioningly, since we will be stronger than them. However, we are not numerous, and there will soon be spaces, vacancies to fill in the higher reaches of the Government. We shall require talented new magicians to help us rule. Great wealth and the relaxations of power await our allies. Well now, you are young, Mandrake, but we recognize your ability. You have the makings of a great magician. Join with us, and we shall provide you with the apprenticeship you have always craved. Think about it – no more experiments in solitude, no more bowing or scraping to fools who are scarcely fit to lick your boots! We will test and inspire you, we will draw out your talent and let it breathe. And one day, perhaps, when Simon and I are gone, you will be supreme . . .'

The voice trailed off, left the image hanging. Nathaniel was silent. Six years of frustrated ambition were etched into his mind. Six years of suppressed desire – to be recognized for

THE AMULET OF SAMARKAND

what he was, to exercise his power openly, to go to Parliament as a great minister of State. And now his enemies were offering it all to him. He sighed heavily.

'You are tempted, John, I see that. Well, what do you say?'

He looked the old magician directly in the eye. 'Does Simon Lovelace *really* think I will join him?'

'He does.'

'After everything that has happened?'

'Even so. He knows how your mind works.'

'Then Simon Lovelace is a fool.'

'John—'

'An arrogant fool!'

'You must—'

'After what he has done to me? He could offer up the world and I'd refuse it. Join him? I would rather die!'

Schyler nodded, as if satisfied. 'Yes. I know. That is what I told him you'd say. I perceived you as you are – a silly, muddled child. Tcha! You have not been brought up correctly; your mind is fogged. You are of no use to us.'

He took a step forward. His shoes squeaked on the shiny floor.

'Well, aren't you going to run, little boy? Your djinni is gone. You have no other power. Would you not like a head start?'

Nathaniel did not run. He knew it would be fatal. He flicked a look at the other tables, but couldn't see clearly what objects they displayed; his enemy blocked the way to them.

'Do you know,' the old man said, 'I was impressed the first time we met – so young, so full of knowledge. I thought Simon was very harsh on you; even the affair with the mites was amusing and displayed an enterprising nature. Ordinarily

406

I would kill you slowly – that would amuse me further. But we have important business in a few moments and I cannot spare the time.'

The magician raised a hand and spoke a word. A shining black nimbus appeared, glimmering and fluctuating around his fingers.

Nathaniel threw himself to one side.

Bartimaeus

39

I hoped the boy could keep out of trouble long enough for me to reach him. Getting in was taking longer than I thought.

Up and down the wall the lizard scuttled; round cornices, over arches, across pilasters, its progress ever more speedy and erratic. Each window it came to – and there were plenty of them in the mansion – was firmly shut, causing it to flick its tongue in frustration. Hadn't Lovelace and Co. ever heard of the benefits of fresh air?

Many minutes went by. Still no luck. Truth was, I was loath to break in, except as a last resort. It was impossible to tell whether the rooms beyond had watchers who might respond to the slightest untoward noise. If I could only find a crack, a cranny to sneak through . . . But the place was too well sealed.

There was nothing for it: I would have to try a chimney.

With this in mind I headed roofwards, only to have my

attention caught by a very tall and ornate set of windows a little way off on a projecting wing of the house. They suggested a sizeable room beyond. Not only that, but a powerful network of magical bars crisscrossed the windows on the seventh plane. None of the Hall's other windows had such defences. My curiosity was piqued.

The lizard sped across to take a look, scales scuffling on the stones. It gripped a column and poked its head towards the window, being careful to keep well back from the glowing bars. What it saw inside was interesting, all right. The windows looked onto a vast circular hall or auditorium, brightly lit by a dozen chandeliers suspended from the ceiling. At the centre was a small raised podium draped with red cloth, around which a hundred chairs had been arranged in a neat semi-circle. A speaker's stand stood on the podium, complete with glass and jug of water. Evidently this was the venue for the conference.

Everything about the auditorium's décor – from the crystal chandeliers to the rich gold trimmings on the walls – was designed to appeal to the magicians' (vulgar) sense of wealth and status. But the really extraordinary thing about the room was the floor, which seemed to be entirely made of glass. From wall to wall it glinted and gleamed, refracting the light of the chandeliers in a dozen unusual tints and shades. If this wasn't unusual enough, beneath the glass stretched an immense and very beautiful carpet. It was Persian-made, displaying – amid a wealth of dragons, chimeras, manticores and birds – a fantastically detailed hunting scene. A life-size prince and his court rode into a forest, surrounded by dogs, leopards, kestrels and other trained beasts; ahead of them, amongst the bushes, a host of fleet-footed deer skipped away. Horns blew, pennants waved. It was an idealized eastern fairy-tale court and I would have been quite impressed, had I not glanced at a couple of the faces of the courtiers. That rather spoiled the effect. One of them sported Lovelace's horrid mug; another looked like Sholto Pinn. Elsewhere, I spied my erstwhile captor, Jessica Whitwell, riding a white mare. Trust Lovelace to spoil a perfectly good work of art with such an ingratiating fancy.[1] No doubt the prince was Devereaux, the Prime Minister, and every important magician was pictured amongst his fawning throng.

This curious floor was not the only odd thing about the circular hall. All the other windows that looked onto it had shimmering defences similar to the one through which I spied. Reasonable enough: soon most of the Government would be inside – the room had to be safe from attack. But hidden in the stonework of my window frame were things that looked like embedded metal rods, and their purpose was not at all clear.

I was just pondering this when a door at the far end of the auditorium opened and a magician walked swiftly in. It was the oily man I had seen passing in the car: Lime, the boy had called him, one of Lovelace's confederates. He carried an object in his hand, shrouded under a cloth. With hasty steps and eyes flicking nervously back and forth, he crossed to the

---

[1] How the weavers of Basra must have loathed being commissioned to create such a monstrosity. Gone are the days when, with complex and cruel incantations, they wove djinn into the fabric of their carpets, creating artefacts that carried their masters across the Middle East *and* were stain resistant at the same time. Hundreds of us were trapped this way. But now, with the magical power of Baghdad long broken, such craftsmen escape destitution only by weaving tourist tat for rich foreign clients. Such is progress.

podium, mounted it and approached the speaker's stand. There was a shelf inside the stand, hidden from the floor below, and the man placed the object inside it.

Before he did so, he removed the cloth and a shiver ran down my scales.

It was the summoning horn I'd seen in Lovelace's study on the night I stole the Amulet of Samarkand. The ivory was yellow with age and had been reinforced with slender metal bands, but the blackened fingerprints on its side[2] were still quite visible.

A summoning horn . . .

I began to see daylight. The magical bars at the windows, the metal ones embedded in the stonework, ready to spring shut . . . The auditorium's defences weren't to keep anything *out* – they were to keep everyone *in*.

It was definitely time I got inside.

With scant regard for any over-flying sentries, I scampered up the wall and over the red-tiled roof of the mansion to the nearest chimney. I darted to the rim of the pot and was about to duck inside – when I drew back, all of a quiver. A net of sparkling threads was suspended below me across the hole. Blocked.

I ran to the next. Same again.

In considerable agitation, I crossed and recrossed the roof of Heddleham Hall, checking every chimney. Each one was sealed. More than one magician had gone to great lengths to protect the place from spies.

---

[2] The only remains of the first person to blow the horn, it being an essential requirement of such items that their first user must surrender himself to the mercy of the entity he summons. With this notable design flaw, summoning horns are pretty rare, as you'd imagine.

I halted at last, wondering what to do.

All this time, at the front of the house below, a steady stream of chauffeured cars[3] had drawn up, disgorged their occupants and headed off to a car park at the side. Most of the guests were here now; the conference was about to begin.

I looked across the lawns. A few late arrivals were speeding towards the house.

And they weren't the only ones.

In the middle of the lawn was a lake adorned with an ornamental fountain, depicting an amorous Greek god trying to kiss a dolphin.[4] Beyond the lake, the drive curled into the trees towards the entrance gateway. And along it three figures came striding, two going fast, the third faster. For a man who had recently been knocked about by a fieldmouse, Mr Squalls was racing along at a fair old lick. Son was doing even better: presumably his lack of clothes encouraged him on his way (at this distance he looked like one big goose pimple). But neither of them matched the pace of the bearded mercenary, whose cloak swirled out behind him as he strode off the drive onto the lawn.

Ah. This might spell trouble.

I perched on the lip of the chimneypot, cursing my restraint with Squalls and Son[5] and debating whether I could ignore the distant trio. But another look decided me. The bearded man was coming along faster than ever. Strange – his paces

---

[3] In a perfect example of most magicians' dreary style, each and every vehicle was big, black and shiny. Even the smallest looked as if it wanted to be a hearse when it grew up.

[4] Inadvisable.

[5] I thought my blows would keep them unconscious for at least a couple of days. But I'd fluffed it. That's what comes of hurrying a job.

seemed ordinary ones, but they ate up the ground at blinding speed. He had almost halved the distance to the lake already. In another minute he would be at the house, ready to raise the alarm.

Getting into the house would have to wait. There wasn't time to be discreet. I became a blackbird and flew purposefully from the mansion roof.

The man in black strode nearer. I noted a flicker in the air about his legs, an odd discrepancy, as if their movement was not properly contained within any of the planes. Then I understood: he wore seven-league boots.[6] After a few more paces, his trajectory would be too swift to follow – he might travel a mile with each step. I speeded up my flight.

The lakeside was a pretty spot (if you didn't count the statue of the disreputable old god and the dolphin). A young gardener was weeding the margins of the shore. A few innocent ducks floated dreamily on the surface of the water. Bulrushes waved in the breeze. Someone had planted a small bower of honeysuckle by the lake: its leaves shone a pleasant, peaceful green in the afternoon sun.

That was just for the record. My first Detonation missed the mercenary (it being difficult to judge the speed of someone wearing seven-league boots) but hit the bower, which vaporized instantly. The gardener yelped and jumped into the lake, carrying the ducks off on a small tidal wave. The bulrushes

---

[6] Potent magical devices, invented in medieval Europe. At the wearer's command, the boots can cover considerable distances in the smallest of strides. Normal (Earth) rules of time and space do not apply. Allegedly, each boot contains a djinni capable of travelling on a hypothetical *eighth* plane (not that I would know anything about that). It was now easier to understand how the mercenary had managed to evade capture when he first stole the Amulet for Lovelace.

caught fire. The mercenary looked up. He hadn't noticed me before, probably being intent on keeping his boots under control, so it wasn't strictly sporting, but hey – I was late for a conference. My second Detonation caught him directly in the chest. He disappeared in a mass of emerald flames.

Why can't all problems be as easy to resolve?

I did a quick circuit, eyeing the horizon, but there were no watchers and nothing dangerous in sight, unless you count the pink backside of Squalls's son as he and his dad turned tail and raced for the park gateway. Fine. I was just about to head off back to the house, when the smoke from my Detonation cleared away, revealing the mercenary sitting in a muddy depression a metre deep, mucky, blinking, but very much alive.

Hmm. That was something I *hadn't* counted on.

I screeched to a halt in mid-air, turned, and delivered another, more concentrated blast. It was the kind that would have made even Jabor's knees tremble a bit; certainly it should have turned most humans into a wisp of smoke blowing in the wind.

But not Beardy. As the flames died down again, he was just getting to his feet, as casual as you like! He looked as if he'd been having a catnap. Admittedly, much of his cloak had burned away, but the body beneath was still hale and hearty.

I didn't bother trying again. I can take a hint.

The man reached inside his cloak and from a hidden pocket withdrew a silver disc. With unexpected speed he reached back and threw – it missed my beak by a feather's breadth and returned spinning to his hand in a lazy arc.

That did it. I'd gone through a lot in the last few days. Everyone I met seemed to want a piece of me: djinn, magicians, humans ... it made no difference. I'd been summoned, manhandled, shot at, captured, constricted, bossed about and generally taken for granted. And now, to cap it all, this bloke was joining in too, when all I'd been doing was quietly trying to kill him.

I lost my temper.

The angriest blackbird you've ever seen made a dive for the statue in the middle of the lake. It landed at the base of the dolphin's tail, stretched its wings around the stone and, as it heaved, took a gargoyle's form once more. Dolphin and god[7] were ripped from their foundations. With a brittle cracking and the rasp of ripping lead, the statue came away. A jet of water spurted from the ruptured pipes inside. The gargoyle raised the statue above its head, gave a bound, and landed on the lakeside bank, not far from where the mercenary was standing.

He didn't seem as fazed as I'd have liked. He threw the disc again. It bit into my arm, poisoning me with silver.

Ignoring the pain, I tossed the statue like a Highland caber. It did a couple of stylish flips and landed on the mercenary with a soft crump.

He looked winded, I'll give him that. But even so, he wasn't anything like the flatness I required. I could see him struggling under the prone god, trying to get a grip so he could shove it away. This was getting tedious. Well, if I couldn't stop him, I could certainly slow him down. While he was still floundering around, I jumped over, unlaced his seven-league boots and plucked them off his feet. Then I threw them as hard as I could into the middle of the lake, where the ducks were busily regrouping. The boots splashed down in their midst and instantly sank out of sight.

---

[7] They were intertwined. Never mind how.

'You'll pay for that,' the man said. He was still struggling with the statue, moving it slowly off his chest.

'You don't know when to give up, do you?' I said, scratching a horn irritably. I was wondering what more to do, when—

– I felt my insides being sucked out through my back. My essence squirmed and writhed. I gasped. The mercenary looked on as my form grew vaporous and weak.

He gave a heave and shoved the statue off. Through my pain, I saw him getting to his feet. 'Stop, coward!' he cried. 'You must stand and fight!'

I shook a dissolving claw at him. 'Think yourself lucky,' I groaned. 'I'm letting you off. I had you on the ropes and don't you forg—'

Then I was gone, and my rebuke with me.

Nathaniel

40

The bolt of jet-black plasm hit the nearest display table. The shaman's head-dress, the pots and pipes, the table itself and a section of the floor all vanished with a noise like something being sucked sharply down a plughole. Foul steam rose from the wound in the floor.

A metre or so away, Nathaniel rolled head over heels and got straight to his feet. His head felt woozy from the roll, but he did not hesitate. He ran for the next display table, the one with the metal cubes. As the old magician raised his hand once more, he scooped up as many cubes as he could and disappeared behind a neighbouring bookcase. The second plasm bolt struck just behind him.

He paused for a moment. Beyond the bookshelves, the old magician made a clucking noise with his tongue. 'What are you doing? Do you plan to toss more mites at me?'

Nathaniel glanced at the objects in his hand. Not mites, but scarcely any better. Prague Cubes: minor conjuror's tricks peddled by low-caste magicians. Each cube was little more than a mite bottled up inside a metal shell with a variety of mineral powders. When released with a simple command, mite and powders combusted in an amusing way. Silly diversions, nothing more. Certainly not weapons.

Each cube had a paper wrap stamped with the famous distilling glass logo of the alchemists of Golden Lane. They were old, probably nineteenth century. Perhaps they would not work at all.

Nathaniel picked one and tossed it, wrapping and all, over the top of the shelves.

He shouted the Release Command.

With a brilliant shower of silver sparkles and a tinny melody the imp inside the cube combusted. A faint but unmistakable fragrance of lavender filled the gallery.

He heard the old magician burst into a hearty chuckle. 'How charming! Please – some more! I wish to smell my best when we take over the country! Do you have rowan flavour? That would be my favourite!'

Nathaniel selected another cube. Party gimmicks or not, they were the only things he had.

He could hear the squeaking of the old man's shoes as he shuffled down the gallery towards the end of his aisle. What could he do? On either side, bookcases blocked his way out.

Or did they? Each shelf was open-backed: on every row, he could see above the tops of the books into the next aisle. If he pushed himself through . . .

He tossed the next cube and ran at the shelf.

Maurice Schyler rounded the corner, his hand invisible inside its wavering bulb of force.

Nathaniel hit the second shelf of books like a high jumper clearing a bar. He muttered the Release Command.

The cube exploded in the old man's face. A starburst of purple sparks zipped and spun, high as the ceiling; a nineteenth-century Czech marching song rang out briefly in accompaniment.

In the next aisle along, fifty books crashed down like a falling wall. Nathaniel sprawled on top of them.

He felt, rather than saw, the third bolt of plasm destroy the aisle behind him.

The magician's voice now carried a slight note of irritation. 'Little boy – time is short! Stand still, please.'

But Nathaniel was already on his feet and hurtling towards the next shelf. He was moving too fast to think, never allowing himself a moment's pause, lest his terror rose up to overwhelm him. His one aim was to reach the door at the far end of the gallery. The old man had said there was a pentacle there.

'John – listen!' He landed on his back in the next aisle, amid a shower of books. 'I admire your resolve.' A leather-bound dictionary fell against the side of his head, making bright lights twinkle across his vision. He struggled upright. 'But it is foolish to seek revenge on your master's behalf.' Another burst of magical force: another section of shelving vanished. The room was filled with thick, acrid smoke. 'Foolish and unnatural. I myself *killed* my own master, long ago. Now, if your Underwood had been a worthy man, I would understand it.' Nathaniel threw the third cube behind him; it bounced harmlessly against a table and did not go off. He had forgotten to say the command. 'But he was not a worthy man – was he, John? He was a drivelling idiot. Now you will lose your life for him. You should have stayed away.'

Nathaniel had reached the final aisle. He was not far from the door at the end of the room – it was a few strides off. But here, for the first time, he stopped dead. A great anger swelled inside him and damped down his fear.

Shoes squeaked softly. The old man shuffled back up the gallery, following the trail of scattered books, checking each side aisle as he went. He saw no sign of the boy. Drawing near the door, he turned into the final aisle, hand raised at the ready—

And clicked his tongue in exasperation. The aisle was empty.

Nathaniel, who had silently clambered back through the shelves to the previous aisle and had now crept up behind him, thus had the element of surprise.

Three cubes hit the magician at once and exploded together at a single command. They were a lime-green Catherine Wheel, a ricocheting Viennese Cannon and an Ultramarine Bonfire, and although the effect of each one individually would have been modest, taken together they became quite potent. A medley of cheap popular ballads sounded and the air instantly became heavy with the flavours of rowan, edelweiss and camphor. The combined explosion blew the old man off his feet and straight into the door at the end of the gallery. He hit it hard, head first. The door caved in; he slumped across it, his neck twisted oddly. The black energy pulsing on his hand instantly snuffed out.

Nathaniel walked slowly towards him through the smoke, cupping a final cube loosely in his palm.

The magician did not move.

Perhaps he was faking it: in a moment he would spring up, ready to fight . . . This was possible. He had to be ready for him.

Closer . . . Still no movement. Now he was adjacent to the old man's splayed leather shoes . . .

Another half-step . . . surely he would get up now.

Maurice Schyler did not get up. His neck was broken. His face sagged against a panel of the door, his lips slightly apart. Nathaniel was close enough to count all the lines and creases on his cheek; he could see little red veins running across the nose and under the eye . . .

The eye was open, but glazed, unseeing. It looked like that of a fish on a slab. A trace of limp white hair fell across it.

Nathaniel's shoulders began to shake. For a moment, he thought he was going to cry.

Instead, he forced himself to remain motionless, waiting for his breathing to slow, for the shaking to die down. When his emotion was safely contained, he stepped over the body of the old man. 'You made a mistake,' he said softly. 'It is not my *master* that I'm doing this for.'

The room beyond was small and windowless. It had perhaps once been a storeroom. A pentacle had been drawn in the centre of the floor, with candles and incense pots carefully arranged around. Two of the candles had been knocked over by the impact of the falling door, and these Nathaniel carefully set upright, in position.

On one of the walls was a gold picture frame, hanging from a nail by a string. There was neither painting nor canvas inside the frame; instead it was filled with a beautiful image of a large, circular, sunny room, in which many small figures moved.

Nathaniel knew instantly what the frame was: a scrying glass far sharper and more powerful than his lost bronze disc. He stepped closer to inspect it. It showed a vast auditorium filled with chairs, whose carpeted floor shone strangely. The ministers were entering it from one side, laughing and chatting, still holding their glasses, accepting smart black pens and folders from a line of servants by the door. The Prime Minister was there, at the centre of a milling throng, the grim afrit still attentively in tow. Lovelace had not yet arrived.

But any moment now, he would enter the hall and set his plan in motion.

Nathaniel noted a box of matches lying on the floor. Hurriedly, he lit the candles, double-checked the incense and stepped into the pentacle – admiring, despite his haste, the elegance with which it had been drawn. Then he closed his eyes, composed himself, and searched his memory for the incantation.

After a few seconds, he had it ready. His throat was a little claggy because of the smoke; he coughed twice and spoke the words.

The effect was instantaneous. It had been so long since Nathaniel had completed a summoning that he gave a little start when the djinni appeared. It was in its gargoyle form and wore a peeved expression.

'You really have got perfect timing, haven't you?' it said. 'I'd just got the assassin where I wanted him, and all of a sudden you remember how to call me!'

'It's about to start!' The effort of calling Bartimaeus had made Nathaniel light-headed. He leaned against a wall to steady himself. 'Look – there in the glass! They're gathering. Lovelace is on his way now, and he'll be wearing the Amulet, so he won't feel the effects of whatever happens. I–I think it's a summoning.'

'You don't say? I'd worked that one out already. Well, come on then – surrender to my tender claws.' It flexed them experimentally; they let off a creaking sound.

Nathaniel went white. The gargoyle rolled its eyes. 'I'm going to have to *carry* you,' it said. 'We'll have to hurry if we want to stop him entering the room. Once he's in, the place will be sealed – you can bet on that.'

Gingerly, Nathaniel stepped forward. The gargoyle tapped a foot impatiently. 'Don't worry on my account,' it snapped. 'I won't strain my back or anything. I'm feeling angry and my strength's returned.' With this, it made a grab, snatched Nathaniel around the waist and turned to leave, only to trip over the body lying in the doorway.

'Watch where you leave your victims! I stubbed my toe on that.' With a bound it had cleared the debris and was leaping through the gallery, spurring itself on with great beats of its stony wings.

Nathaniel's stomach lurched horribly with every stride. 'Slow down!' he gasped. 'You'll make me sick!'

'You won't like this then.' Bartimaeus leaped through the arch at the end of the gallery, ignored the landing and staircase completely and plummeted directly to the hall ten metres below. Nathaniel's wail made the rafters echo.

Half flying, half leaping, the gargoyle negotiated the next corridor. 'So,' it said agreeably, 'you've made your first direct kill. How does it feel? Much more manly, I'm sure. Does it help blot out the death of Underwood's wife?'

Nathaniel was too nauseous to listen, let alone answer.

★ ★ ★

A minute later, the ride came to an end so abruptly that Nathaniel's limbs swung about like a rag doll's. The gargoyle had halted at the corner of a long corridor; it dropped him to the floor and pointed silently up ahead. Nathaniel shook his head to stop his vision spinning, and stared.

At the other end of the corridor was the open door to the auditorium. Three people stood there: a haughty servant, who held the door ajar; the fish-faced magician Rufus Lime; and Simon Lovelace, who was buttoning up his collar. A brief flash of gold showed at his throat, then the collar was adjusted and his tie wrapped in place. Lovelace clapped his companion on the shoulder and strode through the door.

'We're too late!' Nathaniel hissed. 'Can't you—?' He looked to his side in surprise – the gargoyle was gone.

A tiny voice whispered in his ear. 'Smooth your hair down and get to the door. You can enter as a servant. Hurry it up!' Nathaniel ignored the strong desire to scratch his earlobe; he could feel something small and ticklish hanging there. He squared his shoulders, swept back his hair and trotted along the corridor.

Lime had departed elsewhere. The servant was swinging the door to.

'Wait!' Nathaniel wished his voice were deeper and more commanding. He approached the servant at speed. 'Let me in too! They want someone extra to serve the drinks!'

'I don't recognize you,' the man said, frowning. 'Where's young William?'

'Erm, he had a headache. I was called in. At the last minute.'

Footsteps along the corridor; a voice of command. 'Wait!'

Nathaniel turned. He heard Bartimaeus swearing on the cusp of his earlobe. The black-bearded mercenary was approaching fast, bare-footed, ragged cape swinging, blue eyes afire.

'Quick!' The djinni's voice was urgent. 'The door's open a crack – slip inside!'

The mercenary quickened his pace. 'Stop that boy!'

But Nathaniel was already jamming a boot heel down hard on the servant's shoe. The man whooped with agony and his clutching hand jerked back. With a wriggle and a squirm, Nathaniel evaded his grasp and, pushing at the door, squeezed himself through.

The insect on his ear leaped up and down in agitation. 'Shut it on them!'

He pushed with all his strength, but the servant was now applying his full weight on the other side. The door began to swing open.

Then the voice of the mercenary, calm and silky, sounded beyond the door.

'Don't bother,' it said. 'Let him go in. He deserves his fate.'

The force on the door eased and Nathaniel was able to push it shut. Locks clicked into position within the wood. Bolts were drawn.

The small voice spoke against his ear. 'Now, *that* was ominous,' it said.

41

Bartimaeus

From the moment we got inside the fateful hall and its boundary was sealed, events happened fast. The boy himself probably never got a good look at the set-up there before it changed for ever, but my senses are more advanced, of course. I took it all in, every detail, in the briefest of instants.

First, where were we? By the locked door, on the very edge of the circular glass floor. This glass had been given a slightly rough surface, so that shoes gripped to it, but it was still clear enough for the carpet below to be beautifully displayed. The boy was standing right above the edge of the carpet – a border depicting interlocking vines. Nearby, and at intervals around the whole hall, stood impassive servants, each one beside a trolley heavily laden with cakes and beverages. Within this was the semicircle of chairs that I had seen from the window, now groaning under the assembled bottoms of the magicians. They were sipping their drinks and half listening to the woman, Amanda Cathcart, who was standing on the podium in the centre of the hall, welcoming them all there. At her shoulder, his face expressionless, was Simon Lovelace, waiting.

The woman was wrapping up her speech. '. . . Lastly, I hope you will not mind me drawing your attention to the carpet on display below. We commissioned it from Persia and I believe it is the biggest in England. I think you will find yourselves all included if you look carefully.' (Murmured approval, a few cheers.) 'This afternoon's discussion will last until six. We will then break for dinner in the heated marquees on the lawn outside, where you will be entertained by some Latvian sword-jugglers.' (Enthusiastic cheering.) 'Thank you. May I now hand you over to your true host, Mr Simon Lovelace!' (Strained and ragged clapping.)

While she droned on, I was busy whispering in the boy's ear.[1] I was a head louse at this point, which is pretty much as small as I can go. Why? Because I didn't want the afrit to notice me until it couldn't be avoided. She was the only otherworld being currently in evidence (for politeness's sake, all the magicians' imps had been dismissed for the duration of the meeting) but she was bound to see me as a threat.

'This is our last chance,' I said. 'Whatever Lovelace is going to do, take it from me he'll do it now, before the afrit picks up the Amulet's aura. He's got it round his neck: can you creep up behind him and pull it into view? That'll rouse the magicians.'

The boy nodded. He began to sidle around the edge of the crowd. On the podium, Lovelace began an obsequious address:

'Prime Minister, ladies and gentlemen, may I say how *honoured* we are . . .'

---

[1] In both senses. And I can tell you I've been in some sticky places in my time, but for sheer waxy unpleasantness, his ear lobe takes some beating.

We were now at the side of the audience, with a clear run down the edge of the magicians' chairs towards the podium. The boy started forwards at a canter, with me urging him on like a jockey does a willing (if stupid) horse.

But as he passed the first delegate, a bony hand shot out and caught him by the scruff of the neck.

'And where do you think *you're* going, servant?'

I knew that voice. For me it brought back displeasing memories of her Mournful Orb. It was Jessica Whitwell, all cadaverous cheeks and cropped white hair. Nathaniel struggled in her grip. I wasted no time, but motored over the top of his ear and down the soft white skin behind it, making for the grasping hand.

Nathaniel wriggled. 'Let . . . me . . . go!'

'. . . it is a delight and a privilege . . .' As yet, Lovelace had heard nothing.

'How *dare* you seek to disrupt this meeting?' Her sharp nails dug cruelly into the boy's neck. The head louse approached her pale, thin wrist.

'You don't . . . understand . . .' Nathaniel choked. 'Lovelace has—'

'Silence, brat!'

'. . . glad to see you here. Sholto Pinn sends his apologies, he is indisposed . . .'

'Put him in a Stricture, Jessica.' This was a magician at the next chair along. 'Deal with him after.'

I was at her wrist. Its underside ran with blue veins.

Head lice aren't big enough for what I had in mind. I became a scarab beetle, with extra-sharp pincers. I bit with gusto.

The woman's shriek made the chandeliers jangle. She let go of Nathaniel, who stumbled forwards, nearly jolting me from the back of his neck. Lovelace was interrupted – he spun round, eyes wide. All heads turned.

Nathaniel raised his hand and pointed. 'Watch out!' he croaked (the grip on his neck had nearly throttled him). 'Lovelace has got the Am—'

A web of white threads rose up around us and closed over Nathaniel's head. The woman lowered her hand and sucked her bleeding wrist.

'—ulet of Samarkand! He's going to kill you all! I don't know how, but it's going to be horrible and—'

Wearily, the scarab beetle tapped Nathaniel on the shoulder. 'Don't bother,' I said. 'No one can hear you. She's sealed us off.'[2] He looked blank. 'Not been in one before? Your lot do it to others all the time.'

I was watching Lovelace. His eyes were locked on Nathaniel, and I caught doubt and anger flashing across them before he slowly turned back to his speech. He coughed, waiting for the magicians' chattering to die down. Meanwhile, one hand edged towards the hidden shelf in the lectern.

The boy was panicking now; he lashed out weakly at the rubbery walls of the Stricture.

'Keep calm,' I said. 'Let me check it: most Strictures have weak links. If I can find one I should be able to break us out.' I became a fly and, starting at its top, began to circle carefully across the Stricture's membranes, looking for a flaw.

'But we haven't time . . .'

---

[2] The threads of a Stricture act as a seal. They allow no object (or sound) to escape their cocoon. It's a kind of temporary prison, more usually employed on unfortunate humans than on djinn.

I spoke gently to quieten him. 'Just watch and listen.'

I didn't show it, but I was worried myself now. The boy was right: we really had no time.

Nathaniel

'But we haven't time—' Nathaniel began.

'Just shut up and watch!' The fly was buzzing frantically around their prison. It sounded decidedly panicked.

Nathaniel had barely enough room to move his hands, and nowhere near enough to do anything with his legs or feet. It was like being inside a mummy's case or an iron maiden . . . As he had this thought, the terror of all constricted things bubbled up within him. He suppressed a mounting urge to scream, took a deep breath and, to help distract himself, focused on events around him.

After the unfortunate interruption, the magicians had turned their attention back to the speaker, who was acting as if nothing had happened: 'In turn, I would like to thank Lady Amanda for the use of this wonderful hall . . . Incidentally, may I draw your attention to the remarkable ceiling, with its collection of priceless chandeliers? They were taken from the ruins of Versailles after the French Wars, and are made of adamantine crystal. Their designer . . .'

Lovelace had a lot to say about the chandeliers. All the delegates craned their necks upwards, making noises of approval. The opulence of the hall ceiling interested them greatly.

Nathaniel addressed the fly. 'Have you found a weak point yet?'

'No. It's been well put together.' It buzzed angrily. '*Why* did you have to get yourself caught? We're helpless in here.'

Helpless, yet again. Nathaniel bit his lip. 'I assume Lovelace is going to summon something,' he said.

'Of course. He's got a horn for that purpose, so he doesn't have to speak the incantation. Saves him time.'

'What will it be?'

'Who knows? Something big enough to deal with that afrit, presumably.'

Again, panic struggled in Nathaniel's throat, wrestling to be loosened in a cry. Outside, Lovelace was still describing the intricacies of the ceiling. Nathaniel's eyes flicked back and forth, trying to catch the gaze of one of the magicians, but they were still absorbed in the marvellous chandeliers. He hung his head in despair.

And noticed something odd out of the corner of his eye.

The floor . . . It was difficult to be sure with the lights glaring in the glass, but he thought he could see a movement on the floor, like a white wave rapidly travelling across it from the far wall. He frowned; the Stricture's membranes were getting in the way of his vision – he couldn't be sure what he was actually seeing. But it was almost as if something was covering the carpet.

The fly was wheeling about near the side of his head. 'One crumb of comfort,' it said. 'It can't be anything *too* powerful, or Lovelace would have to use a pentacle. The Amulet's all very well for personal protection, but the *really* strong entities need to be carefully contained. You can't afford to let them go running loose, or risk total devastation. Look what happened to Atlantis.'

Nathaniel had no idea what had happened to Atlantis. He

was still watching the floor. He had suddenly become aware that there was a sense of movement all across the hall – the whole flooring seemed to be shifting, though the glass itself remained solid and firm. He looked between his feet and saw the smiling face of a young female magician move quickly past beneath the glass, closely followed by a stallion's head and the leaves of a decorative tree . . .

It was then that he realized the truth. The carpet was not being covered. It was being *drawn back*, quickly and stealthily. And no one else had noticed. While the magicians gazed gawping at the ceiling, the floor below them changed.

'Erm, Bartimaeus—' he said.

'*What?* I'm trying to concentrate.'

'The floor . . .'

'Oh.' The fly settled on his shoulder. 'That's *bad*.'

As Nathaniel watched, the ornately twining border passed below him, then the carpet's tasselled edge itself. It moved off, revealing a gleaming surface below – perhaps made of white-washed plaster – on which great runes were inscribed in shining black ink. Nathaniel knew immediately what they were standing on, and one glance across the room confirmed it. He saw sections of perfectly drawn circles, two straight lines converging at the apex of a star, the elegant curving lines of runic characters, both red and black . . .

'A giant pentacle,' he whispered. 'And we're all inside.'

'Nathaniel,' said the fly. 'You know I told you to keep calm and not bother waving or shouting?'

'Yes.'

'Cancel that. Make as much movement as you can. Perhaps we can attract the attention of one of these idiots.'

Nathaniel jiggled about, waved his hands and jerked his

head from side to side. He shouted until his throat was sore. Around him whirled the fly, its body flashing in a hundred bright warning colours. But the magicians nearby noticed nothing. Even Jessica Whitwell, who was closest, still gazed at the ceiling with starry eyes.

The terrible helplessness that Nathaniel had felt on the night of the fire flooded over him again. He could feel his energy and resolution draining away. 'Why won't they *look*?' he wailed.

'Pure greed,' the fly said. 'They're fixated with the trappings of wealth. This is no good. I'd try a Detonation, but it would kill you at this range.'

'Yes, don't do that,' Nathaniel said.

'If *only* you'd already freed me from the Indefinite Confinement spell,' the fly mused. 'Then I could break out and tackle Lovelace. You'd be dead, of course, but I'd save everyone else, honest, and tell them all about your sacrifice. It would— Look! It's happening!'

Nathaniel's eyes had already been drawn to Lovelace, who had made a sudden movement. From pointing at the ceiling, his hands now descended to the back of the lectern with feverish haste. He drew something out, hurled its covering cloth to the floor and raised the object to his lips: a horn, old, stained and cracked. Sweat beaded his forehead; it glistened in the light from the chandeliers.

Something in the crowd gave an inhuman roar of anger. The magicians lowered their heads in shock.

Lovelace blew.

Bartimaeus

When the carpet drew back and the giant summoning pentacle was revealed, I knew we were in for something nasty. Lovelace had it all worked out. All of us, him included, were trapped inside the circle with whatever he was calling from the Other Place. There were barriers on the windows and, no doubt, in the walls as well, so there was no chance any of us would escape. Lovelace had the Amulet of Samarkand – and with its power, he was immune – but the rest of us would be at the mercy of the being he had summoned.

I hadn't lied to the boy. Without the constraining pentacle, there was a limit to what any magician would willingly summon. The greatest beings run amok if they're given any freedom,[3] and Lovelace's hidden design meant that the only freedom this one was going to get would be inside this single room.

But that was all the magician needed. When his slave departed, he alone of the great ones of the Government would be left alive, ready to assume control.

He blew the horn. It made no sound on any of the seven planes, but in the Other Place it would have rung loud.

---

[3] One of the worst examples was the Mycenaean outpost of Atlantis on the island of Santorini in the Mediterranean. About 3,500 years ago, if memory serves. They wanted to conquer another island (or some predictable objective like that), so their magicians clubbed together and summoned an aggressive entity. They couldn't control it. I was only a few hundred miles away on the Egyptian delta; I heard the explosion and saw the tsunami waves come roaring across to deluge the African coast. Weeks later, when things had settled down, the pharaoh's boats sailed to Santorini. The entire central section of the island, with its people and its shining city, had sunk into the sea. And all because they hadn't bothered with a pentacle.

As was to be expected, the afrit acted fastest. Even as the summoning horn came into view, she let out a great bellow, seized Rupert Devereaux by the shoulders and flew at the nearest set of windows, picking up speed as she went. She crashed into the glass: the magical barriers across it flared electric blue and, with an impact like thunder, she was propelled back into the room, head over heels, with Devereaux spinning limply in her grip.

Lovelace took the horn away from his lips, smiling slightly.

The cleverer magicians had understood the situation the instant the horn was blown. With a flurry of coloured flashes, imps appeared at several shoulders. Others summoned greater assistance – the woman by our side was muttering an incantation, calling up her djinni.

Lovelace stepped down carefully from the podium, his eyes trained somewhere high above. Light danced on the surface of his spectacles. His suit was elegant, unruffled. He took no notice of the consternation all around.

I saw a flicker in the air.

Desperately, I threw myself at the edges of the web that surrounded us, searching for a weakness and finding none.

Another flicker. My essence shivered.

Nathaniel

Many of the magicians were on their feet now, their voices raised in alarm, heads turning from side to side in bewilderment, as thick iron and silver bars slid into position across every door and window. Nathaniel had long since stopped bothering to move: it was clear that no one would take any notice of him. He could only watch as a magician some way in front slung his chair to one side, raised a hand and shot a ball of yellow flame at Lovelace from a distance of only a couple of metres. To the surprise of the magician, the flame altered its course slightly in mid-air and disappeared into the centre of Lovelace's chest. Lovelace, who was staring intently up towards the ceiling, appeared to have noticed nothing.

The fly buzzed back and forth, bunting its head against the wall of the Stricture. 'That's the Amulet's work,' it said. 'It'll take whatever they throw.'

Jessica Whitwell had finished her incantation: a short stumpy djinni hovered in the air beside her; it had taken the form of a black bear. She pointed, yelled an order. The bear moved forwards through the air, paddling its limbs as if swimming.

Other magicians sent attacks in Lovelace's direction: for perhaps a minute he was at the centre of a lightning storm of furious, crackling energy. The Amulet of Samarkand absorbed it all. Lovelace was unaffected. He carefully smoothed back his hair.

The afrit had picked itself up from where it had fallen and, having set the dazed Prime Minister lolling on a chair, leaped into the fray. It flew on speedy, shining wings, but Nathaniel noticed it approached Lovelace on a peculiar circular course, avoiding the air directly above the podium.

Several magicians had by now reached the door of the hall, and were vainly straining at the handles.

The afrit sent a powerful magic towards Lovelace. Either it

went too fast, or it was primarily on a plane he could not see, but Nathaniel only saw it as the suggestion of a jet of smoke that crossed to the magician in an instant. Nothing happened. The afrit cocked its head, as if bemused.

On Lovelace's other side, the black bear djinni was closing fast. From each paw, two scimitar-like claws unsheathed.

Magicians were running helter-skelter, making for the windows, the door, for anywhere at all, accompanied by their host of shrieking imps.

Then something happened to the afrit. To Nathaniel, it was as if he was looking at the afrit's reflection in a pond and the water surface was suddenly disturbed. The afrit seemed to shatter, its form splitting into a thousand quavering shards that were sucked towards a section of air above the podium. A moment later they were gone.

The black bear djinni stopped paddling forwards. Its claws flipped back out of sight. Very subtly, it went into reverse.

The fly buzzed loudly against Nathaniel's ear, shouting in pure panic. 'It's happening!' it cried. 'Can't you see it?'

But Nathaniel saw nothing.

A woman ran past, mouth open in panic. Her hair was a pale shade of blue.

Bartimaeus

The first thing most of them noticed was the afrit. That was the spectacular one, the real curtain-raiser, but in fact plenty had been going on in the previous seconds. The afrit was unlucky, that was all; in her haste to destroy the threat to her master, she got too close to the rift.

The split in the air was about four metres in length and only visible on the seventh plane. Perhaps a few of the imps glimpsed it, but none of the humans could have done so.[4] It wasn't a nice, clean, vertical sort of rift, but diagonal, with jagged edges, as if the air had been torn like thick, fibrous cloth. From my prison, I had watched it form: after the first flicker above the podium, the air had vibrated, distorted wildly and finally snapped along that line.[5]

As soon as the rift appeared, the changes had begun.

The lectern on the podium altered: its substance turned from wood to clay, then to an odd, orange metal, then to something that looked suspiciously like candle wax. It sagged a little, as if melting along one side.

A few blades of grass grew up from the surface of the podium.

The crystal drops of the chandelier directly above it turned to water droplets, which hung suspended for a second in position, shimmering in many colours, then fell to the floor as rain.

A magician was running towards a window. Each line of the pinstripe on his jacket undulated like a sidewinder.

No one noticed these first minor changes or a dozen similar

---

[4] Unless they noticed a faint grey smudge along the line of the rift. This was where light was draining away, being sucked off into the Other Place.

[5] It was the old chewing-gum principle in action. Imagine pulling a strip of chewed gum between your fingers: first it holds and stretches, then gets thin somewhere near the middle. Finally a tiny hole forms at the thinnest point, which quickly tears and splits. Here, Lovelace's summoning had done the pulling. With some help from the thing on the other side.

others. It would take the afrit's fate for them to cotton on.

Pandemonium filled the room, with humans and imps squeaking and gibbering in all directions. As if oblivious to this, Lovelace and I watched the rift. We waited for something to come through.

42

Bartimaeus

Then it happened. The planes close to the rift suddenly went out of sync, as if they were being pulled sideways at varying speeds. It was as though my focus had gone haywire, as it does after a blow to the head — I suddenly saw the windows beyond seven times over, all in slightly different positions. It was most disconcerting.

If whatever Lovelace had summoned was strong enough to disrupt the planes like this, it boded ill for all of us inside the pentacle. It must be very close now. I kept my eye on the rift in the air . . .

Amanda Cathcart passed us, screaming, her bob a fetching blue. A few more changes had been noticed by all and sundry: two magicians, who had strayed too near the podium in a vain attempt to attack Lovelace, found their bodies elongating unpleasantly; one man's nose also grew to a ridiculous length, while the other's vanished altogether.

'What's happening?' the boy whispered.

I did not answer. The rift was opening.

All seven planes distorted like stirred syrup. The rift widened and something like an arm thrust through. It was quite transparent, as if it were made of the most perfect glass; in fact, it would have been wholly invisible were it not for the twisting, swirling convulsions of the planes around it. The arm moved back and forth experimentally: it seemed to be testing the odd sensations of the physical world. I glimpsed four thin protuberances or fingers at the end of the arm: they, like it, had no substance of their own, and were only given form by the rippling disturbances in the air about them.

Down below, Lovelace stepped back, his fingers nervously feeling between his shirt buttons for the Amulet's reassuring touch.

With the distortion of the planes, the other magicians began to see the arm for the first time.[1] They emitted assorted cries of woe that, from the biggest, hairiest man to the smallest, shrillest woman, covered a harmonic range of several octaves. Several of the bravest ran into the centre of the room and coerced their attendant djinn into sending Detonations and other magics galore in the direction of the rift. This turned out to be a mistake. Not one single bolt or blast made it anywhere near the arm; all either screamed off at angles to smash into the walls and ceiling, or dribbled to the floor like water from a dripping hose, the energy taken out of them.

The boy's mouth hung so low and loosely, a rodent could

---

[1] They could only see the first three planes clearly, of course, but that was enough to get the outline.

have used it as a swing. 'That th-thing,' he stammered. 'What is it?'

A fair enough question. What was it, this thing that distorted the planes and disrupted the most powerful magic, when only one arm had actually come through? I could have said something dramatic and eerie like 'The death of us all!' but it wouldn't have got us very far. Besides, he'd only have asked again.

'I don't know exactly,' I said. 'Judging by its caution in coming through, it has rarely been summoned before. It is probably surprised and angry, but its strength is clear enough. Look around! Inside the pentacle, magic is going wrong, things are beginning to change form . . . All normal laws are being warped, suspended. The greatest of us always bring the chaos of the Other Place with them. No wonder Lovelace needed the Amulet of Samarkand to protect himself.'[2]

As we watched, the giant, translucent arm was followed by a brawny, translucent shoulder, more than a metre long. And now something like a head began to emerge through the rift. Once more it was only an outline: seen through it, the windows and the distant trees showed perfectly; around its edge, the planes shuddered in a new frenzy.

'Lovelace can't have summoned this on his own,' I said. 'He *must* have had help. And I don't just mean that old scarecrow you killed, or the clammy one at the door. Someone

---

[2] The entity trapped inside the Amulet had to be at least as powerful as this new-comer if Lovelace was to withstand its force. Even as a long-suffering djinni, I still had a grudging admiration for the ancient Asian people who had managed to capture and compress it.

with real power must have had a hand.'[3]

The great being pulled itself through the gap. Now another arm appeared, and the suggestion of a torso. Most of the magicians were clustering against the periphery of the room, but a few near the windows were caught in a ripple running through the planes. Their faces changed – a man's became a woman's; a woman's a child's. Maddened by his transformation, one magician ran blindly towards the podium – in an instant, his body seemed to become liquid: it slewed in a corkscrew motion up into the rift and vanished from sight. My master gasped in horror.

Now a great, translucent leg emerged, with almost feline stealth and poise. Things were really desperate. Nevertheless, I'm an optimist at heart. I noticed that the ripples emanating from the being changed the nature of every spell they hit. And that gave me hope.

'Nathaniel,' I said. 'Listen to me.'

He didn't answer at first. He was transfixed at the sight of the lords and ladies of his realm running about like demented chickens. After all the events of the previous few days I had almost forgotten how young he was. Right at that moment, he did not look like a magician at all, just a terrified small boy.

'*Nathaniel.*'

A faint voice. 'Yes?'

'Listen. If we get out of this Stricture, do you know what we have to do?'

'But how *can* we get out?'

---

[3] This being was greater by far than all the various marids, afrits and djinn that magicians normally summon. A strong magician can summon an afrit on his own; most marids require two. I was calculating a minimum of four for this one.

'Don't bother about that. *If* we escape, what must we do?'

He shrugged.

'I'll tell you, then. We need to accomplish two things. First – get the Amulet off Lovelace. That's your job.'

'Why?'

'Because I can't touch the Amulet now that he's wearing it: it's absorbing everything magical that comes near him – and I don't wish to be included accidentally. It's got to be you. But I'll try to distract him while you get close.'

'That's kind.'

'The second thing,' I said, 'is that we must reverse the summons to drive our big friend away. That's your job.'

'My job *again*?'

'Yes – I'll help by pinching the summoning horn from Lovelace. It needs to be broken if we're to do the job. But you'll have to round up some of the other magicians to speak the Dismissal spell. Some of the stronger ones are bound to know enough, providing they're still conscious. Don't worry – you won't have to do it yourself.'

The boy frowned. '*Lovelace* intends to dismiss it on his own.' He said this with a touch of his normal vigour.

'Yes, and he's a master magician, highly skilled and powerful. Right – that's settled. We go for the Amulet. If we get it, you head off and seek help from the others, while I deal with Lovelace.'

How the boy would have answered, I'll never know, because at that moment, the great entity stepped clear of the rift and a particularly strong ripple ran out through the planes. It swept through the discarded chairs, turning some to liquid, setting others on fire, and finally reaching the shimmering white Stricture where all this time we had been imprisoned. At its touch, the membrane that enclosed us exploded with a cacophonous bang that sent me flying one way and the boy another. He landed heavily, cutting his face.

Not far away, the great translucent head was slowly turning. 'Nathaniel!' I shouted. 'Get up!'

Nathaniel

His head rang with the force of the explosion and he felt something wet against his mouth. Close by, amid the strident clamour of the hall, a voice called out his birth-name. He stumbled to his feet.

The being was fully present now: Nathaniel sensed its shape, towering high against the ceiling. Beyond it, in the distance, a crowd of magicians huddled helplessly with their imps. And there in front of him stood Simon Lovelace, shouting orders to his slave. One hand was pressed against his chest; the other was outstretched, still holding the summoning horn.

'See, Ramuthra?' he cried. 'I hold the Amulet of Samarkand, and I am thus beyond your power. Every other living thing in this room, be it human or spirit, is yours! I command you to destroy them!'

The great being inclined its head in acceptance; it turned towards the nearest group of magicians, sending shock waves out across the room. Nathaniel began to run towards Lovelace. A little way off, he saw an ugly fly buzzing low along the ground.

Lovelace noticed the fly; he frowned and watched its

weaving, darting progress through the air – first it came close to him, then it drew back, then it came close again – and all the while, Nathaniel was sneaking up behind.

Closer, closer . . .

The fly made an aggressive dart at Lovelace's face, the magician flinched – and at that moment, Nathaniel pounced. He gave a spring and leaped on the magician's back, his fingers wrenching at his collar. As he did so, the fly became a marmoset that snatched at the horn with clever, greedy fingers. Lovelace cried out and gave the marmoset a buffet that sent it spinning, tail over snout; then, bending his back, he tossed Nathaniel over his head to land heavily on the floor.

Nathaniel and the marmoset sprawled side by side, with Lovelace standing over them. The magician's glasses hung crookedly from one ear. Nathaniel's departing hands had ripped his collar half away. The gold chain of the Amulet of Samarkand was exposed around his neck.

'So,' Lovelace said, adjusting his spectacles and addressing Nathaniel, 'you rejected my offer. A pity. How did you elude Maurice? With the help of this thing?' He indicated the marmoset. 'Presumably that is Bartimaeus.'

Nathaniel was winded; it pained him when he tried to rise.

The marmoset was on its feet and growing, altering in outline. 'Come *on*,' it hissed to Nathaniel. 'Before he has a chance to—'

Lovelace made a sign and spoke a syllable. A hulking shape materialized at his shoulder; it had a jackal's head. 'I hadn't meant to summon you,' the magician said. 'Good slaves are so hard to find and, man or djinni, I suspect I shall be the only one walking out of this room alive. But seeing as Bartimaeus is here, it seems wrong to deny you the chance of finishing him off.' Lovelace made an easy gesture towards the gargoyle that now crouched low and ready at Nathaniel's side. 'This time, Jabor,' he said, 'do not fail me.'

The jackal-headed demon stepped forward. The gargoyle gave a curse and darted into the air. Two red-veined wings sprouted from Jabor's back; they flapped once, making a cracking noise like breaking bones, and carried him off in pursuit.

Nathaniel and Lovelace were left regarding each other. The pain in Nathaniel's midriff had subsided a little, and he was able to get to his feet. He kept his eyes fixed on the glint of gold at the magician's throat.

'You know, John,' Lovelace said, tapping the horn casually against the palm of one hand, 'if you'd had the luck to be apprenticed to me from the start, we might have done great things together. I recognize something in you; it is like looking into a mirror of my younger days – we share the same will to power.' He smiled, showing his white teeth. 'But you were corrupted by Underwood's softness, his mediocrity.'

He broke off at this point, as a howling magician stumbled between them, his skin shining with tiny iridescent blue scales. From all across the room came the confused, unsettling sounds of magic distorting and going wrong, as it met the shock waves emanating from Ramuthra. Most of the magicians and their imps were piled up against the far wall, almost one on top of the other in their effort to escape. The great being moved towards them with lazy steps, leaving a trail of altered debris in its wake: transformed chairs, scattered bags and belongings – all stretched, twisted, glimmering with unnatural tones and colours. Nathaniel tried to blot it from his mind; he gazed at the Amulet's chain, readying himself for another try.

Lovelace smiled. 'Even now you haven't given up,' he said. 'And that's exactly what I'm talking about – that's your iron will in action. It's very good. But if you'd been my apprentice, I'd have trained you to keep it in check until you had the ability to go with it. If he is to survive, a true magician must be patient.'

'Yes,' Nathaniel said huskily, 'I've been told that before.'

'You should have listened. Well, it's too late to save you now; you've done me too much harm, and even were I so disposed, there's nothing I could do for you in here. The Amulet can't be shared.'

For a moment he considered Ramuthra: the demon had cornered an outlying pocket of magicians and was reaching down towards them with grasping fingers. A shrill screaming was suddenly cut off.

Nathaniel made a tiny movement. Instantly, Lovelace's eyes snapped back to him. '*Still* fighting?' he said. 'If I can't trust you to lie down and die with all those other fools and cowards, I shall have to dispose of you first. Take it as a compliment, John.'

He set the horn to his lips and blew briefly. Nathaniel's skin crawled; he sensed a change behind him.

Ramuthra had halted at the sound from the horn. The disturbance in the planes that marked its edges intensified, as if it radiated a strong emotion, perhaps anger. Nathaniel watched it turn; it appeared to be regarding Lovelace across the breadth of the hall.

'Do not hesitate, slave!' Lovelace cried. 'You shall do my bidding! This boy must die first.'

Nathaniel felt an alien gaze upon him. With a strange detached clarity, he noticed a beautiful golden tapestry hanging on the wall beyond the giant head; it seemed larger than it should be, in crystal-clear focus, as if the demon's essence magnified it.

'Come!' Lovelace's voice sounded cracked and dry. A great wave rippled out from the demon, turning a nearby chandelier into a host of tiny yellow birds that broke away and flew across the rafters of the hall before dissolving. Ponderously turning its back on the remaining magicians, it set off in Nathaniel's direction.

Nathaniel's bowels turned to water. He backed away.

Beside him, he heard Lovelace chuckle.

Bartimaeus

So here we were again, Jabor and I, like partners in a dance – I retreating, he pursuing, step by synchronized step. Across the chaotic hall we flew, avoiding the scurrying humans, the explosions of misdirected magic, the shock waves radiating from the great being stalking in its midst. Jabor wore a grimace that might have been annoyance or uncertainty, since even his extreme resilience would be tested in this new environment. I decided to undermine his morale.

'How does it feel to be inferior to Faquarl?' I called, as I ducked behind one of the few remaining chandeliers. 'I don't see Lovelace risking *his* life by summoning him here today.'

From the other side of the chandelier, Jabor tried to lob a Pestilence at me, but a ripple of energy disrupted it and it became a cloud of pretty flowers drifting to the floor.

'Charming,' I said. 'Next you need to learn to arrange them properly. I'll lend you a nice vase, if you like.'

I don't think Jabor's grasp of insults extended far enough to take that quite on board, but he understood the tone, and it actually roused him to verbal response.

'HE SUMMONED ME BECAUSE I'M STRONGER!' he bellowed, wrenching the chandelier from the ceiling and hurling it at me. I dodged balletically and it shattered against the wall, to rain down in little lumps of crystal on the magicians' cowering heads.

Jabor did not seem impressed by this graceful manoeuvre. 'COWARD!' he cried. 'ALWAYS, YOU SNEAK AND CRAWL AND RUN AND HIDE.'

'It's called intelligence,' I said, pirouetting in mid-air, seizing a splintered beam from the ceiling rafters and hurling it at him like a javelin. He didn't bother to move, but let it crack against his shoulders and fall away. Then he came on. Despite my fine words, none of my sneaking, crawling, running or hiding was having much effect right now, and looking down across the hall, I saw that the situation was in fact deteriorating rapidly. Ramuthra[4] had turned and was proceeding back across the room towards where the magician and my master were standing. It wasn't hard to see what Lovelace intended: the boy had become too much of an irritant to let him live a moment longer. I understood his point of view.

And still Lovelace held the horn; still he wore the Amulet. So far we had gained nothing. Somehow he had to be

---

[4] I hadn't heard of this particular being before. Unsurprising really, since though there are many thousands of us that magicians have cruelly summoned – and thus defined – there are countless more that merge into the Other Place without any need for names. Perhaps this was the first time Ramuthra had been summoned.

distracted, before Ramuthra got near enough to destroy the boy. An idea came into my mind unbidden. Interesting . . . But first, I needed to shake Jabor off for a while.

Easier said than done, Jabor being a persistent sort of fellow.

Avoiding his outstretched fingers, I ducked down through the air, in the vague direction of the centre of the room. The podium had long since been reduced to a blancmangey sort of substance by the proximity of the rift. Scattered shoes and chairs were strewn all around, but there was no one left living in this area.

I dropped at speed. Behind, I heard Jabor rushing through the air in hot pursuit.

The nearer I got to the rift, the greater the strain on my essence – I could feel a suction starting to pull me forwards; the effect was unpleasantly similar to being summoned. When I had reached the limit of my endurance, I stopped in mid-air, did a quick somersault and faced the oncoming Jabor. There he was, whistling down, arms out and angry, with not a thought for the danger just beyond me. He just wanted to get his claws on my essence, to rend me like one of his victims from old Ombos[5] or Phoenicia.

But I was no mere human, cowering and quailing in the temple dark. I am Bartimaeus, and no coward either. I stood my ground.[6]

Down came Jabor. I hunched into a wrestling pose.

He opened his mouth to give that jackal cry—

---

[5] *Ombos*: city in Egypt sacred to Seth, Jabor's old boss. For a century or two Jabor lurked in a temple there, feeding on the victims brought to him, until a pharaoh from Lower Egypt came and burned the place to the ground.

[6] Or air, really. We were about seven metres up.

I flapped my wings once and rose up a fraction. As he shot under me, I swivelled and booted his backside with all my strength. He was going too fast to stop quickly, especially with my friendly assistance. His wings jammed forward in an effort to stop . . . He slowed . . . began to turn, snarling . . .

The rift exerted its pull on him. An expression of sudden doubt appeared on his face. He tried to beat his wings, but they didn't move properly. It was as if they were immersed in fast-flowing treacle; traces of a black-grey substance were pulled off the fringes of his wings and sucked away. That was his essence beginning to go. He made a tremendous effort, and actually succeeded in advancing a little towards me. I gave him a thumbs-up sign.

'Well done,' I said. 'I reckon you made about five centimetres there. Keep going.' He made another Herculean effort. 'Another centimetre! Good try! You'll get your hands on me soon.' To encourage him I stuck a cheeky foot in his direction and waved it in front of his face, just out of reach. He snarled and tried to swipe, but now the essence was curling away from the surface of his limbs and being drawn into the rift; his muscular tone was visibly changing, growing thinner by the instant. As his strength ebbed, the pull of the rift became stronger and he began to move backwards, slowly first, then faster.

If Jabor had had half a brain he might have changed into a gnat or something: perhaps with less bulk he might have fought free of the rift's gravitational pull. A word of friendly advice could have saved him, but dear me, I was too busy watching him unravel to think of it until it was far too late. Now his rear limbs and wings were sloughing off into liquid streams of greasy grey-black stuff that spiralled through the rift and away from Earth. It can't have been pleasant for him, especially with Lovelace's charge still binding him here, but his face showed no pain, only hatred. So it was, right to the end. Even as the back of his head lost its form, his blazing red eyes were still locked on mine. Then they were gone, away into the rift, and I was alone, waving him a fond adieu.

I didn't waste too much time on my goodbyes. I had other matters to attend to.

Nathaniel

'An amazing thing, the Amulet of Samarkand.' Whether from fear, or from a cruel delight in reasserting his control, Lovelace persisted in keeping up a one-sided conversation with Nathaniel even as Ramuthra stalked remorselessly towards them. It seemed he could not bring himself to shut up. Nathaniel was retreating slowly, hopelessly, knowing there was nothing he could do.

'Ramuthra disrupts the elements, you see.' Lovelace continued. 'Wherever it treads, the elements rebel. And that ruins the careful order on which all magic depends. Nothing any of *you* might try can stop it: every magical effort will misfire – you cannot hurt me, you cannot escape. Ramuthra will have you all. But the Amulet contains an equal and opposite force to Ramuthra's; thus I am secure. It might even lift me to its mouth, so that chaos raged upon me, and I would feel nothing.'

The demon had halved the distance to Nathaniel and was

picking up pace. One of its great transparent arms was outstretched. Perhaps it was eager to taste him.

'My dear master suggested this plan,' Lovelace said, 'and, as always, he was inspired. He will be watching us at this moment.'

'You mean Schyler?' Even on the threshold of death, Nathaniel couldn't restrain a savage satisfaction. 'I doubt it. He's lying dead upstairs.'

Lovelace's self-possession faltered for the first time. His smile flickered.

'That's right,' Nathaniel said. 'I didn't just escape. I killed him.'

The magician laughed. 'Don't lie to me, child—'

A voice behind Lovelace: a woman's, soft and plaintive. 'Simon!'

The magician looked back; Amanda Cathcart stood there, close at hand, her gown torn and muddied, her hair dishevelled and now slightly maroon. She limped as she approached him, her arms out, bafflement and terror etched upon her face. 'Oh, *Simon*,' she said. 'What have you done?'

Lovelace blanched; he turned to face the woman. 'Stay back!' he cried. There was a note of panic in his voice. 'Get away!'

Tears welled in Amanda Cathcart's eyes. 'How could you do this, Simon? Am I to die too?'

She lurched forwards. Discomforted, the magician raised his hands to ward her off. 'Amanda – I–I'm sorry. It . . . it had to be.'

'No, Simon – you promised me so much.'

Sideways on, Nathaniel stole closer.

Lovelace's confusion turned to anger. 'Get away from me,

woman, or I will call on the demon to tear you to shreds! Look – it is almost upon you!' Amanda Cathcart made no move. She seemed past caring.

'How *could* you use me in this way, Simon? After everything you said. You have no honour.'

Nathaniel took another shuffling step. Ramuthra's outline towered above him now.

'Amanda, I'm warning you—'

Nathaniel leaped forward and snatched. His fingers rasped against the skin on Lovelace's neck, then closed about something cold, hard and flexible. The Amulet's chain. He pulled at it with all his strength. For an instant the magician's head was jerked towards him, then a link somewhere along the chain snapped and it came away free in his hand.

Lovelace gave a great cry.

Nathaniel fell back from him and rolled onto the floor, the chain's links colliding against his face. He scrabbled at it with both hands, clasping the small, thin oval thing that hung from the middle of the broken chain. As he did so, he was conscious of a weight being removed from him, as if a remorseless gaze had suddenly shifted elsewhere.

Lovelace had reeled in the first shock of the assault, then made to pounce upon Nathaniel – but two slender arms pulled him back. 'Wait, Simon – would you hurt a poor, sweet boy?'

'You're mad, Amanda! Get off me! The Amulet – I must—' For an instant he fought to extricate himself from the woman's desperate grip, and then the towering presence directly above him caught his horrified eye. His legs sagged. Ramuthra was very close to all three of them now: in the full power of its proximity, the fabric of their clothes flapped wildly, their hair blew about their faces. The air around them shivered, as if with electricity.

Lovelace squirmed backwards. He nearly fell. 'Ramuthra! I order you – take the boy! He has *stolen* the Amulet! He is not truly protected!' His voice carried no conviction. A great translucent hand reached out. Lovelace redoubled his entreaties. 'Then forget the boy – take the woman! Take the woman first!'

For a moment, the hand paused. Lovelace made a great effort and ripped himself from the woman's grasp. 'Yes! See? There she is! Take her first!'

From everywhere and nowhere came a voice like a great crowd speaking in unison. 'I SEE NO WOMAN. ONLY A GRINNING DJINNI.'

Lovelace's face froze; he turned to Amanda Cathcart, who had been gazing at him with a look of agonized entreaty. As he watched, her features slowly altered. A smile of triumphant wickedness spread across her face from ear to ear. Then, in a flash, one of her arms snaked out, plucked the summoning horn from Lovelace's slackening grip and snatched it away. With a bound, Amanda Cathcart was gone, and a marmoset hung by its tail from a light fitting several metres off. It waved the horn merrily at the aghast magician.

'Don't mind if I have this?' it called. 'You won't need it where you're going.'

All energy seemed to depart from the magician; his skin hung loose and ashen on his bones. His shoulders slumped; he took a pace towards Nathaniel, as if half-heartedly trying to reclaim the Amulet . . . Then a great hand reached down and engulfed him and Lovelace was plucked into the air. High, high, higher he went, his body shifting and altering as it did so. Ramuthra's head bent to meet him. Something that might have been a mouth was seen to open.

An instant later, Simon Lovelace was gone.

The demon paused to look for the cackling marmoset, but for the moment it had vanished. Ignoring Nathaniel, who was still sprawled on the floor, it turned back heavily towards the magicians at the other end of the hall.

A familiar voice spoke at Nathaniel's side.

'Two down, one to go,' it said.

Bartimaeus

I was so elated at the success of my fine trick that I risked changing into Ptolemy's form the moment Ramuthra's attention was elsewhere. Jabor and Lovelace were gone and now only the great entity remained to be dealt with. I nudged my master with a boot. He was lying on his back, cradling the Amulet of Samarkand in his grubby mitts like a mother would her baby. I had set the summoning horn down by his side.

He struggled to a sitting position. 'Lovelace . . . did you see?'

'Yep, and it wasn't pretty.'

As he rose stiffly to his feet, his eyes shone with a strange brilliance – half horror, half exaltation. 'I've *got* it,' he whispered. 'I've got the Amulet.'

'Yes,' I replied hastily. 'Well done. But Ramuthra is still with us, and if we want to get help, we're running out of time.'

I looked across at the far side of the auditorium. My elation dwindled. The assembled ministers of State were a lamentable heap by now, either cowering in dumb stupefaction, banging on the doors, or fighting viciously with each other for a position as far away as possible from the oncoming Ramuthra. It was an unedifying spectacle, like watching a crowd of plague rats scrapping in a sewer. It was also highly worrying: since not one of them looked in a fit state to recite a complex dismissal spell.

'Come on,' I said. 'While Ramuthra takes some, we can rouse the others. Who's most likely to remember the counter-summons?

His lip curled. 'None of *them*, by the looks of things.'

'Even so, we've got to try.' I tugged at his sleeve. 'Come *on*. Neither of us knows the incantation.'[7]

'Speak for yourself,' he said slowly. '*I* know it.'

'You?' I was a little taken aback. 'Are you sure?'

He scowled at me. Physically, he was pretty ropey – white of skin, bruised and bleeding, swaying where he stood. But a bright fire of determination burned in his eyes. 'That possibility hadn't even occurred to you, had it?' he said. 'Yes – I've learned it.'

There was more than a hint of doubt in the voice, and in the eyes too – I glimpsed it wrestling with his resolve. I tried not to sound sceptical. 'It's high-level,' I said. 'And complex; and you'll need to break the horn at exactly the right moment. This is no time for false pride, boy. You could still—'

'Ask for help? I don't think so.' Whether through pride or practicality, he was quite right. Ramuthra was almost upon the

---

[7] I hadn't a clue. Words of Command are magicians' business. That is what they are good at. Djinn can't speak them. But crabbed old master magicians know an incantation for every eventuality.

magicians now; we had no chance of getting help from them. 'Stand away,' he said. 'I need space to think.'

I hesitated for an instant. Admirable though his strength of character was, I could see all too clearly where it led. Amulet or no Amulet, the consequences of a fluffed dismissal are always disastrous, and this time I would suffer right along with him. But I could think of no alternative.

Helplessly, I stood back. My master picked up the summoning horn and closed his eyes.

Nathaniel

He closed his eyes to the chaos in the hall and breathed as slowly and deeply as he could. Sounds of suffering and terror still came to him, but he shoved them from his mind with a force of will.

That much was relatively easy. But a host of inner voices were speaking at him, and he could not shut their clamour out. This was his moment! This was the moment when a thousand insults and deprivations would be cast aside and forgotten! He knew the incantation – he had learned it long ago. He would speak it and everyone would see that he could not be overlooked again. Always, *always* he had been underestimated! Underwood had thought him an imbecile, a fool with barely the strength to draw a circle. He had refused to believe his apprentice could summon a djinni of any kind. Lovelace had thought him weak, childishly soft-hearted, yet likely to be tempted by the first cursory offer of power and

status. He had refused to accept that Nathaniel had killed
Schyler too: he had gone to his death denying it. And now
even Bartimaeus, his own servant, doubted that he knew the
Dismissal spell! Always, always, they cast him down.

Now was the moment when everything was in his hands.
Too often before he had been rendered powerless – locked in
his room, carried from the fire, robbed by the commoners,
trapped in the Stricture . . . The memories of these indignities
burned hot inside him. But now he would act – he would
show them!

The outcry of his wounded pride almost overwhelmed
him. It pounded on the inside of his skull. But at the deeper
core of his being, beneath this desperation to succeed for his
own sake, another desire struggled for expression. Far off, he
heard someone cry out in fear and a shudder of pity ran
through him. Unless he could bring the spell to mind, the
hapless magicians were going to die. Their lives depended on
him. And he had the knowledge to help. The counter-
summons, the Dismissal. How had it gone? He'd read the
incantation, he *knew* he had – he'd committed it to memory
months before. But he couldn't concentrate now, he couldn't
bring it to mind.

It was no good. They were all going to die, just as Mrs
Underwood had died, and again he was about to fail. How
badly Nathaniel wanted to help them! But desire alone was
not enough. More than anything else he had wanted to save
Mrs Underwood, bring her from the flames. He would have
given his life for hers, if he could. But he had not saved her.
He had been carried away and she had gone for ever. His love
had counted for nothing.

For a moment, his past loss and the urgency of his present

desire mingled and welled within him. Tears ran down his cheeks.

Patience, Nathaniel.

Patience . . .

He breathed in slowly. His sorrow receded. And across a great gulf came the remembered peace of his master's garden – he saw again the rhododendron bushes, their leaves glinting dark green in the sun. He saw the apple trees shedding their white blossom; a cat lying on a red-brick wall. He felt the lichen under his fingers; saw the moss on the statue; he felt himself protected again from the wider world. He imagined Ms Lutyens sitting quietly, sketching by his side. A feeling of peace stole over him.

His mind cleared, his memory blossomed.

The necessary words came to him, as he had learned them sitting on the stone seat a year or more ago.

He opened his eyes and spoke them, his voice loud and clear and strong. At the end of the fifteenth syllable, he split the summoning horn in two across his knee.

As the ivory cracked and the words rang out, Ramuthra stopped dead. The shimmering ripples in the air that defined its outlines quivered, first gently and then with greater force. The rift in the centre of the room opened a little. Then, with astonishing suddenness, the outlines of the demon crumpled and shrank, were drawn back into the rift and vanished.

The rift closed up: a scar healing at blinding speed.

With it gone, the hall seemed cavernous and empty. One chandelier and several small wall lights came on again, casting a weak radiance here and there. Outside, the late afternoon sky was grey, darkening to blue. The wind could be heard rushing through the trees in the wood.

There was absolute silence in the hall. The crowd of magicians and one or two bruised and battered imps remained quite still. Only one thing moved: a boy limping forwards across the centre of the room, with the Amulet of Samarkand dangling from his fingers. The jade stone at its centre gleamed faintly in the half-light.

In utter silence, Nathaniel crossed to where Rupert Devereaux sprawled half-buried under the Foreign Minister, and placed the Amulet carefully in his hands.

Bartimaeus

43

Typical of the kid, that was. Having carried out the most important act of his grubby little life, you'd expect him to sink to the ground in exhaustion and relief. But did he? No. This was his big chance and he seized it in the most theatrical fashion possible. With all eyes on him, he hobbled across the ruined auditorium like a wounded bird, frail as you like, straight for the centre of power. What was he going to do? No one knew; no one dared to guess (I saw the Prime Minister flinch when the boy held out his hand). And then, in the climactic moment of this little charade, all was revealed: the legendary Amulet of Samarkand – held up high so all could see – handed back to the bosom of the Government. The kid even remembered to bow his head deferentially as he did so.

Sensation in the hall!

What a performance, eh? In fact, almost more than his

ability to bully djinn, this instinctive pandering to the crowd suggested to me that the boy was probably destined for worldly success.[1] Certainly, his actions here had the desired effect: in moments, he was the centre of an admiring throng.

Unnoticed in all this fuss, I abandoned Ptolemy's form and took on the semblance of a minor imp, which presently (when the scrum drew back) hovered over to the boy's side in a humble sort of way. I had no desire for my true capabilities to be noticed. Someone might have drawn a connection with the swashbuckling djinni who had lately escaped from the government prison.

Nathaniel's shoulder was the ideal vantage point for me to observe the aftermath of the attempted coup, since for a few hours at least the boy was the centre of attention. Wherever the Prime Minister and his senior colleagues went, my master went too, answering urgent questions and stuffing his face with the reviving sweetmeats that underlings brought him.

When a systematic headcount was made, the list of missing was found to include four ministers (all fortunately from fairly junior posts) and a single under-secretary.[2] In addition, several magicians had suffered major facial and bodily distortions, or been otherwise inconvenienced.

The general relief quickly turned to anger. With Ramuthra gone, the magicians were able to set their slaves against the magical barriers on the doors and walls and quickly burst out

---

[1] If magicians rely on theatrical effects to overawe the people, they also use much the same techniques to impress and outmanoeuvre each other.

[2] Amanda Cathcart, Simon Lovelace and six servants had also vanished into the rift or the mouth of Ramuthra, but in the circumstances the magicians did not consider these significant losses.

into the house. A thorough search was made of Heddleham Hall, but apart from assorted servants, the dead body of the old man and an angry boy locked in a lavatory, no one was discovered. Unsurprisingly, the fish-faced magician Rufus Lime had gone; nor was there any sign of the tall black-bearded man who had manned the gatehouse. Both seemed to have vanished into thin air.

Nathaniel also directed the investigators to the kitchen, where a compressed group of under-cooks was found trembling in a pantry. They reported that about half an hour previously,[3] the head chef had given a great cry, burst into blue flame and swelled to a great and terrifying size before vanishing in a gust of brimstone. Upon inspection, a meat cleaver was found deeply embedded in the stonework of the fireplace, the last memento of Faquarl's bondage.[4]

With the main conspirators dead or vanished, the magicians set to interrogating the servants of the Hall. However, they proved ignorant of the conspiracy. They reported that during the previous few weeks Simon Lovelace had organized the extensive refurbishment of the auditorium, keeping it out of bounds for long periods. Unseen workers, accompanied by many oddly coloured lights and sounds, had constructed the glass floor and inserted the new carpet,[5] supervised by a

---

[3] i.e. at exactly the moment Lovelace perished.

[4] So, once again, our paths had crossed without a definitive confrontation. A pity really; I was looking forward to giving Faquarl a good hiding. I just hadn't quite had time to get round to it.

[5] As well as no doubt creating the secret mechanism in an adjacent room, which pulled back the carpet from the floor and triggered the bars upon the windows. Certain types of foliot are very gifted at construction jobs; I used to have a band of them under me when working on the walls of Prague. They're good workers, provided they don't hear the sound of church bells, in which case they down tools and crumble into ashes. That was a drag on festival days – I had to employ a bunch of imps with dustpans and brushes to sweep away the pieces.

certain well-dressed gentleman with a round face and reddish beard.

This was a new clue. My master eagerly reported sighting such a person leaving the Hall that very morning, and messengers were immediately sent out with his description to alert the police in London and the Home Counties.

When all was done that could be done, Devereaux and his senior ministers refreshed themselves with champagne, cold meats and jellied fruits and listened properly to my master's story. And what a story it was. What an outrageous yarn he told. Even I, with my long experience of human duplicity, was flabbergasted by the whoppers that boy came up with. To be frank, he *did* have a lot of things to hide: his own theft of the Amulet, for example, and my little encounter with Sholto Pinn. But a lot of his fibs were quite unnecessary. I had to sit quietly on his shoulder and hear myself referred to as a 'minor imp' (five times), a 'sort of foliot' (twice), and even (once) as a 'homunculus'.[6] I ask you – how insulting is that?

But that wasn't the half of it. He recounted (with big, mournful eyes) how his dear master, Arthur Underwood, had long been suspicious of Simon Lovelace, but had never had proof of any wrongdoing. Until, that was, the fateful day when Underwood had by chance perceived the Amulet of Samarkand in Lovelace's possession. Before he could tell the authorities, Lovelace and his djinn had arrived at the house

---

[6] *Homunculus*: a tiny manikin produced by magic and often trapped in a bottle as a magician's curio. A few have prophetic powers, although it is important to do exactly the *opposite* of what they recommend, since homunculi are always malevolent and seek to do their creators harm.

intent on murder. Underwood, together with John Mandrake, his faithful apprentice, had put up strong resistance, while even Mrs Underwood had pitched in, heroically trying to tackle Lovelace herself. All in vain. Mr and Mrs Underwood had been killed and Nathaniel had fled for his life, with only a minor imp to help him. There were actually tears in his eyes when he recounted all this; it was almost as if he believed the rubbish he was spouting.

That was the bulk of his lie. Having no way of proving Lovelace's guilt, Nathaniel had then travelled to Heddleham Hall in the hope of somehow preventing his terrible crime. Now he was only happy he had managed to save the lives of his country's noble rulers, etc., etc.; honestly, it was enough to make an imp weep.

But they bought it. Didn't doubt a single word. He had another hurried snack, a swig of champagne, and then my master was whisked away in a ministerial limousine, back to London and further debriefing.

I went along too, of course. I wasn't letting him out of my sight for anything. He had a promise to keep.

44

The servant's footsteps receded down the stairs. The boy and I looked around.

'I preferred your old room,' I said. 'This one smells, and you haven't even moved in yet.'

'It doesn't smell.'

'It does: of fresh paint and plastic and all things new and fabricated. Which I suppose is quite appropriate for you – don't you think so, Mr *Mandrake*?'

He didn't answer. He was bounding across to the window to look out at the view.

It was the evening of the day following the great summoning at Heddleham Hall, and for the first time my master was being left to his own devices. He had spent much of the previous twenty-four hours in meetings with ministers and police, going over his story and no doubt adding lies with each retelling. Meanwhile, I'd remained out on the street,[1] shivering with impatience. My frustration had only increased when the boy had spent the first night in a specially provided dormitory on Whitehall, a building heavily guarded in numerous ways. While he snored within, I'd been forced to skulk outside, still unable to engage him in the necessary chat.

But now another day had passed and his future had been decided. An official car had driven him to his new master's

---

[1] Government offices tend to be full of afrits and search spheres, and I feared they might take exception to my presence.

472

home – a modern riverside development on the south bank of the Thames. Dinner would be served at half past eight; his master would await him in the dining room at eight fifteen. This meant that Nathaniel and I had an hour all to ourselves. I intended to make it count.

The room contained the usual: bed, desk, wardrobe (a walk-in one, this – swanky), bookcase, bedside table, chair. A connecting door led to a tiny en-suite bathroom. There was a powerful electric light set in the pristine ceiling and a small window in one wall. Outside, the moon shone on the waters of the Thames. The boy was looking out at the Houses of Parliament almost directly opposite, an odd expression on his face.

'They're a lot nearer now,' I said.

'Yes. She'd be very proud.' He turned, only to discover that I had adopted Ptolemy's form and was reclining on his bed. 'Get off there! I don't want your horrible— Hey!' He spotted a book tucked into a shelf beside the bed. '*Faust's Compendium!* My own copy. That's amazing! Underwood forbade me to touch this.'

'Just remember – it didn't do Faust any good.'

He was flipping the pages. 'Brilliant . . . And my master says I can do minor conjurings in my room.'

'Ah, yes – your nice, sweet, new master.' I shook my head sadly. 'You're pleased with her, are you?'

He nodded eagerly. 'Ms Whitwell's very powerful. She'll teach me lots. And she'll treat me with proper respect, too.'

'You think so? An honourable magician, is she?' I made a sour face. My old friend Jessica Whitwell, rake-thin Minister for Security, head of the Tower of London, controller of the Mournful Orbs . . . Yes, she was powerful, all right. And it was no doubt a sign of how highly the authorities thought of Nathaniel that he was being entrusted to her tender care. Certainly, she would be a very different master from Arthur Underwood, and would see to it that his talent didn't go to waste . . . What it would do to his temperament was another question. Well – no doubt he was getting exactly what he deserved.

'She said I had a great career ahead of me,' he went on, 'if I played my cards right and worked hard. She said she would supervise my training, and that if all went well they'd put me in the fast stream and I'd soon be working in a ministerial department, getting experience.' He had that triumphant look in his eyes again, the kind that made me want to put him over my knee. I made a big show of yawning and plumping up the pillow, but he kept going. 'There's no restriction on age, she said, only on talent. I said I wanted to get involved with the Ministry for Internal Affairs – they're the ones who're hunting the Resistance. Did you know there was another attack while we were out of London? An office in Whitehall was blown up. No one's made a breakthrough, yet – but I bet I could track them down. First off I'll catch Fred and Stanley – and that girl. Then I'll make them talk, then I'll—'

'Steady on,' I said. 'Haven't you done enough for a lifetime? Think about it – two power-crazed magicians killed, a hundred power-crazed magicians saved . . . You're a hero.'

My slight sarcasm was wasted on him. 'That's what Mr Devereaux said.'

I sat up suddenly and cupped my ear towards the window. 'Listen to that!' I exclaimed.

'What?'

'It's the sound of lots of people not cheering.'

He scowled. 'Meaning what?'

'Meaning the Government's keeping this all very quiet. Where are the photographers? Where are the newspapermen? I'd have expected you on the front page of *The Times* this morning. They should be asking for your life story, giving you medals in public places, putting you on cheesy limited edition postage stamps . . . But they aren't, are they?'

The boy sniffed. 'They have to keep it quiet for security reasons. That's what they told me.'

'No, it's for reasons of not wanting to look stupid. "TWELVE-YEAR-OLD SAVES GOVERNMENT"? They'd be laughed at in the street. And that's something no magicians ever want, take it from me. When that happens, it's the beginning of the end.'

The boy smirked. He was too young to understand. 'It's not the commoners we have to fear,' he said. 'It's the conspirators – the ones who got away. Ms Whitwell says that at least four magicians must have summoned the demon, so as well as Lovelace, Schyler and Lime there must be at least one more. Lime's gone, and no one's seen that red-bearded magician at any of the ports or aerodromes . . . it's a real mystery. I'm sure Sholto Pinn's in on it, too, but I can't say anything about him, after what you did to his shop.'

'Yes,' I said, putting my hands behind my head and speaking in a musing sort of way, 'I suppose you *do* have rather a lot to hide. There's *me*, your "minor imp", and all my exploits. There's *you*, stealing the Amulet and framing your master . . .' He flushed at this and made a big show of going off to investigate the walk-in wardrobe. I got up and followed him. 'By the way,' I added, 'I notice you gave Mrs Underwood a starring role in your version of events. Helps salve your conscience, does it?'

He spun round, his face reddened. 'If you have a point,' he snapped, 'get to it.'

I looked at him seriously then. 'You said you would revenge yourself on Lovelace,' I said, 'and you did what you set out to do. Perhaps that takes away a little of your pain – I hope so; I wouldn't know. But you *also* promised that if I helped you against Lovelace, you'd set me free. Well, help has been dutifully given. I think I saved your life several times over. Lovelace is dead and you're better off – in your eyes – than you've ever been before. So now's the time to honour your promise, Nathaniel, and let me go.'

For a moment he was silent. 'Yes,' he said, at last. 'You did help me . . . You did save me . . .'

'To my eternal shame.'

'And I'm . . .' He halted.

'Embarrassed?'

'No.'

'Delighted?'

'*No.*'

'A teensy bit grateful?'

He took a deep breath. 'Yes. I'm grateful. But that doesn't alter the fact that you know my birth-name.'

It was time to iron this out once and for all. I was tired; my essence ached with the effort of nine days in the world. I had to go. 'True,' I said. 'I know your name and you know mine. You can summon me. I can damage you. That makes us quits. But while I'm in the Other Place, who am I going to tell? No one. You should *want* me to go back there. If we're both lucky, I won't even be summoned again during your lifetime. However, if I am –' I paused, gave a heavy sigh – 'I promise I won't reveal your name.'

He said nothing. 'You want it official?' I cried. 'How about this? "Should I break this vow, may I be trampled into the sand by camels and scattered among the ordure of the fields."[2] Now I can't say fairer than that, can I?'

He hesitated. For an instant, he was going to agree. 'I don't know,' he muttered. 'You're a de— a djinni. Vows mean nothing to you.'

'You're confusing me with a magician! All right, then –' I jumped back in anger – 'how about this? If you don't dismiss me here and now, I'll go right downstairs and tell your dear Ms Whitwell exactly what's been going on. She'll be very interested to see me in my true form.'

He bit his lip, reached for his book. 'I could—'

'Yes, you could do lots of things,' I said. 'That's your trouble. You're too clever for your own good. A lot has happened because you were too clever to let things lie. You wanted revenge, you summoned a noble djinni, you stole the Amulet, you let others pay the price. You did what you wanted, and I helped because I had to. And no doubt, with your cleverness, you could devise some new bond for me in time, but not quickly enough to stop me telling your master right now about you, the Amulet, Underwood and me.'

'Right now?' he said quietly.

'Right now.'

'You'd end up in the tin.'

'Too bad for both of us.'

For a few moments we held each other's gaze properly, perhaps for the first time. Then, with a sigh, the boy looked away.

---

[2] An old Egyptian vow. Be careful when you use it – it invariably comes true.

'Dismiss me, John,' I said. 'I've done enough. I'm tired. And so are you.'

He gave a small smile at this. '*I'm* not tired,' he said. 'There's too much I want to do.'

'Exactly,' I said. 'The Resistance . . . the conspirators . . . You'll want a free hand trying to hunt them down. Think of all the other djinn you'll need to summon as you embark on your great career. They won't have my class, but they'll give you less lip.'

Something in that seemed to strike a chord with him. 'All right, Bartimaeus,' he said finally. 'I agree. You'll have to wait while I draw the circle.'

'That's no problem!' I was eagerness itself. 'In fact, I'll gladly entertain you while you do it! What would you like? I could sing like a nightingale, summon sweet music from the air, create a thousand heavenly scents . . . I suppose I could even juggle a bit if that tickles your fancy.'

'Thank you. None of that will be necessary.'

The floor in one corner of the room had been purposely left bare of carpet and was slightly raised. Here, with great precision, and with only one or two fleeting glances at his book of formulae, the boy drew a simple pentacle and two circles with a piece of black chalk he found in the drawer of his desk. I kept very quiet while he did so. I didn't want him to make any mistakes.

At last he finished, and rose stiffly, holding his back. 'It's done,' he said, stretching. 'Get in.'

I considered the runes carefully. 'That cancels Adelbrand's Pentacle, does it?'

'Yes.'

'And breaks the bond of Perpetual Confinement?'

'Yes! See that hieroglyph here? That snaps the thread. Now do you want to be dismissed or not?'

'Just checking.' I skipped into the bigger circle and turned to face him. He readied himself, ordering the words in his mind, then looked at me severely.

'Take that stupid grin off your face,' he said. 'You're putting me off.'

'Sorry.' I adopted a hideous expression of malady and woe.

'That's not much better.'

'Sorry, sorry.'

'All right, prepare yourself.' He took a deep breath.

'Just one thing,' I said. 'If you were going to summon some-one else soon, I recommend Faquarl. He's a good worker. Put him to something constructive, like draining a lake with a sieve, or counting grains of sand on a beach. He'd be good at that.'

'Look, do you *want* to go or not?'

'Oh yes. I do. Very much.'

'Well, then—'

'Nathaniel – one last thing.'

'*What?*'

'Listen: for a magician, you've got potential. And I don't mean the way you think I mean. For a start, you've got far more initiative than most of them, but they'll crush it out of you if you're not careful. And you've a conscience too, another thing which is rare and easily lost. Guard it. That's all. Oh, and I'd beware of your new master, if I were you.'

He looked at me for a moment, as if he wanted to speak. Then he shook his head impatiently. 'I'll be all right. You needn't bother about me. This is your last chance. I have to be down for dinner in five minutes.'

'I'm ready.'

Then the boy spoke the counter-summons swiftly and without fault. I felt the weight of words binding me to the Earth lessen with every syllable. As he neared the end, my form extended, spread, blossomed out from the confines of the circle. Multiple doors opened in the planes, beckoning me through. I became a dense cloud of smoke that roared up and outwards, filling a room that became less real to me with every passing instant.

He finished. His mouth snapped shut. The final bond broke like a severed chain.

So I departed, leaving behind a pungent smell of brimstone. Just something to remember me by.

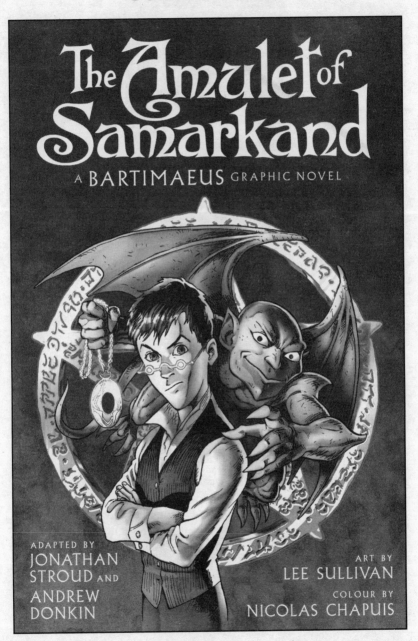

'I was compressed into a rather tawdry bottle and turned into a cheap sideshow attraction, possibly for all eternity. Those were the downsides. As for the upsides . . . Well, I couldn't see any just yet.'

Demon extraordinaire, Bartimaeus, is stuck as a spirit slave doing dead-end jobs in King Solomon's Jerusalem. The shame of it! Solomon's ring of legend, which affords its master absolute power, has a *lot* to answer for.

But with the arrival of Asmira, an assassin girl with more than just murder on her mind, things start to get . . . interesting. Throw in a hidden conspiracy, seventeen deadly magicians and some of the most sinister spirits ever to squeeze inside a pentacle, and Bartimaeus is in the tightest spot of his long career. He's going to have to use every ounce of magic in his ever-shifting body to wriggle his way out of this one.

A spell-binding addition to the internationally acclaimed, best-selling *Bartimaeus* sequence.

978 0 385 61915 8